Martin WALKER

A Shooting at Chateau Rock

Quercus

First published in Great Britain in 2020 by Quercus
This paperback edition published in 2021 by

Quercus Editions Ltd
Carmelite House
50 Victoria Embankment
London EC4Y 0DZ

An Hachette UK company

A CIP catalogue record for this book is available
from the British Library

MMP ISBN 978 1 78747 770 4
OME ISBN 978 1 78747 771 1

10 9 8 7 6 5 4 3 2 1

Typeset by CC Book Production
Printed and bound in Great Britain by Clays Ltd, Elcograf S.p.A.

MIX
Paper from
responsible sources
FSC® C104740

Papers used by Quercus are from well-managed forests
and other responsible sources.

A7 061 083 5

Martin Walker is a prize-winning journalist and the author of several acclaimed works of non-fiction, including *The Cold War: A History*. Martin and his family have had a home in the Périgord region of France since the 1990s and have become ever more connected to this gastronomic heartland of the country by friends and neighbours, dog and chickens, garden and countryside. Among their friends is the local village policeman (and Martin's tennis partner) who inspired the series of mystery novels based around Bruno, Chief of Police.

Also by Martin Walker

THE DORDOGNE MYSTERIES

To Gerard Fayolle and Gerard Labrousse, two fine men
and excellent mayors whose work taught me most of what
I know about the health of local democracy in the Périgord.

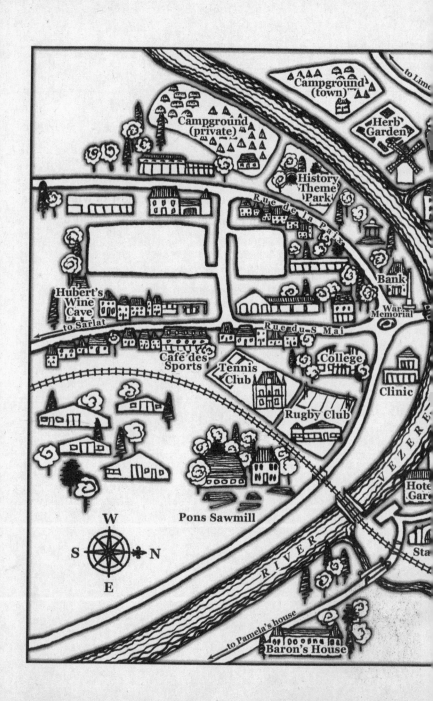

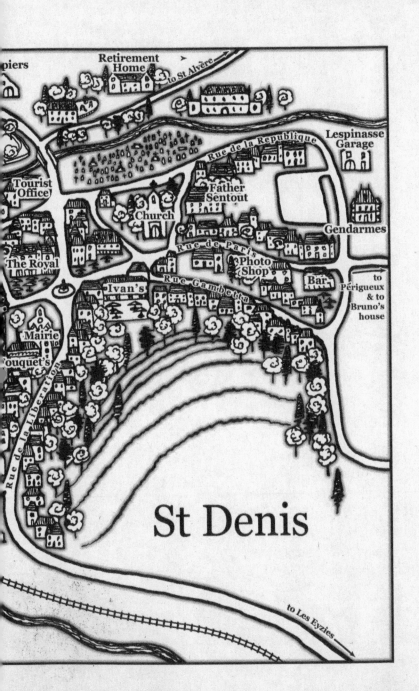

1

Two days after his father's funeral a distraught Gaston Driant came to the Mairie of St Denis, asking to see Bruno Courrèges, the town's chief of police. Bruno assumed that Gaston, an old acquaintance from the town tennis club, was still in shock at the dreadful nature of his father's death. The old man, a widower, had been alone on his remote farm when he had suffered a fatal heart attack, and had not been found for several days. Patrice, the postman, liked to visit his older customers from time to time to see how they were, and he'd always found a friendly welcome at Driant's home, along with a glass of his home-made *gnôle*, a notorious firewater that Bruno had learned to treat with great respect. When Patrice's knock went unanswered, he had opened the kitchen door. Two cats had darted out and then Patrice had reeled back from the smell. Then he had thrown up when he saw what the cats, desperate for food, had done to the dead farmer. Once he'd recovered, he'd called Dr Gelletreau, whom he knew had been Driant's physician, and waited outside in the fresh air for his arrival.

Gelletreau had come within the hour, accompanied by an ambulance. Once he had seen the body he wrote a prescription for sleeping pills for Patrice, along with an instruction for the

1

post office to grant him three days' leave. Given the circumstances, Gelletreau's death certificate, citing a heart attack as the cause of Driant's demise, had understandably gone unquestioned. And as the doctor later told Bruno, he had been treating Driant for heart trouble for the past several months and the previous month had written an authorization for a pacemaker to be installed in Driant's chest.

Bruno was surprised when Gaston firmly refused his offer to take him down for coffee to Café Cauet saying, 'This is going to be official, Bruno, so we'd better stay here in your office. I just came from a new *notaire* in Périgueux for what I understood to be the reading of Dad's will. He'd sent a letter for me that was waiting at the funeral parlour. My sister, Claudette, was with me, she came down from Paris. We were stunned by what the *notaire* told us. Anyway, on the drive back here we agreed I should come and see you as an old friend. I mean, you know the law and we don't.'

There was nothing left of his father's estate, Gaston explained. Without telling his children, Driant had sold the farm and put all the money into an insurance policy that would pay for him to spend the rest of his days in an expensive residential home for the elderly. He was due to go there in September. The *notaire* said that Driant had insisted on spending one last summer on the farm he'd inherited from his father.

'Claudette and I can't believe that Dad didn't tell us what he planned to do,' Gaston went on. 'And we don't understand why he went to this fancy *notaire* in Périgueux when the whole family had always used Brosseil for wills and such. I was going to see Brosseil right after going to sit with Dad in the funeral parlour but that was when I found the letter from the *notaire* in Périgueux.'

Bruno nodded in understanding. Brosseil had followed in the footsteps of his father and grandfather as the local *notaire* in St Denis. He knew everybody in the district and everybody had always used him for wills, property sales and official paperwork. Brosseil was something of a character, fussy and prim in dress and manner and exhibiting a vanity so ridiculous that it was almost endearing, a private joke that the whole town enjoyed. But Bruno knew that his work was meticulous and that he was as honest as the day was long.

'And this retirement home is not like Dad at all,' Gaston went on. 'My sister looked it up on her phone. It's an old chateau that was turned into a hotel and now it's a very grand home for the elderly. The fees start at four thousand euros a month That's more than double what I earn. And because my dad's dead, this home gets to keep all the insurance money. It all seems very fishy to Claudette and me and we agreed that I'd ask you about it.'

Bruno took down the names and addresses of the *notaire*, the insurance agent and the residential home and made a photocopy of the *notaire*'s letter to Gaston.

'Let me look into this,' he said. 'How old was your dad?'

'Seventy-four next birthday, in November. But apart from what Gelletreau said about his heart, he seemed in good shape when I saw him last, still kept up the farm. I came up here in March as usual to help him with the lambing. And that's another thing: what's going to happen to the sheep and ducks and chickens?'

3

After being laid off when the local sawmill had closed a couple of years earlier, Gaston had found a job in Bordeaux as an ambulance driver. Bruno had written him a reference, citing Gaston's clean driving record and his years as a volunteer fireman which had brought him some qualifications in first aid. Gaston was raising two daughters who were still in secondary school so he'd probably been hoping for a decent inheritance when his father died.

'He'd never mentioned these plans to you or Claudette?' Bruno asked.

Gaston shook his head. 'When we were talking over dinner at lambing time he said he wanted to stay on the farm as long as he could and then go to the retirement home here in St Denis where he knew everybody. I can't understand what got into him.'

'Leave it with me,' Bruno said. 'I've got your address and phone number so I'll let you know what I find out. All I can say at this stage is that usually in cases of old people changing their wills there has to be a formal declaration signed by a doctor and a lawyer that establishes the change is being made freely and of his own volition and that he's in full possession of his faculties. If there is no such declaration, you might have a case. But going up against a *notaire* and an insurance firm would probably be a very lengthy and expensive affair.'

'*Merde*,' Gaston grunted. 'It's always the same. One law for the rich and another for the rest of us.'

'In this instance, Gaston, if there is no such attestation the law could be on your side. And you know the Mayor and I will back you. Again, my condolences on your loss. I liked your dad.

4

He was always a regular at the rugby games and at the hunting club dinners. And that *gnôle* he made was the best *eau de vie* in the valley, even if it wasn't really legal. I hope at least he left you a few bottles.'

'One or two, but he drank most of that rocket fuel himself and I can't say I blame him,' Gaston said, rising to shake Bruno's hand.

Bruno's first stop was just down the hall at the registry. There he consulted the commune's *cadastre*, the detailed map showing each property lot, its owner and the tax data. The new ownership had not yet been registered. Driant's farm was listed as sixty-two hectares, which would be big for a vineyard but was small for a sheep farm, mostly woodland and poor pasture up on the plateau. What surprised Bruno was that Driant had made an application for a construction permit to build four new houses on his land. He had described them in the application as cottages for farmworkers, which was what such applications usually said even when the real intention was to sell them off as holiday homes.

Bruno had never heard of Monsieur Sarrail, the *notaire* in Périgueux, but from the letterhead he knew he was in a fancy location on the Rue du Président Wilson in the centre of the city. When he looked up the agent for the insurance company Bruno found that he had an address in the same building. That was interesting. He checked the website of the retirement home and was startled to see a handsome chateau near Sarlat that he recognized. He'd been invited to dinner there one evening by his friend the Baron some five or six years ago, when it had been a newly restored four-star hotel with a dining room that was said to be aiming for a Michelin rosette. The meal had been a touch too *nouvelle cuisine* for Bruno's taste, the portions small and the plates over-decorated in an effort to appear artistic and inventive. Bruno and the Baron had thought it pretentious. They'd never been back.

As a retirement home, it offered what were described as full medical services, a registered nurse, a physiotherapist and a masseuse on the premises, and a resident doctor who also sat on the management board. It advertised itself as a 'luxury establishment for the discerning customer, modelled on an exclusive private club'. It boasted its own cinema, a spa, a nine-hole golf course and a manager who had previously been on the staff of the Hotel Crillon in Paris.

The chef was said to have served his apprenticeship at a restaurant in Geneva that Bruno had heard of, and had then been a sous-chef at the Relais Louis XIII in Paris. Bruno had been taken there for dinner one evening by his old flame, Isabelle, and had eaten the finest quenelles of his life. Why on earth would Driant want to go to a grand retirement home like that, where the old sheep farmer would be sneered at by the other inhabitants and probably also by the staff? Subscriptions by application, the website said.

Bruno found the manager's name on the website, called the Hotel Crillon in Paris and asked for the head of security. He introduced himself and found that he was speaking to a former detective of the Préfecture de Police of Paris, who had heard of Bruno from their mutual friend J-J, the chief detective for the *département* of the Dordogne. Bruno said he was checking on a luxury retirement home in his region which claimed that the manager had worked at the Crillon. The old detective laughed at the name. The man in question had indeed worked there for a few months as one of several junior assistant concierges, whose main duty was to take care of the guests' baggage and to collect and deliver their laundry and dry cleaning. He had been competent, the detective said, but had been asked to leave after one affronted female guest complained that he had offered his services as a gigolo.

Bruno then phoned J-J at police headquarters in Périgueux to ask if he knew anything about the *notaire* or the retirement home, and whether this sounded like some kind of insurance scam.

'I haven't heard about the retirement home, but this is nothing new in the *notaire* system,' said J-J. 'He's the first one here but there are several in Paris, a *notaire* who forms a partnership with an insurance agent, an accountant and an investment adviser to offer full financial consultancy, usually for rich people. They call it wealth management. So far I've heard nothing bad about the guy in Périgueux but it's not really my field. I can have a discreet word with a colleague from the *fisc* if you like.'

Bruno felt reassured. The *fisc* was the slang term for the *brigade nationale de répression de la délinquance fiscale*. Although they sometimes worked closely with the police they were not police officers, since they applied the fiscal code and reported to the Ministry for the Budget and Public Finances, not to the Interior Ministry. Bruno told J-J what he'd heard about the manager of the retirement home from J-J's friend at the Crillon and left him laughing.

Bruno then went to ask Claire, the secretary at the Mairie, if the Mayor was free. The Mayor must have heard him since he called through the half-open door to tell Bruno to come right in. Bruno explained what he'd heard and asked if the Mayor knew anything about Driant applying for a construction permit.

'Yes, and he got it approved by the council,' the Mayor said. 'It was a matter of professional courtesy. Driant served two terms on the council for the commune, before your time, Bruno. You know how councillors tend to support one another's projects, and with all these retirees coming here from the rest of France and Europe we're getting a housing shortage. But I agree it sounds odd. I'll find out what my colleague in Sarlat knows about this retirement home. It doesn't sound at all like the kind of place Driant would have enjoyed.'

'You know Driant's farm,' Bruno said. 'What do you think it would be worth?'

'They'd never sell it these days for raising sheep, not since Brussels cut the hill farm subsidies. Driant had one of the last of them,' the Mayor replied. 'The house and barns alone might fetch a hundred and fifty thousand, but only if somebody wanted to make it into a small hotel and *gîtes*. I assume that's what the construction permit was for. It would depend on how much repair work would be needed. But the place has a great view. It could be popular in summer with the right management. Maybe you should talk to Brosseil, then find out whether Driant had sworn a statement of competence and we'll talk again.'

Bruno found the fussy little *notaire* in his office on the Rue

Gambetta. Short and getting plumper, Brosseil was always so neatly dressed in a suit and tie with a flower in his buttonhole that he had a reputation as something of a dandy. In St Denis few men wore ties to work, not even the Mayor. Brosseil was respected rather than liked. His wife, one of the dwindling number of women in town who stayed at home and prepared the traditional daily lunch rather than take a formal job, was a faithful churchgoer and a stalwart of the Action Catholique charity.

Bruno, however, knew Brosseil had hidden depths. He had heard from female friends that the *notaire* was a star of the dance floor, the best ballroom performer in town. He went twice a week with his wife to nearby clubs in Bergerac and Périgueux, where they and their fellow enthusiasts could twirl to their hearts' content. Bruno could just about waltz but had no idea of the difference between a quickstep and a foxtrot. He simply circled the room, moving his feet in time to the music while trying not to step on his partner's toes. But he recalled from the last *pompiers* ball that Brosseil had indeed been the master of the dance floor. Bruno's friends Pamela, Fabiola and Florence had each returned starry-eyed from their waltzes with Brosseil, saying he was such a skilled partner that they had never danced so well.

'This comes as an unpleasant surprise,' Brosseil said after Bruno had explained the reason for his visit. 'It's not considered good form to go poaching in other *notaires*' districts and Driant was my client. It's also a breach of professional courtesy not to let me know that the old will had been superseded. I drew up and filed Driant's original will for him. How he heard of this new *notaire* in Périgueux I have no idea. This means that in effect Driant has disinherited his children.'

The insurance aspect of the deal was also questionable, Bruno was told. Under the usual actuarial tables, Driant could have expected to live another five to ten years, so the fees of the retirement home could reach as much as five hundred thousand euros. And the farm could only hope to recoup that money if it was sold with the gîtes as a going concern. But building the four gîtes would cost at least three hundred thousand, plus repairs to the farm, building a swimming pool, terraces, a proper parking lot, furniture . . .

'The numbers don't add up – they wouldn't get their money back. I can't see any reputable insurance firm agreeing to such a deal,' Brosseil said, ticking off each new expense on his well-manicured fingers. 'Unless, of course, they somehow knew that the old man had heart trouble. For someone of that age, any insurer would want to see medical records before agreeing to a contract. So I agree with Driant's son. It sounds fishy. Have you spoken to the Mayor about this?'

'He was the one who suggested I should talk to you. What do you know about this *notaire* Driant used?'

'Not much,' Brosseil replied. 'Sarrail is new to the region. I heard he came from Marseille or Nice, somewhere on the coast. He's obviously well-financed, judging from the office he's leased. Still, with so many retirees moving to the Périgord and the new hotels and restaurants being launched, he probably knows the region is a promising market. I'll ask around. If I learn anything useful I'll let you know.'

Brosseil paused, tapping a finger against his lip. 'It might be useful to get hold of whatever documents Driant signed with this insurance firm and with the retirement home. I checked on the registry of wills when I heard of his death and no new will had been registered that would invalidate the old one. That's why I'm surprised Driant's son went to Sarrail rather than to me. As far as I know Driant's original will is still valid and along with his son I'm named as an executor. I can certainly request a copy of any financial agreements he made that would affect the will. The more I think about this, the more irregular it appears to be.'

'Please do that. But could Driant have signed a new will, invalidating the old one, just before he died?' Bruno asked. 'If so, the registry might not have had time to be updated.'

'That's possible but they are usually pretty quick. I can check. And if you're in touch with Gaston, ask him why he went to Sarrail. How did he know Sarrail was involved in his father's estate? Did Sarrail contact him?'

'Sarrail sent a letter to the funeral parlour. It was waiting for Gaston when he got there,' said Bruno. He pulled out his notebook and scribbled down the questions Brosseil had raised. At the back of his mind another question was starting to surface. The crucial evidence in all this might turn out to be the death certificate signed by Dr Gelletreau, which listed a heart attack as the cause. Bruno would have heard if there had been an autopsy. Gelletreau may have made some kind of post-mortem examination but more likely the doctor, almost as old as Driant, had simply filled out the form on the basis of Driant's age and history of heart trouble. If so, since the old man had been cremated, any contrary evidence was no longer available.

As he went back to his office, Bruno pondered calling his friend Fabiola who was by far the best doctor in town and always willing to help him. Phoning her at the town clinic, where she worked with Gelletreau, did not seem like a good idea. Bruno knew he'd be seeing her that evening when they went out to exercise the horses. He could ask her opinion then. He knew she was fond of the elderly doctor, even while she had limited respect for his skills.

As he entered his office his desk phone was ringing. It was Brosseil to say that he had checked again with the registry of wills and Driant's new will had been registered on the previous Tuesday, having been signed and formally approved on the Friday, three days earlier. Bruno checked the calendar. Patrice had found Driant's body on the Friday after the will had been registered. The funeral had taken place on the following Tuesday. It was now Thursday.

'It sounds as though Driant may have died on the very day the will was formally registered,' Bruno said. 'Which is the crucial date for the will: the day it was signed or the day it was registered?'

'The day it was signed and witnessed,' Brosseil replied. 'But that's irrelevant since we don't know the exact date and time of death. Meanwhile, I've just written to Sarrail to request copies of the deeds of sale for Driant's farm, the insurance contract and also evidence that the sale of the livestock has been properly registered. That's very important in these days of European subsidies and regulations.'

'Tell me more,' Bruno said, and scribbled down notes as Brosseil explained the arcane procedures that only a country *notaire* accustomed to dealing in livestock sales would be likely to know.

'What if the *notaire* and new owner haven't followed these procedures with the livestock?' Bruno asked when Brosseil had finished.

'In a really serious case, the entire sale could be in question and the *notaire* involved could lose his licence. He could even be sued for professional negligence by the new owner. However, in this case they probably have a way out by saying that Driant agreed to take care of the formalities about the livestock but died before doing so. That's the way I'd play it and I imagine these men aren't fools.'

'What happens if Sarrail won't let you have those documents?'

'Deeds of sale for properties and livestock and wills are public documents which have to be filed and registered at the Préfecture. One way or another, we'll get copies of them. Whether we can get the *notaire* is another matter.'

2

Bruno had no idea whether a crime had been committed or whether Gaston had simply been another victim of some fancy legal footwork against which he had no redress without launching a lawsuit he could not afford. As a country policeman, Bruno adhered to an unwritten code that required him to do his best for his neighbours and also for their live-stock. So as he drove his police van up into the hills towards St Chamassy, enjoying the pure pleasure of this fresh green landscape in May, he was wondering if anyone had taken care of the sheep and chickens. The cats, he knew, could fend for themselves.

When he pulled into Driant's farmyard he saw a truck that he recognized. It belonged to Marc Guillaumat, another elderly sheep farmer who lived a few kilometres away on the other side of the valley. He had been a friend of Driant's since their schooldays. Bruno found him filling the water troughs at the chicken coop, shook hands and asked if he needed any help.

'No, I've just about finished,' Marc said. 'I thought I'd better keep an eye on the lambs until somebody decides what to do with them, and when I got here I found there was no water for the chickens and ducks. The sheep can feed themselves up here this time of year on the pasture but there's a lot of foxes with young to feed so I was worried about the lambs.'

Just beyond the duck pond, Bruno saw a flock of sheep clustered close together with four sheepdogs lying on their bellies, tongues out, watching the newly shorn ewes whose lambs huddled beneath them. Up here on the plateau, the farmers usually kept the fleece on their flocks until April or even later.

'Two of them are my dogs and the others, the bitch and her pup, belonged to Driant,' Guillaumat said, following the direction of Bruno's gaze. 'He trained them well. Nobody took them away so they've kept watch on the lambs but I don't think his dogs have been fed since young Gaston came up here the morning of the funeral. I had some dog biscuits in the truck and they leaped on them like they were starving.'

Bruno raised his eyebrows. Mistreatment of dogs angered him.

'I thought Gaston would come back and tell me what he planned to do with them all but I haven't heard from him. He gave me Driant's shotgun as a keepsake but that was all. The sheep troughs were bone dry when I got here. I suppose they could use the duck pond but look at it, damn near dry. It's not right, Bruno. I'll be giving Gaston a piece of my mind when I see him.'

'It's kind of complicated but it turns out Gaston and his sister don't inherit,' Bruno said, explaining Driant's decision.

'I was wondering if he'd do something crazy like that,' Guillaumat said. 'One time earlier this year I came to visit and he had some fancy young woman with him, foreign, from the way she spoke. She wore a short skirt and too much make-up. Then

I saw her here again later and I asked him about her. He said she was from his insurance company, but he always was one for the ladies. He got lonely after his wife died. Apart from me and a few chums at the rugby club I don't think he had many friends. Mind you, he was always at that Club du Troisième Age, but that was to meet women. '

'When did you see this young woman?' Bruno asked.

'The first time was in March after the lambing and then again in early April, when I came to see him about getting the fleeces shorn. We always shared the work. It's easier with the two of us. And with his fleece money he always went down to one of those massage parlours in Bergerac.' Guillaumat gave a short, harsh laugh. 'After a few drinks he used to boast that he could still do the business, just like his old ram.'

Bruno nodded, grinning. 'If the new owners don't want the sheep, would you like to have them? They might even pay you to take them off their hands.'

Guillaumat shook his head. 'I don't have the pasture and it's the same with the only other two sheep farmers left around here. And I don't know anybody who could afford to buy them. If it wasn't for the subsidies, we'd starve. I suppose the new owners will just ship them down to the abattoir.' The old man paused and spat. 'They'll be in for a shock when they find out it costs as much to slaughter them as they'll get for the meat.'

'Would you want the ducks and chickens?' Bruno went on. 'The new owners probably don't even know they exist.'

'Maybe the ducks because I could get a few euros for them but not the chickens. There's no point. With these European regulations we're not allowed to sell the eggs in the markets any more. But I'll take the geese. Come December I can get fifty, sixty euros for each one.'

'Will you keep an eye on the sheep until I can find out what the new owners want to do? I'll make sure they pay you for your time.'

'In that case, certainly. I'll come by every couple of days.'

'By the way, how did you learn about Driant's death?' Bruno asked.

'In the market, I ran into Dr Gelletreau. Funny thing was, I'd called the doc when I couldn't get through to Driant because he wasn't answering his phone. He sometimes forgot to recharge it. But Gelletreau said not to worry because he'd just been in about getting a pacemaker for his heart.'

The old farmer waved and drove off. Bruno found the door to the farmhouse open, the rotten-sweet smell of the old man's death still lingering so he opened the available windows and looked around. Somebody had emptied the ancient fridge and washed the plates, stacking them in the dryer on the sink. There were two wine glasses, two water glasses, two side plates, two dinner plates and two soup bowls. Had Driant not been alone for his last meal?

There were four rooms on the ground floor – the kitchen, a primitive bathroom, a seldom-used parlour with thick dust on the window sills, and an untidy study with a desk piled with unopened mail. A narrow staircase led upstairs to one large bedroom, two small ones and a junk room filled with ancient trunks and women's clothes hanging on rails in plastic sacks. They looked very old-fashioned, as likely to belong to Driant's mother as to his late wife. It seemed that Driant had slept in the main bedroom, since the bed was unmade and a pair of grubby striped pyjamas hung from the post at the foot of the bed. One pillow still had the depression that showed where Driant had lain his head. The other looked clean enough but when on a hunch Bruno turned it over he saw a stain that looked like lipstick. He bent down to sniff and caught the faintest of scents. Inside a drawer of the bedside table he found a small bottle without the usual pharmacist's label containing lozenge-shaped blue pills. Beneath them were two well-thumbed porno magazines and a vibrator.

There was no landline phone in the house and Bruno could find no mobile phone, even after leafing through the mess in the study. But there was a mobile phone bill from Orange, on which a quavering hand had scrawled 'paid'. In a drawer he found a cheque book, with counterfoils showing payments to Orange, the Trésor Public of St Denis and the local supermarket. Bruno took the cheque book, leaving a signed receipt, noted the number of the mobile phone and tried calling it. No result, not even the message service. That was odd, since the payments were up to date. There was little more to be done in the house so he made sure the sheepdogs' feeding bowls were filled with biscuits and croquettes he found in the barn.

Still angry at the neglect of the animals Bruno drove straight to Périgueux to confront Sarrail, the *notaire*. A young woman in the outer office looked startled at his arrival and asked if he had an appointment.

'The police don't make appointments, *mademoiselle*,' he said briskly and strode past her to the open the door which carried Sarrail's name.

He found a sleekly groomed man in his thirties speaking a foreign language and Bruno heard the phrase, '*Da, konyechno, vsyo pariadke*.' It sounded Slavonic, perhaps Russian. He was wearing a pinstriped suit, a brilliantly white shirt and a silk tie that looked expensive. He was sitting behind a very modern desk of steel and glass that carried a large computer screen, a notepad and a Mont Blanc fountain pen. He was rising angrily at the intrusion until he took note of Bruno's uniform. He gestured to Bruno to take a seat, turned away and spoke again briefly in Russian before putting down the phone and asking how he could help.

'Monsieur Sarrail?' Bruno asked. The man nodded. 'Where did you learn your Russian?'

'At school, but I kept it up. I have some Russian clients. And who would you be?'

Bruno handed him a business card and explained that he was investigating a complaint from Driant's son about his father's new will. Had there been any formal statement of his fitness to do so?

'Because of his age, I insisted on it,' said the *notaire*, an educated voice with a slight northern accent, from Lille or maybe Belgium. He sounded calm and self-assured. Behind him on the wall was a large modern painting that featured battling superheroes from comic books rendered in harshly clashing colours of orange, pink and green.

Monsieur Driant had appeared before a panel of three qualified assessors in Périgueux, Sarrail explained, and went on to name them. One was a psychologist from the local hospital, the second was Maître Debeney from the Palais de Justice and the third was François Maunoury, currently serving his third term as city councillor. The new will was handled in the usual way. The assessors satisfied themselves that Monsieur Driant was competent to sign it. Sarrail had then read the will aloud. Driant confirmed in the presence of the assessors that this was a precise statement of his intentions. Then he read it aloud and signed it.

'At my suggestion Driant then read out the act of sale and the insurance policy and his letter of application to the retirement home and showed them the home's letter of acceptance,' Sarrail went on. 'The assessors asked him whether he intended in effect to disinherit his two children and he replied in the affirmative. I forget his exact words but Driant said they had each moved away and he seldom saw them and so he felt he could not count on them to see him through his old age so he wanted to make his own arrangements. He also made a disparaging remark about his daughter's lifestyle. I felt it proper to add that the children were not disinherited. All his other goods, including a small life insurance policy along with his furniture and personal possessions and vehicle went equally to his children. It was all completely above board and after some more questions, the assessors were satisfied that Monsieur Driant knew exactly what he was doing. Each of the three signed the will as witnesses.'

'When was this?' Bruno asked, thinking Sarrail's remarks sounded carefully rehearsed.

'Twelve days ago.'

'Very shortly before he died,' said Bruno and paused, as if reflecting. 'Did you register the new will?'

'Yes, but not that day. The meeting with the assessors was on a Friday afternoon so I formally filed it on Monday. It was registered on the following day.'

'And how did you learn of his death?'

'I read it in *Sud Ouest*. I at once wrote to his son at the address of the funeral parlour in St Denis, where the paper reported that the body had been taken. What exactly was this complaint from the son? I can imagine he wasn't happy with the new will but that's not unusual among families.'

'Did you visit Driant's home? Around here that's usual in the case of a *notaire* who drew up the will.'

'No, I didn't, because the farm was not part of the will. It had already been transferred to a new owner, the insurance company. It is now in their hands. Some of the contents were bequeathed to his children but I gather they had already taken those when they visited the farm.'

'What do you plan to do about the livestock?' Bruno asked. 'There are more than a hundred sheep, almost as many lambs and the old ram, not to mention the ducks, chickens and sheep-dogs. There'll be trouble if they're not taken care of.'

There was a long silence and Bruno could see the *notaire* was thinking carefully and then he began scribbling on his notepad before he answered, 'Again, that's the responsibility of the new owner but I'll look into it and make sure they are disposed of without delay. Thank you for informing me. Is there anything else?'

Convinced that the *notaire* couldn't care less about the sheep, Bruno wanted to press the matter. He asked for the name and address of the new owners and the lawyer simply referred him to the insurance agent in the same building, information Bruno already had.

'Would you have the name of the young woman from the insurers who visited Monsieur Driant in April?' Bruno asked.

'No, but you might try the agent himself,' came the curt reply.

'The last time Gaston Driant saw his father a few weeks ago, the old man had said he planned to live and work on the farm as long as he could and then go to the retirement home in St Denis where he knew people,' Bruno said. 'Gaston couldn't understand why his father had suddenly chosen this much more expensive place without even letting his son and daughter know.'

'I see,' said Sarrail. 'There could be many reasons for that, not even allowing for the resentment with which Monsieur Driant spoke of his children during the assessment process. As long as he was judged to be in his right mind, it is not for the *notaire* to question his client's wishes. And there's no question about Monsieur Driant's competence. If you'd like to speak with any of the assessors I can give you their names and phone numbers and print out a copy of their assessment for you. Will that be all?'

'Are you in contact with the insurance agent?' Bruno asked. 'He seems to share your address.'

'Monsieur Constant and I sometimes work together if a client needs insurance advice,' Sarrail replied cautiously. 'Why?'

'You might want to let him know that wilful neglect of livestock is a criminal offence. I've been up to the farm and those animals have been left without food or water. This can be a serious matter if, as in this case, the animals and farm in question are receiving subsidies from public funds.'

'I see. I'll try to let Monsieur Constant know about this but he's out of the office, travelling on business. Of course, it's an issue for the insurance company, not him personally. I imagine such matters are outside his usual sphere. Do you have any suggestions I might pass on? Coming from a rural commune I imagine you know more about this than I do.'

Sarrail uncapped the fountain pen and held it poised over the notepad.

Bruno explained that the new owner should either sell them, and he would find livestock markets listed at the Préfecture, or take them to a licensed abattoir to have them killed and sell the meat. Before this he would have to put together the necessary forms for each animal, and inform and get approval from the local livestock agent. His name and address would also be on file at the Préfecture.

'The laws of wilful negligence and mistreatment of animals also apply to the sheepdogs, ducks and chickens,' Bruno added. 'But I'm not sure whether they qualify for subsidies under the new hill farm rules.'

Sarrail said nothing but began scribbling notes.

'As the *notaire* who handled the will, did you also take care of the sale of the farm to the insurance group?' Bruno asked. He was starting to enjoy this. 'If so, you will naturally have filed details of the new owner of the livestock with the proper authorities both at our own agriculture ministry and with the European Commission. And of course you'll have ensured the new owner had a proper licence to be the owner of subsidized livestock that may be used for human consumption.'

'I see,' said Sarrail, avoiding Bruno's question about drawing up the deeds of sale. 'I'll pass all this along to Monsieur Constant. But I'm confident that the proper formalities will have been observed by Monsieur Driant, although that might have been interrupted by his unfortunate death.'

'I hope you understand, *monsieur*, that any failure to meet the livestock regulations could throw the whole sale of the farm into question, quite apart from the legal liabilities for taking due care of the animals. I will naturally try to reach Monsieur Constant himself but I count on you to ensure he is aware of these concerns and that he faces serious charges. Please ask him to contact me as soon as possible. May I wish you a very good day, Monsieur Sarrail. And by the way, welcome to the Périgord.'

Bruno rose and left, trying to suppress a grin at the thought of these city-slickers learning to their cost that animals had rights, too. He tried the door of the insurance agent in the next door office. It was locked and there was no response to his knock. He scribbled a brief message on his business card explaining that Monsieur Constant should contact him at once and pushed it under the door.

For the first time, he began to think that there might be hope for Gaston and his sister to inherit something after all. Back in his police van, he called his friend Maurice, the regional livestock commissioner at the sub-Préfecture in Sarlat, whom he knew from festive evenings after rugby games, and asked whether the Driant farm sale had been registered with him. No, it had not, Bruno was told. But it certainly should have been. Bruno then told Maurice, with only a little exaggeration, that without him and old Guillaumat, Driant's sheep might have died of thirst by now. Bruno explained the whole story and agreed to meet Maurice at the farm the following morning at eight.

Then he called another friend, Annette, a young magistrate in Sarlat, and asked if she would draw up a summons against the agent of the insurance company for mistreatment of livestock, with himself as witness of negligence.

3

Back in his office, Bruno found a message from Brosseil asking him to call. He rang the number and learned that Brosseil had just heard from a colleague that one of the more celebrated small chateaux in the area was up for sale, the business being handled by a fancy agency in Paris that was better known for its art sales. Bruno thanked him for the news and sat back in his office chair, staring out across the bridge over the River Vézère and along the ridge that flanked the valley to the north. The chateau was on the far side of that ridge, about five kilometres from St Denis, and Bruno sometimes passed it when exercising his horse.

The place was known as Chateau Rock. It enjoyed quite a reputation in the neighbourhood that dated from the first arrival of its rock star owner Rod Macrae, and the widespread assumption that drug-fuelled orgies with groupies and exotic sports cars would become regular features of local life. Older inhabitants of the region professed to be shocked but their younger counterparts were thrilled. This would put St Denis on the map! Even the appearance of the heavily pregnant Madame Macrae and their sedate Volvo estate had not stilled the salacious expectations of the locals, nor the way teenage boys would dare one another to creep through the undergrowth to spy on the rock star's private life. By the time Bruno arrived in St Denis the novelty and the fantasies had long faded. But the region was glad to have a famous inhabitant and a faint echo of the chateau's old notoriety remained.

Bruno was surprised at his ignorance of Macrae's decision to sell. He thought he knew the family better than that. He had visited Chateau Rock regularly, when Rod Macrae and his wife Meghan held their annual birthday party for their two children, born on the same day although three years apart. Bruno knew them both, for they had each spent years in the tennis classes he ran for the local youngsters.

The children, Jamie and Kirsty, had both gone to the junior school in St Denis and then to the town's *collège* until the age of fifteen when each of them had been sent to a boarding school in England. Jamie, the elder by three years, was now at the Royal College of Music in London and Kirsty was hoping to go to Edinburgh University in the autumn. Bruno knew Rod quite well from the local rugby club, less for his appearance at local matches than through his almost religious attendance at the broadcasts of the Six Nations matches on the club's big screen. Whenever Scotland was playing he brought along a litre bottle of Scotch whisky for all to share. In Bruno's early years in St Denis, when the recording studio that Macrae had built in the chateau grounds was still busy, he had been invited to attend the post-recording party that Macrae always threw after some new album was complete. But there had been no such party for some years, Bruno reflected, wondering if this decline had inspired Macrae's decision to sell. On impulse, Bruno picked up the phone to call him and was answered by Macrae's wife, Meghan.

'I just heard the news that you're selling but I hope you stay in the area,' he began. 'We'd miss you.'

'I'm going back to Britain,' she said. 'I'm not sure about Rod. He's still thinking what to do. But now the kids are grown and moving out, the place is too big. We're getting a divorce while I'm still young enough to start a new life. We'll have a last family summer here before, though.'

'I'm sorry to hear that,' Bruno replied. 'I half-expected Jamie and Kirsty to turn up one day to start new families of their own.'

'They love it here so they might, but not at Chateau Rock. Still, they'll be here this summer. Jamie is giving some concerts for Musique du Périgord Noir. And he'll be recording his first CD. Rod calls it his studio's last gasp.'

'And you're also staying on through the summer? It all sounds surprisingly amicable for a divorce.'

'It is amicable and we'll stay friends. At least I hope so. I'm still fond of him but I was a child bride, Bruno. Rod's getting on for seventy and I'm not quite forty yet. I have no intention of spending the rest of my life as his unpaid nurse.'

'Are you going back to Scotland?'

'Rod might do that but I'm off to a teacher's training college just outside London. You remember I took that degree in French and Spanish through the Open University? With one year of training I can be a full-time teacher and I'm looking forward to that. I haven't yet decided where to go. My sister lives in Manchester so I might move there.'

Bruno wished her luck. He'd always been impressed by Meghan even before she'd begun volunteering to give English conversation classes at the local *collège*.

'Please give Rod my regards and I might come up tomorrow to say hello. Are Jamie and Kirsty back yet? I'd like to see them again.'

'Kirsty flies in tomorrow afternoon and Jamie is driving down from Paris with some of his musician friends sometime in the next few days. He's a bit vague about it. You'll be very welcome whenever you want to stop by.'

Bruno went down the hall of the Mairie to inform the Mayor of the news. The immediate reaction of the wily old politician was to regret that no local estate agent had been hired.

'It's best to keep these matters within the community,' the Mayor said. 'Local knowledge is always important, as you know, Bruno. I'd hate to see the fees from a sale like that going to some big firm in Paris. Do you know how much they are asking for the chateau?'

'Not yet,' said Bruno. 'I'll try and find out tomorrow. But I'm also concerned about the vineyard. I'd hate for us to lose that.'

Macrae had acquired almost five hectares of ragged and ill-maintained vines with his property and at first had hopes of marketing bottles of his own Chateau Rock. But after some disappointing years hiring part-time winemakers he had allowed the town vineyard to manage it on their joint behalf. Julien, who ran the vineyard, and Hubert who ran the town's celebrated wine store, had been delighted with the deal. They reckoned on getting at least fifteen and maybe twenty thousand bottles a year from Macrae's vines and he was happy with five thousand euros in cash each year and all the bottles he wanted for his own consumption.

'I recall that it's a *bail agricole*,' said the Mayor. 'Any new owner will have to honour that or buy us out.'

St Denis was officially an agricultural commune, which gave farmers special rights and all the inhabitants outside the *zone urbaine* were entitled to keep geese and chickens, goats and horses. Newcomers were sometimes surprised and even offended that they had no legal recourse against the owners of the cockerels who woke them at dawn, or the donkeys which brayed their way through mating seasons. More than once, a new arrival who proved less than neighbourly in his dealings with nearby farmers would find a host of cackling geese appearing near his bedroom window during the night.

Moreover, such a commune allowed for a *bail agricole*, a special agricultural lease that ran for nine years, with an automatic renewal for another nine years unless formal notice was given on either side eighteen months before the lease expired. An agricultural lease could be verbal and only required a notary's intervention if it extended beyond twenty years.

'A Paris *notaire* might not know much about these farm leases,' the Mayor said thoughtfully. 'How long has the current lease been going?'

'It will be two years in November, just after that *vendange* when we launched the town vineyard,' Bruno replied. 'And the lease is verbal. You and I were there to witness it when Macrae and Julien shook hands.'

'Even though he's never turned up for board meetings, Macrae is on record as a director of the company,' the Mayor added, stroking his chin in the way he did when thinking hard. 'And he signs the company's annual reports, which means he cannot claim to be unaware of the *bail agricole*.'

'I think he only became a director because Kirsty enjoyed working in the vineyard,' said Bruno, wondering where the Mayor was heading. Most of Bruno's savings were invested in the town vineyard which made a modest profit every year, employed half a dozen locals and would soon pay off the bank loan the Mayor had negotiated to buy out Julien's failing business.

'Every school holiday Kirsty was out there in the vines, pruning in winter, trimming in springtime, picking in September,' Bruno went on. 'Julien even offered her a job but Macrae always insisted she should get a degree first. She starts at Edinburgh University this autumn and I imagine she'll be there during this year's harvest.'

The Mayor waved aside Bruno's remarks.

'It will be up to us to ensure that due account of our lease is taken in the event of a sale,' he said, adopting a pious air that Bruno recognized. It meant the Mayor was up to something. 'We have a duty to consider the interests of the town vineyard. After all, the town has made significant investments and improvements there, clearing out dead vines, replanting new ones, taking on new staff. Until we took it over, that vineyard was a liability. And now it will doubtless enhance the value of Macrae's property.'

Bruno nodded. 'And let's not forget that we've started the

process of turning it into an organic vineyard,' he said, grinning as he realized the way the Mayor's mind was working.

'Indeed, nothing could be more important than the new owner recognizing the ecological stewardship the town vineyard has displayed,' the Mayor replied. 'It's a great responsibility. They might be well advised to come to an amicable arrangement to let us take over the vineyard altogether.'

The Mayor smiled at Bruno. They understood one another perfectly. The Mayor did not need to spell out all the endless little obstructions an experienced mayor, armed with an agricultural lease, could deploy to ensure that the vineyard remained firmly and probably permanently within the town's control.

'I suppose it will depend who buys the property,' Bruno said. 'Given the history of Chateau Rock it's likely to be another foreigner. If so, we should make him or her very welcome and suggest that the mutually advantageous partnership between the new owner and the town vineyard continues for many years to come. And we have some time. The sale won't go through until October since the Macraes want a last family summer together at the chateau.'

'Good,' said the Mayor. 'Let's keep this to ourselves for the moment, though you could let Hubert and Julien know about it in confidence. If there are any further improvements to be done in the vineyard now is the time.'

'There's that experimental corner where they are trying the new rootstock. You remember that warning Hubert gave us about the way climate change is affecting our Merlot.'

Local winemakers had recognized that the hotter summers

32

were shortening the growing season for certain grape varieties, Merlot most of all. Some who kept good records reckoned that it was ripening a month earlier than thirty years ago and contained more sugar which meant more alcohol in the wine. Some of the red wines were now being labelled as having fifteen or even sixteen per cent alcohol, which was creeping into the territory of sherry and madeira and other fortified wines.

Producing a balanced blend with the usual Cabernet Sauvignon or Cabernet Franc grapes was becoming a challenge. It was no good picking the Merlot early; the grapes would not have time to produce the phenols and tannins that give it character. One or two of the Bergerac vineyards were even planning to phase out Merlot altogether. But winemakers tended to be instinctively conservative, with many of the traditionalists reckoning that with skilful management of the leaf cover over the Merlot grapes they could slow their ripening. Giving up Merlot would be a last resort, so closely and traditionally were the wines of Bergerac and the whole of the Bordeaux region linked to this iconic grape. The wines of Pomerol, some of them – like Château Petrus – among the most expensive wines in the world, were traditionally made entirely from Merlot grapes.

Like many other growers in the region, the town vineyard was steering a middle course, hoping for the best but preparing for the worst. They continued to plant Merlot while at the same time experimenting with new varieties of grapes that were better adapted to the heat.

'I think I'll ask Pamela if we can take the horses that way

on this evening's exercise,' Bruno said as he left the Mayor's office. 'I'd like to see how those new grapes are coming along.'

And so later that day, his uniform on a hanger back in his police van, Bruno was on horseback in his riding clothes and boots when he drew rein and stepped down from the saddle. Patting his horse on the neck he led Hector through one of the rows of new vines, pausing every few metres to lift some foliage and examine the grapes, hard as little bullets this early in the season but already warm to the touch. It seemed to Bruno, still an amateur in the winemaking business, like a promising harvest so long as the weather remained good and no thunderstorms came to pepper the grapes with hail. Those little pellets of ice could flatten and destroy an entire vineyard overnight.

'What are you looking for?' Pamela called down from her seat on Primrose, her favourite horse. She pulled gently on the reins to stop Primrose from following Bruno. Primrose tried a tentative nibble on some of the new grape leaves and Pamela turned her away.

'Nothing in particular,' Bruno replied. 'Just the general condition of the grapes. They're coming on well.'

'When I first came here, all the rows of vines seemed to be neatly trimmed like soldiers on parade and all the rows between them were weeded and bare,' she said. 'It all looked much more tidy than the vineyards today.'

'That's because we're going organic, avoiding chemical fertilizers and sprays,' he said, looking up and grinning at her. An excellent horsewoman, who had taught Bruno how to ride, she looked magnificent. 'The vineyard may seem a little untidy but organic wines are the future. The more life in the soil, the better the wine.'

Bruno remounted and they trotted over the low crest where Chateau Rock came into view, about three hundred metres away. The original medieval stone tower loomed over the two wings. One had been added in the seventeenth century and the other in the nineteenth. Oddly, the most recent structure looked to be the oldest part of the building, a mock-medievalism on the outside and more modern comforts within being the fashion of the Third Empire. This was the wing where the Macraes put their guests and held their dinners and parties. Its broad terrace led to the swimming pool and tennis court. Beyond the court was the old barn, once used to dry tobacco. Now it housed the recording studio.

The family lived in the other, older wing whose plumbing and bedrooms had been thoroughly modernized when Rod Macrae had first bought the place. This family wing opened onto a tidy but sprawling vegetable garden. Scaffolding had been erected and the whole façade was evidently being overhauled and the windows repainted ahead of the chateau going on sale. Bruno had expected to see at least one of the Macraes on the terrace, enjoying the evening sun over a glass of wine, but the place seemed deserted. Maybe they were out to dinner.

'There's Félix with the rest of the horses,' Pamela said from behind him. Bruno turned away from the chateau to follow the direction of her finger to see the stable lad with a string of horses on a leading rein behind him. Pamela waved, nudged her heels against Primrose's sides and set off at a brisk walk down the gentle slope to the hunters' track below. Bruno gave Chateau Rock and the valley stretching below a final look and followed her to join the others.

4

This wasn't one of Bruno's regular Monday evening dinners, when he gathered with his friends at the riding school run by Pamela and Miranda. But the Baron had been on the river half the morning and had rung around to propose an impromptu fish supper. A bucket full of fresh trout stood beside the barbecue which he and Jack Crimson, Miranda's father, were stacking with dried vine twigs. From an upstairs bathroom window came the sound of children laughing and splashing and speaking the strange Anglo-French patois that Miranda's two boys spoke together with the children of Florence, a local teacher.

Fabiola was on duty at the medical centre until eight but her partner, Gilles, had already arrived with a large bowl holding at least a kilo of fresh strawberries from their garden. He had some of the early season Gariguette but most of his offering were Charlottes, and Bruno's favourites, the small and intensely sweet and perfumed Mara des Bois. Gilles had embraced with enthusiasm the Périgord's reputation for producing the finest strawberries in France. It was the only region in Europe to have its own trademark protection.

Balzac, Bruno's basset hound, greeted his master's return

with his usual sonorous howl of welcome and trotted along at Hector's heels until they reached the stables. Along with Félix, Bruno and Pamela rubbed down the horses, refilled their water troughs and mangers, changed in the poolhouse and had a refreshing dip in the swimming pool before rejoining the others. In the past, May had been too early for all but the most hardy to use the open-air pool. But Pamela had taken advantage of a new state programme that subsidized solar panels and battery systems. With new panels now installed on all the roofs of the barns and stables, the riding school had energy to spare to sell back to the national grid and also to heat her swimming pool.

Miranda's father, Jack Crimson, had set the table on the terrace under the trellis of vines. Bruno looked to see whose wines Jack had bought on his latest foray into the Bergerac vineyards. His weekly expeditions of research were now taking Jack to wine-makers that were new to Bruno and his friends. So it was today. Bruno had heard of the sweet, golden Monbazillac wines of the Domaine de Pécoula but he'd never tasted their dry white wines and looked forward to doing so.

Each one of them fell into a separate task without being asked, so accustomed were they to working together. Bruno took the bucket of trout into the stable and began to gut and clean them in the stable sink. Pamela had gone to the kitchen to slice lemons for the fish and to peel garlic and potatoes. Felix took the bucket of fish guts to the compost box. It had a sealable lid so the foxes could not get inside. He buried the guts deep in the box and forked some grass cuttings on top.

'How goes the new book?' Bruno asked Gilles, who was

hulling the strawberries he'd brought. They had first met during the siege of Sarajevo when Gilles had been an eager young reporter for *Libération* and Bruno had been wearing the blue helmet of a United Nations peacekeeper. Now retired from a distinguished career with *Paris Match*, Gilles had wooed and become the partner of Fabiola.

'It's tough, when most people in France hardly know Ukraine is still a war zone. And most of the rest think Russians and Ukrainians are two different peoples, when half the Ukrainians have relatives living in Russia. Ukraine's foreign minister was born and educated in Russia and his father-in-law is the Russian general who seized Crimea. It's complicated.'

'Politics usually are,' said Bruno. 'But I thought you'd almost finished the book.'

'Me too, but events on the ground keep changing. I may have to go back there for a week or two. I'm trying to arrange an interview with a guy called Stichkin, a judo friend of Putin when they were boys in St Petersburg. Stichkin was born in Ukraine but counts himself as a patriotic Russian. He's as rich as Croesus and I'm told he helped finance and organize the Russian takeover of Crimea and eastern Ukraine.'

'Fabiola won't like you going back,' Bruno said. He recalled Fabiola saying she'd first realized she was in love with Gilles when he was in Kiev covering the occupation of the Maidan by young Ukrainians protesting their pro-Russian President's blocking of an association agreement with Europe. It had turned into a slaughter with dozens of the protesters gunned down by mysterious snipers. For several frantic hours, Fabiola had not known whether Gilles had survived.

'She's not happy about it but she says she understands.'

'She says that because she loves you and knows that you want to get the story.'

'It's more than a story, Bruno,' Gilles said sharply. 'People here say Europe has known peace for seventy years but it's not true. You and I were in the Balkan wars in the nineties and now we have the Ukraine war today. And all along the Mediterranean coast there are wars and revolts and refugees. Those Maidan shootings triggered everything: the Russian occupation of Crimea, the separatist war in eastern Ukraine, Russia's first massive disinformation campaign on social media to try and put the blame on the protesters.'

'I remember the Russians leaking that recording they'd made of some high American diplomat saying "Fuck the EU" to the US ambassador in a phone call.'

'Victoria Nuland, assistant secretary of state for Europe,' said Gilles, grinning now. 'I remember thinking it was refreshing for people to hear how top officials really spoke to each other – and about each other. Anyway, I think we'd better join the others.'

Bruno had brought Pamela a dozen eggs from his chickens when he arrived to exercise the horses and Miranda had hard-boiled them before rounding up the children for their bath. In the kitchen Bruno peeled eggs, cut them in half and spooned out the solidified yolks. He chopped some *allumettes*, thin strips of smoked bacon, and fried them in their own fat while Pamela passed him some mayonnaise she'd made. He used a fork to crumble the hard egg yolks, added salt and pepper and two spoonfuls of Dijon mustard and then stirred in the bacon bits and the mayonnaise before spooning portions, the size of walnuts, into the halved egg whites. He set them out on a large plate and sprinkled a small amount of paprika onto the *oeufs mimosa* before taking them out to the terrace and putting the dish in the centre of the table. He draped a dishcloth over the bowl to keep away any flies.

Félix came in with two new lettuces from the garden and a bowl of radishes, already washed in the stable sink. Jack placed the opened bottles of wine onto the table with some jugs of water from the spring and then came a sound like a cattle stampede as the four children thundered down the stairs from their bath. They stood dutifully to be kissed by the adults and then dashed outside to find Balzac. A few moments later Florence and Miranda followed, their lipstick freshened and their hair tidy and not a trace of the sauna-like conditions and heaps of bubbles their children had enjoyed.

'I need a drink,' Miranda declared, and Bruno poured splashes of crème de cassis into half a dozen wine glasses, filled them with white wine and handed around the kir, their usual pre-dinner apéritif.

'I have a message for you from the choirmaster, Bruno,' said Florence. 'He needs to talk to you about the programme for the summer concerts. We're singing Beethoven's choral fantasy for the Musique en Périgord concert and he wants to know if that suits you for the open-air event as well.'

'I thought you were doing your standard programme of Handel, Tchaikovsky and the Mozart piece, what is it – '*Laudate Dominum*'? Bruno said, knowing how much Florence enjoyed singing the soprano role. 'I think people like the familiar old favourites.'

'I tend to agree but you'd better discuss it with him. And now the pool is warm enough, when do you plan to start teaching the children to swim? Remember, you promised them.'

They arranged to meet on Sunday morning when Bruno would join them for breakfast at eight.

Gilles's phone rang out with the opening bars of the Piaf song 'La Vie en Rose'. He answered briefly, put his phone away and reported that Fabiola had a late patient and they should not wait. Bruno began sawing off slices from the big round *tourte* of bread from the Moulin and the children were called to table. The Baron laid all but one trout on the barbecue and joined them, asking the youngsters if they recalled the lesson he'd given them on how to eat a fish while avoiding the bones. Their mouths full of fresh bread and *oeufs mimosa*, they nodded silently and dinner was under way.

Bruno looked around the table at his friends. The Baron he had known for more than a decade, since he'd first come to take up the job of policeman at St Denis. They had met at the rugby club, again at the tennis club and then at the hunters' club, three of the crucial associations that helped bind together the community of St Denis.

Jack Crimson he had known slightly for some years, at first accepting his claim to have been a boring civil servant and diplomat enjoying his retirement in France. It was only in subsequent criminal cases, the first after Jack's home was burgled, that Bruno had learned he had been more than just a diplomat. Crimson had retired after running Her Britannic Majesty's Joint Intelligence Committee and had contacts with senior figures in security and intelligence on both sides of the

Atlantic. One of them, to Bruno's surprise, had turned out to be the shadowy General Lannes from the staff of France's Minister of the Interior who appeared from time to time in Bruno's life when matters of state security erupted in the peaceful Périgord.

When he'd first met Pamela, she was known locally as 'the mad Englishwoman' who parked her horse and did the cross-word puzzle of the previous day's *Times* over a croissant and coffee in Fauquet's café. She spoke unnervingly correct French and watered her horse in the river at the end of her morning rides, dressed English-style in riding coat and jodhpurs with her red-gold hair spilling out from beneath her riding cap. It was after he had lost Isabelle, the woman he still thought of as the great passion of his life, that Bruno had come to know Pamela better and started their initially happy but later interrupted affair.

The interruption had been Pamela's idea, insisting he needed to find a woman who would, unlike her or Isabelle, settle down with him and raise a family. Bruno had agreed, wondering whether such a paragon would ever appear who combined maternal instincts with the fiery spirit and independence of Isabelle or Pamela. When such a perfect woman failed to appear, Pamela had welcomed him back to her bed but only at times of her choosing.

Bruno's eyes lingered on the last of the grown-ups at table, Florence, the single mother of the two toddlers Dora and Daniel, whom Bruno adored. He had met her as a downtrodden divorcee. She had been working under an odious boss – who harassed her – as a quality controller in a local truffle market.

43

Learning that she had a degree in chemistry, Bruno had helped her to find a job teaching environmental science at the St Denis *collège*. Her confidence had soared. Florence had launched the school's computer club and been elected to the regional council of the Teachers' Union. She was now on the Mayor's list for the next council elections, which would make her into one of Bruno's bosses.

They had just begun to clear away the plates from the main course when a horn tooted and Fabiola's Renault Twingo turned into the stable yard. She parked and walked briskly towards them declaring she was starving before kissing everyone and sitting down to devour the last two *oeufs mimosa*. The Baron rose to put her trout on the still-glowing embers of the grill and Jack poured her a glass of white wine, which she sank in three gulps before holding out her glass for more.

'Sorry I'm late. One of the usual local hypochondriacs,' she said. 'These *oeufs* are delicious, Bruno. And your trout looks super, Baron, and I love this wine you brought, Jack. What were you all talking about before I came along to interrupt?'

'Food, wine and horses,' Pamela replied. 'The essentials of a healthy life.'

'So you haven't heard the gossip about the Macraes at Chateau Rock?' Fabiola went on. 'I'm told they're getting a divorce and selling up.'

'Where did you hear that?' asked Pamela.

'From my hypochondriac. It seems her husband had been teaching the Macraes' daughter to drive but she texted him today to ask if she'd be capable of passing her test this summer because the whole family would be leaving France. So that means Chateau Rock will be going on sale. I wonder how much they'll want for it?'

It was remarkable, thought Bruno, as the discussion went on, how fascinated people were by the price of properties that had nothing to do with them. As they were all leaving, he took Fabiola aside to ask her about Gelletreau signing Driant's death certificate.

'Professional courtesy means that I couldn't possibly comment, Bruno,' she said crisply. 'Driant was not my patient and it's clear that he did have heart problems. Gelletreau told me that the approval for the pacemaker he'd recommended finally came through on the day of the old boy's funeral. Why do you ask?'

She and Gilles were hovering by their car, poised to leave. Bruno explained briefly the concerns of Driant's children and the unusual choice of the expensive new retirement home.

'The one near Sarlat?' Gilles asked. 'I've been there. They have what they call a literary salon, but it's really a book club. They invited me along last month to talk about my book and sign some copies. They gave me an excellent dinner. It's an impressive place, feels like a stately home, beautifully restored and the library where I spoke was well stocked.'

'I've heard of the place, too,' said Fabiola. 'One of the doctors on their board came to see us with a glossy brochure. Apparently they were visiting all the doctors and clinics in the region, trying to drum up business by claiming they were the only place in the region offering full medical services. They even invited us to lunch there to take a look at the facilities. I think Gelletreau went.'

'He's not known to turn down the offer of a free lunch,' Bruno said, grinning.

'Gelletreau may be getting on in years but he's not a bad doctor,' Fabiola replied, quite sharply. 'Quite the opposite. He has a great deal of experience and he genuinely cares for his patients, checks with the pharmacies that they are taking what he prescribes. And he still makes house calls which is more than you can say for a lot of doctors these days.'

'I'm not criticizing your colleague,' Bruno said, choosing his words with care. 'Gelletreau is my doctor and I have no complaints. But he tends to focus on the obvious – remember that case when he said it was a heart attack and you found out it was cyanide poisoning? That's why I'm wondering how much of an examination he made before stating that Driant had died of a heart attack.'

'Come on, Bruno. An old man with heart trouble, on beta blockers, about to get a pacemaker, what more do you expect?' she retorted. 'There was nothing that sounded at all suspicious about the death and from what I heard of the state of the body when Gelletreau found it, I'm not sure I'd have probed any deeper. And as for the retirement home, maybe the old man was so concerned about his health that he decided he'd rather go to a place with on-site facilities to take good care of him. That seems perfectly understandable to me.'

'I'm told Driant was a bit of a ladies' man and I found some pills in his bedside drawer that looked like Viagra. Could that have affected his heart?'

'Maybe. Who prescribed them?'

'No pharmacy label. It could have been mail order.'

Fabiola grimaced. 'That could have been a problem. What about drugs?'

'None that I saw. Why?'

'If there was any sign of cocaine, that could have been very dangerous in his condition, even fatal. But since he was cremated there'll be no forensic evidence so we'll never know. Maybe Gelletreau should have checked, but if there were no grounds for suspicion . . .' Her voice trailed off and she shrugged. 'Goodnight, Bruno.'

5

At eight the next morning Bruno met Maurice, the livestock commissioner, at Driant's farm. Balzac was with him, on a leash in case the lure of the sheep or the prospect of new friendships with the sheepdogs proved too tempting. Bruno wanted no distractions as he explained his concerns about the welfare of the livestock.

'And the buyer is an insurance company? They should know better,' said Maurice, shaking his head. 'I suppose they can always plead that the old man should have taken care of the paperwork but it's two weeks since he died so that's not much of an excuse. And the deed of sale was two weeks old. That's not good. And in all this time no representative of the new owners have been here to check on the livestock? That's not just irresponsible – it's criminal negligence.'

Bruno nodded agreement. 'The only people who have been here since the old man was found dead have been his son, who fed and watered the stock, and then yesterday I came here and met Guillaumat from across the valley who was doing the same. I filed a statement of mistreatment to Annette, the Sarlat magistrate we've worked with before.'

'Right, I'll visit Guillaumat next to take a statement from

him and then I'll talk to Annette. It will be up to her whether I file a complaint through the Commission or add mine to yours. I presume this *notaire* who handled the sale hasn't much experience with farming.'

Bruno smiled and shook his head. 'I'm told that what he does is called wealth management.'

'He can probably expect to lose some of that wealth in fines,' said Maurice, with a contemptuous snort. 'Honest farmers who have to deal with all this paperwork will be delighted to read in the paper that some financial guys are getting rapped.'

'How much can the fines be?'

'Depends on the court but it's usually between fifty and a hundred euros for each animal. A hundred ewes, almost as many lambs, so at most it could be twenty thousand. By the way, I don't like the look of some of the lambs so I'll take them to our vet. They need lots of water when they come off their mother's teat.'

'You'd better let Guillaumat know how many you've taken. I've asked him to come over every day or two to take care of the animals. I presume we can bill the new owners for that.'

'Certainly, and I'll bill them for my time as well. If had my way, these bastards would go to prison. They're not fit to deal with livestock.'

They said goodbye and Bruno headed to Chateau Rock, sad at the sale but still looking forward to seeing Rod Macrae, a guitarist whose riffs and songs had been part of the soundtrack of his boyhood. When Rod stood up from the garden chair on the chateau terrace he was as tall and as skinny as he'd been in his days of rock music fame several decades earlier.

He still dressed the same way, black jeans tucked into high-heeled boots, a Stetson perched on the back of his head and a denim shirt with a black leather waistcoat that was shiny with constant wear. With the lines of age etched deep into his face, Macrae looked even more cadaverous. Bruno assumed he was wearing the hat out of vanity – he knew Rod to be bald on top – but he'd grown out the grey hair on the sides of his head to keep his trademark ponytail. And he still kept a hand-rolled cigarette smouldering on his bottom lip as he had in his days on stage.

'Ça va, Bruno?' he asked in a slow, almost lazy voice. He reached out to shake hands before bending to greet Balzac.

'This is one hell of a fine-looking dog,' he said, scratching Balzac at that spot on his chest the hound couldn't reach. Balzac almost purred with pleasure. 'He's pure-bred, ain't he, a real pedigree hound?'

'Yes, from the best hunting pack in France, I'm told. I was lucky to get him.'

'I know the story, after your last dog was killed in the line of duty, somebody in the government arranged for you to get this one. You planning on breeding him? I only ask because I think it might be time for me to get a dog in this new life I'm heading for and I can't think of a finer companion than someone like this.'

Bruno was surprised by the idea but saw the sense in it from Macrae's point of view. 'He's still a bit young for breeding, and I'm supposed to contact someone from the hunting pack when it's time,' he said. 'They want to pick out the right mate for him. Maybe I should give them a call.'

'I'd really like one so be sure to let me know.'

'I was sorry to hear you're selling up,' Bruno said. 'You'll be missed, all of you.'

'We're not all going. The kids want to keep a foothold here so we're fixing up the farm worker's cottage at the far side of the vineyard. It's on the edge of the property so it's easily carved out from the sale of the chateau. It shouldn't cost much and we're planning to cut that stand of timber on the other side of the hill. Oak and acacia, good burning wood that should sell for more than enough. '

'What about water and electricity?'

'That's not a problem. We can easily bring in power and water access from the recording studio up the slope. It's just a matter of hooking it up, putting in a new septic tank and fixing the roof. The timber can pay for all that. The kids say they'll clean it out and redecorate the place this summer, if they get the time. I know they'll be practising for that tennis tournament of yours. And I'm not sure if you know that Jamie will be giving a concert at the music festival. I'd like to record his first CD here in the studio. So we'll go out with a bang.'

'Is Jamie still playing classical guitar?'

Macrae nodded. 'That's his thing, but he's also pretty good on piano. And he's taken up singing at the Royal College, choral stuff.'

'What about Kirsty? What's she going to study?'

'She was going to read languages, adding Italian and Spanish to her French and becoming an interpreter but it seems that computers are taking over so there's not much demand. She might change to politics or law. It all seems a bit up in the air for Kirsty, but Jamie is set on a career in music.'

'Following in the family footsteps,' Bruno said. 'What about you? Will you go back to Scotland?'

Macrae shrugged. 'Maybe, it kind of depends on the deal we get for the chateau. Meghan wants enough out of the sale to buy a place of her own and we want to do the same for each of the kids. I'll keep what's left.'

'That's generous of you.'

'Not really. I get the royalties from the music. Golden Oldie stations play my stuff and other people are still doing my old songs. The royalties add up – Britain, America, Germany, Australia, even some from France – I do okay.' He spat out the stub of the cigarette and ground it into the earth with his boot. 'But I have to admit I'll miss this place.'

'Is Meghan here?'

'She had to go see the *notaire* about separating the cottage from the rest of the property. Brosseil called this morning to say that under French law it was more complicated than we thought. We may have to end up selling it to the kids for a nominal sum.'

'I'm glad they're staying,' Bruno said. 'Jamie and Kirsty have all their school friends here. Half the kids in town learned to speak English from Meghan's classes at the *collège*.'

Macrae nodded and began to roll another cigarette from the tobacco pouch he kept in his waistcoat pocket. 'She's planning on going to teacher training college in England and making a career of it.'

He paused, licking the cigarette paper and then lighting it. 'I think she's doing the right thing. She's still a young woman, doesn't want to be stuck with an old fart like me. Still, it's a wrench. The only woman I ever stayed with. Hell, the only one I could have stayed with.'

Bruno groped for something to say. He and Macrae had been friendly for years but they had never shared anything personal or private.

'Have you got any plans?' Bruno asked.

'Not unless someone asks me to do a comeback tour but I'm getting too old.'

'Didn't seem to stop Leonard Cohen.'

'Yeah, well, my style is a bit different. I've been working on writing a few songs, just playing around with my guitar, indulging myself like old men do.'

'That's good. I'd be interested to hear them,' said Bruno, who remembered as a boy hearing the surging, infectious chords of Macrae's group and his raucous voice on the radio. 'I grew up with some of your records. One of the guys in my unit in the army had all your songs on a cassette.'

'That was a long time ago,' Macrae said. 'This new stuff I'm working on is different; songs and ballads more than the old heavy rock. Just me and my guitars. When Jamie was here over Christmas he and I played some numbers together. Mainly I'm just having fun, but maybe I can make something out of them. We'll see.'

'I'd like to hear them, the new songs,' Bruno said.

'Yeah? That's nice of you.' Macrae nodded vaguely, making

no commitment but looking pleased. 'Let's go see what the lady from Paris has been doing. She's filming the place with a drone. Apparently it's the thing now for high-end property sales.' He began heading across in a slow, rolling stroll that reminded Bruno of the way cowboys walked in films of the old West. Maybe it was the boots.

A young woman dressed in casual chic shook hands with Bruno and asked him to call her Nathalie. In the shade at the side of the chateau, out of the direct sun, she turned on the small screen on the control panel. She had done a high shot of the whole property, then dipped the drone down to float slowly over the vineyard and the gardens before circling around the chateau itself. She had taken the drone around the buildings, once clockwise and once anticlockwise, and then paused it to hover over the medieval tower before focusing on some special features like balconies and the ornate doorway.

The film ended by lowering the drone to each of the terraces, front and rear. Nathalie had set the scene, arranging wine glasses and a bottle on the table at the rear of the house, and plates and cutlery as if for a family lunch on the main terrace at the front. And from each table, she had taken long, panning shots of the view the outdoor diners would enjoy.

'That should attract a lot of potential buyers,' Bruno said, impressed. It was a great deal better than the usual snapshot of properties for sale that he saw in the estate agents' windows in St Denis.

'Looks good to me,' said Macrae. 'Anything more you need or shall we go and enjoy this bottle on the back terrace?' He raised the open bottle of wine.

'I'd rather you showed me round the inside first,' said Nathalie. She handed Bruno a business card with her photo on one side and her contact details on the other, including the permit number for her drone. 'Perhaps you could let me know if there are any local restrictions on the drone,' she said, and then turned back to Macrae.

'I'll need to take measurements and take some photos, maybe think about styling some of the rooms. At this price level, clients tend to have definite ideas about the way they want their fantasy chateau to look. Sitting rooms need to be elegant but anonymous, dining rooms should be baronial and kitchens should look medieval but with modern fittings, that sort of thing. Maybe we could borrow this beautiful basset hound for the day. He's just the kind of dog that adds that touch of class, with a suggestion of hunting.'

She turned to Macrae. 'Do you have a shotgun? Or a gun room? Maybe we could have a shot of the dog in the kitchen, a shotgun leaning against the sink and a couple of game birds lying there, waiting to be plucked.'

Bruno and Macrae exchanged baffled glances. 'You can borrow Balzac if you think it will help, so long as you get him back to me at the Mairie before six. But we're out of the hunting season, though we could shoot a couple of pigeons.'

'We've got some rabbits I shot early this morning when I saw them eating their way through the garden,' said Macrae. 'And Meghan should be back soon. I think this is something you'd better work on with her. Meanwhile, I'll show you around indoors.'

'And I'd better get back to work,' Bruno said, rising and telling

Balzac to stay. 'But you'd better tell any prospective buyers the dog won't come with the house.'

Macrae grinned and went into the house. He came out with a small, square envelope, and handed it to Bruno. 'Here's a CD of my latest stuff. Let me know what you think.'

Bruno drove off. He slipped the CD into the slot of the player in his van, wondering what sort of music Macrae had been making. He'd been a classic rocker, not heavy metal but steady, driving rock with a hint of country. Bruno recalled that some of the songs were almost ballads. He remembered Macrae had played bass, and had done some of the vocals with that urgent, yearning voice. And he'd been the song-writer, which probably explained why he'd done well out of the royalties.

There was a steady bass leading into the first song but then a rhythm guitar came in with a drum track, sounding like country, and then that voice, familiar but aged by countless thousands of cigarettes and no doubt a great deal of wine and whisky. It was slow, melodic, a little mournful, and while Bruno could not quite make out the drawled English words the mood felt right. What surprised Bruno was the solo, a different guitar altogether and using a slide, the metal glove on a finger that changed the sound into something sharper and leaving a lingering, almost plaintive tone behind it.

The second number was a classic ballad, a love song, and this time Bruno caught the words of the chorus – 'Watching you sleep.' Again he heard the different guitars and the melody was sweet and new. He liked it and told himself he'd play it again when he had time to note down the words or when he saw Pamela so she could translate. He hit the fast-forward button to get to the duets with Jamie, intrigued by how the old man would balance his son's classical guitar.

He recognized the notes of the Spanish classic, Rodrigo's 'Concierto de Aranjuez'. At home, he had a CD of Paco de Lucia playing it on guitar while backed by an orchestra, the delicacy of the guitar against the deep sound of the strings and the sharp counterpoint of the clarinet. But this was different. Bruno tried to work out how it had been done. He assumed that Jamie had played the classical guitar but then Macrae had laid down a separate bass guitar track to play the orchestral role and then used a steel guitar with a slider instead of the clarinet. It was different, not so different as to be odd or ungainly, but instead sounding fresh and genuine.

Was this only something that Macrae could put together in a recording studio, Bruno asked himself, or might the father and son be able to reproduce this live on stage? What a coup it would be for the Périgord if Macrae's first comeback event were to be staged here in St Denis, an open-air concert on the riverbank.

If Macrae wanted publicity, Bruno could certainly arrange that, through *Sud Ouest* and the local radio and TV stations. They would jump at the chance, and once word got around, the riverbank would be packed with people. He might even be able to stage it on a Tuesday evening, when the town held its popular *marché nocturne*, filling the flat land behind the medical centre with benches and tables and stalls selling food. Just across the river from the stage where the free concerts were held, the diners at the night market would be able to see and hear the performance, or eat first and stroll across the bridge to the concert. Excited by the prospect, Bruno pressed the replay button to hear Macrae's music again.

When he reached the St Denis *collège* Bruno climbed the steps to Florence's apartment but there was no reply. He walked to the school's science lab, where he found Florence running the popular computer club she had founded. A dozen pupils were at work on laptops and desktops and Florence's two young children leaped up to greet him from the corner where they had been playing with a tablet.

They dragged him to the small chairs where they had been sitting to show him the electronic painting they'd been making, a rather geometric version of a dog in brown, black and white, with long ears, sniffing at some red flowers. It was evidently meant to be Balzac. Bruno admired it and told them to save it so that when they next saw his dog they could show him his portrait. Bruno wasn't sure that Balzac would recognize himself but the children already seemed more at home with computers than Bruno could ever be.

He offered Macrae's CD to Florence, asked if she could copy it for herself and email a copy to their friend Amélie in Paris, a magistrate with a splendid voice who would be singing at the riverfront concerts in July.

'Let me know what you think,' he said. 'It's new songs that Rod Macrae has been working on and a duet with his son. I think it's pretty good but I'm not sure how to copy it.'

Florence gave him a pitying look, put the disc into the tower of a desktop, downloaded it and then pressed a few keys before explaining that she was emailing a copy to Amélie and another for herself.

'It's his copyright so I thought I'd better password-protect it and I'll let Amélie know the password separately,' she said. She handed him back the disc. 'If you like, I can send a copy to your phone so you'll also have it there and I'm sure we can find an app that will transcribe and then translate the lyrics for you.'

'Really? You can do that on my phone, translate the words from the music?'

Florence gave him that pitying look again. 'Maybe you should start sitting in with us here at the computer club and learn a few more of the basics.'

Feeling suitably chastened, Bruno drove to the Mairie to collect Balzac and was pulling into his own driveway when his phone vibrated. He checked the screen. It was Annette, the Sarlat magistrate.

'Filing the mistreatment charge has been delayed, Bruno,' she began. The Procureur in Périgueux and my boss here in Sarlat are arguing about jurisdiction, who brings the prosecution. If you want to hurry things up, I suggest you talk to your friend on *Sud Ouest* and get some animal rights enthusiasts involved. Nothing speeds up lawyers like bad publicity.'

Bruno made three calls. The advantage of being a country policeman for so long was his range of contacts. So his first call was to the local secretary of SPA, the Société Protectrice des Animaux. The second was to the head of Jeunes Agriculteurs, an energetic young man whom he'd taught to play rugby.

The third was to Philippe Delaron, the local correspondent of *Sud Ouest*, and he made sure Philippe had the first two phone numbers and the number of Sarrail's office. *That should work,* he thought.

6

After his dawn run through the woods with Balzac and a brisk thirty minutes exercising the horses at Pamela's riding school, Bruno was showered, shaved and dressed in uniform ready to perform his traditional stroll through the Saturday morning market. But the ritual of coffee and croissant at Fauquet's, with a corner of croissant for Balzac, was not to be missed and only after that did Bruno begin his patrol of the market, greeting friends, enjoying the sight of the stalls loaded with fresh strawberries, cherries, radishes and all the bounty of early summer. Bruno's nose twitched at the familiar smell of the chickens turning slowly on their row of spits on the rotisserie. He felt the heat from the grill as he paused to greet Raoul, who wore a thin singlet and a cotton headband to keep the sweat from his eyes.

'Hot work,' said Bruno, shaking hands as he admired the rows of quail, pigeons, chickens and capons on the grill. He always marvelled that Raoul managed to sell them all. 'It's good standing here in winter but not so much now.'

'You get used to it,' said Raoul, taking a swig from a bottle of water and then turning to attend to a customer.

Bruno walked on to find his friend Stéphane, who was sitting

61

at a folding table behind his cheese stall with Michel, who sold the best fruit and vegetables, and Germinal, who was selling wines from the town vineyard. The table was placed strategically at the point where their three stalls backed up against one another and they were enjoying their usual *casse-croûte*, the meal of cheese and bread and pâté that the market people relished all the more, having started loading their vans before six in the morning. A half-empty glass of red wine stood before each of them. Without waiting to ask, Germinal took from his stall another glass to pour Bruno a welcome drink while they passed on the market gossip. He finished his wine, thanked them and moved on, pausing when he saw Meghan scurrying across the bridge towards the market, empty shopping bags in both hands and across her shoulders.

'*Bonjour*, Bruno,' she said, presenting her cheek to be kissed. 'I had to park miles away, behind all the camping cars. And I'm in a panic. We just got a call from Jamie to tell us he's arriving this evening from Paris with a minivan full of friends. And Kirsty flies into Bergerac airport this afternoon so I'm going to have to shop to feed them all tonight and tomorrow. Rod's in his damn studio, working, and I have beds to make, bathrooms to clean. He's got no idea how much work goes into getting ready for a houseful of guests. What the hell do I feed them all?'

'You know the old rule: when in doubt, roast chicken.'

'Yes, but two of Jamie's friends are vegetarian, maybe even vegan.'

'No problem,' said Bruno, who always enjoyed thinking of menus. 'It's warm enough to eat outside so give them gazpacho to begin, then a couple of roast chickens from Raoul to save you cooking. You buy some cheese from Stéphane and some cherries and strawberries from the market. The asparagus is great this year, served with melted butter for most of the guests and lemon for the vegans. I saw you already have lots of lettuce in your *potager* at home.'

'I was thinking of going to the bio stall for different kinds of vegetable pâté, hummus and tofu,' Meghan replied. 'And lots of bread.'

'Good idea. And why not get some soy sauce, ginger, mung beans and mushrooms and make a big Chinese-style stir fry. With a bag of potatoes, another of onions and a third of carrots plus lots of fruit, pasta bread and rice, that's the vegetarians taken care of. Now that's settled, let me get you a coffee at Fauquet's first, then we can go shopping and I'll help you carry the bags to the car.'

They took a table on the terrace shaded from the sun by a large orange parasol and ordered coffee for Bruno and a hot chocolate and croissant for Meghan. He asked what she thought of the drone video of Chateau Rock.

'I thought it was great, really stunning, and I loved the styling stuff she did indoors, like a cross between a baronial mansion and a classy hotel. I've no talent for that kind of thing but I can't wait for Kirsty to see it. She's different, really gifted that way, got the artistic gene from her dad, I expect.'

'Has Kirsty sorted out her course at university?'

'That's one of the things that's worrying me,' Meghan said. She looked as if she'd dressed in a hurry or come straight from gardening, in grubby jeans and a checked shirt that had seen better days. This was unusual, thought Bruno; she normally dressed with care. Her hair was straggling from a loose bun, a style that didn't suit her. Still, she smiled as Balzac rested his head on her knee and gazed up at her with appealing eyes. Bruno knew his dog was thinking of Meghan's croissant.

'She said she's made a decision and wants to come and let us know, which makes it sound as though it's not something that we'll want to hear. Rod's already in a bad mood, after the woman from the estate agents said he should forget about asking for three million and set his sights a lot lower.'

'He'll cheer up when the kids arrive,' said Bruno.

'I'm not so sure,' she said. 'He's unhappy about this divorce, although he says he understands and he accepts it. He doesn't like being alone, never has. At least now he's back making music, which I'm very pleased about. But he says he'll really miss his recording studio when the chateau is sold. I can tell what he's thinking – everything seems to be going wrong for him at once and it's all my fault. I feel guilty but I owe it to myself to live for me for a change, and not just for Rod and the kids. I got married so young.'

'You're entitled to your own life, Meghan. Rod told me he understands that.'

'Understanding it and accepting it are two very different things,' she said, her voice sounding tired.

'Maybe there's a new future for him in music,' Bruno said. 'He gave me a CD of his latest songs and I think they're great. I was planning to come up to ask him if he'd like to give one of our riverbank concerts.'

'That would cheer him up. Why not come and tell him that and then join us all for dinner this evening? Jamie and Kirsty will be really pleased to see you which might help smooth things over and I know Rod will be bucked up if you tell him you like the new songs.'

'I'm having trouble making out the words in English,' Bruno said. 'But I also really liked that duet he played with Jamie, the concerto. Rod told me the other day he's hoping he and Jamie can put together some more music this summer and he's planning to record Jamie's first solo CD. And, yes, I'd love to come to dinner this evening but wouldn't I be in the way with all Jamie's guests?'

'Quite the opposite. And bring this little fellow,' she said, caressing Balzac and giving him a piece of her croissant. 'Just the sight of him makes everybody smile.'

'In that case, I'll be there, but let me make the gazpacho and I'll bring it with me. So that's less bother for you in the market.'

'You're a lifesaver, Bruno,' she said, leaning forward to plant a kiss on his cheek. 'It's funny, but even in that uniform I can never think of you as a policeman.'

'I won't wear it tonight. I wouldn't want to intimidate Jamie or his friends,' he said, smiling.

'Their friends seem interesting; one of them is a girl that Jamie seems very keen on. Another is at the Royal College with Jamie. The others are all at the Paris Conservatoire where they've been rehearsing for these summer concerts they're doing all over the region.'

'You must have had an interesting youth with Rod and his band,' Bruno said, glad of the chance to ask Meghan some questions that had left him curious for years. 'Were they at the height of their fame when you got to know him?'

'Looking back, I think they were past their peak by then, but I didn't really know. He was still famous, or at least the band was, and I loved their music. I was just sixteen, although I told Rod I was older when we met. And he told me he was only in his thirties. In fact he was forty-five. The local paper had a competition and the prize was to meet the band and then to be allowed to go backstage after the show. I was the lucky one and went with my kid brother and we all sort of hit it off and one thing led to another.'

'Were you still at school?'

'I'd just left and was training to be a hairdresser and I was starry-eyed. Me with a real rock star! And I think Rod was ready to settle down. Life on the road is pretty exhausting and the band was in that phase where they knew they were starting to break up but stayed together for the sake of the money, so the music suffered. Some of them blamed me, which made the arguments worse. I was pregnant by then. We spent days on the bus, going from gig to gig, nobody talking except when some of them started making snide comments when I had to stop the bus to be sick on the side of the road. I don't know why they call it morning sickness. I had it all the time.'

'Was that when you came here, very pregnant with Jamie?' Bruno said.

'Yes. Rod had been here a couple of times before he met me, staying with friends from music. Pink Floyd, Deep Purple, 10cc – several of them had places down here back then and doubtless they had some wild times. But Rod had fallen in love with the landscape and the food and wine and he was fascinated by the caves. He still goes off to visit them, buys books on pre-history, even collects old flint tools. After the rains sometimes he goes walking, looking to see if some new ones have been unearthed.'

'I wish I'd known that,' said Bruno. 'I do the same, it's amazing how beautiful some of them can be, those perfect leaf shapes.'

Meghan nodded politely but seemed to want to get back to her story. 'Anyway, when the band broke up, we hit the Périgord trail for a new life together. And it worked, we were happy and raising the kids but when they went away to school in England it started to change, for both of us. Even though I'd started giving those English classes at the *collège* we had time on our hands. Rod was getting visibly older, the chateau felt almost empty and far too big, needing too much work to keep the place up. That's why I did that Open University degree and then I realized I could start a new life on my own. Does that sound selfish?'

Bruno shook his head. 'You only have one life.'

'That's what I tell myself, and I suppose it's what I'll tell Kirsty when she lets us know whatever it is she's decided to do. I've got a feeling she wants to stay in France rather than go to university in Edinburgh. She was born here, after all.'

'So she's a French citizen. She could go to university here.'

'I hadn't thought of that. But why not?'

Meghan sat up and collected her bags. 'I'd better get the shopping done. Potatoes, asparagus, strawberries and the rest. At least thanks to the town vineyard we've got lots of wine at home.'

Bruno was heading back into the Mairie when he was hailed. He turned and saw Brosseil waving at him from the bio stall, with a rose in his lapel, wearing patent leather shoes and dressed as carefully as if he were off to a ballroom dancing contest. Bruno went across, shook hands and waited while Brosseil put his change into a small leather pouch that he slipped back into a trouser pocket.

'The *notaire* in Périgueux sent me a copy of Driant's new will along with the other documents that he swore before the three assessors,' Brosseil said. 'They only arrived this morning and I thought you'd like to see them.'

'Thank you,' said Bruno. 'Do they tell us anything new?'

'Not really, except that Sarrail handled both the will and the sale, which isn't exactly illegal but it's not recommended, for obvious reasons. It also means he's responsible for ensuring the livestock regulations were observed – and we know they weren't. We also now have the name of the insurance company that was involved. And it came with an invitation for me to visit the retirement home tomorrow afternoon. They're holding an open house, probably trying to drum up business among the local *notaires*.'

'They've already been doing that with the doctors around here,' said Bruno. 'Gelletreau got a free lunch out of it.'

'We *notaires* only seem to be getting refreshments, whatever that means. From three until six. Obviously we're seen as less worthy than the medical men.'

'Or perhaps they suspect you are all men of unquestioned probity and therefore less liable to be seduced by their blandishments,' Bruno replied, smiling. 'Are you going?'

'No, but I thought you might be interested in taking a look for yourself, if you think it's worthwhile following this up. I'm not sure it is. It looks as though they did what was legally required for Driant to file a new will but it still leaves a nasty taste in the mouth so I've filed a complaint with the *notaires*' association over the livestock. There may be one remaining issue – I'd never heard of the insurance company, Euro-Trans-Med. They have offices in Cyprus, Malta, Monaco, Luxembourg. I'll look into that when I have a chance.'

'Tell me,' said Bruno. 'Even if the new will was legal and Driant was deemed competent by the proper authorities, are there any grounds at all for the will to be contested?'

'Yes, if there's evidence of inherent fraud in the dispositions under the new will, which is why you might want to check the credentials of the insurance company. Or if there is any evidence that Driant was acting under constraint or improper pressure such as blackmail. But I can't say I see any signs of that.'

7

Thinking he'd better try to wrap up the loose ends in the Driant case, Bruno called the medical centre to ask if Dr Gelletreau was free. He was with a patient but his shift was about to end so Bruno strolled across the bridge to the clinic and glanced through one of the well-thumbed glossy magazines as he waited. They mostly contained celebrity gossip and photos of Britain's royal family and various lesser stars among Europe's old rulers, from Belgium and Sweden to Monaco and some German princelings he'd never heard of. Bruno wondered whether these publications represented the doctors' own subscriptions or came from patients. Or maybe there was some central depository that stored magazines until they were deemed sufficiently ancient to be distributed around the waiting rooms of France. Beneath the glossies, he found an ancient issue of *Pèlerin*, a Christian monthly he had thought long since discontinued. He was halfway through a moderately interesting article on pilgrimages to Lourdes when Gelletreau appeared.

'You wanted to see me, Bruno?' said St Denis's oldest doctor, ushering him into the consulting room, where Bruno explained the concerns of Driant's family and asked if Gelletreau was confident of his diagnosis of heart failure as the cause of death.

'Short of an autopsy one can never be certain,' came the reply. 'But I'm confident, yes. Driant was my patient for years and he'd had heart troubles, arrhythmia and palpitations. He was on blood thinners, then beta blockers and I'd recommended that a pacemaker be inserted. I didn't think a heart attack was imminent but in view of his lifestyle I wanted to take no chances.'

'His lifestyle?'

Gelletreau smiled and leaned forward. 'Just between us, I can tell you he was a *chaud lapin*, damn near insatiable, or as much as he could be at that age.' *Chaud lapin*, literally 'hot rabbit', was the French phrase for any man who was sexually active, eager and indiscriminate.

'That's why he joined that club for the Troisième Age, so he could meet women, usually widows, who were prepared to accommodate him,' Gelletreau went on. 'He was always pressing me to give him a prescription for Viagra, which in view of his heart condition I refused to do. He may have got some through the internet although I'd warned him against it. You can do a lot for patients but you can't force them to take your advice. Frankly, the only thing that surprised me about his death was that he was alone and not in bed. That's probably how he'd have wanted to go, although I doubt whether that's what his kids would like to hear. What are they worried about?'

'Apparently he signed up to move to that fancy new retirement home near Sarlat.'

'Really? The one at the chateau? That's a surprise.'

'I thought he might have heard of it from you,' Bruno said.

'I gather they were contacting all the local doctors to offer their services.'

'It's a very fine place but probably far beyond the financial reach of most people around here. But Driant knew about it already. He came to see me with a pamphlet about the place that he'd found at that Troisième Age club he went to and asked what I thought. I said it was very expensive but that having medical care permanently available was probably a good thing and it seemed to have a decent social life. They invited me to lunch when they took me round on a tour. The food was excellent.'

'It seems Driant went along to look the place over and signed up.'

Gelletreau smiled again. 'He probably saw all the single widows there and reckoned he'd found himself a happy hunting ground.'

'So you didn't recommend it?'

'No, what I recommended was what I prescribed for him: installing a pacemaker to get his heart beating normally. I can't swear to his dying of a heart attack but I'd be stunned if there'd been any other cause. It was obvious to me that he'd died at once, otherwise he'd have tried to reach his phone. There was no need for an autopsy; nothing suspicious, just the sad death of a man who lived alone.'

Bruno nodded, making a private note to look into Driant's missing phone, and stood to take his leave, when Gelletreau asked, 'Where are you going with this, Bruno?'

'Just trying to put the minds of his two children at rest. They'd been expecting an inheritance but he signed an insurance deal to pay for the place in that retirement home that left very little for the heirs.'

Gelletreau grunted. 'I didn't know that. It seems he was even more of an old fool than I'd thought. Was this insurance deal all above board?'

'It looks that way. He made out a new will and was declared competent to do so by a tribunal of assessors in Périgueux.'

'I see. I'm sorry for his children. I knew them both quite well, treated them when they were growing up. Indeed, his daughter Claudette was one of the first babies I brought into the world when I arrived here. An impressive girl, very bright, always reading, she seemed almost to live in the public library. Driant could never reconcile himself to her way of life.'

'How do you mean?'

'Claudette went to university in Paris where she discovered or perhaps realized that she was gay. She became very feminist and then very successful with a high-powered management consultancy job in Paris.' Gelletreau shrugged and sighed and then sat back comfortably in his chair, the pose of an accomplished raconteur. 'She couldn't wait to get away from the farm and her father could never forgive her for not presenting him with a clutch of grandchildren. He was already a grandpa through Gaston's kids but he was an old-fashioned man. Women should be getting married, looking after their husband and staying at home to produce lots of children – that was his view and he held to it very firmly.

'I know it saddened him, both the way Claudette lived and the estrangement, but at least she came to the funeral so I give her credit for that,' Gelletreau went on. 'He was proud of her in his way, but he couldn't express it. I understand his views because that was the way I was brought up. But I understand Claudette's position too; times change and we have to change with them. Driant didn't see it that way.'

'Except for the Viagra,' Bruno said, with a rueful smile.

'That was about the only aspect of modern life he had time for,' Gelletreau said, chuckling. 'I think he knew his way of life was over. Now that they've slashed the hill farm subsidies it can't go on, even though he was barely in the cash economy. He used the subsidy money for his phone and electricity and buying diesel for that old truck. He lived on his mutton, his chickens and that patch of *potager* for his potatoes and cabbages. He burned his own timber in a wood stove he used for warmth and cooking. And he got his pocket money from selling that firewater he made.'

'The best *gnôle* in the valley,' said Bruno.

'Indeed it was and I'm glad I have a few bottles to remember him by. Every time he came to see me he left me a bottle. In fact . . .'

Gelletreau bent down and reached into the cupboard of his desk and brought out two glasses and an unmarked litre bottle two thirds full of a colourless liquid. He uncorked it and poured out a generous glass for each of them.

'Here, let's drink to the memory of the old boy,' he said, handing Bruno a glass. He clinked his own against it and then each of them murmured, 'To Driant.'

'Hah!' said Bruno once the fire in his throat subsided. 'Nobody makes it like that any more.'

'More's the pity,' said the old doctor. He emptied his glass, and then stuck out his tongue to lick the last of the spirit from his bushy white moustache.

'By the way,' said Bruno, 'when you went there and pronounced him dead, did you see his mobile phone?'

Gelletreau shrugged and poured himself another slug. 'No, I don't think so, but it never occurred to me to look.'

Bruno walked back to his office, thinking about what he should say before he called Gaston Driant's number in Bordeaux. He felt obliged to report that there had been a new legal will and that his father had been deemed mentally competent to sign it. And that Dr Gelletreau was sure of his death certificate. But how far should he raise possible false hopes about the legality of the sale?

'I don't know if you were aware of it but his doctor had been treating your dad for heart trouble,' he began when Gaston answered his phone. 'The doc had recently recommended that he should be fitted with a pacemaker, so it looks as though there's not much question about the cause of death.'

'No, I didn't know that,' Gaston said. 'He never mentioned it. But that was his way. He kept a lot of things to himself so I'm not surprised.'

'I'm not sure how much further we can continue the enquiry, Gaston,' Bruno continued. 'I'm sorry, but your dad seemed pretty sure that he wanted to go to the new retirement home. He went there for a look around and told Gelletreau that he liked what he saw. Still, I gather he left you and your sister some personal items and family jewellery in the new will so it's clear he was thinking of you.'

'I suppose so, Bruno, and thanks for looking into it. What's going to happen to the sheep and lambs?'

'That's up to the new owner. The *notaire* assured me that he'll take care of it though we may be able to get them for negligence. I think they'll send the lot to a local abattoir. But if you want to start raising chickens yourself I'm sure there would be no objection if you took them away.'

'It's a nice thought, Bruno, but we haven't got the space in the garden, let alone enough room in my car to move them all, and it would cost me a tankful of petrol to come up again. Feel free to take any of the chickens you want and give the others away if you can find a home for them. I'd rather that than send them off to some butcher. Dad was fond of those birds and the eggs were pretty good.'

'Aren't you going to take some of the furniture? That was all left to you and Claudette, along with his tools.'

'I took the tools plus some small things we remembered, mementoes, really, some of the plates and cutlery, the books and family photo albums. Frankly, my wife took one look at the furniture and said we should have burned the carpets right then and there. I had enough trouble from her when I suggested we might keep his sheepdogs. She really put her foot down. Still, I took the rocking chair he'd made for himself, even though she's banished it to my garden shed.'

'Just one last thing, or rather two. Did you ever find your dad's mobile phone?'

'No, but I can't say I was looking for it. Do you have the number?'

'Yes, thanks. I found it on an old bill. If you want to read your dad's new will I can get you a copy but it might not be easy reading. Your dad was a bit harsh about your sister's lifestyle. Gelletreau said he could never reconcile himself to it.'

'That's true enough, although I'm sad to say it.' He spoke quickly, as though wanting to end the call. 'Well, that seems to be the end of it and I appreciate what you've done.'

After Gaston hung up, Bruno thought that was the end of the matter until J-J called to invite Bruno to lunch in Périgueux along with J-J's friend from the *fisc*.

'I told you I'd check with him and it turns out he was already interested in this Périgueux *notaire* of yours, Sarrail, having come across his name in some other funny business. Any new developments at your end?'

'Not really. I just interviewed the doctor who pronounced him dead of a heart attack and he's sure of his diagnosis. The old man already had heart trouble and was scheduled for a pacemaker. The one bit of news is that I've got the name of the insurance company that was supposed to pay out for Driant to go to the fancy retirement home: Euro-Trans-Med. It seems to be based in Cyprus, Monaco, Malta and Luxembourg. Our local *notaire* had never heard of it.'

'Nor have I,' J-J said. 'But my antennae start to twitch whenever I hear of something involving money that's based in Monaco. I think the man from the *fisc* will be more than interested in that.'

'What day is this lunch? Remember Tuesday is our market day so I'll be stuck in St Denis until midday at the earliest.'

'I know, that's why I've arranged the lunch for Wednesday. My friend will take the train from Bordeaux that gets in at eleven thirty so I've booked us a table for noon.'

'Where are we eating?' Bruno asked.

'Where do you expect three cops to eat in Périgueux? Where I can eat *tête de veau*? And I seem to recall that last time we ate there you raved about that turbot dish they do in a *pot-au-feu* with the scallops.'

'Ah, the Hercule Poirot,' Bruno said. 'That lovely old room with the arches just over the square from the cathedral. What was it, fourteenth century or something? Is your friend an Agatha Christie fan?'

'Of course, and better still, his name's also Hercule, Hercule Goirau. You probably know him by reputation. He was the one who cracked that big wine scam a couple of years ago, sent a couple of *négociants* to prison. You remember, the one with the fake labels of Châteauneuf du Pape that went to China. He's head of the Bordeaux office these days, and not a man you'd want to have looking into your accounts. He's got quite a reputation so I hope you're up to date with your taxes.'

'You hardly make it sound like a lunch I should look forward to,' said Bruno, laughing. 'Even though I'm far too poor to have tax problems.'

'I'm kidding. Hercule is all right, even gave me a few investment tips. But you know these boys from the *fisc*, brains like adding machines. Still, he likes his food and wine so you'll have to admit that proves he's sound at heart.'

8

Making gazpacho was for Bruno much more important than preparing a simple soup. It marked the moment when spring had turned indisputably into summer, when he routinely ate in the open air and the garden provided most of his meals. He put on Macrae's CD as he washed, trimmed and deseeded the vegetables before cutting them into chunks and putting them into his blender. He usually prepared a soup for six or eight people, but today he'd make enough for three separate days to help Meghan with her brood of hungry young guests, and another for himself.

One peeled cucumber, one red and one yellow pepper and a half kilo of ripe, plum tomatoes went into the blender with five tablespoons of olive oil, two glasses of Bergerac sec white wine and a glass of water. He added salt, pepper, three well-chopped cloves of garlic, a third of a *bâtard* of *pain aux céreales*, and one of two small loaves of brown bread he'd bought to thicken the soup. He tasted the result, added a pinch more salt, a tablespoon of tomato purée and a small glass of oloroso sherry and gave the now full blender another brief whir.

Bruno poured the result into a big glass jar, and repeated the entire process three times more. He put all four jars into his fridge, three for Meghan and one for himself. He poured two tablespoons of olive oil into his largest pan and chopped the remaining *bâtard* into crouton-sized chunks and put them into the oven to crisp.

He found himself enjoying Macrae's new songs even more this time, and especially the duet of the Rodrigo concerto that he'd played with his son. When it ended, Bruno put his original version by Paco de Lucia into his player and found that he preferred it but that the Macrae adaptation stayed in his head, perhaps because like so many of his generation he was accustomed to the sound of an electric guitar. When had they become common? he wondered. Probably in the 1950s. Had they been available in their day would not Mozart and Beethoven have written for an instrument so distinctive? With his thoughts on this track, he reflected that the saxophone was also a relatively new instrument and where would jazz be without it?

But this was no day to lounge around indoors, Bruno chided himself, and went out to his garden, taking the hoe to start weeding between the rows of vegetables he'd planted earlier in the year. Balzac watched him for a moment and then bounded off to visit the ducks and chickens and to patrol the grounds. Bruno paused to watch him and then raised his eyes to the view that stretched out ahead, the field of pasture that rose to the next ridge, and then rose again to another yet higher crest. On and on went the landscape, rising and falling, some with trees and others with bare moorland, until the highest ground Bruno could see stood out starkly against the bright blue sky to the east.

It was a view he never tired of, but he went back to his weeding, breaking off only when he remembered that he had still to unload the washing machine that he'd filled before making the soup. He brought the wet clothes out in a big wicker basket and pegged them out to dry on the lines he'd strung between the trees. Then he whistled for Balzac, ready to set out on a stroll along the ridge and enjoy the afternoon until it was time to head for the riding school to give Hector his evening exercise. He'd barely set out when he was interrupted by a phone call from Amélie in Paris.

'Those songs from Rod Macrae, they're great,' she began. 'Will he be around when I come down?'

'Yes, all through the summer, and his kids, too. His son, Jamie, is the classical guitarist on the instrumental track.'

'Do you think he'd mind if I performed that one, "Watching You Sleep", when I come down? I'd give him the credit and everything but I think it's beautiful. Do you know him well enough to ask for me?'

'Yes, I'm going to his place for dinner this evening. I can ask him then.'

'I'll send you two songs I've recorded at home, just a recording app on my laptop but he might like to hear what another singer makes of it. I mean, I'm not normally this forward but –'

'Oh yes, you are, Amélie,' Bruno interrupted, a chuckle in his voice. 'You're wonderfully forward in the nicest possible way.'

'I'm not sure if that's a compliment or what but I'll email you two songs, one of them with my voice doing a very gentle backing track, like a chorus. And the other is my version. Ask him what he thinks. And don't forget to tell him I think the songs are terrific and his voice is great. It's way past time for him to make a comeback.'

'I won't forget,' Bruno replied. 'I was going to give Rod exactly the same advice this evening, but whether he takes it – I don't know. He's depressed because his wife wants a divorce. But at least he has the prospect of an alternative future through music and his son is ready to join him in that.'

It was a conversation that stayed with Bruno as he drove to Chateau Rock. As was so often the case when he discussed a problem with someone else, he'd begun to see things a little differently and found himself able to put his new perception into words. Whether Macrae wanted to pay the slightest attention to Bruno's advice would be up to him, but also, Bruno reflected, on the way that Bruno delivered it. In Bruno's experience the best way to deliver advice was to make it sound like something else. So if Bruno let Macrae think he was doing St Denis a favour by singing at the town concerts he might be more tempted to try it.

Bruno had always got on well with Rod and Meghan but his real connection was with their children. He smiled to himself as he realized how much he was looking forward to seeing them on the brink of adulthood, and to meet this girl that Jamie was said to be interested in. It was Kirsty who came bounding forward, almost like a puppy, to hug him as he climbed out of the Land Rover. She bent down to caress Balzac and tell him what a fine boy he was, and then hugged Bruno again. Like her brother, she took after her father, the same tall and rangy build. Not a conventionally pretty girl, she had good eyes, a generous mouth and thick, brown hair with a natural curl. She'd grow into her looks, Bruno thought.

'You're looking well,' he said. 'Something has made you happy – and if it's love, whoever he is, he'd better be worth it.'

'No, it's not that. It's that I've finally decided what it is I want to do, and it's not law and it's not Edinburgh.'

'Don't keep me in suspense. Have you told your mum and dad?'

'I've told Mum, and she sort of agrees, but I'm waiting to tell Dad until he's more relaxed after dinner and I'm counting on you to help him see things my way. I want to go to Bordeaux university and do a degree in wine and make that my career. It's a four-year course, with the prospect of vacations working in Australia, California, Chile, Italy – and it means that in the long run I'll have the option of staying here in the Périgord where I was born.'

'Having seen you working in the vineyard every time you come back, I can't say I'm really surprised,' said Bruno. 'And it's not as though you don't know what you're getting into, always at the mercy of the weather. But I have to say I've never met anyone who makes decent wine who isn't fundamentally happy about their life.'

'Will you say that to Dad?'

'Of course. Is Jamie here yet?'

Kirsty shook her head. 'Still on his way in a van with his friends. Dad's in the recording studio, polishing some stuff he wants to do with Jamie when he gets here, and Mum's in the kitchen.'

'I'm looking forward to meeting this young woman Jamie is keen on,' he said. 'Your mum mentioned her. Do you know her?'

'Yes, Galina. She came to London for a long weekend to visit

83

Jamie and we had dinner at some gastro-pub. She'd never seen one before. She's quite shy, very pretty and from an extremely rich family. She stayed at the Ritz in a suite that cost more per night than I live on in a month. And Jamie says she's a brilliant musician.'

'Is she French?' Bruno asked.

'No, originally Russian, I think, but she hasn't lived there for years. Jamie says she's got a European passport, from Cyprus, I think.'

She helped him carry in the three jars of gazpacho, the box of croutons and the kilo-sized box of *aillou* he'd bought at Stéphane's stall. Gazpacho was never complete, Bruno believed, without a spoonful of the blend of crème fraîche and *fromage blanc*, herbs and garlic, that his friend made fresh each day. In the kitchen they found Meghan grappling with a mountain of peeled potatoes, carrots and courgettes and worrying whether she should leave the cheese out or put it back in the fridge.

'Should I put the vegetables in the oven now, do you think?' she asked Bruno nervously, her hands half-raised as though not quite sure what to do with them. Her face was red and her hair was hanging in tendrils. 'Oh dear, I've got to go and shower and change yet. Thank heavens you're here, Bruno. And with the gazpacho, bless you.'

'Oh, Mum, the others are still on the way. There's lots of time,' said Kirsty, a daughter who looked fully grown but was still young enough that she'd not learned to hide her exasperation with her elders.

'I imagine the first thing they'll want when they get here is a bathroom, or several bathrooms,' said Bruno. 'I'll put the gazpacho away and catch up with Kirsty while you go and change. I'm sure Kirsty's right – you've got lots of time. And if they do turn up early, I'll look after the vegetables while Kirsty sees them settled and gets them all a drink. Then you can make your big entrance as the lady of the chateau.'

Bruno grinned at her and made an extravagant bow to make Meghan laugh. She'd barely gone upstairs, still smiling, when Rod came in through the kitchen door, mobile phone in hand. Jamie had just called him to say the minivan was passing Niversac, which meant they were about thirty minutes from arriving. And there would be six people, not five as expected.

'Jamie says they're a bit tight-packed in the van,' said Rod, helping himself to wine. 'They have the guitar and cello case up on the roof rack with the suitcases.'

'You mean it's a sextet?' Bruno asked.

'Basically it's a string trio, a cello played by one of Jamie's pals at the Royal College with a violin and a viola from the Paris Conservatoire. Jamie plays guitar and he can also play piano, and then there's his girlfriend who plays the flute. The sixth guy is some out-of-work distant cousin of hers so he's coming as the driver, roadie and bag carrier. It will be good to have a houseful of young people.'

There was a lot of contact between the musical schools of Paris and London, Rod explained. Jamie had told him that the pupils and teachers encouraged them to spend a term or two in the other capital and the summer music festivals in each country offered a way to make some pocket money and improve their performance skills.

'What about you?' Bruno asked. 'Are you going to be

performing? I really liked your new songs and that duet you played with Jamie. I'd love to see you doing your new songs at one of our riverside evenings in St Denis. And there's a young jazz singer, a friend of mine, who liked "Watching You Sleep" so much she made a backing track for it. Have a listen.' Bruno pulled out his phone.

'I wasn't planning to share that stuff just yet. That was for your ears only.'

'Sorry, you didn't say so and I was so enthusiastic about it . . .'

'That's okay. Let's hear what she's done with it.'

Bruno pressed Play and even through the tiny phone speakers the voices of Rod and Amélie blended well together. She sang along with him on the chorus lines but in the separate verses she just let her voice croon discreetly, almost as a separate instrument.

'She's good,' said Rod, nodding. 'I like it. Email it to me and I'll play it through my own speakers in the studio, get a better idea of how it works. She's got a great voice. Where's she from?'

'Guadeloupe, but she sang in clubs in Canada when she was putting herself through university there and she's living in Paris now. She'll be here for a week, singing at our evening concerts and also doing a special show of Josephine Baker songs at Chateau des Milandes. They're planning to make a recording and the whole concert is going to be televised. I can get you tickets, if you want.'

'I'd like to see that, thanks.'

Behind her father, Kirsty was trying to send some kind of discreet signal to Bruno, putting her finger to her lips in a universal code for silence. He assumed that she did not want him to raise her decision to abandon law for the profession of wine. He nodded briefly, then asked, 'What is Meghan planning to do with these heaps of vegetables?'

'Drizzle them with olive oil and bake them in the oven,' said Kirsty. 'It's not fancy but it will do the job.'

'In that case we'd better start slicing the potatoes and carrots. They'll take longer than the courgettes.'

Bruno and Kirsty set to work as Rod lounged against the sink, watching them. Kirsty suggested he might help by setting the big table on the terrace. Dinner plates, side plates, soup bowls, knife and fork and two spoons each, Kirsty suggested.

'And don't take them out one and two at a time. Put them all on a tray, Dad,' she said, with a hint of barely controlled impatience in her voice. It reminded Bruno that, much as he longed to be a father, there were aspects of the parent–child relationship that he found unsettling. But then Rod was old enough to be Kirsty's grandfather, he thought, and then caught himself. He wasn't much younger than Rod had been when Jamie was born.

9

Barely had they all finished their tasks when there came the toot-toot of a car horn from the drive. Meghan descended the stairs looking every inch the lady of the chateau. She was wearing a magnificent kaftan of heavy silk and had her hair piled up high. She flung open the double doors and stood waiting on the terrace for her son to bound up and hug her. Only then did Jamie introduce his companions.

'Ah, Balzac, great to see you,' Jamie said, as the basset hound jumped up to greet him, Balzac's habit with old friends. Even after all this time Bruno had been unable to train him out of it.

'Bertie you met in London, *Maman*. Ippo, Pia and Galina are brilliant musicians and friends from Paris. And Sasha who's getting down the cello from the roof is Galina's cousin. We're all dying for a pee and a shower and we're all starving. Hi, sis,' he added, embracing Kirsty and then hugging his father.

'Bruno, grand to see you as well,' Jamie said, embracing him. 'I knew you must be here when I had to fend off Balzac's assault.'

Rod was shaking hands with each of the guests and asked the plump Frenchman with the curly hair, 'Is your name really Ippo?'

'It stands for Hippolyte,' the young man replied in excellent

English. 'I was named for Hippolyte Taine, the historian and a distant relative of my mother. And thank you for inviting us to stay here. It's very kind of you.'

'This place is magnificent,' Pia, the young Frenchwoman, said to Meghan. She was the BCBG type, *bon chic et bon genre*, good style and good class, instantly recognizable from the dress, accent and hairstyle of the well-born and fashionable young *Parisienne*. Hippolyte was the male version. Bertie was different. He was big, athletic and with muscles that suggested regular visits to the gym. But nobody had ever taught him how to dress. He was wearing nylon tracksuit bottoms that stopped at his impressive calves. On his feet were gaudy trainers and he wore a cheap-looking white polo shirt with red, white and blue stripes on the collar. He carried his mobile phone in a pouch on his belt, rather than the way Pia wore hers, casually stuck into the hip pocket of very tight designer jeans.

Bertie was the only one who joined Bruno to help Sasha unload the van. Sasha was lean and tough-looking. Despite the heat of the day he was wearing a long-sleeved denim shirt that did not quite conceal the tattoos on his forearms when he reached up to take the cello case from Bertie. Sasha was a good decade older than the others. There were calluses on the sides and knuckles of his hands that suggested he did a lot of karate. His dark hair was cut very short and his trainers looked new and very expensive indeed, as did his Rolex Oyster watch. He may have been out of work, but his last employment had clearly been lucrative. Unlike Bertie, he ignored Balzac's friendly approach and his face remained expressionless throughout the introductions and unloading.

Galina had shaken hands with Kirsty, Meghan, Rod and Bruno, in that order, had murmured a few polite words to each one and then bent down, hiding her face behind a fall of fine blonde hair, to concentrate on Balzac. Bruno, who noted that she was wearing a Cartier Tank watch, wasn't sure whether she genuinely liked the dog or was doing so to avoid human contact. Balzac, of course, was entranced and not simply because he always liked women.

Kirsty and her mother showed them to their various rooms and Rod and Bruno began opening wine bottles and placing them on the side table on the terrace. With a view down to the pool and tennis court, it was a sheltered and pleasantly warm spot in the sun that was still a couple of hours from setting. Bruno went into the kitchen, put the vegetables into the oven and started boiling water for the asparagus. He poured one of his jars of gazpacho into a tureen and took it out to the table. Rod, wine glass in hand, was staring down at a view he must have known by heart.

'I'll really miss this place,' he said. His wine glass was empty and as if he'd just realized it, he stretched out an arm for a bottle and poured himself a refill. 'I'll miss Meghan, too. Christ only knows where I'll end up.'

'I'm no expert but those new songs of yours should ensure you won't have to worry about your future,' Bruno said. 'You must know they're good; different from what you used to do but I think they're better, more real, a lot of life behind them. Maybe you should do a comeback tour. I'd stand in line to be a paying customer.'

'Thanks, Bruno.' Rod gave a hollow laugh. 'I'll believe you. Thousands wouldn't. What did you think of our house guests?'

'A polite and well-brought-up bunch of young people but the older man, Galina's cousin, seemed somewhat out of place in that company.'

Rod nodded. 'That's what I thought. Not the kind of guy I'd hire as a roadie.' And then, very softly, as if for Bruno's ears alone, he added, 'I'd be a bit wary of meeting him alone in a dark alley.'

Footsteps and loud young voices heralded the arrival of the guests and the terrace became crowded as glasses chinked and bowls of nuts and olives were passed around. Meghan was chatty and cheerful, evidently enjoying being the hostess, so Bruno went into the kitchen.

'Good for you,' said Kirsty, joining him. 'Where are those chickens?' She opened the fridge and pulled them out, still wrapped in tinfoil, as they had come from Raoul. 'Oh God, they haven't been carved.'

'Get me a sharp knife and I'll do it,' said Bruno. He tested the knife she passed him, a Solingen. It sliced the chicken breasts perfectly. Kirsty went to a drawer and pulled out a dozen white linen napkins, murmuring, 'Dad always forgets the napkins.' She took them out to the table and announced that dinner was about to be served.

Since nobody else seemed to think of it, Bruno put the *aillou* into a bowl with a teaspoon, put the kettle on to boil for the asparagus and checked his watch. He took a pack of butter from the fridge and cut cubes into a saucepan which he put onto the oven top beside the asparagus pot so they would warm rather than melt and went out to the table. Rod was sitting at the head and the other end was empty. So Bruno sat there with Kirsty and Galina on either side of him and Sasha beside Galina. They were talking in low tones, almost whispering, in a language Bruno thought must be Russian.

With the food and wine vanishing fast, Bruno thought the gathering must, to an outsider, have looked enviably convivial. But at the table he felt the atmosphere was brittle and strained. He knew Kirsty was worried about telling her father her plans, that Rod was unhappy about the divorce and the loss of this place he loved. But the good spirits and energy he'd expected from the young musicians seemed forced. He'd assumed that Ippo and Pia were a couple but Pia seemed to be cooling on Ippo and being more than friendly to Bertie. Perhaps it was because Ippo was paying more attention to Kirsty than Pia appreciated. Above all, Sasha seemed to cast a gloom over Galina, and her withdrawal behind that screen of long hair created a corner of stiff silence at Bruno's end of the table.

Bruno excused himself to go to the bathroom but instead on an impulse he went to the rental van to check the documents. They were made out to Alexander Kozak, age thirty-five, with a Maltese passport and driving permit. That had to be Sasha. He returned to the terrace. At once Meghan rose, asking Kirsty to help gather the soup bowls and told the guests to help themselves to the bread and vegetable pastes, the hummus and tofu on the table. Bertie was the only guest who rose and began to help stack bowls and take them into the kitchen. Bruno headed to the kitchen to put the asparagus into boiling water. The stalks were slender and very fresh so he reckoned no more than five minutes. He blanched them with cold water and slid the saucepan with the softened butter onto the flame.

'You know what you're doing,' said Bertie, standing by the stove to watch.

'Practice,' said Bruno. 'Is Bertie short for Albert?'

'No, it's because I'm from Alberta in Canada.' Bertie bent down to open the dishwasher door and started to fill it. 'Nobody can pronounce my first name so they call me Bertie. I don't mind.'

'So what's your real name?' Bruno asked, glancing down and seeing a small tattoo on Bertie's upper arm as he reached into the dishwasher. It seemed to be a trident, or perhaps a yellow hand with three fingers raised on a blue background.

'Matviyiko – it's Ukrainian,' Bertie replied. 'My ancestors came to Canada before the First World War. There are well over a million of us Ukrainians in Canada.' He seemed to notice Bruno's interest in the tattoo and said, 'It's the Ukrainian emblem.'

'I have a friend who's writing a book about Ukraine – the Maidan revolution,' said Bruno. 'He was there as a journalist for *Paris Match* when the shooting broke out, says it was the scariest story he'd ever covered. He's been back a couple of times, to Kiev and Crimea, researching.'

'Really?' said Bertie, eagerly. 'I'd like to meet him, see what he thinks about what really happened. I knew someone who died there but so much disinformation has been pumped out that a kind of mythology has grown up around the Heavenly Hundred, the people who got killed there.'

'I'll see if he can meet us for coffee,' said Bruno and they exchanged phone numbers. Then Bruno put the asparagus into a big bowl, their bright green hue set off by the lemons that he'd cut into quarters and placed around the rim of the dish.

The cheese board kept the conversation rolling, as those who ate it told the vegans what they were missing in Stéphane's Tomme d'Audrix, a Trappe d'Echourgnac from a local abbey and one fresh and one *demi-sec* goat cheese. The vegans countered that the quality of the lettuce from the garden could not be appreciated by the cheese-eating barbarians and everyone fell with delight on the strawberries. By this time, the ten of them at table had sunk as many bottles between them although Bruno had been holding back since he had to drive home. Nobody seemed to ask whether the wine from the town vineyard that Rod served was vegan or even organic. When Kirsty began serving coffee, Bruno thought it might be time to go, but Rod and Jamie brought out their guitars and Galina produced a flute.

'Mum and Dad and Kirsty haven't heard this before,' said Jamie. 'In Paris Galina and I have been working on a version of Schubert's *Ständchen* for flute and guitar. It's usually done as a song with piano but it's such an adaptable and lovely piece that we thought we'd try it.'

Bruno didn't know the music but the gentle guitar seemed to him to match the sharper tone of the flute. It was a flute as he had never heard it before, the notes less soft than usual, almost piercing. Bruno was so intent on Jamie and Galina that it took him a moment to realize that Rod had picked up a guitar and started playing a soft bass line to run beneath the main theme.

When the piece ended, the table applauded and Galina gave a brief curtsy. She stood and tossed her head, her blonde hair flying back to reveal a face that in the candlelight took on a classic, cool beauty until she transformed it with a smile that became brilliant as the applause went on and she exchanged proud glances with Jamie.

'We'll do one more Schubert, his famous opus one hundred, which is usually performed by strings with a piano,' Jamie said. 'You'll see from the very different tone of this piece why I think that Galina is the best flautist I've ever heard. Some of you might know this Schubert piece from the Stanley Kubrick film, *Barry Lyndon*.'

Jamie bent to his guitar and then glanced up at the girl, an almost worshipful look on his face. 'I learned that from Galina, who knows almost as much about movies as she does about music.'

Bruno saw both Kirsty and her mother shift their gazes sharply to Galina, as if Jamie had revealed more perhaps than he had intended of his feelings for the young woman. Jamie had already turned his eyes back to his guitar and started playing what seemed a military march, a steady beat, while the flute broke in, keeping the same rhythm but then breaking away as though in search of freedom, or possibly of leadership. This was not music as Bruno had ever known it or even thought of it before, being utterly intimate, the players within touching distance of him and having just shared a glance whose intensity Bruno could still feel.

What an extraordinary difference, Bruno thought, between the music he listened to on the radio or on his CD player, music he appreciated and enjoyed and sometimes felt transported by, and this far more powerful and personal closeness and human connection between the musicians. Music for him had been a pleasant backdrop, sometimes an exciting addition to his life. But suddenly he became aware how for talents such as these it could become all-consuming, a passion. Bruno found himself on his feet as they ended, applauding until his hands were sore, knowing he had tears in his eyes and a lump in his throat.

10

Bruno awoke at seven with the music still in his head and jogged through the woods with Balzac. Stopping only to buy breakfast at Fauquet's, he arrived at Florence's apartment shortly after eight. He was carrying a sack of oranges and a paper bag containing two *pains aux chocolat* for the children and two croissants, the pastries still warm from the oven. Balzac was standing at his side, eyes fixed on the paper bag with its tantalizing smells as they waited for Florence to answer the doorbell.

She opened the door and before Bruno or Florence could say a word, the twins exploded onto the doorstep in their haste to embrace Balzac. There was just time for Bruno to kiss Florence before Daniel and Dora began clutching his leg, demanding to be picked up in the usual way, one in each arm. They were growing so fast, Bruno wondered how much longer he'd be able to play this trick. He handed Florence the bag with the pastries and the sack of oranges, murmuring how much better the juice was when freshly squeezed, and bent his knees so he could pick each of them up. With their arms warm around his shoulders and clutching his collar he walked through to the familiar kitchen. It was set for four, with coffee for him and Florence.

'We've got new swimming trunks,' said Dora. 'Mine are red.'

'And mine are blue,' announced Daniel. 'I wanted to sleep in mine but Mummy said we should save them for today.'

'Have you been practising in the bath like I told you?' he asked, putting them down on their chairs.

'Yes, and I held my breath underwater while Mummy counted to ten. Then I stayed down for three more seconds,' said Daniel.

'And we've been practising holding our breaths in bed,' said his sister.

'That's good,' said Bruno, standing at the sink, cutting the oranges in half and starting to squeeze out the juice, enjoying the sharp smell of the fruit. 'What's the longest time you managed?'

'I counted to ten twice,' said Daniel. 'But I think I might have counted a bit faster in the second ten.'

'Whatever you give to Balzac, make sure there are no bits of chocolate in it because that's not good for dogs,' Bruno told them. 'That means all the more chocolate for you.'

They each tore off a corner about the size of Bruno's thumbnail. He joined them at the table, pouring out the fresh orange juice and then tearing off a generous portion of his own croissant. Balzac's mouth was visibly watering. The orange juice disappeared quickly and Daniel and Dora slipped down to the floor and solemnly handed Balzac his small portion.

By nine, they were sitting alongside Balzac on the pool steps at the shallow end. The children's feet were dangling and splashing in the warm water as Félix demonstrated how he could swim up and back down the pool underwater. Bruno was trying not to stare at Florence in a fetching green bikini.

Time to start the swimming lesson! He slipped into the water and swam a length freestyle before returning on his back, floating and paddling with his hands.

'You see?' he said. 'I floated all the way back down the pool. Your body wants to float. Your chests are full of air that wants to rise in the water. Now, put your goggles on, and then crouch down so you're underwater and with your eyes open blow out a little breath. Then come up and tell me what you saw. One, two, three – go.'

The children sank down, bounced back up, scrambled onto the pool steps where their heads were well above water and cried out, almost in unison. 'Bubbles.'

Balzac barked to welcome their return and began licking the water from their arms.

'I saw bubbles going up to the surface,' said Dora.

'That's why I said the air in your chest wants to go up just like the bubbles. That's how you float,' Bruno said. 'If you lie on your backs and paddle a little with your hands and wave your feet gently up and down, you'll float just like I did. Do you want to try that?'

'Me first,' cried Daniel. 'I know the rule is ladies first but I want a go for once.'

Dora agreed, albeit reluctantly.

Daniel kicked off from the steps, his face just above the water, his hands paddling and his legs waving. Bruno had his hands beneath the boy, not touching but to make sure he didn't lose his confidence, and despite one splutter when a wavelet washed across his face, he persevered and headed slowly up to the deep end, Bruno swimming beside him. When he reached the far end, Bruno helped him grab the side of the pool and hold on. Standing in the shallow end, Florence was clapping her hands. And then Fabiola and Gilles arrived, both in shorts and T-shirts, to join in the applause.

'Well done, Daniel,' Bruno said. 'You can float and you can travel all the way to the deep end on your own. That's wonderful for your first try. Now it's Dora's turn. Will you swim beside her, Félix, as she joins us up here?'

Dora set off, pushing too hard with her feet against the steps and her head went underwater. Bruno's heart was in his mouth and he saw Florence move towards her. But Dora surfaced, began paddling gamely and made it all the way to join Bruno and her brother.

'I didn't have to hold her up once,' said Félix as he came up to them. 'Now let's see you both go all the way back. I'll be there to let you know when you're at the steps.'

Bruno followed them, doing a slow breaststroke as the two children floated and paddled their way back to the shallow end where Balzac and their mother were watching from the steps.

'That's wonderful, darlings,' called Florence. 'You're swimming already.'

Bruno climbed out and tossed into the pool two oblong floats of plastic foam he'd bought at the supermarket and dived in after them. He surfaced by the children and asked, 'Do you know how a frog moves in the water?'

'He kicks with his powerful legs,' Daniel answered.

'Your legs are much more powerful, so I want each of you to put your hands on a float and practise the frog kick up to the end of the pool. Can you do that?'

They set off, kicking their legs and going much faster than they had on their first length up the pool. When they reached the end, Bruno told them to put the float onto the side of the pool and float back, but this time using the frog kick.

'But only kick gently this first time,' he said as they set off. 'Don't forget to paddle with your hands.'

They pushed off on their backs, their faces tight with determination and Bruno feared he was pushing them too fast. He stayed close to them all the way, encouraging them with praise and saying they were almost there, until they reached the steps at the shallow end where Florence was now sitting at the poolside applauding their progress. When they stood up, beaming with pride, Florence hugged them both then jumped into the pool to hug Bruno.

'I never expected you'd get them swimming today,' she said, still holding him. Bruno was conscious of her breasts pressing against his chest. Then she turned to hug Felix and thank him for his efforts. By now Miranda's children had arrived and dived into the pool. Bruno turned and made his way easily to the deep end and back, slowing as he saw how crowded it had become since Gilles and Fabiola had donned swimsuits and joined the throng.

Florence climbed out of the pool and said she had to leave to get to her choral service. She went back into the house to change. When she returned, soberly dressed, she was carrying Bruno's phone.

'I heard it ringing but it stopped before I could find it in your shirt,' she said. 'I thought I'd better bring it in case it's urgent.'

Bruno clambered out of the pool, dried himself roughly on a

towel and took the phone. It was the Mayor, calling him from home. He'd left a message asking Bruno to call at his home at his earliest convenience. What could that be about on a Sunday morning when the Mairie was closed and Bruno was supposed to be off duty?

The Mayor picked up immediately.

'*Bonjour*, Bruno. Brosseil came to see me to tell me what he knew about this business with Driant and his will. He said that you might be going along to the open house this afternoon at the retirement home. I wonder, would you mind if I came along as well? I'm curious.'

Bruno replied that the Mayor was welcome to join him.

'Perhaps you'd like to join me in a late salad lunch here before we head off. You can brief me on what you know so far about this affair. Brosseil said you were looking into the matter, to see what could have persuaded Driant to leave his children with nothing. And on a fine day like this, the prospect of a glass of cool kir seems especially enticing.'

Bruno explained that he had to watch Florence's children for an hour but that she'd be back by one so he could join him after that.

Back at the poolside, he asked Gilles if he felt like meeting a young Canadian-Ukrainian who was interested in his book, one of the group of musicians staying at Chateau Rock. Might he have time for a coffee?

'Not today, Bruno, I'm enjoying the pool. Maybe in the week, perhaps market day when I do the shopping. Give me his phone number. What's his interest, exactly?'

'He was talking about all the different versions of what

happened in the Maidan, who did the shooting, and said something about disinformation. He was hoping you might bring some clarity to it.'

'I wish I could,' Gilles said. 'Despite hundreds of hours of video from mobile phones and forensic reports and three-dimensional models of the place to see where the bullets came from, there's still a lot of controversy. At first everyone blamed the Berkut, the paramilitary police who supported the pro-Russian government. But then it seemed that at least some of bullets came from buildings occupied by the protesters. Then some Georgian mercenaries came forward and said they'd been paid to shoot at both sides to trigger a wider battle. The Kremlin disinformation machine went into overdrive, claiming they'd been hired by the Americans. By that time most of the Berkut guys had taken part in Russia's takeover of the Crimea.'

'Bertie, this Canadian musician, spoke of the Heavenly Hundred. Were there really that many shot?'

'Altogether, over several days, more than that. When I went to the Kiev morgue on the last day of January, there were twenty-six unclaimed bodies,' said Gilles. He looked around to see if Fabiola was in earshot and kept his voice low.

'I haven't told her the half of it,' he said. 'On the three worst days, February eighteenth to twentieth, there were eighty-six deaths from gunfire and another fifty died in the fire that was deliberately set in the Trade Union building. It was chaos, the police targeting journalists, wrapping nails around stun grenades and tossing them at the press. One guy I knew was burned alive when he took shelter under a car and then its gas tank blew up. Remember how we learned that in Sarajevo? Never hide under a car.'

'*Mon Dieu*, I didn't know it was that bad.'

'Nor does Fabiola. Let's go and enjoy the pool and thank our lucky stars that we're here in the peaceful Périgord.'

11

Bruno found the Mayor enjoying the sun on his terrace, the Sunday newspapers on the table before him and some political debate between two local deputies playing on the radio beside them.

'Why we were foolish enough to elect either of those two to represent us in the National Assembly I have no idea,' the Mayor said, rising to greet him and switching off the radio. 'Let's get a drink.' Bruno followed the Mayor into the kitchen, picking two wine glasses and a bottle of crème de cassis from the cupboard as the Mayor began opening a bottle of Bergerac sec. 'And how is Florence? You know she's going on the list for the council at the next election? She's well-known and respected after the success of that computer club she started at the collège. I think she's very likely to be elected.'

He took the wine glasses out to the terrace on a tray, then pulled his pipe and tobacco pouch from the pocket of his cardigan.

'I thought you'd given up your pipe under pressure from Jacqueline,' Bruno said as they clinked glasses. The Mayor and Jacqueline seemed now to be an established couple, living together at the Mayor's house. A spare bedroom had been made into a study for Jacqueline, while the Mayor worked in his own study on his magnum opus history of St Denis. Jacqueline, who was half-American, spent one term each year teaching history in New York and another at the Sorbonne in Paris.

'Yes, I did but now I'm back on my pipe, at least in the privacy of my home,' the Mayor said, puffing away as he applied a match and the familiar scented smoke began to drift in Bruno's direction. 'This is Jacqueline's term to be teaching at Columbia. But she'll be back next month and I'll stop the day before she returns. In the meantime, I have the pleasure of feeling like a naughty schoolboy. I know you won't inform on me,' he said with a wink at Bruno.

The thought surfaced at the back of Bruno's mind that perhaps he had been invited here less to attend the open day than because the Mayor was lonely. He changed his mind when they arrived at the chateau, for the invitation had attracted not only the local *notaires* but also most of the mayors up and down the valley. The Mayor didn't need Bruno to accompany him.

'Did I forget to tell you I have my own invitation, Bruno?' the Mayor said, nodding greetings right and left. 'Kind of the owners to offer their hospitality to us humble elected servants of the public.'

They strolled through the gardens in front of the chateau. They were laid out in geometrically shaped lawns intersected by gravel paths and topiary in the formal style that had distinguished French gardens since Louis XIV had built Versailles. They walked around the wing of the chateau, a nineteenth-century building with fake battlements and towers with conical roofs. Behind it they found several well-tended *potagers*, each fenced off to create a plot about ten metres square and with a name painted on the gate to each one. Several of them were being worked by elderly people and the Mayor paused at one such gate bearing the name Drouon, to study the white-haired man who was wielding a hoe and asked, 'Is that really you, *mon vieux*?'

'*Mon Dieu*, Mangin, are you planning on joining us here?' asked the gardener, leaning his hoe against a wheelbarrow and coming to the gate to shake hands. An elderly mongrel who had been dozing by the gate opened one eye and then went back to sleep.

'No, just visiting. I'm curious about the place. Let me introduce our *chef de police*, Bruno Courrèges. Bruno this is Pierre Drouon, who was already a ten-year veteran mayor of Terrasson when I was first elected. Pierre taught me almost everything I know about politics. It's a pleasure to see you, old friend. We last met at your wife's funeral.'

'That's why I'm here. Life became very lonely and I heard about this place from my doctor. I've been here since it opened. As you see, I have my own garden. I heard your wife died, so please accept my condolences. Are you thinking of joining us?' he asked again.

'Not just yet. I'm still Mayor of St Denis.'

'Well, when the time comes, you'd be very comfortable. They organize book clubs, theatre visits, film nights and a wonderful masseuse.'

'I'll bear it in mind. Are you in the chateau?'

'No. Because of the dog I'm in the new block over there through the trees. You can't have a chateau room if you want to keep a pet. But I take my meals there.'

'Well, I won't keep you from your garden, *mon vieux*.'

The Mayor strolled on, Bruno at his side, along a path through the trees and towards the new block, a long terrace of stone-built cottages with the classic red roofs of the Périgord. Two wings thrust forward to form a handsome courtyard with rustic tables and chairs where people were drinking tea and playing chess or watching a play area evidently designed for visiting grandchildren. The only sound was of the children's voices. Bruno counted twenty doors in the long terrace, ten more in each of the wings.

The Mayor led the way back to the main entrance and they went in to view the public rooms. The entrance hall was imposing and the large dining room looked more like a res-taurant than the canteen Bruno knew at the *maison de retraite* in St Denis. A magnificent lounge was furnished with what looked to be genuine antiques and led into a comfortable, well-stocked library.

'I could certainly be comfortable here,' murmured the Mayor as they went back to the lounge where visitors were gathering for what was billed as a short speech of welcome by the director followed by questions and a reception. The lounge filled fast and more chairs had to be brought in from the hall and library. In a low voice, Bruno informed the Mayor what he had learned of the director from the Hotel Crillon.

As the Mayor chuckled, Bruno saw an unexpected couple coming into the lounge: Philippe Delaron of *Sud Ouest* and Nathalie, the real estate agent. She was carrying a clipboard on which she was scribbling notes as she walked, Philippe whispering into her ear. Before Bruno could head across to greet them, one of the staff tapped a fork against a wine glass and asked them to welcome the home's director who would explain the philosophy of the Château Marmont.

The director was in his thirties, dressed in a dark suit and bow tie. He welcomed the guests and went on to say that he made no apologies for the expense of the place, since it was designed to offer a quality of living and service that was far beyond the capabilities of the public sector. But it was fitting that those who had worked hard and been successful should see no decline in their quality of life after retirement. The questions were mostly predictable, about pets and family visits, but one female questioner raised a laugh when she asked if any marriages had taken place among the inmates.

'We've been open for less than a year but we have already celebrated two, with one more taking place next month. It will be celebrated in our own private chapel here in the grounds,' the director replied with a smile, to a scattering of applause. 'We pride ourselves on offering the fullest possible social life to our guests.'

'That will bring them in,' murmured the Mayor into Bruno's ear.

Then a man with long white hair, a beard and a scholarly air asked if they had any special facilities for those suffering from Alzheimer's disease.

'Let me answer that,' said a middle-aged man who had been standing to one side. 'I'm Dr Jean-Michel Dumouriez and I'm the chief medical consultant here. I visit each day and I'm permanently on call to support our resident medical team. Of course we have arrangements for our guests with any kind of serious illness to be treated privately in the most advanced facilities available. To my surprise, we have seen no case yet of the kind you mention. I suggest this may be because of the lively social and intellectual life that we offer our guests. What's more, the spa, gymnasium and gardens we provide help our guests keep in the best possible physical condition.'

Beside Bruno, the Mayor raised his hand and called out, 'I have a question, and perhaps an indelicate one.' Since he was one of the better-known of the local figures, his intervention caused a small stir.

'Many of us will remember what happened to the stock markets and in some cases to our savings in 2008, and in other years of financial turmoil. I'm sure I'm not alone in suspecting we may have another crash or crisis in the not-too-distant future. What happens to those who find themselves no longer able to afford your considerable fees?'

'Thank you for that important question and I'm sure it will be on many minds,' the director replied smoothly. 'We've arranged with a leading insurance group a solution under which our guests may use current savings or the sale of shares or property to buy an insurance policy. This would cover the residential and medical fees, or the fees in a specialized medical facility, for the policy holder's remaining years.'

'How would that work, exactly?' the Mayor asked.

'Each solution has to be tailor-made to the individual taking out the policy, depending on their age, medical condition, disposable funds and so on,' the director went on. 'Many of our guests have life insurance policies that are due to pay out in the not-too-distant future. Depending on the date and amount, these funds can be applied to the new insurance policy. This removes all cares and concerns about the guest's right to a stable, comfortable residence with us for the rest of the guest's life.

'And now,' the director continued, 'let us invite you to take a glass of champagne and some canapés and we thank all of you for your interest and your visit.'

As he spoke, waitresses in long black skirts and white dress shirts with black bow ties entered the room bearing silver trays with glasses of champagne, mineral water and fruit juice, followed by several more carrying trays of mini vol-au-vents, Vietnamese *nems*, and open sandwiches of smoked salmon and foie gras. *No expense spared*, thought Bruno. He and the Mayor helped themselves and began circulating around the room, greeting several acquaintances and political colleagues of the Mayor and hearing how impressed they all were.

Bruno made his way across the room to greet Nathalie and Philippe and murmured, 'I know why Philippe is interested in this place but what brings you here, Nathalie?'

'Given rising longevity, it's an interesting concept. Brosseil told me about this event and suggested that if the new home was a success, the organizers might be looking to expand and start looking for a new chateaux. That's where I come in. And what brings you here, Bruno?'

'I came to keep my Mayor company and I think I'd better get back to him.'

He returned to find the Mayor surrounded by a group of colleagues, all discussing the director's remarks, the way he'd handled the questions and whether the place would prove a lasting success.

'I was particularly impressed by his response to your question, Mangin,' said another former Mayor. 'Trust you as a former member of the Senate to get to the heart of the matter: how to afford it and what happens when the savings run out. And the way this damn government is running the economy, that could happen to many of us.'

'Thank you,' the Mayor replied with a slight bow. 'But I'm afraid the director moved on too quickly with the champagne before I could ask my follow-up question. And as you know, old friend, the follow-up is often the one that addresses the crucial and the unanswered point.'

'And that is?'

'What happens to our heirs, to our sons and daughters and grandchildren? Such a policy may take care of us for the rest of our days, but it clearly threatens to leave our heirs bereft of the kind of inheritance that most of us here enjoyed, whether in land or property or as life insurance policies. I inherited my house and a tidy sum from the thrift and generosity of my own parents. And so did you, my dear colleague,' said the Mayor, fixing his questioner with a stern eye. 'And what will our children say of us when we devour the patrimony of the family, perhaps built up over several generations, to finance our own declining years in luxury? And what if we die the very year that we move in? So my final question is this: if we devote all our savings to a place such as this, how on earth will we sleep at night, knowing that our own children will find it hard to forgive us? I for one don't wish to think of them standing over my grave and cursing me for my selfishness.'

12

Bruno returned from his morning run with Balzac the next day, and from long habit switched on his radio, toaster and the kettle for his coffee, in that order. He gave Balzac two of the dog biscuits he made himself, loaded fresh coffee grounds into his cafetière and put a spoonful of honey and crumbled a third of a cinnamon stick into his mug. By the time he'd pressed down the plunger the radio had delivered the news he'd been waiting for. The third item was Philippe's story in *Sud Ouest* about charges being filed against an insurance group for the neglect of two hundred sheep and lambs at one of the last hill farms in the region. The newspaper was quoted as saying that the charges came after 'a highly unusual sale and insurance deal by the farmer to buy lifetime residency in a luxurious retirement home'.

'Obviously there was a problem here because of the unexpected death of the farmer, Monsieur Driant, who lived alone and whose body was not found for some days,' came the emollient tones of Sarrail, the Périgueux *notaire*. 'Monsieur Driant had undertaken to complete all the necessary paperwork for the sale of the farm and livestock but his unfortunate death interrupted that process, as we shall explain to the court. Suitable arrangements for the livestock are being made.'

Best of all, thought Bruno, was the Procureur saying that the legitimacy of the sale of the farm might have to be reconsidered, given that the rules on the sale and care of livestock had apparently been ignored. He couldn't help grinning as he loaded Balzac into his van and set off to exercise the horses. He was looking forward to reading Pamela's copy of *Sud Ouest*.

Bruno pondered what Sarrail might mean by 'suitable arrangements'. At Pamela's place, he scanned Philippe's detailed story, spread over two inside pages, with photos of two of the lambs looking sickly in Maurice's arms. The animal protection society was demanding criminal charges be brought against the neglectful insurance company. The *Jeunes Agriculteurs* were vowing to warn every farmer in the region against these 'predatory financial groups', and the Mayor of St Denis was quoted warning against 'luxury retirement homes that financed themselves by disinheriting whole families'.

'Do I detect your hand behind all this?' Pamela asked, reading over his shoulder in the stables. 'I heard something about it on the radio earlier.'

'Me?' asked Bruno innocently. 'It's the free press doing its job.' He checked Hector's saddle girth and mounted. Then, with an idea forming about the fate of Driant's sheepdogs, he suggested that they take the horses on a different ride today, up to the plateau to call at Driant's farm to see what was happening to his sheep.

Thirty minutes later, they dismounted and hitched their horses to a fence post at the farm. Two men whom Bruno didn't know were trying to persuade the flock of sheep and lambs to climb a ramp into a livestock truck. On the truck's door was the logo of an abattoir at St Astier, some fifty kilometres away. Driant's two sheepdogs were stretched out on his porch, watching the vain antics of the men as the sheep wheeled and sprinted away, evading all attempts to load them. Balzac, who had followed the horses, went across to the porch to renew his acquaintance with Driant's dogs, then lay down beside them to watch.

'You'll need good sheepdogs for that,' Bruno told the two men, as they turned and eyed him and Pamela. Except for his riding cap, he was in police uniform.

'We can't do anything with those two dogs on the porch,' one of the men said, coming forward to shake hands and introducing himself as Henri, owner-driver of the truck. He presented a printout of an email from Constant's insurance agency, ordering the sheep and lambs taken for slaughter. 'Your dog seems to know them. Can you do something?'

'I wouldn't know how to work with those sheepdogs. They were trained by the old farmer who used to live here. Are you planning on taking them, too? And what about the chickens?' Bruno asked.

'Nobody told us anything about dogs or chickens,' came the reply. 'Normally we just back up to an enclosure where the sheep are kept and push them in, but this lot are running loose and we're getting nowhere. Time's money for me and I've three more jobs to do today.'

'If I can find another shepherd to bring his own dogs, will you give him twenty euros for his trouble?' Bruno asked, taking out his phone.

The man said yes. Bruno made the call, and ten minutes later

Guillaumat arrived with his dogs and the sheep were loaded with brisk efficiency, Driant's dogs rising from the porch to join in the fun. Guillaumat was given a twenty euro note and the truck drove off.

'You sure you can't take the dogs?' Bruno asked the old shepherd, who shook his head sadly, saying, 'I suppose they'll have to go to the animal rescue pound.'

He turned to see Pamela on the porch, making friends with the two sheepdogs. The mother stayed with her. But the younger dog, after a friendly lick of Pamela's hand, trotted off to join Balzac, who was playing one of his favourite games, running in and out between the horses' legs. The horses accepted this patiently. Hector bent his great head down to Balzac's level to nuzzle the dog, who often slept in Hector's stall when Bruno stayed the night at Pamela's. Hector then gave the young sheepdog an amiable sniff. Pamela's horse, Primrose, followed suit. It looked as though his idea might be bearing fruit.

'I remember you saying you were thinking of getting a watchdog for the stables,' he said to her. 'They're a mother and son, so I'd hate to see them parted. Or shot, which is what I expect the lawyers would do to them.'

'They're good dogs,' said Guillaumat. 'And the young one seems friendly with the horses. He's called Beau and his mother is Bella.'

'Why don't we take them to the riding school?' Pamela said. She glanced at Bruno. 'Since I suspect you planned this all along, you'll have to make lots more of those dog biscuits of yours.'

'With pleasure.' He turned to Guillaumat. 'I doubt whether

Beau and Bella would follow us back. Would you do me a favour and drive them to the riding school? You might want to take some of the chickens for your pains.'

'I already told you I can't use them,' said Guillaumat. 'But there's a couple of bantam cocks that I can take and raise for my table. Driant was particular about his hens. He's got some Rhode Island reds, Leghorns and a couple of Golden Comets, all good layers. His cockerel is a young *Gallus domestique*, a fine bird, about eighteen months old so he's fully mature and the hens are used to him. He can handle ten or a dozen, no problem.'

'How about having your own chickens?' Bruno asked Pamela. 'You've got that fine bit of pasture far enough from the house and *gîtes* that the cockerel's morning call won't be a problem. It's big enough for a score or more chickens to scratch around and feed themselves. We can get Félix's dad to put a fence in and this evening I can help him build a chicken coop. And Miranda's kids will enjoy having them, going down each morning to collect the eggs.'

Pamela gave him a wry smile. 'Why do I think you've had this in mind all along, Bruno?' she asked. 'But yes, why not? And I'm sure people who rent the *gîtes* will enjoy having fresh eggs. Let's do it.'

Guillaumat picked out the bantams and put them into a cardboard box that he placed on his passenger seat. He and Bruno rounded up the rest of the chickens and loaded them into the back of the truck. He put the two sheepdogs onto the back seat and climbed in.

'Before you go,' said Bruno. 'Remember you told me about that young woman you met here with Driant, the one with the foreign accent who said she was from the insurance company? Could you describe her for me, age and height, hair colour, that sort of thing?'

'A bit shorter than me, very dark hair, slim build, at least from her legs and I could see plenty of them,' said Guillaumat, seeming to enjoy the memory. 'She wore a lot of make-up and had amazing eyebrows, perfect, as if they were painted on. Until she said she was with the insurance I thought she might have been a model, or . . . er . . .' His voice trailed off and he glanced at Pamela as if embarrassed.

'You mean you thought she might have been an expensive prostitute,' Pamela said, smiling at the old man.

'Well, I did wonder,' he said. 'Knowing Driant.'

'When you said a foreign accent, was her French good?' Pamela asked

'Yes, excellent, better than mine with the grammar. She spoke with a lot of breathiness of voice, with a sort of cough when she said the words *chaque* and *roc*. Made me remember the Algerian war, the way those Arabs spoke.'

That was interesting, thought Bruno, thanking Guillaumat and saying they'd see him at the riding school. Bruno and Pamela mounted their horses and rode back at a steady trot, Balzac bringing up the rear, with Bruno feeling relieved that Pamela had solved the problem of Driant's dogs. The chickens had been a happy afterthought.

He thought about what they'd need for the chicken coop. He had a big roll of chicken wire at home but he should buy some cement and metal stakes. He would need to bury the wire deep but he could borrow a digger from Michel at the public works.

He had plenty of planks in his barn that he'd rescued years ago from a neighbour's ruined tobacco-drying barn. Four posts of seasoned wood, ten centimetres square, would suffice for the frame of the coop, each sunk into a bucket filled with pebbles and cement. His old planks would provide the roof and walls and there was straw in the stables. Waterproof felting would be good to add to the roof but he remembered there was a roll at the back of Pamela's stables. If he made a sloping roof he could put some corrugated plastic on top and a gutter to catch the rainwater.

Once they reached the stables Bruno took Guillaumat to one side.

'That young Arab woman who was visiting Driant – did you notice what kind of car she was driving?'

'Oh yes, a nice one, one of those new Volkswagen Beetles, a convertible, in blue. Of course she had the hood up when I saw it.'

Bruno thanked the old man and sent him on his way, then drove himself home to collect the planks and chicken wire. He stopped at the local sawmill to buy the baulks of wood and then again at Bricomarché for some bags of cement and a piece of two-metre square corrugated plastic for the roof. By chance, the Baron was there, buying light bulbs. He immediately volunteered to help, and at once bought a junction box, an outdoor lamp and electric wire to mount above the door to the chicken coop. Bruno then picked up Félix's father, who joined them for a promise of half a dozen eggs a week. He called Michel, who offered to bring the digger to Pamela's place at lunchtime.

Bruno and Félix's dad dug the post holes and dropped in

four of the big plastic buckets in which Pamela bought oats in bulk for her horses. They used stones and half-bricks to hold the posts in place, poured in cement and then unrolled the chicken wire to see if there was enough. It would make a generous enclosure of ten metres by twenty. Bruno left Félix's dad and the Baron sawing the planks for the walls of the coop and screwing them onto battens, while he went back to his office to deal with paperwork.

He first called the prosecutor's office and was told that Sarrail had been served with a demand that he present himself for an interview but that Constant, the insurance agent, was said to be out of town until the following week. Then Bruno called Constant's office to find out if there was a number where he could be reached and the phone was answered by a young woman. He identified himself, saying he had good news – that he had seen the sheep and lambs taken from the farm and added that he had found new owners for the sheepdogs.

'That's excellent news and very kind of you,' came the reply, and there was something about the breathy catch in the way she pronounced the word 'excellent' that made him think of Guillaumat's description.

'I've been trying to reach Monsieur Constant about this every day since we got news of Monsieur Driant's death.'

'*Chaque jour*? Every day?' she replied.

And Bruno heard it distinctly, that slight Arabic cough on the word *chaque*.

'I didn't catch your name,' he said. 'Are you a colleague of Monsieur Constant?'

'I'm Mademoiselle Saatchi, Lara Saatchi,' she said. 'I'm an

associate agent here and I'm running the office while Monsieur Constant is in our Monaco office. I was the one who organized the abattoir for the sheep and I'm very relieved that has now been done. We've had such trouble with this business of the farm because of Monsieur Driant's unfortunate death.'

'I think you met Monsieur Driant's friend, another sheep farmer called Guillaumat, when you visited the farm last month,' he said.

There was a pause before she spoke. 'Everything was handled by Monsieur Constant in person.'

'I see,' he replied. It wasn't quite a denial. This was not the time to push too hard, but he could try a little nudge. 'We're trying to identify the young woman, claiming to be from the insurers, who was visiting Monsieur Driant when his friend, another sheep farmer, called at the farm. Right now, it seems she may have been the last person to see Monsieur Driant alive, so you'll understand why we are anxious to question her. Do you have another female associate in the office?'

'You would have to ask Monsieur Constant about that,' she replied. 'He's in charge of personnel.'

'Of course. Do you have a number for him at the Monaco office, or a cell phone? There are still some legal matters to clear up.'

She gave him the number of the Monaco office, pleaded an imminent interview with another client, thanked him for his help and ended the call. Bruno was left staring at the dead phone in his hand. He felt sure this was the woman Guillaumat had seen. She might well have been the last woman to see Driant alive. But what did that mean, and what did it prove?

Bruno could not be sure whether he was making mountains out of molehills. Even if there was something to his suspicion that Driant's death had been extraordinarily, even suspiciously convenient for Sarrail and Constant, the cremation meant there would be no proof. Bruno knew his biases might be getting in the way, that there was something about Sarrail's city-slicker smoothness that offended him. And he had no grounds for suspicion against this woman Lara except for that catch in her voice when she'd used the word *chaque*.

At least he could check on that. He could ask J-J to send a plain-clothes cop to watch outside the office and snatch a photograph of her that he could show to Guillaumat or take Guillaumat to identify this young woman for himself. But first he called the Monaco number, to be told that Constant was travelling to the Luxembourg office. He took the number, called Luxembourg, identified himself and requested a callback from Constant the moment he arrived, on urgent legal business. The man was infuriatingly and probably deliberately elusive.

Bruno told himself to calm down. Just because Constant and Sarrail didn't give a damn about the livestock they had so casually acquired did not make them criminals. And just because he suspected that Gaston Driant and his sister had been victims of an injustice did not mean he could do anything about it without real proof. He'd already found one small lever against Sarrail and Constant – their careless mistreatment of animals – that he'd already been able to use to embarrass them publicly. And if he could find more evidence that would help turn the Procureur's questioning of the sale into a powerful case, the Driant heirs might yet have justice. He'd keep on probing. If Guillaumat recognized Lara Saatchi, that would be an excuse to call her in for questioning.

Content that he had a plan, Bruno dealt with various emails and told the Mayor's secretary that he'd be back later that afternoon. He drove home for more tools before heading to the riding school to help finish the work on the chicken coop. The first thing he saw was Michel's mechanical digger, scooping out the ditch in which the enclosure's chicken wire would be buried. Up towards the main house, Bruno saw Balzac leading the two sheepdogs on a tour of their new home, each of them stopping at each corner and fence post to raise a leg and mark their territory. That would help keep foxes away!

The Baron and Félix's father had assembled the coop's walls and the sloping roof and attached the corrugated plastic to it. The coop was now ready to be fixed to the four main posts once the cement was dry. The two men were already working on the floor. Bruno took off his jacket, picked up his sledge-hammer and began hammering in the iron stakes, one every three metres, while the Baron attached the chicken wire. The bottom half-metre of the wire was sunk into Michel's ditch and Pamela brought successive wheelbarrow loads of broken bricks and stones to help keep the wire in place against burrowing foxes.

By the time Michel had finished the ditch, Félix's dad had the fresh cement ready to pour onto the broken bricks. Michel waved goodbye, taking with him a bottle of Pamela's Scotch in thanks. Bruno sank the final stake just a metre short of the stable wall. Pamela brought the last wheelbarrow of rocks and bricks and stood back to watch as the final cement was poured.

'You've all done wonders. I can't believe it's finished already,' Pamela said. 'But why the gap beside the stable wall?'

'We'll make a door of wood frame and chicken wire so we can go in and feed them,' Bruno replied. 'Once the chickens are settled here you can leave it open in the day and let them roam free. When they get used to their new place they'll make their own way back at dusk.'

'Will the chicken coop be ready for them to sleep there tonight?' Pamela asked.

'No, we have to let the cement in the post holes dry thoroughly overnight so the frame is stable enough to attach the coop. Once that's done, I'll attach some gutters under the slope of the roof with a downpipe into a cistern so you'll always have rain water for their drinking bowls. But for tonight, I think they can shift for themselves in the stables.'

He glanced at the yard, where the chickens were pecking at the straw and the small piles of fresh horse manure, and pottering in and out of the stables. 'They've made themselves at home already,' he said. 'And the horses don't seem to mind.'

'I'm very impressed with all of you,' she said. 'Why don't I go and prepare some lunch for you while you men finish the door?'

'*A vos ordres, madame,*' said the Baron, giving her a mock salute.

Half an hour later, the door was finished.

'Time for lunch,' said Bruno.

Pamela had made a simple stew from minced beef, vegetables and a can of tinned tomatoes with some potatoes on the side and a magnum of red wine from the town vineyard. She joined them to eat and attacked the food with the same hungry appetite as the three men.

'Will I get fresh eggs tomorrow?' she asked.

'The birds need to settle first,' said the Baron. 'You might get one or two, though.'

She brought out the cheeseboard and a bowl of salad, fresh lettuce and rocket in walnut oil and a splash of white wine. Dessert was *affogato*, strong espresso coffee poured over vanilla ice cream.

'Lovely,' said the Baron, leaning back and patting his tummy. 'If all workers were fed like this by their bosses, there'd be no strikes.'

'You're getting this because I can't afford to pay you,' Pamela replied, and brought out the cognac.

13

Back in his office Bruno felt in no mood to work so he looked up the number for the *132ème bataillon cynophile*, the French military kennels at Suippes. The place was home to four specialized companies of troops and to the largest assembly of military dogs in the world. It was the place that raised and trained the two thousand war dogs currently deployed by the French armed services. There were two companies of troops training to deploy with guard and patrol dogs. A third company worked with dogs being trained to detect mines and explosives and a fourth was training them to find narcotics.

Bruno had seen these war dogs at work in Bosnia, when he'd been attached to the United Nations peacekeepers. He'd been deeply impressed at the way they and their handlers guarded military compounds, ran security patrols, detected minefields and guarded suspects. He had heard from old friends who were still in the military that the use of war dogs had expanded dramatically in Afghanistan, where French troops had been deployed as part of the NATO forces, and had seen how much more use the American troops had made of dogs. They had proved invaluable on night patrols, in guarding prisoners and in searching vehicles for car bombs. Their main new task was to search in advance of patrols and convoys for the IEDs, Improvised Explosive Devices or roadside bombs, that the Taliban favoured.

The canine specialist base at Suippes had gone into overdrive to keep up with the fast-growing demand for war dogs and for the sniffer dogs increasingly deployed at airports and rail stations. There were now three hundred dogs being trained there every few months. The French and British troops had followed the American military in equipping their war dogs with harnesses carrying a camera and microphones and sending them to search for the human ambushers and snipers. The allied war dogs had been so effective that the Taliban had started targeting the animals, shooting them on sight and sending in their own dogs to attack them. In response, the allied dogs were given thick, spiked leather collars to protect them against the Afghan hounds.

Bruno also knew that the NATO forces in Afghanistan were under orders to play down the role of the war dogs in the media, wary of the effect on public opinion at home. Instead, the military public relations teams focused on the use of tracked robots and drones, but Bruno knew most of the troops preferred to rely on the dogs. They weren't rendered useless by dust storms and nor were they vulnerable to the small plastic-covered mines that the Taliban laid around their IEDs, specifically to knock out the robots. While Bruno knew himself to be as soft-hearted as anyone else when it came to one of the dogs being wounded or killed, he understood that preventing human casualties took precedence. At least now the French military no longer euthanized dogs at the end of their active service but allowed them to retire with their human handlers.

When his call was answered, Bruno asked for the adjutant's office. Every old soldier knew that while officers come and go, the adjutant's top sergeant was always the person who knew how to get things done.

'Yeah, I remember. You're the cop with the basset hounds,' came the answer when Bruno identified himself. 'Your old dog is listed on the memorial here, killed in action. What can we do for you?'

Bruno explained that when the *bataillon* had arranged for a new basset hound puppy to be delivered to him, it had come with the message that they would want to breed from him in the future. Since his dog was now getting to be old enough, he was calling to ask whether that requirement still remained in force.

'We don't use bassets here, although I'd like to. They're not all that easy to breed. I've got your file up on my screen now. I see you got a *Croix de Guerre*. They're pretty rare in these peaceful times. Your dog came from a litter from the hunting pack at Cheverny. You called him Balzac, right?'

'That's right, Balzac. But why do you say they are hard to breed?'

'Bassets sometimes need a little human help to get things to fit, that's why most breeders use artificial insemination these days. It's also economics. You can get more pregnancies from a single stud male that way, and a top pedigree stud doesn't come cheap. I can give you the phone number of the master of hounds at Cheverny and you could talk to him. Or I may have a better idea.'

'Go ahead.' When a *sergent-chef* came up with a better idea, Bruno knew that it was worth paying attention.

'You're in the Dordogne, is that right? We had a *caporal-chef* here, terrific woman, great with dogs, a lifer who did her twenty years and retired around the time your last hound was killed. In fact, I think she was the one who arranged your replacement basset and she's a real fan of the breed. Now she runs a kennel, raising them in the Dordogne, near Excideuil. Her name is Claire Mornier and I'm sure she'd like to hear from you. Give her warmest best wishes from Sergent-Chef Plarin, and tell her we all miss her, particularly the dogs. Let me know how it turns out.'

'I certainly will,' said Bruno. 'But why don't you train bassets at Suippes? They're brilliant sniffer dogs.'

'Don't tell me, I know,' Plarin replied. 'I'd use them for sniffing out explosives and narcotics and as trackers but the problem is that they're just too popular, too lovable for our kind of work. Whenever you get a crowd, at an airport or a station, kids gravitate towards the bassets. You don't get that kind of distraction with the German shepherds. And some of the troops don't like to use them because they don't look menacing enough.'

'But bassets hunt wild boar and foxes,' Bruno objected. 'They're brave and relentless.'

'I know, I know, I believe you. Claire used to say the same. But that's just the way it is. You were in the army long enough to know that. I'll text you Claire's number.'

Bruno thanked him, ended the call and sat back to reflect on the curious ways of the military, the importance that so many soldiers attached to the way they and their weapons looked and how they lived up to the warrior image of themselves. He could understand that the beguiling looks of a basset hound might not quite match the desired military style. They were making a mistake. Anyone who had hunted with bassets knew that along with bloodhounds they had the best nose of any dog. They were designed that way, their long, floppy ears perfect for stirring up the grass to release any lingering scent. Bruno's former dog, Gigi, had once identified and tracked down a burglar from a blurred fingerprint left on a pane of glass a month earlier. After that incident, Bruno had done some research and learned that while humans had only some twenty million smelling cells, dogs usually have over two billion, with bassets closer to three billion.

And it wasn't just their sense of smell, Bruno knew. Humans can hear sounds from zero to twenty kilohertz, while bassets have a much higher range, able to hear up to seventy. Even when asleep in Bruno's bedroom, Balzac would wake and alert him if a passing fox even thought about investigating the chicken coop. Bruno smiled at the memory and in that almost telepathic way he had, Balzac lifted himself from his seated position, stretched and yawned and then nuzzled at Bruno's leg. Maybe he was just scratching but Bruno didn't think so. He bent down to stroke his dog's back and pat his side.

Bruno wondered whether their close bond would change once Balzac had been at stud. Would he develop some more special canine relationship with his mate, or with their pups? He had no idea. It was startling, Bruno thought, how little we knew of these utterly different beings with whom we had been so close for some thirty thousand years.

Bruno had trained his dog in the usual way, with treats and

praise when he did the right thing. He never beat Balzac, and even now he still persevered, raising his hand, palm forward, and frowning as he spoke a crisp '*Non*,' to try and teach his dog not to jump up in eager friendship each time he saw a familiar face. But Balzac's cheerful instincts usually got the better of his training.

'How do you feel about meeting a lady basset and making some puppies?' he asked his dog. Balzac stared back at him, trying to figure out what this human tone of voice meant. Bruno caressed his dog's head in reassurance. 'You think you're ready to be a father?'

'Do you think he understands the question?' came a voice, Bruno had been so focused on his dog that he hadn't noticed that the Mayor was standing in the doorway. Bruno's former dog, Gigi, had been the son of the Mayor's own basset, Montaigne, named for the sixteenth-century philosopher who was the Périgord's most famous son. Montaigne had been known as the best hunting dog in the valley. Bruno remembered seeing Gigi stand over the plot in the Mayor's garden where he and Bruno had buried the old hound. The Mayor had suggested that Gigi could smell his parent's long-dead remains. At the time, Bruno had been sceptical, but he'd kept silent, not wanting to disturb the Mayor's memories.

'I'm thinking of breeding him,' Bruno said.

'I'm glad to hear it – about time,' said the Mayor. 'That pedigree is too special not to be continued. But in the meantime, what did you learn from Macrae?'

'He's hoping to sell the place for three million but the agent says he'll be lucky to get two and a half. His kids want to keep a foothold here so he's doing up a cottage near the vineyard for them. And he's making music again, writing songs, doing duets with his son. I listened to a CD he gave me. It's pretty good and I'm hoping he'll start his comeback at one of our free concerts.'

'Good,' said the Mayor, turning to leave. 'Keep me informed. And make sure you find a good dam for Balzac. He deserves the best.'

On an impulse, Bruno turned to his computer and googled 'basset hound pedigree puppies' and was startled to see that prices went as high as fifteen hundred euros. That was close to his monthly salary. In St Denis, you could rent a three-bed-room house for three or four months for that kind of money. But that would mean selling the pup to a stranger and Balzac losing any connection with his pup. Pamela's business partner, Miranda, had two sons who adored Balzac. They would love to have a dog of their own, and the same with Florence's children.

He picked up his phone and called Claire Mornier. When she answered, he conveyed Sergeant Plarin's greetings and intro-duced himself, thanking her for her role in sending him Balzac.

'*Chef de Police* Bruno Courrèges,' she said. 'I'm so glad you called. How's Balzac doing? I saw that story in *Sud Ouest* about him catching that Irish terrorist. He looked wonderful in the photo.'

'Balzac's on great form, sitting beside me as we speak.' At the mention of his name, Balzac gave a cheerful bark and then laid his head on Bruno's foot. 'When I first got him, he came with a message that the battalion at Suippes might want to breed from him when he was old enough.'

'That was me,' she said. 'I was already close to finishing my time and I knew I'd want to start breeding bassets and Balzac has a wonderful pedigree, including the Stonewall Jackson breed. It descends from the bassets the Marquis of Lafayette presented to George Washington when he went over to help him defeat the English.'

'Do you think Balzac is ready to breed?'

'Certainly, he's nearly two years old. That's perfect. Leave it another year and some of them get a bit confused about what to do. I've got a lovely brown and white bitch, Carla. I named her after the ex-President's wife because I'm a fan of her music but not so much of her husband. Carla's formal name for the Kennel Club is Diane de Poitiers and she likes Carla Bruni's music, too. I think they find it restful. I never play heavy rock or pompous classical stuff for them.'

'Balzac likes music as well. He even likes my singing and sometimes howls along when we're in the car.'

'It sounds like these dogs are made for each other. Carla is just a little older than Balzac and has recently started her third time on heat.'

'How do we go about this?'

Claire explained that Carla would be on heat for three weeks. She would like to do the breeding on day eleven and leave them together for a couple of days. A month after that she should be able to hear the puppies' heartbeats with a stethoscope. Pregnancy normally lasted about two months.

'If you waive the stud fee,' she went on, 'you get to choose the pick of the litter if there are seven pups or fewer. Eight or more and you get a second pup. If she doesn't get impregnated, you might want to get a vet to examine Balzac and then we can try again in six months' time.'

'That sounds fine. I don't need the stud fee. So I should bring him up to you in what, a few days from now?'

'Let me check the calendar ... Yes, Sunday would be good and I presume that will be a day off for you? You could bring Balzac here Saturday afternoon, get him used to the place and I have a spare room where you could stay. Bring a friend if you like. It's a double bed with its own bathroom. That way you can help me feed the pack and we'll introduce Balzac to the gang before we sit down to enjoy a *p'tit apéro* and I'll cook us dinner. I'll be delighted to see Balzac again. I still think of him as a puppy although I'm sure he's full grown. He was a lovely little fellow, always good-natured and inquisitive. I'm glad he's gone to someone like you.'

'I'll bring wine and some of our foie gras, maybe a few eggs from my chickens and salad from the garden,' he said, warmed by her kind welcome.

'Sounds like a feast.'

Bruno ended the call feeling cheerful about Balzac's intended date, and about Claire. She seemed very competent and was obviously devoted to dogs. He checked his watch. Knowing it was his turn to make the Monday night communal dinner, he had started his preparations over the weekend.

14

Bruno always took his cooking seriously but the Monday night dinners for his friends at the riding school were special. Sometimes he wondered whether the rotation of the role of chef brought out in him some spirit of competition to outdo the others. This time he planned to begin with fresh asparagus from his garden, then follow this with a dish he'd encountered at the home of Momu, the maths teacher at the local *collège*. Despite his Algerian heritage, Momu was more French than most people Bruno knew, reading *Le Monde* every day and always being the first in St Denis to read the Prix Goncourt winner. Although Momu and his family usually ate French food, he was proud of his Middle Eastern heritage. The dish he'd shared with Bruno was a classic: lamb shanks with walnuts and pomegranate. Momu claimed to have learned how to make it at his mother's knee and Bruno had found it delicious and tantalizingly different.

Bruno had started on Saturday with his pestle and mortar. He had first ground and then mixed together in a bowl one and a half teaspoons of ground cinnamon, the same amount of ground turmeric, a teaspoon of ground cumin and half a teaspoon of ground cardamom. The spices were then rubbed into three kilos of trimmed lamb shanks, one for each of the eight adults at dinner with small ones for the children. He left the spiced meat in his fridge for the rest of the day.

After his return from the retirement home on Sunday, Bruno had browned the shanks in olive oil over a medium-high heat, drained them on absorbent paper and cleaned the pan. Then he had gently fried three thinly sliced onions, adding salt and freshly ground black pepper, until they were soft and transparent.

Next he had added six sprigs of thyme, six crushed garlic cloves, three wide strips of lemon zest and two bay leaves, stirring everything into the onions for two minutes. He sprinkled into this two tablespoons of plain flour and stirred until all the flour was absorbed. Then came the wine, a large glass of Bergerac red. He brought the dish to a simmer and stirred until it thickened. Then he slowly poured in a litre of chicken stock, a quarter-litre of pomegranate juice, and half that amount of pomegranate molasses that Momu had said he would find in the local health food shop. Bruno had let this simmer for five minutes.

He had arranged the lamb shanks in a deep roasting pan and poured the onion, stock and pomegranate mixture over them to reach three-quarters of the way up each shank. He covered the pan with foil and put it in the oven, turning occasionally, for an hour and forty minutes, until the meat was almost falling off the bone. He removed the pan from the oven and let it cool.

He had run the braising liquid through a sieve into a saucepan and added a quarter kilo of shelled walnuts before simmering the liquid over medium-high heat until it had been reduced by a third. He tasted it and added a little more ground pepper. Were he serving it that day, he'd have arranged the lamb on a warm platter, and then spooned the walnuts and sauce over the shanks. But Bruno knew from Momu that lamb improves if braised a day ahead and it also made it easier to skim off the fat. So he'd left it overnight, planning to take the dish to Pamela's the next day.

For dessert he had planned something special as a treat for the Baron, which he made late Monday afternoon. He plucked almost a kilo of cherries from the tree in his garden and stewed them gently in a little water with a tablespoon of honey. He let the cherries cool in individual glasses, reserving six tablespoons of the juice to add to the dish when he served it. He poured half a litre of whipping cream and a third of that quantity of crème fraîche into a saucepan, stirring over a gentle heat. He removed two tablespoons to a separate bowl and beat two large egg yolks and a whole egg into it. He added the zest of a lemon to the main saucepan which he brought slowly to the boil and immediately turned off the heat. Pouring a little hot cream onto the egg mixture, he whisked hard.

Then, slowly, he tipped the egg and cream mixture back into the saucepan, whisking continuously. He added a tablespoon of sugar and over a medium-low heat, he gently heated the egg cream to thicken it, stirring attentively, careful not to let it boil. When it seemed thick enough, he turned off the heat and let it cool before drizzling it over the cherries. Once the cream had set, he packed the glasses carefully in a cardboard box with separate compartments that he normally used to store wine glasses and drove to the riding school.

At Pamela's, after serving the asparagus, he reheated the lamb shanks in their sauce and began to prepare the couscous. He brought to the boil half a litre of duck stock and fifty grams of butter. He stirred in the couscous, covered the pan and turned off the heat, letting it sit for five minutes before adding two large spoonfuls of olive oil, one of lemon juice plus salt and pepper. He stirred it all together with fifty grams of grated parmesan cheese. Feeling a little nervous, he took the lamb shanks and couscous to the table.

'It smells wonderful,' said Pamela, loyally. 'What's that rich fruit I smell?'

'I think it's pomegranate and if it's the dish Bruno and I once enjoyed at Momu's house, it's a real treat,' said the Baron.

Fabiola was the first to taste it. 'Good heavens, it's glorious,' she declared. 'Try some of that sauce with the couscous.'

The children, fresh from the bath taken after running around the stables chasing chickens, were just as enthusiastic. Jack Crimson announced that it was the best meal Bruno had ever cooked for them.

'A good job I brought some of that Cuvée l'Odyssée from Clos de Breil,' Jack added. 'You need a wine of that depth to go with a meal like this. Did you really get this recipe from Momu? I'll have to get to know him better.'

The whole dish was devoured, lamb, couscous and all, until only the bones were left. Bruno carefully picked out the three biggest and gave one each to Balzac, Beau and Bella who had been sitting patiently at the foot of the table, drooling.

'I'm glad you put me in touch with Bertie from Canada,' said

Gilles. 'We met this morning for coffee, and he copied me some emails his cousin had sent from Kiev before he was killed.'

'Killed? I didn't know that,' said Bruno.

'He was killed in the fighting in Odessa in May,' Gilles replied. 'Bertie says he's never forgiven his parents for refusing to let him go to Kiev, although he was just a schoolboy at the time. I told him his parents were right – more than six thousand people were killed in Ukraine that year.'

'That puts our own political troubles in perspective,' murmured the Baron into the silence that fell over the table.

'Time for dessert,' said Bruno.

Over the cherries, which went down just as well as the lamb shanks, Bruno recounted his visit to the retirement home on the previous day, saying he agreed with Gilles that the place had been well restored and he'd found the overall system impressive. But when he described the question and answer session, quoting from memory the Mayor's final speech, the whole table fell silent. Bruno understood why.

For the Baron, well into his seventies and a wealthy man, the luxurious retirement home might have been designed with him in mind. That was probably also the case for Jack Crimson but Miranda, however, was eying her father coolly. For her and her children, inheritance was a deeply personal issue. For Pamela, who until her mother's death had faced the prospect of supporting an elderly parent who no longer even recognized her, it was a question that struck close to home. They wouldn't be sitting in this riding school without the legacy from Pamela's mother. For Fabiola, who believed passionately in a high quality health service being available to all for free, with no extra privileges for the rich, it was a reminder that even the fine French health system could not afford to provide quality homes for all the elderly. On a schoolteacher's salary, living in subsidized housing and raising two small children with little prospect of saving enough to buy a house of her own, Florence must have been wondering what hope she had of leaving them much of a legacy.

Félix had gone back to his Périgueux lycée that morning. Bruno could imagine the young man changing the mood and making them all smile by reminding them that it was irrelevant as far as he was concerned. His parents lived in social housing and he was unlikely to inherit anything except his father's old boots and some pots and pans.

Bruno reflected that while he had a house to pass on and his shares in the town vineyard, he had nobody to whom he really wanted to leave his bequest. The only will he'd ever made was the one he had been required to draft while in the army, where he'd left everything to his aunt in Bergerac, who had taken him into her home from the church orphanage. He'd never been happy there, the poor relation living on the charity of people just as poor, and he had escaped into the army as soon as he could. His aunt was now in a state-run retirement home and any bequest to her from Bruno would go to his cousins, to whom he'd never been close.

He should visit Brosseil to make out a new will, he thought. He'd kept putting it off, hoping that he'd meet a woman who would become his wife and they would raise children together and leave their worldly goods to them. But he was beginning to wonder whether that would ever happen. And he had faced the prospect of death more than once in his work in recent years. He could always change his will later, of course, if the right woman came along. In the meantime, he had better make a will that reflected his current thoughts and priorities. And who better to be his heirs than these friends who had become his family? He could leave his modest bank account to a local charity and his house, the Land Rover and his shares in the vineyard to Florence's two children and Félix.

By eight the next morning, Bruno was patrolling the market. He enjoyed being there as the stalls were being erected and loaded with the fresh fruits and vegetables that were coming in profusion from the market gardens. He went for his customary coffee and croissant at Fauquet's, standing at the counter and skimming through that day's *Sud Ouest* as he exchanged greetings with the regulars and the Mairie employees enjoying a quick coffee before the working day began. As the clock on the Mairie tower struck nine, he was at Brosseil's door and thirty minutes later he emerged, his new will drafted, signed, witnessed and on its way to the national registry.

Back in the market, he found Kirsty shopping, her brother trailing behind her carrying the bags. Galina and Sasha strolled along beside them, munching hot *nems* from the Vietnamese stall. Bruno was told that Pia, Ippo and Bertie were all enjoying a second croissant at Fauquet's, having raved over their first.

'How about some practice before our club tournament?' Bruno asked Kirsty and Jamie. 'I'm doing a training session for the junior team at the tennis club at four thirty. They'd love to knock some balls around with you two when I tell them you were our stars just a few years ago.'

'Can Galina come too?' Kirsty asked. 'She's a much better player. I heard she wiped the floor with Jamie at her club in Paris. Why don't we have a doubles match after the training session, girls against guys?'

Bruno agreed and Galina at once added, 'And it would be great if you could come, please, to the chateau this evening where we are rehearsing again the concerto. I'd like that. You can help us eat the food Kirsty has been buying.'

Galina spoke a fluent if imprecise French with an unfamiliar Slavic accent. She might have been Russian or Polish, but her remarks were peppered with colloquial French terms. He had to smile at hearing her call the chateau a *baraque*, which traditionally meant a wooden hut but was now used for any kind of residence. From her slang, using *blé* for cash and *ouf* for something great, Galina had obviously spent most of her time with younger French people.

'I warn you, Bruno, get ready for a surprise,' said Jamie. 'Galina is a really hot player.'

As he spoke, Bruno saw Florence hurrying over the bridge towards them, coming from the *collège*. She usually shopped at the market at this time when she had no lessons scheduled. He waved her across and introduced her to the young people, telling them she was the soprano in the town choir.

'Please tell your father I think his new songs are terrific,' Florence told Jamie and Kirsty. 'Bruno let me hear them, along with that guitar duet he played with you, Jamie.'

'It wasn't really a duet since we didn't play it together,' said

Jamie. 'I played it and then he overdubbed his tracks. But yeah, I thought the result was great.'

'Why not join us for supper and tell Dad yourself?' Kirsty intervened. 'They're going to be rehearsing the "Concierto de Aranjuez". Bruno is coming.'

'That's very kind but I have the children to feed and put to bed . . .'

'Come on, Florence, you'll enjoy it,' said Bruno. 'They can stay at the riding school tonight, or one of the girls from school will babysit. I can pick you up and drive you back.'

'Well, in that case, I'd love to come if I can arrange a babysitter. What time?'

Florence hurried off to complete her shopping while the others continued theirs. Bruno went to his office to deal with email and paperwork until midday, when the market began to close. He made a last patrol, bought bread, cheese, pâté and strawberries and drove to Les Eyzies for one of his regular lunches with his colleagues, Louis from Montignac and Juliette on her home turf. Still quite new at policing, Juliette was shaping up well. Bruno had never had a more helpful colleague. Louis was very different, resentful of Bruno's promotion, too fond of his drink, but mercifully close to retirement. Bruno recounted the story of Driant's inheritance and the new retirement home, asking them to let him know if they came across anything involving Sarrail or Constant. He also reminded the others to stay in touch with Maurice, the livestock commissioner, on any sales of farms.

Bruno had been wondering whether this new system, which put him in charge of the whole valley, was proving useful. He worked well with Juliette and they would have cooperated when necessary anyway. Louis needed careful handling, but he knew his district and had proved useful on several occasions. At least Bruno's promised pay rise had come through, although it hardly made up for the extra administrative duties he now faced. And these regular lunchtime meetings kept him in touch with matters up and down the valley. If Constant and Sarrail were looking for more new clients for their retirement home, he'd probably hear about it.

15

Bruno spent the afternoon doing more paperwork, the worst part of his job. When the Mairie clock struck four he packed up and drove to the tennis club. He changed into his whites and joined the junior tennis team, four boys and four girls, all under the age of sixteen, for his weekly coaching session. He had trained each one of them except for one new arrival, a Dutch girl named Lotte, who was probably the best player of them all and Bruno suspected that she would be beating him before the season was over.

Balzac sat just outside the court, watching the progress of each ball as though eager to join the game. From time to time the dog glanced back to the clubhouse and parking lot. Perhaps, like Bruno, he was wondering what might have delayed their friend the Baron, who usually joined them to help coach the youngsters.

Despite his weekly games on the covered court, Bruno felt a little rusty after the winter, or perhaps the youngsters were serving faster. Certainly one of the boys was hitting the ball a lot harder this year and Naomi, the pharmacist's daughter, had somehow developed a way to send the ball kicking higher than he'd expected. But he soon warmed up and began shouting out to them to toss the ball higher or to make more of their follow-through.

The minivan arrived bringing Jamie, his sister and Galina, all in tennis gear. Sasha gave Bruno a casual wave but stayed by the van in his normal dress. Bruno saw that Galina was carrying a very professional-looking bag that must have held three or four racquets. She had pulled her hair back from her face into a ponytail and she looked animated and cheerful. They all greeted Bruno and then Jamie and Kirsty went to watch the juniors, leaving Bruno and Galina alone.

'You are *flic*, and yet you teach sports?' asked Galina.

'Yes, and rugby in winter,' Bruno replied grinning. 'If not for sports, Kirsty and Jamie might have embarked on a lifetime of crime by now.' He saw that Galina looked blank and added, 'That was meant to be a joke.'

'I understand. But your joke is not very funny, I think. Jamie is a fine man and Kirsty is also a good person, and their parents are kind. Why you think their children might have become different?'

'Do you think children always grow up like their parents?'

She seemed to consider this light-hearted question seriously. 'Usually, I think. But not always. Children can learn what not to do if they do not like one of their parents and try not to grow up like that.'

'Is that what you did?' he asked from simple curiosity. She gave him a startled look, nodded and then shrugged in reply and went to join Jamie and Kirsty.

Bruno followed her and invited the three of them to use

the covered court to knock up until the juniors had finished, but the juniors who had been playing singles decided to play doubles and leave one of the open courts for Bruno's friends. They soon stopped playing, though, and gathered round to watch when they heard the power of Galina's strikes, even while warming up. After she'd made a few practice serves, Bruno knew he'd never faced a service that fast. He was going to be way out of his league.

But Jamie and his sister decided to play together, Galina won the toss and offered the ball to Bruno. He shook his head. He wanted to watch her serve. Her first service was not nearly as fast as her practice, but it kicked high and spun, forcing Kirsty to scramble to return it. She looped the ball high and Galina smashed it down the centre between the two siblings. Her next serve to Jamie was very fast indeed. He managed to return it, hard and low to Bruno, who had an easy volley to make it thirty–love. Galina's third serve was almost slow, but placed perfectly in the corner and spinning wide of the receiver. Kirsty just reached it, made a decent cross court return and Galina slammed it down the sidelines too fast for Jamie to react. Her final serve was an ace, right down the middle and screamingly fast. A love game.

The juniors gathered around the court applauded and Bruno was tempted to join in as he took his place on the baseline to receive Kirsty's first serve. The only game that went to deuce was Bruno's service and Galina won that with two brisk volleys. They won the set by six games to love and Bruno reckoned he could claim at most three points of the thirty or so that had been played.

'You're the finest player I've ever shared a court with,' he told Galina as they shook hands at the end of the set. Where Jamie and Kirsty looked as though they'd played a very hard set, Galina looked as cool and unruffled as she had before the game. The junior players were still gathered at the gate of the court to meet her. A couple had pens and pads of paper to get her autograph and ask where she usually played.

'Would you do us the honour of taking part in our club tournament in August?' Bruno asked her. 'The prize is modest but just watching you would raise the game for the whole club.'

'Why not?' she answered. 'I enjoy playing like this, trees all around, a simple country club and a hard court, no crowds and no pressure. It reminds me why I loved this game when I was a child. Will you be my partner in this tournament?'

'I think you should play with someone much better than me,' he said. 'Or maybe with one of our juniors. They could learn a lot. But tell me, where did you learn to play like that?'

'When I won my first junior championship, my father sent me to a tennis academy in Florida,' she said as Jamie and Kirsty crossed the court to join them. 'It was very hard and I began almost to hate the game. Then a friend told me it was not the game but the intense competition that I disliked so now I only play when and where I want.'

'What did you think of that, Bruno?' cried Jamie, shaking hands to congratulate the winners. 'Now you know what a shock I had when I first played Galina.'

'She's extraordinary,' he replied, turning back to Galina when the two Macraes went into the changing rooms to shower. 'Where did you win the junior championships?'

'Cyprus first, then Ukraine.'

'Why those two countries?' Bruno asked.

'I am now citizen of Cyprus, but was born in Donetsk, in Ukraine, so I was also citizen there. I could qualify for the two. My father tried to insist I become tennis professional but my mother is a musician, piano, and she understood that I wanted music to be my life. Tennis should be for play, for fun.'

'Is that what you meant about not wanting to grow up like your father?'

'Yes, of course. I would never want to drive a child as he pushed me. But I understand his ambition for me and I try to forgive him. He is just as hard on himself, which is why he is successful. He says he had to be strong, to succeed in the Soviet Union and in the bad time that came after. He tells me that since I didn't know those years, I could never understand. He is right, I think.'

'Did you grow up in Ukraine?' Bruno asked.

'No, in Moscow until I was twelve. And again I was lucky. My mother put me in a school that had a strong reputation for music. It was when he saw I could play tennis that my father took an interest in my future. Putin likes to play, so tennis was very much in fashion with the *siloviki*, the people of influence in the Kremlin.'

'I have a feeling that you may be more like your father than you think,' said Bruno. 'It must have taken remarkable self-discipline to become so good at both tennis and music.'

Galina stared at him in surprise. They were interrupted by

the two Macraes coming out from the clubhouse, their hair still wet from the shower.

'We'd better get back, Bruno,' said Kirsty. 'Aren't you going to shower, Galina?'

'No, I did not sweat,' Galina replied. 'I'll come back with you rather than make you wait for me.'

'Okay, Bruno, we'll see you with Florence, around seven.'

Bruno was changing after his shower when his phone rang. It was Albert, the captain of the *pompiers* and one of the two professional firemen in what was mainly a volunteer team.

'Bad news, Bruno. It's the Baron,' Albert began. Apparently some young idiot on a motocross bike had skidded into his car. The airbag exploded and slammed his head back, causing concussion. Bruno's old friend was on his way to Périgueux and Fabiola was with him.

'She says he should be okay but at his age she wants him in the hospital and put through a scanner. Don't go up there, she said to tell you. You'd just be in the way and she'll call you as soon as she has any news.'

'What about the kid who hit him?'

'A broken leg. He's in the same ambulance. It's young Thibaudin, the one whose dad works at the holiday village. His mother's on the way to be with him.'

'Thanks for letting me know. Where did this happen?'

'Just fifty metres from the Baron's house, about an hour ago. Raymond was coming back from the supermarket, saw the crash and called us. The Baron had a nose bleed so it looked worse than it probably is.'

Bruno went and told the youngsters who were having a drink at the bar. They were all fond of the Baron, who helped drive them to away games. They might even have to start thinking about finding a replacement for him, Bruno thought.

When he arrived at the riding school, Pamela said she'd already heard the news about the Baron's crash and had invited Gilles to have supper with her and Miranda and Jack.

'Please join us,' she said. 'It's going to be onion soup, a big lasagne I made, salad and cheese and then the new cherries, straight from the tree. We've got a fine crop this year and they're delicious.'

It was that cusp of the seasons for Pamela, just before her gîtes were solidly rented out from June and after the last of her cookery courses had left the previous week. This was the time her gîtes had to be thoroughly cleaned and any minor repairs and repainting done, and the maréchal made his annual visit to replace horseshoes. The first foal was due to be born any time in the next few days to Jenny, an American quarter horse that had come with the stables when Pamela and Miranda had bought the place. Two more foals were expected over the summer.

'Normally I would but Florence and I are invited to Chateau Rock this evening to hear them rehearse their concert and I feel obliged to be there.'

Pamela raised her eyebrows. 'I thought you went there for dinner on Saturday to hear them.'

'This is a different programme, normally done with a small orchestra rather than a string quartet, guitar and flute.'

'And why Florence?' she asked coolly, eyebrows still raised. Bruno saw that Pamela seemed unhappy about this and wondered why. She and Florence were good friends and Pamela knew about Florence's love of singing.

'Because she's the lead soprano in the choral music they'll be performing together,' he said, patiently. 'Anyway, I just dropped by to let you know about the Baron and I'll see you in the morning to exercise the horses.'

She nodded briskly, muttered something about preparing dinner, and turned on her heel, leaving Bruno to wonder what was troubling her. Maybe it was the stress of the pregnant mare. He went after her and put his head around the kitchen door.

'Would you like me to come back after the rehearsal and sit up with you and the mare tonight?' he asked.

Pamela was standing at the kitchen sink, her back to him. 'No, thank you,' she said, her voice stiff. 'It's good of you to offer but the mare and I will do better on our own.'

Bruno drove back to St Denis to collect Florence. He waited until they were in his Land Rover before telling her of the Baron's crash.

'Don't you want to go see him in the hospital?' she asked.

'Fabiola said not to go, but I'll try to see him tomorrow unless they send him home. Fabiola said she thought they'd let him go after giving him a scan.'

'Even a mild concussion can be serious at his age.'

'He's a tough old bird,' Bruno said, trying not to reveal his concern.

The evening began as it had on his previous visit; he and

Kirsty took over the cooking. Kirsty had prepared a green salad and defrosted one of Bruno's gazpachos. She said she planned a simple spaghetti, and she'd bought two apple pies in the market. Bruno glanced at the vegetable basket and the two tins of tomatoes and told her to leave the sauce to him while she and Meghan introduced Florence.

Bruno had never made a meatless spaghetti sauce before but shrugged and got on with it, slicing onions, garlic and courgettes. He topped and tailed some fresh green beans and fried them all in olive oil before adding salt and pepper. He threw in the tomatoes and left the sauce on a very low heat before joining the others. He sat chatting with Rod and Meghan, watching the sun go down. Rod told Bruno they'd go to the studio after dinner so he could record the rehearsal.

'If it's good, I'll print up some CDs they can sell at the concerts,' Rod said as Kirsty went back to the kitchen. 'We took some photos of them all earlier today which we can use as a cover. They want to call themselves the Chateau Rock Ensemble, which pleases me.'

Kirsty brought out the gazpacho and Bruno began slicing the big *tourte* of bread. With the musicians in a fine, excited mood it was a much more convivial evening than the previous one. Bruno's spaghetti was declared a success, even by the non-vegetarians, and the meal ended quickly with the musicians keen to get to the recording studio.

Bruno sat to one side with Kirsty, Meghan and Florence as Jamie's guitar began with the gentle, fluid notes of the opening and then Galina's flute came in boldly. Bruno saw that the two soloists had their eyes fixed on one another in a look that conveyed a perfect understanding. He realized with a small start that he felt no envy, even though he had never known such intimacy with another, except perhaps in love-making.

16

Bruno arrived at the hospital in Périgueux early the next day to visit the Baron in the hospital, but despite wearing his police uniform he was told to come back after lunch. He drove back to the centre of the city, parked in the square beside the cathedral and exchanged his uniform jacket for a red windcheater. He walked back along the Rue Taillefer and crossed the road at Place Bugeaud into Rue du Président Wilson. Just before a bank, he entered an office building and climbed the stairs to the third floor, where Sarrail and Constant had their offices. He pulled out his phone, set it to camera and tried the door to Constant's office. It was locked and there was no reply to his knock.

Back on the street, Bruno noticed a beauty parlour with a small sign that promised expert eyebrow treatments. Bruno could understand what was meant by threading, however the offer of sugaring baffled him. He recalled that Guillaumat had spoken of the eyebrows on the young woman who had visited Driant, so he went in. He was greeted by a woman of around his own age, carefully made-up with sculpted eyebrows and improbably red hair. She closed the account book she was checking and smiled to reveal perfect teeth. He pulled aside his jacket to reveal the police badge and her smile faded but she managed a polite, '*Bonjour, monsieur.*'

'*Bonjour, madame.* I believe you have a client, Mademoiselle Lara Saatchi.'

'Yes, Lara from the new insurance agency upstairs. Is she all right?'

'That's what we're trying to establish. Would you have her home address or mobile number, please?'

'The number, certainly.' She turned to the computer screen at her side, pressed some keys and read out the number. 'No home address, I'm afraid, only the office.'

'Thank you, we'll start there. In case she's not able to answer you might have a credit card receipt,' he said, smiling. 'We can get the address from that.'

She pulled a large box file from a shelf beneath her desk, skimmed through and showed him a receipt for a credit card from Banque Nationale de Paris. He took a note of the number and gave her his business card. 'If you want to verify my credentials, please call Commissaire Prunier.'

He called Lara's number, reached her voicemail and left a message asking her to call him back urgently.

'Is there a problem with Lara?' the woman asked.

'I hope not, but we do need to check with her on an important matter,' he said, smiling again. 'I'll get onto the credit card company for her home address.'

'They might not have it,' she said. 'She uses a company credit card, from the insurance agency.'

'A generous employer,' he said. 'And her eyebrows are a credit to your skills, *madame.* By the way, what is sugaring?'

'It is a traditional method for removing unwanted hair with sugar, lemon juice and water. People like it because it's natural, organic.'

'Thank you, *madame*. One learns something every day. *Au revoir*.'

He strolled back along the Rue Taillefer towards the cathedral and spent a happy half hour browsing in Henri Millescamp's antiquarian bookshop. Amid the leather-bound classics, collected sermons and nineteenth-century cookbooks he was pleased to find a memoir of a boat trip down the Vézère by two Englishmen on the eve of the Grande Guerre. It would make an unusual birthday gift for Pamela. Satisfied with his morning, he went to the restaurant Hercule Poirot, where he was meeting J-J and the man from the *fisc*, Goirau.

Bruno was glancing through the book when the door of the restaurant opened and J-J stood back to let Goirau precede him. Goirau was of average height and pencil-slim with close-cut grey hair. He was wearing a dark suit, blue shirt and a *papillon*, a bow tie, patterned in diagonal stripes of red, white and blue. When he shook hands, Bruno noted that his nails were manicured. There was something about his self-possession and his calculating glance that reminded Bruno of some of the career *sous-officiers* he had known in the army, men who were much more dangerous and more capable than they looked.

Goirau smiled with satisfaction when they were steered to what was clearly the best table in the restaurant, nestled under the medieval vault. He studied the menu with care, and like J-J and Bruno, he chose foie gras to begin, followed by the tête de veau. The important matter of ordering done, Goirau got down to business.

'Gustave Sarrail is a Belgian citizen from Charleroi, but did his studies in Lille and then Paris before moving down to Menton in the nineties, just as the Russian nouveau riche began looking to buy property on the Riviera.' He paused to taste the wine J-J had ordered, a lovely Montravel red from Château Moulin-Caresse that Bruno always enjoyed.

'How agreeable to find a wine as good as this with such a charming name,' Goirau said, smiling.

It was a remark that made Bruno like the man more but he remained wary. So far in his career, Bruno had encountered few members of the *fisc* but he'd heard legendary tales of their skills, of people who played chess in their heads without looking at the board, filled in a sudoku grid after a cursory glance and watched the CAP stock market in Paris, making fortunes from their investments.

'Sarrail enrolled in intensive Russian language classes, the first French *notaire* to do so, hired a pretty Russian girl as his assistant and began to make his fortune,' Goirau went on. 'He didn't come up on our screens until we realized that a great deal of this Russian money was dubious in origin and that he was one of a small group of *notaires* who worked closely with the private banks that were handling much of it. We suspected that he was getting it laundered through banks and investment companies the Russians had opened in Cyprus. Once the euro currency arrived, it all became much easier and Sarrail prospered, in particular because he became closely associated with an oligarch now based in Europe called Igor Ivanovich

Stichkin. He's an ex-military who turned businessman and an old acquaintance of Putin. He was born in the Russian-speaking eastern part of Ukraine that Putin has since virtually reoccupied, a project which Stichkin backed with cash for the pro-Russian militia.'

Bruno controlled his surprise at the name he'd heard from Gilles, and said nothing.

Goirau explained that this was Stichkin's way back into Putin's favour. A shrewd man who had long since realized that the Kremlin's favours came at an ever-higher price, he had quit Russia in 2007, during Putin's second term. He left his wife in Moscow but took with him his daughter and as much of his money as he deemed prudent. He bought himself Cypriot citizenship and a house in Limassol, an apartment in Monaco and a luxurious yacht to cruise back and forth from one to the other. Unless one is a French citizen, there is no personal income tax in Monaco, but the corporate taxes are quite high. So Stichkin kept his investment trusts in Cyprus and Luxembourg and took his income in Monaco.

'This neat solution was devised for him by the ingenious Monsieur Sarrail and the European context is important to this,' Goirau went on, tapping a finger on the table for emphasis. 'We larger countries are having more and more trouble with the little ones: Malta, Cyprus, Monaco, Luxembourg, each of which seeks prosperity through the financial sector and makes life easier for the rich.

'Then we came across a PowerPoint presentation that Sarrail delivered to an investment conference in Luxembourg which we found interesting.' Goirau paused as the first course of foie gras arrived, with a small glass of Monbazillac to accompany it. The conversation turned to the food and Goirau did not resume his account of Sarrail's presentation until the plates were cleared.

Sarrail's lecture had stressed that European demographics would shape the future. Europeans had almost stopped breeding. Only Ireland, France and Britain were anywhere near reproducing themselves and even there, growing life expectancy meant that for the foreseeable future the fastest-growing age group would be the over-sixties. There would be fewer and fewer young people to pay the taxes to finance the pensions and health care of the elderly. Since the European welfare states could therefore no longer afford their traditional generosity, catering to the elderly would be a huge growth business for the private sector. High-quality retirement homes offering comfort, good food, health care on tap and an interesting social life would be an excellent investment.

'Stichkin decided to invest in a pilot project, the one near Sarlat that interests you, Bruno,' said Goirau. 'His investment funds financed it and Sarrail can't afford to let it fail. Stichkin would never forgive him.'

'It sounds like a reasonable and legal investment idea,' Bruno said, cutting at the flesh that had been rolled around the veal tongue and then cooked for at least five hours. It was a classic dish that he seldom ordered but today, with his companions choosing it, he'd felt in the mood for it. To his delight, instead of the conventional *sauce ravigote*, it was served with the rich broth in which it had been cooked.

'Yes, but they may have their timing wrong,' Goirau said,

putting down his knife and fork and fixing Bruno with a sharp eye. 'France's health and retirement model may be under pressure but it's a long way from collapse. And their target market of wealthy old people have other options. A lot of them have second homes in the sun. Morocco or the Caribbean. They have airports nearby so they can come and go and their children and grandchildren can visit them easily. They have doctors and hospitals on hand, golf courses and a choice of restaurants. Above all, they like to mix with their own familiar social circle rather than take their chances in a retirement home full of strangers.'

'So the project is failing?' J-J asked, dipping a chunk of bread into the broth before popping it into his mouth.

'It's not doing well, maybe sixty per cent occupancy, and some of their new customers may not have quite the level of culture and manners that they'd hoped for.'

That would probably apply to Driant, Bruno thought. 'Are there any other cases of customers taking out this insurance policy like Monsieur Driant and then conveniently dying?' he asked.

'Not that we know of – I'm hoping you might help us, but I should add that Stichkin, as you can imagine from his past, has a reputation as a very hard man. There are rumours about people who have crossed him simply disappearing, perhaps from that yacht of his.'

'Who were these people who disappeared?' J-J asked.

'A couple of foolish burglars in Cyprus who made the mistake of breaking into his house when he was away,' said Goirau. 'There's no proof, of course, and the Cyprus police don't seem very concerned about the burglars' fate. They were just two of the fifteen thousand refugees who washed up on the island, mainly Syrians. The island has had more refugees per capita than Italy or Greece.'

A silence fell and Bruno wondered what was becoming of this Europe that had been launched with such high hopes and idealism. After a while, he asked, 'Constant, this insurance guy who shares offices with Sarrail – doesn't he have to have some kind of licence? He has to file his taxes. Doesn't his paperwork leave a trail for you to follow?'

'Yes and no,' Goirau answered. 'He's an agent, not an insurer. He should supposedly be looking for the best deal for his clients. He can pick any insurer who is licensed to operate in Europe, from the giants like Axa and Allianz to smaller, local ones. There are more than a hundred in Luxembourg alone, where Constant is officially resident and where he pays his taxes. And there are more than two hundred in Cyprus. Stichkin himself has one, or rather some of his investment trusts have minority shareholdings, which combined could give him effective control.'

'What's the problem with Stichkin?' J-J asked. 'You said he pulled out of Russia with his money and became a European citizen. When you first mentioned him to me I checked and he's not on any of our sanctions lists. Do we assume he's fairly clean?'

'I certainly don't assume that,' said Goirau. He explained that Stichkin had left a lot of money in Russia but he didn't abandon it. He still had important shareholdings in banks and insurers, in a big nickel company, and in a major car distributor.

'He must have close to a billion euros there, if not more.

162

That gives the Kremlin a great deal of leverage over him if they want to use it, which may explain his sudden enthusiasm for Ukrainian politics,' Goirau went on. 'And he had family there, a younger brother, nephews and nieces. More leverage. But since he was born in Ukraine Stichkin was not officially listed as Russian, so he appeared clean, at least on the surface. That gives him a freedom of action in the West that the Kremlin may well find useful. I'd be surprised if he isn't still doing them some discreet favours, just to make sure his Russian funds don't get confiscated. That's standard Kremlin procedure for oligarchs who don't toe the line. There are lots of precedents. In certain cases, they go to jail or die, sometimes in suspicious circumstances. But Stichkin still seems close to Putin. Like most dictators, the older they get, the more they trust only immediate family or their oldest friends.'

'You make it sound as though this Stichkin business is about much more than a retirement home,' said Bruno.

'Of course, and it's about much more than French taxes. We don't like the way some of these small countries like Cyprus and Malta sell residence visas and passports for suitable sums. But if we're going to be able to do some clearing up and tighten the rules at the European level, we're going to need evidence that will persuade our partners.'

'How do you expect to get that evidence?' J-J asked, in a way that made Bruno suspect that J-J and Goirau had rehearsed this. Perhaps others would be given similar briefings to the one Bruno was receiving.

'There are a number of ways. Perhaps Stichkin could be made to worry about the Kremlin's attitude towards him and come to us for protection, then he might tell us all that he knows. Or if we found sufficient evidence of money-laundering or other offences, we could put pressure on him. Or if a member of his team were to start secretly helping us and telling us Stichkin's every move, that would be ideal. Delicate certainly, and dangerous perhaps, but perfect for us.'

Goirau paused to take a slow, appreciative sip of wine, and then glanced from J-J to Bruno. 'Finally, there is the personal angle. He has an only child, a daughter, who is studying music at the Paris Conservatoire. And young people these days seem to lead such unruly and wayward lives.' Again he paused, shaking his head and glancing meaningfully at Bruno. 'Sex and drugs – so many risks.'

Mon Dieu, *I know what's coming*, Bruno thought, *and I don't like it*. Goirau could only mean Galina. Rather than mention her, he said, 'This is France, a law-abiding country where we don't target the innocent. So I presume you must be thinking of his tame *notaire*, Sarrail. You want him to turn informer?'

Goirau winced. 'I don't like to use such loaded terms. I prefer to think of it as inviting him to do his civic duty by helping the French authorities.' His keen blue eyes turned towards Bruno. 'That's where I think you might be best placed to help us, Bruno,' he said. 'Your role will be to pursue your enquiries on behalf of Driant's children and demand copies of every relevant document. What I'd really like is some indication that Sarrail is involved in the ownership of the retirement home. If we can find that, while he was also acting as the *notaire* for the sale of Driant's land, the conflict of interest could lay him open to a lawsuit from Driant's children for breach of trust.'

Goirau leaned forward and gripped Bruno's hand that was resting on the table. 'I should add that I greatly admire your own imaginative use of the livestock regulations in this business so far. But you haven't gone far enough. This gives you an excellent lever and I count on you to use it.'

'In hunting terms,' Bruno said, 'you want me to flush the game towards you while you wait for it to come under your gun.'

'Somewhat dramatic in expression, Bruno, but yes, that is pretty much what I'm expecting you to do. Not just me and not just the Finance Ministry – the Interior Ministry is equally interested in Stichkin from a security aspect. And bearing in mind his role in Ukraine, your friends of the *piscine* are also interested,' he added, using the slang term for French intelligence because its traditional building was near the pool of the French swimming association.

Goirau sat back, a smugness settling over his features before he spoke again. 'It turns out we have a mutual acquaintance in General Lannes. These days, he and I work together increasingly now that fiscal matters often blur into national security.'

'Our old friend the Brigadier,' said J-J, rolling his eyes at Bruno as if to indicate this involvement of the shadowy General Lannes came as news to him as well.

'Feel free to call him, Bruno,' said Goirau. 'And Lannes asked me to let you know that the usual letter seconding you to the minister's staff has been sent to your Mayor. With his best regards to you, of course. That means you'll be covered under the emergency regulations. You won't need to lose time applying for search warrants.'

Bruno sat back, took a deep breath, looked from J-J back to Goirau and sighed. Then he picked up his glass and sipped, gaining time as he thought what to say.

'You've confirmed many of my own suspicions about Sarrail and Constant so of course I stand ready to help,' he began. 'But there are some things I need from you. I want every security camera in the Rue du Président Wilson checked for film of a young woman, tall, slim, dark hair, probably Arab origins. She gives her name as Lara Saatchi and she works for Constant. She drives a blue VW Beetle convertible and I would bet she regularly parks it in the underground garage around the corner, and you have surveillance cameras in there. I have a witness who saw her with Driant at his farm not long before his death, supposedly from heart failure. I need that film to show it to my witness because she could be the last person who saw Driant alive. I also want a full forensic turnover of the Driant farm to see if any trace of this young woman can be found.'

'But Driant died of natural causes, a heart attack,' said J-J. 'And he was cremated.'

'I'm not sure. That's why I want a full forensic search of his farm.' Bruno tore a page from his notebook, scribbled down the number of Driant's mobile phone and handed it to J-J. 'I also want a full readout of Driant's phone for the three months up to his death. His phone was missing from his house. I asked a magistrate in Sarlat to apply for the warrant but apparently the livestock regulations aren't sufficient for such a telephone search. As for Constant, here's the number of his company credit card, issued to Lara Saatchi.'

He added her name, mobile and credit card numbers to the page torn from his notebook and saw Goirau's eyes light up.

'That should help you look into Constant's accounts. And one last thing . . .' Bruno added. 'There's a young Ukraine-born student at the Paris Conservatoire, a very gifted flautist named Galina. She has just turned up in St Denis with a bunch of student musicians to play in some concerts at local festivals. She's accompanied by a cousin who looks to me like a professional bodyguard. Could she be in any way related to this enquiry of yours?'

'She's Stichkin's daughter, his only child,' said Goirau. 'How interesting that you know her.'

'Her boyfriend is a friend of mine, a fine musician and a decent guy. So if you want my cooperation, you'll leave Galina out of this,' said Bruno, folding his napkin and rising from the table. 'Thank you for lunch and now if you'll excuse me, I have to visit a sick friend in hospital.'

17

Bruno took from his van the bag with clean clothes, tracksuit and trainers that he'd picked up from the Baron's home, and found his friend sitting by his hospital bed in a dressing gown. His face was badly bruised around the eyes and nose but he'd been given a clean bill of health and a lunch he described as 'tolerable'. To the Baron's annoyance, since he hated the white whiskers that revealed his age, the doctors had ordered him not to shave until the facial swellings went down. Bruno waited while the Baron dressed in the bathroom.

'Thanks for picking me up,' he said as Bruno drove back through the city centre. 'I'd have waited for hours for an ambulance to take me home.'

'No problem, I had a meeting in town anyway.'

'You're on a new case? Still involving Driant's death?'

'In a way. I should have asked how well you knew him.'

'We went to school together, played on the same rugby team. One by one, the friends of my youth are going. He and I weren't bosom pals but even the ones you weren't close to, you miss them.'

'You know he hadn't been speaking to his daughter?'

'Because of her sex life? I'd heard that. He was old-fashioned that way. Are you suspicious about his death?'

'I'm not sure. He did have heart problems. I'm certainly curious. There are some open questions, including about his own apparently active sex life.'

'Lucky him, at his age. I remember he told me Viagra had changed his life.'

'It might have ended it,' said Bruno. 'Gelletreau refused to prescribe it because of his heart condition. But Driant got hold of it anyway. I saw some of those blue lozenge-shaped pills in his bedside drawer when I searched the house.'

'It's easy enough. I often get ads on the internet for it. They must know my age.' The Baron paused. 'If it helps, there was a massage parlour in Bergerac he talked about.' He paused again. 'Evidently you suspect something. Can you tell me about the case?'

Bruno gave a guarded summary, without mentioning the *fisc*. He started at the beginning with the visit from Driant's son, and described his and the Mayor's visit to the retirement home before explaining his difficulty in reaching the elusive Sarrail and Constant.

'Why don't I try?' the Baron asked. 'I'm a likely candidate for this Château Marmont home of theirs. I'm the right age, wealthy enough. They'd jump at the chance to sign me up and I can go in wearing a wire, if you like. I owe that much to Driant's memory and all the time I knew him.'

'Let me think about that,' said Bruno. 'We seldom use wires these days. They're clunky, too easily spotted and legally speaking that requires authorization from a magistrate.'

When Bruno got back to his office in St Denis after dropping off the Baron at his home, he found an email from J-J with an attachment of the list of calls to and from Driant's phone. Almost all of the numbers were identified by the registered name of the subscriber, the only exceptions being those phones using prepaid cards that were bought over the counter, but at least the point of sale was listed. Most of the calls were predictable: connections to Driant's son, the St Denis medical clinic, to other farmers, feed suppliers and vets. Several calls had been made to and from the offices of Constant and Sarrail and to the new retirement home. But there were two kinds of calls Driant had made that seemed odd. The first was regular calls to an 08 number, which carried a premium charge. Bruno called it and found it was a sex chatline. The other was four calls to a massage parlour in Bergerac. Bruno called a colleague, an inspector in the Bergerac police, who laughed when Bruno asked what was known about the place.

'It's not what you'd call a medical establishment, more personal relaxation massage,' he was told. 'And you know what that means. Don't tell me you're interested, Bruno.'

'No, I'm working on the case of someone who died in possibly suspicious circumstances and he made several calls to the place. Is it on your map?'

'Not really. It's discreet, not known as a brothel, seems to be well run, causes no trouble so we turn a blind eye. Was this guy elderly, living alone?'

'That's right.'

'That's the usual clientele, old guys getting a little personal service. The place is run by a local woman, middle-aged, used to be a nurse, no criminal record. Most of the girls seem to be foreign.'

'Would you mind if I came down, asked a few questions about the old man?'

'Not at all, be my guest. Do you want any back-up?'

'No thanks, I'll keep it low-key and let you know if I learn anything interesting.'

Forty minutes later, with his tie off and a red civilian jacket over his uniform, Bruno parked in a dowdy side street near the station in Bergerac and entered the only modern-looking shop on the strip. It was sandwiched between a small hardware store and a tired-looking *boulangérie* whose window carried cream cakes that had seen better days. A handwritten notice offered a sack of stale bread for pets at two euros.

'*Bonjour, monsieur*, always a pleasure to see a new client,' said the woman at the front desk. She wore a white coat, had dyed blonde hair and lipstick that matched her fingernails. Her eyebrows were black, and sculpted in the way he'd seen at the beautician's in Périgueux. There was something familiar about her but he could not place it.

'*Bonjour, madame*,' he replied, but before he could pull aside the jacket to show his badge, she suddenly eyed him intently and said, 'I know you. Wait, it will come to me. School – you're Benoît. Remember me? Cécile? You could never stop looking at my boobs. And not just looking.'

Bruno broke out in delighted laughter. 'Cécile! *Mon Dieu*, your breasts were the first ones I ever saw, the first ones I ever held and kissed. I'll remember them to my dying day. We were what, fifteen?'

She stood and presented her cheek to be kissed, and he gave her an affectionate hug. She sat down, still smiling, but with something steely in her eyes as she said, 'You're a cop these days. From time to time I see your photo in the paper. Is that what brings you here?'

'Afraid so.' He sat down on a bench along the side wall and glanced at a poster offering Thai, Swedish and deep tissue massage.' It's about a client of yours, an old man in his seventies called Driant who died a couple of weeks ago.'

'I read about it. Heart attack when he was alone at his farm, it said in the paper. What makes you think he came here?'

'He told one of his old friends about you, and there were four calls to here on his phone. Don't worry, Cécile, this isn't official. And I'm not here for a freebie.'

'That makes a nice change for a cop. Yes, he came here a few times. Always wanted a different girl.'

'How many do you have?'

'Is this between you and me, Benoît? Off the record?'

'Yes, I'm just looking for background.' He smiled, less to reassure her than at hearing himself called by the name he'd been given at the church orphanage, a name he hadn't used since his schooldays.

'There's a Vietnamese woman who pretends to be Thai, an Albanian blonde who pretends to be Swedish, a Congolese girl and a Syrian, a new one. Plus a couple of part-timers, French girls who really are masseuses. And then there's me, the qualified nurse with the credentials.'

'And whatever extra services the girls offer is between them and the client, is that how it works?'

She shrugged. 'Clients want their privacy. I don't go behind closed doors. But if a guy wants to pay extra for a hand job or something more, that's their business.'

'I see you charge fifty euros for a massage. How do you split that?'

'Don't tell the *fisc*, Benoît, but it's half for me and half for the girl.'

Bruno did the sums in his head and gave a low whistle. 'Five girls, even at just four clients a day each you're making over two thousand a week.'

'Less than half that after the rent and taxes and a few pay-offs. And you wouldn't believe how much I spend at the launderette every day, all the sheets and towels. I have to buy new ones every few months. Massage oil is a bastard to get out.'

'How's your life, Cécile? You married? Kids?'

'Once widowed, once divorced, with a daughter who works on the railway who's just made me a grandmother. I had her at eighteen. And a son in Bordeaux training to be an architect.'

'Good for you! I haven't got any kids yet. Never found a woman who wanted to settle down with me.'

'Don't look at me, Benoît,' she said, returning his smile. 'Sometimes I wonder how you and I might have turned out. But I've had more than enough of men.'

'So, what can you tell me about Driant?'

'As I said, he wanted a different girl every time. From the time he was in there, I suppose it was hand jobs. He was a sweet old guy, very courteous, tipped well. The girls had no complaints. When he called, it was always to ask if we had someone new. What do you know about this business?'

'Nothing at all.'

'I could write a history from the women in this game. Back in the nineties they came from the Yugoslav wars, Bosnians and Serbs. Then it was Ukrainians and Russians. After the Americans went crazy we started getting the Afghans and Iraqis and lately it's been the Syrians. You show me a war and I'll tell you what new girls turn up in the business, selling the only thing they have to get by. So you tell me who comes next. Probably those poor girls risking their lives on leaky boats to get across the Mediterranean.'

Bruno sighed and nodded. 'I see what you mean. Tell me, did Driant pay in cash?'

'Yes, but most guys do. Wives can read credit card bills.'

'Did you learn anything about him? Did you chat while he was waiting?'

'Not much. He clammed up when I tried to find out if he was using Viagra because that worried me a bit, thinking he might have a heart attack in one of those back rooms someday. At least the old guy would have died happy. But we hadn't seen him for well over a month. He used to be a regular, always came mid-week in the daytime when it was quiet. Then he stopped. Until I saw his death in the paper I didn't know what had happened.'

'I think maybe it was lambing time. He was a sheep farmer.'

As she rolled her eyes, Bruno went on, 'Could I talk to the women who attended to him, find out what it was he wanted, how he reacted?'

Her eyes turned hard. 'Is that relevant, Benoît? Or is it just your dirty mind?'

'No, Cécile. The death certificate says he died of a heart attack but there are reasons we have to double-check that. I want to know if he ever collapsed here or had any health trouble, if he was always able to perform or if he used any drugs.'

'I'm not aware of anything apart from Viagra. A lot of guys take that. The masseuses would have called me in if he'd had any health problems. When we got chatting on a break, a couple said they liked him, felt sorry for him.'

'So nothing unusual?'

'Not unless you'd call a topless massage with a hand job unusual,' she said, smiling. 'Quite a lot of clients try to get more but my house rules stop at that.'

Bruno chuckled and Cécile sat up. 'You went off into the army when you left school? How did that work out?'

'It was great until I got shot, invalided out. When I came out of hospital I became a cop. I'm happy enough.'

'You always were a decent guy, Benoît. Who knows, if you'd stayed on at school and I hadn't hooked up with that bastard Didier and got pregnant, you and I might have made it work.'

'Didier?' he exclaimed. 'The butcher's son with the big ears? You were the best-looking girl in school. How on earth did you end up with him?'

She grimaced. 'He had his own car, simple as that. That's where he got me pregnant and that's what killed him, eventually. He died drunk, running into one of those log piles on the road to Cadouin. They think he fell asleep. Left me with the little girl and pregnant with the boy. So I buckled down and went to nursing school while raising them. I thought it was a real profession. I hadn't realized it meant wiping a lot of bottoms, which was exactly what I was doing at home with little Mo-Mo, now my big Maurice. So I went into physiotherapy, did a massage course and here we are.'

Bruno nodded slowly and they stared at one another for a long moment and then the door opened and a man shuffled in, late middle-age and wearing a floppy hat that hid half his features. Bruno rose, raised a hand in thanks and farewell and left Cécile to her customer. Back in his Land Rover he checked his phone – he'd turned off the sound when he had been in the massage parlour – and found a text message from Yves, the head of the forensic team attached to J-J's office. Yves was at Driant's farm and they had something. Bruno texted back that he was on his way.

Yves came out of the farmhouse wearing a snowman suit with bootees and a plastic hat, saying his team were still at work and he and Bruno should stand on the doorstep. J-J had been checking locations on Lara Saatchi's phone and had found three occasions when she was connected to the cell phone tower closest to Driant's farm. He read out the dates. Bruno pulled out his phone to check the calendar. Today was Wednesday. Driant's funeral had been the previous Thursday and he'd been found by Patrice the postman on the Friday before that. Time of death had been estimated by Dr Gelletreau at some time between the previous Sunday evening and Tuesday at the latest.

'The last time her phone was here was that Sunday evening, from just before six until just after nine,' Yves said. 'She could have been there when he died. We could even be looking at a murder but with the body cremated we'll never prove it, not unless she confesses.'

'Where is she now?' Bruno asked.

'The last location we had was this morning in central Périgueux but then it went dead. She must have taken out the battery. We have an automatic trace for when she turns it back on.'

'Are you finding anything else in there?'

'Cosmetic traces in the bathroom and long black hairs on a towel. Lots of fingerprints and somebody washed up some dirty dishes. They were wiped clean but we have prints on the handle of the dishwashing brush.'

'That could be Driant's son or daughter,' said Bruno. 'They came to pick up some family souvenirs. But neither of them has black hair.'

'I'll go back in,' said Yves.

'Can you keep an eye open for any sign of cocaine?' Bruno asked. 'I checked with a doc – that could have been what killed him.'

Yves raised an eyebrow but nodded as he went back inside. J-J's voice was excited when he answered Bruno's call, the way he sounded when he was on the trail and the quarry was close.

'I think we've got an image of your Lara Saatchi,' he began. 'We went by your description but then we got confirmation from that woman you mentioned in the beauty shop by her office. She identified her in each film, one from the parking garage and the other from the bank.'

'Yves and I just checked the dates when her phone was at Driant's farm,' said Bruno. 'Her last visit coincides with the likely time of death so Yves said to tell you we might be looking at a possible murder. Send the best images you have to my phone and I'll take it to the farmer who saw her at Driant's place. We have cause enough to have her picked up for questioning.'

'I'm not sure about that just yet, Bruno,' J-J said. 'If I say we may be investigating a homicide we'd have to bring in a magistrate and that screws up Goirau's plan. It's Sarrail and Stichkin he's after, not the office assistant. After a death certificate of heart failure and the cremation, we'd never get a conviction anyway. Even if the old man died when this Saatchi woman was there we might not get more on her than failure to report a death.'

'It's your call,' said Bruno. 'I think it's suspicious that she's dropped off the map. Yves said she must have taken the battery out of her phone. By the way, I visited that massage parlour Driant called four times. He was a regular customer, no health incidents and the girls liked him. He was also a regular caller to a sex chatline.'

'And he was what, seventy-four and still at it like a teenager?' Bruno could hear him chortle down the line. 'There's hope for us all yet. What's your next step?'

'I'll leave you to track down Sarrail and Constant. You have better resources than I do and I'm not sure what progress I can make unless we have them back in Périgueux where I can reach them and start putting pressure on. Meantime, once I get those images of Saatchi I'll show them to my witness for a positive ID.'

'What about the other guy that's connected to Sarrail, the accountant? And isn't there some investment advisor in those offices as well? You could have a crack at them?'

'On what grounds?' Bruno demanded, trying to keep his

irritation under control. 'As far as we know there's no direct connection between them and Driant or the retirement home. We have probable cause to ask questions of Constant about the insurance and Sarrail about his work as *notaire*, but not those others, or at least, not yet. And I'm no accountant, I wouldn't even know what to ask. Surely that's the responsibility of Goirau and the *fisc*. You can't just send me in blind.'

'Goirau wants me to fit you up with a wire when you go to see them.'

'On what grounds, J-J? Without a magistrate taking over the case and authorizing it, that's not legal, and you know it. I'm really not comfortable with the way Goirau thinks he can use us as a kind of battering ram to put pressure on Stichkin. That's not what we do. We're officers of the law. We uphold it, we don't use it for some bureaucrat's convenience.'

'*Merde*, Bruno. *Tu me casses les couilles*,' J-J almost shouted and then ended the call.

Bruno shrugged and stomped off through the farmyard to the pasture where the sheep had been, looking across the valley that he loved and knowing that this was his responsibility, this place and its people. He hadn't liked Goirau and didn't like Goirau's operation nor his arrogantly casual assumption that J-J and Bruno worked for him. And, Bruno thought, it would be him and J-J in trouble if this all went wrong.

His phone beeped. It was J-J sending over the video clips of Saatchi. As he looked at them it rang again, an incoming call. It was J-J again.

'Sorry,' he said. 'My big mouth. And I don't like Goirau's scheme either. But from what you say about the Saatchi woman being at Driant's farm around the time he died, we have reasonable cause to investigate. But I won't ask the Procureur to open a dossier and appoint an investigating magistrate, not yet.'

'Fair enough. But we do have grounds to haul her in for questioning. That's why I'm heading over to a farm across the valley to show Saatchi's photo to my witness who met her at Driant's place.'

'Good, that works for me. And then? What are you planning to do next? Knowing you, Bruno, you'll have something in mind.'

'Then I have to finish building a chicken coop.'

18

When Bruno called at Guillaumat's farm, he confirmed that the images of Lara Saatchi on Bruno's phone were indeed the young woman from the insurance firm whom he'd met at Driant's place. As Bruno left, he told himself there was little he could now do until J-J confirmed that Sarrail or Constant were back in Périgueux. In the meantime, as well as finishing the chicken coop, he had to prepare for taking Balzac to the breeding kennels on Saturday.

It would be a big day for his young dog and Bruno knew he was feeling a little nervous on Balzac's behalf. He'd have to pack an overnight case, and perhaps he should make a new batch of Balzac's dog biscuits as a gift to Claire Mornier. Or should he take flowers to the female owner of the dam his Balzac was about to mount? There was a dilemma of etiquette, he thought, and laughed at himself, happy to be back in his usual good mood after the row with J-J. Bruno knew that J-J was a loyal friend and good colleague and felt equally uncomfortable with the way Goirau from the *fisc* was trying to use them both.

Which reminded him, J-J had introduced him to someone Bruno knew he should have told about Balzac's coming weekend. He pulled off the road and called her cell phone.

'Bruno, lovely to hear from you,' came the familiar, beloved voice that reminded him again how much he missed this woman. 'I was thinking of you just this very morning. It's our first real summer's day here in Paris and I was walking to work through the Tuileries gardens on the way to the Ministry, looking across the river at the Musée d'Orsay and remembering that time we went there. Happy days. And how are you?'

'I'm well, thanks, Isabelle, and you sound good but I'm calling about Balzac.'

'Is he all right?' She sounded concerned.

'He's fine, never better. But he has a big weekend coming up. You remember when you first brought him to me as a pup and told me about the military kennels at Suippes, how they wanted to breed him when he was fully grown? Well, his big day will be this weekend.'

'*Mon Dieu*. How time flies – a puppy and now he's going to be a father. Where will this take place? At Suippes?'

'No, at a kennel north of here close to the Limousin border, run by a breeder called Claire Mornier who was a corporal at Suippes when we first got Balzac. She was the one who arranged for us to have him. Now she's done her twenty years with her pension and breeds dogs for the military. I'll be going there Saturday and staying overnight. They like the dogs to have more than one, er, mating.'

'Like master, like dog, as I well recall,' she said with that light, warm laugh that he knew so well. 'Do you think Balzac would like me to be there?'

'We always said he's as much your dog as mine and you know how he loves to see you.' As he waited for her response, Bruno could hear the sound of pages being turned and computer keys being clicked.

'I can come out Saturday, but I have to be back by Monday,' she said. 'You said you'll be staying overnight, do you have a hotel booked?'

'No, she has a room for visiting owners,' he said, and then added, tentatively, 'I can book you a nearby hotel if you like.'

'Nonsense, I want to be on hand for Balzac, and with you, of course, Bruno. You know how much I miss you, and the Périgord, and Balzac.'

'And I you,' he replied, delighted at the prospect. 'I could meet your train at Limoges or at Brive.'

'How far is this place from Brive airport? That looks more convenient and faster for me. Oh, wait. There's a plane from Orly that gets in at seven on Saturday evening which is too late and it has a lousy return time. Trains look better; there's one that gets me to Brive at two on Saturday and leaves at four on Sunday. How does that sound?'

'Perfect. We'll meet you at Brive station on Saturday. Claire has offered to make dinner so I'll bring some wine, foie gras, salad and cherries from my garden.'

'Can I bring anything? How on earth do we celebrate a dog's first mating?'

'The promise of a second,' he replied, laughing.

'Until Saturday, *je t'embrasse*,' she said.

Feeling wonderful, Bruno whistled most of the way back to the riding school where he waved at Miranda as he passed the paddock where she was supervising a circling ring of children on ponies. He greeted Balzac, who had spent the day there since the morning ride. Balzac followed his master to the coop, the two sheepdogs keeping a respectful distance behind. Inside the chickens' enclosure, Bruno checked that the four support posts were firmly placed and secure. He took his saw and battery-driven drill from his Land Rover and then cut to length and screwed in the cross-braces. He then attached the four sides of the coop, ensuring that the rear posts were ten centimetres higher than the front, to give a sloping roof so rainwater could flow.

The plank roof fitted perfectly. He screwed it in and covered it with waterproof felt, attaching it with rubber washers and fat-headed screws to prevent leaks. Over that he laid corrugated plastic, used bolts and washers to attach it and then mounted the gutter to catch the rainwater. He fitted the downpipe and placed it to drain into the largest bucket he could find. He'd get a proper cistern, holding five hundred litres, later in the week.

He made a ramp so the chickens could climb up into their coop, fixed it to the doorway and then fed into the coop the two perches the Baron and Félix's dad had made earlier. He slid old wine boxes full of straw beneath the perches, checked that the outer wire and stakes were secure and that the door to the enclosure latched properly. Then he washed in the stable sink, gave Hector an apple from the barrel and headed for Pamela's office where he found her in jeans and a sweatshirt, her hair piled up with a couple of pencils, doing her accounts.

'Great news,' she exclaimed, leaping up to give him a kiss of welcome. 'The *gîtes* are now booked up for the whole season which means we'll be in profit this year with enough over to give me and Miranda a very modest salary, probably just a little more than minimum wage.'

'Congratulations,' he said, hugging her in return. 'Your business plan assumed you wouldn't be in profit until year three. That's wonderful. And you've bought those new horses and the ponies and launched the cookery school. That means you're well ahead of your schedule.'

'And I have a glorious new foal who was born without any trouble at all. She'll grow up to be lovely and when the schoolkids turn up they'll all fall in love with her. I already have and so have Jack and Miranda and her boys.'

'I have a surprise for you,' he said. 'Follow me.' Taking her hand, he led her behind the stable to where the new chicken enclosure and coop waited to be admired.

'The only question is, what colour should I paint it?' he asked. 'Would you like blue to match your shutters and the stable doors? Or something different? I could just give it a coat of weatherproof varnish so it blends in with the stables.'

'Blue, please. And thank you, it's lovely and I had two eggs this morning. Now come and see the foal. Her mother's already let her make friends with the sheepdogs and Balzac.'

'I'll be away this weekend,' he said, and explained about taking Balzac to the breeding kennels.

'That'll be quite a step for him. We'd better remember to keep him at your place when Bella goes on heat. I dread to think what a basset-sheepdog cross would look like.'

Bruno laughed and as they went to the further stable to admire the foal, he suggested they might want to ride to

Chateau Rock that evening so Pamela could meet the musicians. She asked if any of them rode and Bruno knew that Jamie and Kirsty both did. He pulled out his phone to call the chateau and Kirsty answered. She would love to ride, and then put down the phone to ask the others, coming back on the line to say that Jamie, Galina and Sasha would join them. Pamela went off to don her riding clothes while Bruno began saddling the six horses, leaving his own Hector until last.

Half an hour later, with the spare horses on a leading rein, they arrived at Chateau Rock where the entire household turned out to watch the departure, with Galina almost dancing with glee at the prospect. It was soon evident that she was by far the best rider among the newcomers, almost as good as Pamela. Jamie and Kirsty were decent riders, having learned at the riding school before Pamela bought it. Sasha was evidently a beginner but insisted on joining them.

Pamela set an easy pace down the slope past the vineyard and into the valley at Paunat where she followed a farm track that skirted the line of trees shading the stream. They crossed at a ford, shallow at this time of year, and then rode up through the woods on a bridle trail towards Pezuls, reaching the ridge that led to Sainte-Alvère where they could canter. Sasha was soon trailing behind while Galina leant forward on the big Warmblood gelding she'd chosen, gave him rein and moved quickly into a gallop. Hector was not a horse to let another take the lead and they were soon neck and neck, leaving the others behind.

They stopped at the road for the others to catch up and

Bruno dismounted to warn oncoming traffic as they all crossed and then rode on towards St Avit before turning back towards Chateau Rock. Bruno checked his watch when it came into sight and was surprised to see that they had been out for only an hour. Rod, Meghan and the others were standing on the terrace and waving, a bottle of champagne and some glasses on the table to welcome them back.

'That was a wonderful end to a perfect day,' exclaimed Galina, looking more lively than Bruno had ever seen her as she dismounted to thank Pamela. 'We went to the Lascaux cave this morning, had lunch at Domme with the most beautiful view in the world. Then Jamie took us down through the trees to a ruined castle like from a fairy tale.'

'It was the ruined castle of Commarque and she loved it,' said Jamie, coming up behind Galina and hugging her, his arms locked around her waist. She nestled happily into him. 'We thought we'd better show her the region.'

'This is the loveliest countryside I've ever seen, and so romantic,' Galina said. 'I think I could stay here for ever and Jamie and Kirsty say there is so much more to see.'

'Sarlat,' said Kirsty.

'Limeuil,' chimed in Jamie.

'Milandes,' said Pamela as Bruno burst out, 'Monbazillac.'

'We'll have time to see everything while you're here,' said Jamie, nuzzling her and kissing the corner of her mouth.

Rod and Meghan were beaming, delighted to see their son so happy. Bruno, however, noticed that Kirsty was watching this with a quizzical eye until she was distracted by Sasha who, instead of descending from his horse, began to fall. He toppled with an almost comic slowness. Bertie let out a massive belly laugh and Bruno saw with alarm that Sasha's left foot was still caught in the stirrup. Panicking, Sasha grabbed at the horse's mane, putting much of his weight on it. The usually tranquil mare was startled. She bucked and jumped forward, dragging Sasha who had landed hard on his back. His head bounced hard on the ground as the horse gathered speed.

Bruno leaped to grab the bridle and calm the horse and at once Pamela was beside him, crooning as she stroked the horse's neck to soothe the alarmed mare. Pia ran down from the terrace to attend to the dazed Sasha, checking his pulse and looking into his eyes.

'Don't just stand there laughing, Bertie, you idiot,' Pia snapped, glancing up at Bertie standing with the others on the terrace. 'Get some dishcloths and water. Do something useful for once. His pupils are tiny. I think he may have a concussion.'

Bertie flushed but turned and went to the kitchen, Kirsty going with him. The horse was calm so Bruno left her to Pamela and went to join Pia. 'How's his pulse?' he asked.

'Fast but not racing. I think he'll be all right but I only did a first-aid course. I'm no expert.'

'You're right about the pupils but he's facing the sun,' Bruno said. He put his hand over Sasha's eyes. 'See, they're getting bigger now that they're in the shade.'

Bertie arrived bare-chested, slopping water from a bucket and handing Pia his T-shirt. 'Best I could do,' he muttered as she began bathing Sasha's face and holding him back as he tried to sit up. Moments later Kirsty was there with clean dishcloths and smelling salts.

'*Yav pariadky*,' Sasha said, sounding groggy. '*Poosti menya. Vsyo normalno.*'

'He says he's okay and you should let him up,' Bertie said.

'No, you just lie there and rest a bit, Sasha,' Pia said, ignoring Bertie. She folded his T-shirt and put it under Sasha's head and then put a soaked cloth on his forehead.

Bertie leaned down and pulled his T-shirt away, muttering something Bruno didn't quite catch about Russians and hard heads. Then he said something that sounded like Russian and, quick as a cobra, Sasha reached out an arm, grabbed Bertie's ankle and yanked hard to send him toppling before rearing up from the ground and throwing a punch towards Bertie's solar plexus. Even as he fell Bertie managed to twist away, caught Sasha's forearm and used the momentum of his own fall to try to pull Sasha down. It didn't work. Sasha went with the pull and Bruno just managed to get there in time to prevent Sasha from landing hard with his knees in Bertie's belly. Instead, Sasha's knees landed on grass. He turned again, his eyes murderous and fixed this time on Bruno.

'Stop,' Bruno roared in his best parade ground voice. He put up his hands, palms forward. 'Stop,' he yelled again. 'Both of you.'

Sasha kept his eyes fixed on Bruno but began to relax.

'That voice,' he said. 'You were soldier, yes?'

'Yes,' said Bruno. 'Like you.'

Sasha nodded slowly, let his hands drop and said, 'You did the right thing. Thanks. Maybe I buy you a drink.'

Then he turned to Pia. 'Thank you, Pia. You are a good woman. You deserve better than that piece of Ukrainian shit.'

He threw the prone Bertie a contemptuous look and stomped off into the chateau.

Bruno helped a shamefaced Bertie to his feet. His back and arm were grazed but the worst damage had been to his pride.

'That wasn't very clever, Bertie,' he said. 'Sasha is a trained soldier and if you look at his hands you can see he does karate. He could have really hurt you, big as you are. Worse still, starting a fight like that was very rude to your hosts.'

Bertie looked sullenly at Bruno but then Pia came up to him and began dabbing at his grazes with a damp cloth. 'Bruno's right, Bertie,' she said gently. 'You started it. You really should apologize.'

'Okay,' he said, and looked up at Rod and Meghan. 'I'm sorry. But I think Sasha should apologize to the horse.'

That broke the tension. Everybody laughed, more from relief than humour. Pamela brought the horse back, and said she'd better be going.

'Do you go riding every day?' Galina asked.

'Morning and evening, we have to exercise the horses,' said Pamela, smiling at her. 'We usually start about seven at this time of year, later in winter. And we ride again at about six, when the heat of the day is fading. You're a good rider so feel free to join us any time.'

'There's champagne waiting here for everybody,' said Rod. 'And your apology is accepted, Bertie. And Bruno, thanks for breaking it up. You certainly deserve a glass of champagne.'

'I'll help Pamela hitch the horses to the railing and join you,' said Bruno.

'Would you like to stay for dinner?' Meghan asked as Rod poured out champagne and handed around glasses.

'That's so kind, but we have to take the horses back while it's still light,' said Pamela. 'But anyone who wants to ride out at seven tomorrow morning will be welcome, and I'll provide some breakfast.'

'Yes, please,' Galina said, pirouetting out of Jamie's arms and taking a glass from his father. 'Let's do it, Jamie. I promise to wake you at six thirty.'

Bruno finished his glass, thanked Rod, and said, 'We'll see you all on Friday evening when you're rehearsing in the church at Audrix ahead of your first performance there.'

'I'm taking everyone to the auberge afterwards,' said Galina. 'I want to thank Jamie's parents for their hospitality. So please join us for dinner after the music. I know that your friend Florence is coming with some of her choir.'

'I'd like that, thank you,' Bruno replied. 'How about you, Pamela?'

'Yes, gladly.'

'Good, that's a date,' Bruno said while undoing the hitch that held the horses and putting his hands together to make a lift for Pamela to climb into the saddle. 'And I expect to hear that Galina has been to Monbazillac and the vineyards by then.'

'And don't leave out Château des Milandes for the falconry and the Josephine Baker museum,' added Pamela as Bruno swung himself onto Hector's back.

The trail was wide enough for Bruno to move up and ride alongside Pamela, the other horses trailing behind.

'I owe you a dinner,' he said. 'For the one I missed yesterday evening. 'Would you like to go to Ivan's?'

'No thanks, not tonight, I don't feel like going out again. You don't owe me anyway, the number of times I've dined at your place. Fabiola said she might pick up a pizza when she gets off at eight. You know Gilles is in Paris, seeing his editor. Why not join us? You can tell us about that mysterious Galina and her even more mysterious chap who could hardly ride but looked like he was on duty. Do you think he's her bodyguard?'

'Yes, I'm almost certain of it.'

'How exciting. She must be an heiress or the daughter of someone important. Did you say she's Ukrainian?'

'With a Cypriot passport,' Bruno replied, not wanting to go into details of her father and his wealth.

'She seemed very keen on Jamie and he's obviously smitten with her. How well do you think he knows her?'

'Jamie was on an exchange in Paris for the summer term at the Conservatoire so they'll have known each other for two or three months. The first time I saw them at Chateau Rock I was struck by the way they played music together, like a mystic communion between them, as though each understood the other in an extraordinary and intense way. I found it quite humbling to watch.'

'How do you mean, humbling?'

'As though they had reached a sort of blending of minds that we mere mortals can never hope to achieve. I wonder if only highly gifted musicians can attain that, or maybe brilliant mathematicians or even poets – people who seem to operate on a higher plane than ordinary people like me.'

'Oh, Bruno, you have your moments,' she said with a laugh. 'And now let's canter. I can almost taste that pizza.'

19

When Bruno arrived at his office the next morning after a pleasant ride with Galina and Jamie, but without Sasha, he found a copy of Yves's forensic report in his email. The blue pills in Driant's bedside drawer were indeed Viagra, and the packet carried coding that indicated it had come from a mail-order service in Holland. The key findings were fingerprints on the opened foil condom wrapper found beneath Driant's bed which matched prints taken from the desk and other items in Lara Saatchi's office. And there were traces of cocaine on the wrapper so this could now be classed as a possible homicide. Yves was still waiting for a lab report on the long strands of black hair found on one of Driant's towels, but he was certain that it matched some hairs taken from a hairbrush in Lara's office desk.

There was no added note from J-J saying that the case was now being handed to a magistrate who could order Lara *mis en examen*, detained for questioning. When Bruno checked, J-J had not even opened a case file. Bruno tried to think what was holding J-J back, other than Goirau and the *fisc*. Lara could be detained pending possible charges of failing to report a death and at least required to account for her movements and Driant's state of health when she had last seen him. There was also clear evidence to suggest that she had a sexual relationship with the old man while also dealing with him as a business client. This in itself raised the suspicion that the insurance contract had been improperly obtained and that Driant's heirs had thus been cheated out of their inheritance. Bruno had little doubt that if they brought a civil case against the insurers, they would win. So why was J-J being so cautious? Bruno picked up his phone and called him.

'When I briefed Prunier and said I wanted to get a warrant to bring her in for questioning, Prunier said I was being too hasty,' J-J said, referring to his boss, the Commissioner of Police for the *département*. 'Prunier didn't say so but he gave me the clear impression that he was under pressure, from both Goirau at the *fisc* but mainly from our old friend the Brigadier. You know Prunier, he's a decent guy and he clearly wasn't happy about this. What's more, he stressed that you had now been seconded to the Brigadier's staff so this was now above his pay grade and well above mine.'

At least he'd been authorized to keep watch on the offices to see if Lara, Constant or Sarrail returned, J-J added. But for the moment, there would be no formal case file and no request to the Procureur to appoint an investigating magistrate.

'So I'm on my own, without even getting a briefing from the Brigadier,' Bruno said. 'This stinks. What am I supposed to do?'

'Wait until the Brigadier contacts you. Your Mayor has acknowledged receipt of the Brigadier's letter seconding you so you're now legally under his orders.'

'Again.'

'Again,' agreed J-J, with a short, bitter laugh.

'Despite the forensic report and my eyewitness?'

'Despite all that. But think this through, Bruno. You'll hear from the Brigadier when it suits him but you know Driant's son and daughter. It looks to me as if they have a wide-open civil case against the insurance company and against the retirement home. Persuade them to get a good lawyer. As a matter of course he will file a court request for available police documentation. A judge can order us to turn over Yves's forensic report and your report on your witness identifying Mademoiselle Saatchi. If I were you, I'd file that report to me in writing as soon as you can.'

'Which lawyer in Bordeaux would you recommend?' Bruno asked. 'That's where Gaston lives, Driant's son.'

'You remember Maître Duhamel, the lawyer who was acting for the mother of that American girl who died in the well? He's a real bastard, but that's what you want.'

Next, Bruno called the Baron, asked him how he felt and was told that he'd already been checked that morning by Fabiola and was in the best of health. Bruno asked if the Baron recalled his suggestion the previous day of going to see Sarrail and said it could be helpful. Then he went in to see the Mayor, asked to discuss something in confidence and laid out the entire story, Driant and Lara, Goirau and the *fisc*, J-J and Prunier, Stichkin and the Brigadier.

'And since you're now under the orders of General Lannes, we can presume that this has become a matter of national security,' said the Mayor, filling his pipe and leaning back in his chair. He called for Claire, his overly inquisitive secretary, and asked her to search out the property tax records for Driant's farm, going back to the time he inherited it.

'That will stop Claire listening at the door,' said the Mayor, with a conspiratorial wink. 'I think J-J is right. Driant's heirs should pursue this in the civil courts. Knowing Driant's children, I think it might make more sense to talk to his daughter, a professional woman with, I presume, some financial resources of her own. I know Duhamel, the lawyer J-J suggests; I can easily give him a call at home to assure him this will be worth his time.'

The Mayor put aside his pipe, leaned forward and tapped the surface of his desk with a forefinger. 'I don't like this at all. It's not right that people can be cheated out of their inheritance by some young woman seducing an elderly gentleman of my commune and our police are held back from investigating. So go ahead, Bruno. As you say, you have as yet received no orders from the Brigadier. You can even say you're acting on my suggestion.'

The Mayor applied a new match to his pipe, and then through the smoke fixed his gaze on Bruno, who caught the light of battle in his eye.

'Now, if things get tricky, and they probably will, as a former Senator I can arrange for some discreet consultations about setting up a Senate commission of enquiry into the role of foreign finance in our insurance industry. It won't happen, of course, but it will set the cat among the pigeons. Or I could have a question sent to the Health Minister on the licensing system for luxury retirement homes of dubious ownership. That would have a similar effect. And I could prepare the ground with some judicious leaks to the media. Should I have a quiet word with Phillippe Delaron, since he's already floated part of the story? Or you could do it?'

'It would have more weight coming from you,' said Bruno.

'Consider it done,' said the Mayor. 'It's about time these over-zealous types in our security services were reminded that they work in a democratic republic that is governed by laws that are made by our elected representatives in the Assemblée Nationale and the Senate. Will that do, Bruno?'

'Very well, Monsieur le Maire, and thank you.'

'Don't thank me, Bruno. I think this is going to be rather interesting. I'll call that cunning lawyer now. And please draft a summary of the affair as you know it for me.'

Back in his office, Bruno wrote the summary and sent it to the Mayor. Then he quickly wrote a report on Guillaumat's identification of Lara Saatchi and sent it to J-J, as requested. He took the opportunity to add a paragraph pointing out that forensic and cell phone evidence meant that Lara had been the last person to see Driant. Noting the cocaine on the condom wrapper, he proposed that Lara be detained for questioning in an apparent homicide.

He sat back, thinking, and then used the special secure phone he had been given by the Brigadier in a previous operation to call the Brigadier's office. He left his name with a duty officer and requested a briefing on what he was now expected to do. After that he called Gaston Driant's cell phone, explained briefly that he now thought that he and his sister had been victims of an injustice but wanted to inform her personally. Gaston gave Bruno her numbers, landline and mobile. Bruno called the mobile number, introduced himself and asked if she was able to speak privately.

'Go ahead,' she said, a brisk voice.

Choosing his words with care, Bruno explained that he believed that she and her brother had been cheated and that there was evidence in police files that might not suffice for a criminal case but would certainly give great weight to a civil case in which he, as chief of police, would be ready to testify. He gave her the name and phone number of Duhamel, adding that the Mayor would personally brief the lawyer and press him to take the case.

'What would this lawyer cost?' she asked.

'I'd imagine that having spoken to our Mayor, a former Senator with the influence that implies, he would accept a retainer of a thousand euros. Once he files a statement of claim in court, he can apply for access to relevant police records. However, I think you might be able to get informal sight of an important forensic report before then.'

'And what would that report show, Bruno?'

'That the insurance agent employed a young woman who had sexual relations with your father in the course of getting his signature on the contract. You might even be able to argue that the use of Viagra and cocaine before sex may have provoked his heart attack.'

'Jésu-Maria,' she exclaimed. 'Are you serious? My dad – coke?'

'One thing at a time,' said Bruno. 'We both know your brother doesn't have the financial resources for the lawyer's retainer. I assume that you do.'

'Correct.'

'You are aware that the *notaire* and insurance company are already facing legal action for negligent treatment of your father's sheep?'

'Yes, Gaston told me about the story in *Sud Ouest*. I feared that might be the end of the matter.'

'I have not let this matter drop, *mademoiselle*. I want to see justice done, and you and Gaston receive your proper inheritance.'

'Thank you, Bruno. Please call me Claudette and not *mademoiselle*. I remember your first few weeks as village *flic*. I was home on vacation and Dad took me to the rugby game and you were playing. He pointed you out and said you were the best number six he'd seen play for St Denis since he was on the team. And you know that he used to play at number six?'

'I didn't know that, I'm touched. May I have your private email, Claudette?'

She gave it and Bruno sent a copy of his own summary of the case, including Yves's report, telling her over the phone never to reveal the source. But it would allow her lawyer to demand the full reports.

'How much can I tell Gaston?'

'Up to you,' he said. 'You know him best and how far he can be discreet. But you realize all this is sensitive.'

'Indeed, I'm just looking at your summary now. *Mon Dieu*, you've put some work into this. *Merde*, this implies my dad might have been murdered for his money!'

'Not quite that. But it's very strong evidence of highly improper if not fraudulent manipulation of an old man on the part of the insurers And we'd have to prove the cocaine was brought by the young woman.'

'Do you know where I work, Bruno?'

'Gaston said you're a management consultant.'

'Yes, but my main client is the Ministry of Health, with special focus on managing the challenges of longevity. So you'll understand why I think I'd better let Gaston put his name to this case, rather than mine. I can pay the retainer, of course.'

'Very wise,' said Bruno as he saw the green light flash on his other phone that meant someone from the Brigadier's office was calling. 'I have to go. We'll speak again.'

He answered the secure phone and heard the Brigadier's familiar voice saying, 'I'm surprised you want a briefing, Bruno. As I recall you go your own way whatever I might suggest.'

'As a former soldier I always respect the chain of command, sir,' he replied.

'Stop it, Bruno. I'll tell you what we want you to do in good time. But keep up the pressure on these two men in Périgueux, the *notaire* and the insurance agent. That's how we'll get to Stichkin.'

'You know I went horse-riding with his daughter this morning?'

'No, but we knew you did so last night,' the Brigadier said breezily. 'We're monitoring her phone and she told Daddy. She also informed him she's in love. Stay close to Galina, she may be the key to this whole operation, her and this insurance fraud you've been working on. Oh, and Bruno, give my warm regards to Isabelle when you see her on Saturday, and give Balzac a pat from me. My best wishes for a successful mating, stand by for further instructions and keep a very watchful eye on that so-called cousin of Galina's. He's a spook, Putin's watchful eye, ex-Spetsnaz and as hard as nails.'

The call left Bruno wholly uncertain of his mission, or rather, his small part in the much larger mission the Brigadier and the French security agencies had in mind. But he had been told to stay in touch with Galina and to watch out for Sasha. He knew that Spetsnaz, *Voyska spetsialnovo naznacheniya*, were Russian military special forces, an arm of GRU military intelligence. *Mon Dieu*, he thought, to have such a professional killer in the Périgord, acting as Galina's watchdog, meant that the Kremlin put great importance on Stichkin's daughter. That implied that Stichkin himself was an object of serious attention from both French and Russian intelligence.

Not for the first time since his initial encounter with the Brigadier, Bruno felt way out of his depth. But he had his orders: to stay close to Galina and to pursue the insurance fraud, which meant depending on J-J to track Lara, Constant and Sarrail. For that he had to wait. He checked his watch. It was close to noon, when the mothers would be gathering outside the *maternelle* to pick up their children and he liked to be there when his other duties permitted. He picked up his *képi*, donned his jacket and headed across the square and down past the fire station to the infant's school, to greet the mothers and hold up the traffic so their prams, buggies and children could pass.

Strolling back up the narrow alley alongside the church he heard organ music from within and slipped inside to hear the opening notes of Mozart's '*Laudate Dominum*', which Bruno knew from the choir's annual performance at the riverbank concerts he organized. Florence was standing in the centre of the choir, gazing up to the vaulted roof of the ancient church and her clear sweet voice began to fill the great space.

'*Laudate dominum omnes gentes*,' she began. 'Praise the Lord, all nations and all peoples, for he has bestowed his mercy upon us . . .'

And then the full might of the twenty voices of the choir came in to join her at 'Glory to the Father, the Son and the Holy Ghost' until her soprano soared away again on 'As it was in the beginning, is now and ever shall be.' Then in full voice the entire choir roared out, '*Et in saecula saeculorum*. For ever and ever, Amen.'

Bruno felt a warm sense of peace flow over him, and tears pricking at his eyes. It was partly the simple beauty of the music, and partly the familiarity of the village church and the choir composed of his friends and neighbours, the sense that generations before him had found comfort and solace here. His last time here had been for Driant's funeral. As the last echoes of the music died away he knew it was fitting that he was now seeking justice for that old man who had played rugby for this town just as Bruno had, and for Driant's heirs.

He felt rather than heard the church doors open and some people enter. He did not look up but then saw Galina, Jamie and Rod slip into the pew beside him.

'Will they continue?' Galina whispered, almost in his ear, and then she knelt and crossed herself in an unusual way, putting her first two fingers and thumb into a point and touching first her forehead, then her stomach, then her right shoulder and finally her left.

'They are rehearsing a concert and they usually sing Tchaikovsky's "Hymn of the Cherubim",' he whispered back.

She turned to stare as if surprised, and then murmured '*Slava*

Bogu' and crossed herself the same way again, as the first pure and high notes came from the women alone before the deep male bass joined them. They all sat in silence when the music ended and the choirmaster began talking to the singers. Bruno turned his head and saw tears streaming down Galina's face, a wet handkerchief clutched in one hand, and Jamie's hand clutched just as firmly in the other.

'I'm glad you heard it,' said Bruno and glanced at Jamie as Rod rose and they all began to file out of the pew and into a sunlight so bright it made them blink. 'What brings you all here?'

'We were showing Galina around the neighbourhood,' said Jamie, putting his arm around his girlfriend, who folded her body against him but gazed up at the front of the church. 'We took her to the abbey at Cadouin and then to Limeuil and the Chapel of St Martin, where we'll be performing. She was stunned by the place and the frescoes, and then we sang so she could hear for herself that the acoustics are perfect. Just by chance we decided to stop here for lunch at Ivan's before going on to the museum at Les Eyzies, and after we'd parked by the gendarmerie and were strolling back past the church, Galina heard the music so we slipped in.'

'It was fate that I should hear this Russian music here, almost like a message from heaven,' said Galina, her eyes still raised to the cross atop the church spire. 'And so many beautiful churches, in every village we see. It tells me that this Périgord is a very spiritual place and that I am welcome here. It calms my soul to think that this can be my home.'

Bruno tried not to show his surprise as he and Rod quickly

exchanged glances. Jamie, by contrast, was nodding in understanding. Rod cleared his throat, took his tobacco pouch from
his waistcoat pocket and rolled a cigarette.

'Well, it was certainly a lucky chance that we came upon
such beautiful music,' he said, lighting up and blowing out a
plume of smoke. 'But now it's time for lunch. You know Ivan's
place, Bruno. Perhaps you'd like to join us. What's his *plat du
jour* going to be?'

'Thursday, that's usually *blanquette de veau*, but Ivan always
has a vegetarian plate, and if you haven't been there for a
while, you're in for a surprise.'

Sasha had suddenly appeared and joined the group. As Bruno
stared, Sasha slipped an expensive-looking mobile phone into
his pocket. He noticed Bruno watching him and nodded coldly.

They'd turned and begun walking up the Rue de Paris towards
Ivan's when Bruno's phone vibrated. It was the Baron. He signalled to the others to go on without him.

'We've hooked him,' said the Baron, gleefully.

'How do you mean, hooked him?'

'I'm meeting Constant, the insurance man, in the Glycines
bistro outside Les Eyzies at two.'

20

Bruno thought fast. He should be able to follow the insurance agent to find out where he was staying, confront him and demand to know Lara's whereabouts. But the meeting being held in Les Eyzies, just fifteen minutes from St Denis, gave him another idea. He called Juliette, his counterpart in that town, and explained that he'd be grateful if she could arrange to wear civilian clothes, watch for Constant at Les Glycines and then follow him on her motorbike. She'd met the Baron at dinners at Bruno's home, so she'd have no trouble spotting the insurance man. And be sure to get his car details and registration, Bruno added. Juliette was his nominal subordinate and he could have made it an order but he disliked pulling rank unless he had no choice. Knowing Juliette she'd jump at the chance of something out of the usual routine.

'The chef fancies me so I can probably even get Constant's credit card number if you want,' she said cheerfully. 'I assume this is the bastard who abandoned those animals at the farm?'

'That's him, and it's looking much more serious than that,' he said. 'I'll be in my Land Rover and in uniform. I'll stay at a distance. I don't want him to know he's being followed and we can stay in touch on our mobiles.'

Next he called J-J to say the quarry had been sighted. Should he simply be followed? Or could Bruno detain him for questioning?

'What have you heard from the Brigadier?'

'He told me to keep up the pressure on Constant and Sarrail and to stay close to Stichkin's daughter. I'm about to have lunch with her. But I've just learned that Constant has an appointment near here and I've put a tail put on him.'

'I'd better check with the boss and let you know. This doesn't sound time-critical if you're off to lunch. Where are you eating?'

'Ivan's. Blanquette de veau today.'

'I'm envious. I'll be lucky to get a ham and cheese baguette from the canteen.'

'But I'm not having the veal. Ivan has a new girlfriend so there's an alternative menu. You'll have to come and try it.'

The culinary education of St Denis had begun with the Belgian girl Ivan had met on holiday and brought back to offer St Denis some happy months of mussels cooked in various delicious ways. Then Ivan encountered a Spanish *señorita* who returned with him and added paella and *cochillino asada*, a whole roast suckling pig, to Ivan's menu. Bruno cherished the memory of the German, or perhaps Austrian, *fräulein* who cooked *Wiener Schnitzel* to perfection. Mandy, the young Australian woman who cooked Thai and Malay food, had become a good friend who often returned from her wine course in Bordeaux to give a demonstration at Pamela's cooking school. The new chef who shared Ivan's bed and his kitchen had arrived in the Vézère valley under her own steam, stopped at Ivan's for her lunch, returned for dinner and moved in.

Her name was Miko and she came from Osaka in Japan,

where she taught English and French at a high school. She had won an Eiffel scholarship to get a master's degree in French culture at the University of Bordeaux and had used her spring vacation to explore the Périgord. She'd returned to Bordeaux for the summer semester, where she'd persuaded her professor that she had a unique opportunity to study French cuisine. Her irrefutable argument was that no serious understanding of France's culture was possible without in-depth appreciation of its food and its cooking. It may have helped that her professor came originally from Bergerac and needed little persuasion that the Périgord was the true home of French cuisine. Now back with Ivan until her course resumed in September, Miko had begun, after the urgent pleadings of Ivan's customers, to add a daily Japanese dish to Ivan's menu.

Bruno had tried Japanese food while on a visit to Paris and had not been greatly impressed. He had thought the miso soup to be a little bland and he could think of many more interesting things to do with fish than eat it raw. At Miko's suggestion, Bruno had tried her *shogayaki*, thinly sliced pork loin in a sweet sauce of garlic, ginger and *mirin*, a sugary rice wine. Having enjoyed that, he had been delighted by a salmon dish, steamed inside foil with a sauce she called *ponzu*. It was made of soy sauce, lemon and orange juice and *mirin*, along with *katsuobushi*, some dried tuna flakes, and *kombu*, strips of dried kelp.

Devoted to the classic food of the Périgord, Bruno would never admit it in public but he was proud of his own daring in embarking on new cuisines. And he recognized that without Ivan's romantic encounters he would probably never have ventured beyond the occasional Italian meal and Pamela's surprisingly good English dishes like steak and kidney pie and her magnificent Scottish breakfast of eggs, bacon, black pudding, grilled tomatoes, mushrooms and potato scones.

He went into the bistro and saw that Rod had saved a seat for him. Miko came forward with a pad in her hand to take his order. She had learned to present her cheeks for his greeting rather than bow. She was more than a head shorter than Bruno, slim and easy-going, and today she wore bright blue tights, a short and flaring pink skirt that complemented the current colour of her hair, and a white turtleneck sweater with the words *Hell's Devils* in gothic lettering. This, she claimed, was the height of Tokyo fashion. Bruno grinned at the sight of her.

'Are you offering a dish today, Miko?' he asked.

'Prawn tempura with udon noodles, and cucumber soup. You will like the soup, it has *kombu* stock. I will add crème fraîche for you.'

'It's delicious, Bruno,' said Roberte from a table by the door. She ran social services at the Mairie and was lunching with Sylvie who ran the dry cleaners.

'I'll have that, please,' he said, and joined Rod's table, where Jamie and Galina immediately asked to change their order to try Bruno's choice. Sasha said he'd join them.

'Make it five,' said Rod. 'She only just took our order for the veal as you came in so it should be no problem.'

Bruno went to the kitchen hatch to change the order.

'Japanese food in the Périgord, there's a surprise,' said Galina.

Bruno explained about Ivan. Jamie recalled that the last time he'd eaten here the Spanish woman had made a heavenly dessert.

'*Leche frita*,' said Rod. 'I remember it well. And I loved the Wiener Schnitzel, hammered so thin it overflowed the plate, and that wine that was served with it, what was it, Bruno?'

'Grüner Veltliner; Hubert still stocks it at the *cave*.'

'So now we have to send Ivan to Kiev,' said Galina, beaming at Jamie. 'He should find a woman who will make *borscht* and *gribi v'smetane*, mushrooms in sour cream.'

'Can you make those?' Jamie asked.

'They are winter foods, so if you still love me this winter I will make them.'

'I plan to love you for much longer than that,' said Jamie.

Galina lifted a hand to stroke his face while Jamie's father glanced at Bruno, his eyebrows raised. Bruno gave Rod a smile of reassurance. The love affair between Jamie and Galina had been no secret and anyone who had seen them play music together must have been struck, as Bruno had been, by the power of the attraction between them. Even Sasha did not look at all surprised.

The cucumber soup was delicious. Then Miko brought a teapot with five small ceramic cups and poured out a fragrant green tea, and Ivan followed her with a decanter of his house white and five glasses. He put them down, shook hands around the table, welcomed Galina and Sasha as newcomers and Rod and Jamie as old friends, and said the house white from the town vineyard went very well with Miko's food.

'Enjoy your meal,' said Ivan, and returned to his kitchen from which Miko appeared carrying four plates on one arm and a fifth on the other. On each plate were three giant prawns in a light, crispy batter, a steaming bowl of udon noodles and a smaller bowl of a light brown sauce for dipping the prawns.

'*Bon appetit*,' she said, and took away the soup bowls.

Bruno picked up one of his prawns in batter by its tail, dipped it briefly into the sauce and took a bite, followed by a forkful of noodles. The others followed suit, pronounced the food delicious and devoured the meal in appreciative silence, broken only by murmurs of pleasure and sips of wine.

'It is so sad that you are selling Chateau Rock,' said Galina quietly to Rod, once she had finished. 'Jamie and Kirsty are also very sad and so I think are you. Is it only your wife who wants to leave?'

'She doesn't want to leave so much, but she wants to make her own life back in Britain, teaching,' said Rod. 'She wants a house of her own so we'll have to sell the chateau to pay for that. And to be fair it's a lot of work, running the chateau and the garden. Now that Jamie and Kirsty are grown, she wants the chance of a new life while she can, rather than being stuck here with an old man like me to look after.'

'You can make a comeback with your new music and use that money for your wife's new life,' Galina said. 'Jamie has let me listen to it and I like it very much. I think you will have a big success.'

'I'd still have the cost of running the chateau and it's a very big place to look after on my own, even if I were younger. And Jamie and Kirsty may be back from time to time, so we'll have the cottage for them, but they wouldn't be living at the chateau.'

'You could hire a housekeeper and a gardener, rent out part

of the chateau, or rent out the whole place, live in the cottage and use the recording studio,' Galina went on firmly. 'You would be miserable away from here where you have settled, where you have friends. Where would you go, alone back to Scotland? I think you need to think again about this, Mr Macrae. There are other solutions. You could rent it out for musicians every summer, there are so many of us who come here for the festivals. And then you could record their music while still making your own.'

'Do you think so?' Rod asked, looking animated.

'There are three of you who want to keep Chateau Rock – you, Jamie and Kirsty,' said Galina. 'I never heard of one outvoting three before.'

A silence fell. Galina stared challengingly at Rod, until Jamie and Bruno spoke at once. 'I don't think this is the place . . .' Jamie began as Bruno said he had to get back to work.

Bruno rose, put fifteen euros on the table, bowed back to Miko when she came to scoop up the money, waved at Ivan and went out to his police van. He drove home to pick up the Land Rover and tried to focus on the confrontation with Constant but the scene with Galina kept distracting him, along with that earlier remark about belonging here and wanting to stay. Did that mean she had marriage in mind or just residence? She was only in her early twenties and so was Jamie, which struck Bruno as young to be making great commitments.

Once at home, he took off his uniform jacket and laid it on the rear seat of the Land Rover with his *képi* and checked that his long lens binoculars were in their case. Was it really only a year ago that Balzac as a puppy could still fit into that case when Bruno went riding? He slipped on the familiar red jacket that made him look civilian and called Juliette.

'I'm at Les Glycines, in civvies, and I have a spare helmet,' she said, her voice almost bubbling with excitement. 'No sign of the Baron yet but there's a guy of about thirty eating alone and reading through a stack of documents. I think it may be him.'

'Well done, Juliette. Stay out of sight,' he said, and took the back road through St Cirq and past the campground where there was a place he could park out of sight but keep an eye on Les Glycines. At a few minutes before two he spotted the Baron's venerable Citroën DS cruising past the railway station and parking near the hotel. A slim figure carrying a crash helmet came out of a side entrance and disappeared. That would be Juliette.

21

Bruno waited for forty long minutes wondering how to play his meeting with Constant. Keep up the pressure on him, the Brigadier had ordered. Frighten them, Goirau from the *fisc* had said. He knew he could do it but Bruno didn't like such tactics. On the other hand, he didn't like Constant, Sarrail and Lara and their methods even more. They might tell themselves it was only hard-nosed business but to Bruno it was outrageous. And abandoning livestock without food and water was unforgivable. *If only it had been Fabiola who had been called to Driant*, he thought. She would never have signed off on a verdict of a heart attack like Gelletreau, not without taking a thorough look at the body.

The Baron and Constant came out of the front entrance, shaking hands, and then Constant strolled with him to admire the Baron's veteran car before climbing into his own vehicle. Through the binoculars Bruno saw a man of about thirty with neat, short hair and a suntan. He was wearing a business suit and carrying a briefcase that looked as if it had cost more than Bruno earned in a month. He was a little plump and there was a flash of gold on his wrist as he raised his arm to wave the Baron farewell. His Audi drove off sedately enough, Juliette's motorbike following him at a discreet distance.

Bruno trailed them through Meyrals and past St Cyprien on the way down to the Dordogne valley and realized that Constant was heading for Château Marmont, the retirement home. Juliette had parked at the junction where a turnoff led through some woods to the chateau when Bruno drew alongside and thanked her.

'Are we going to arrest him?' she asked.

'No, we're going to make him panic, and I need you to be ready to follow him again if he leaves in a hurry after I do. So just hang on and I'll explain it all later, I promise.'

He drove up to the chateau, parked, put on his uniform jacket and *képi* and went to the front desk. A young woman in a black business suit rose from behind an antique table, just like the receptionist at an expensive hotel. 'Can I help you, *monsieur*?'

'I'm here to see Monsieur Constant, *mademoiselle*.'

'Who shall I say wishes to see him?' she said, about to pick up a phone.

'You don't,' Bruno said, putting his hand down on the phone. 'It's a surprise. Where do I find him?'

She looked startled for a moment, then recovered. 'I'm afraid, *monsieur*, that such an intrusion –'

'No, *mademoiselle*,' Bruno said loudly as an elderly, well-dressed couple, passing through the hall, stared at him. 'Any more delay and I'll have a squad of armed gendarmes here who will tear the place apart in search of him. Your choice.' He took his mobile phone from his pocket.

The young woman glanced at the couple, who had stopped and were watching, fascinated, and then said, 'He has the

Diderot suite, third floor, at the end of the corridor, turn left as you leave the elevator.'

'Thank you, *mademoiselle*,' Bruno said politely. 'But if you call him to warn him, you'll be arrested.'

He went up the stairs and knocked firmly on the door. As it opened, he pushed it hard with his shoulder, sending Constant stumbling backwards. Before he could regain his balance, Bruno frogmarched him to an easy chair and thrust him into it. He then took a straight-backed chair from its place by a desk, pushed its back close up against Constant's legs and sat down, straddling the chair and locking the man in place.

'What on earth – '

'Where is Lara Saatchi?'

'I have no idea.'

'She's supposed to work for you.'

'No, she works for a colleague, Monsieur Sarrail.'

'So why does she work out of your office in Périgueux?'

'I have the extra room in my office. I let Sarrail use it as a favour.'

'So why is she helping to draw up your insurance contracts by having sex with gullible old men?'

Constant's mouth flapped open and closed and opened again. 'I don't understand.'

'You can't have forgotten Monsieur Driant, not after that heavy fine you're facing for leaving his livestock without food or water. We don't like cruelty to animals here in the Périgord. But that's not your problem now, Constant,' Bruno went on, his voice hard. 'You're in real trouble. Lara Saatchi was the last person to see Driant alive but I doubt she left him that way. We have her fingerprints all over his place, including on the condom they used. I imagine she provided the cocaine we found. That's probably what killed the old guy. I suppose you knew about Driant's heart trouble. Conspiracy to commit murder for financial gain will be the charge. Sexy young insurance agent screws an old man to death for his money with you as the pimp. The newspapers will love it. You're going to be famous, you and Sarrail and Lara Saatchi. Sex, drugs, murder – and cruelty to animals.'

Constant closed his eyes and he seemed to slump as his face went white. For a moment Bruno wondered if the man was going to throw up.

'Is that how you usually do business, Constant? Let me see your papers.'

Stunned into silence, Constant took out a wallet and handed Bruno a *carte d'identité* that gave his first name as Benjamin, born in Neuilly, a wealthy Paris suburb, age thirty-three. Bruno slipped it into his pocket.

'When did Lara Saatchi start working for you?'

'She works for Monsieur Sarrail but she's worked with me since late last year when we opened the Périgueux office. She'd worked with him before, in Monaco.'

'Tell me about Trans-Med-Euro.'

'It's an international insurance group, one of my clients. I'm their agent.'

'So why is Lara Saatchi seducing old men into signing your contracts?'

Constant's eyes glanced at the door, the window, and then he looked down before he said, 'I only know that she sometimes helps with paperwork.'

'Where is she now? And why is her phone turned off?'

'I have no idea why, nor where she is. I want to talk to a lawyer.'

'You're going to need one.' Bruno leaned forward. 'May I?' He plucked Constant's phone from his shirt pocket and its screen came alive. He touched the phone icon and pressed the log function which showed previous calls.

'You can't do that . . .' Constant's protest must have sounded feeble, even to him.

'Can't do what? I asked your permission. You didn't object until you realized I might find something you want to hide. So let's go down to the gendarmerie where I'll arrest you for obstruction of justice and put you into the cells until I get a warrant. Or how about I call the gendarmes to come here and arrest you and march you out through the dining hall, the library, the lounge, and you still spend the night in the cells. Which do you prefer?'

'This is surreal. I'm an insurance agent.'

'You're a liar, Constant,' said Bruno casually, skimming through the call logs. 'You said you had no idea where Lara was. This shows you called her this morning and then she called you. And another call to Sarrail and you've been making a lot of calls to a Monaco number. And to a three-five-seven number. That's Cyprus. You do get around. And who is this Stichkin with a satellite phone number? You called him twice yesterday and again today.'

'He's the owner of the insurance group.'

'And where is your partner in crime, Sarrail?'

Constant swallowed. 'He's at the Monaco office.'

'Address?'

Bruno scribbled down the address and then pulled out his own phone and called Juliette.

'Are the gendarmes here yet?' he demanded, holding the phone tight against his ear so Constant couldn't hear Juliette's startled questions. 'We've only got the small fry here, so I want the European arrest warrant for Sarrail delivered to the Monaco police by the end of today.' He read out the address Constant had given him and added, 'You might add Lara Saatchi's name to the warrant. I suspect that's where she's hiding. And see if they know whether Stichkin's yacht is in Monaco.'

Bruno closed his phone, took a page from his notebook, then wrote out and signed a receipt for Constant's phone and identity card. 'If we don't round up Saatchi and Sarrail by tomorrow morning, we'll just have to make do with you.'

Bruno brushed aside the questions of the manager, the former junior concierge of the Hotel Crillon, as he strode through the entrance hall before driving down to join Juliette. He held up Constant's phone.

'Can you download his call log, messages and address book?' he asked. 'When I opened it there was no password.'

'I can do it back at the office. What was that about arrest warrants in Monaco?'

'Just obeying my orders to frighten him a little. I think I owe you dinner, you and the Baron. Are you free this evening? My place at seven, very informal. Please download the stuff from the phone and print it out and thanks for your help. Okay?'

She nodded, looking solemn, and gazed after him as Bruno drove off and headed back to his office, where he phoned the

Baron, to thank him for his help, invite him to dinner and to ask him how the meeting had gone.

'Nothing very urgent, I'll tell you over dinner,' the Baron said. 'Constant is a smooth little devil and I wouldn't trust him a millimetre but he'd done a fair bit of research on me. Is it just you and me for dinner?'

'No, we'll be joined by that young policewoman from Les Eyzies, Juliette. You've met her before at my place. She's involved – I got her to follow Constant after he left you.'

Bruno called J-J to report on his meeting with Constant and gave him the two mobile numbers he'd found for Constant and Lara Saatchi. Yves would have a way of tracking their whereabouts, or at least their nearest cell tower. Bruno promised to send J-J a copy of the phone logs and warned him to expect a call from Maître Duhamel on the civil case being brought by Driant's son. Then he went shopping for chicken thighs from the bio shop and a *pain campagnard* from the Moulin. Putting the chicken in the fridge in the Mairie kitchen, he ran into the Mayor.

'Cooking tonight?' the Mayor asked hopefully.

'Yes, can you join us?' asked Bruno, who could take a hint. 'It's just me, the Baron and Juliette.'

'With pleasure,' said the Mayor.

Bruno excused himself when he heard his desk phone ring, and found Maître Duhamel on the line. He sounded very pleased at the prospect of a lawsuit against an insurance company, which presumably had very deep pockets. Bruno briefed him and put him in touch with Brosseil, whose own testimony against Sarrail might be useful to the lawyer.

Twenty minutes later he was cantering along the ridge above the valley on Hector, with Balzac at his heels, and feeling the wind blow away his self-doubts about his treatment of Constant. He knew it was standard police procedure but it was not the way he liked to work.

Back at his home, he fed his chickens, picked some onions and salad from his garden, took a jar of pâté from his store cupboard and set the table before taking a quick shower and changing into jeans and a corduroy shirt. It was warm enough for them to take their *p'tit apéro* on the terrace so he set out four glasses and a bottle of crème de cassis on the outdoor table, then dusted the chairs. He took a bottle of Château du Rooy dry white wine from the fridge to stop it being too cold and then went to his cherry tree and picked enough fruit for four.

In the kitchen, he chopped two shallots and three cloves of garlic. He seasoned the chicken thighs with salt and pepper and took some of his home-made duck stock from his fridge. In the garden, he picked a handful of fresh tarragon, put some to one side for garnish and chopped the remainder. In a casserole dish he began gently to sauté the shallots in butter. Once they were soft, he added the garlic and the chopped tarragon, a generous wine glass of the stock and a less generous glass of dry white wine and brought it to a low simmer. Then he added the chicken, put the lid onto the pot and put it into the oven on high heat for fifteen minutes, then lowered the heat to medium. Another forty minutes and they'd be just right.

He fed Balzac and refilled his water bowl and sat down to watch the subtle approach of twilight while awaiting his guests. It fell so slowly at this time of year, a very gradual but steady diminution of brightness. Sometimes out here reading he hadn't noticed the dying of the day until suddenly he could no longer make out the words on the page.

As always, Balzac was the first to hear the distant sound and was standing in welcome at the head of the lane when Juliette's motorbike appeared. She parked, took off her helmet, caressed Balzac and then shrugged off her black leather jacket to reveal a bright pink sweatshirt. She handed Bruno a large, fat envelope.

'Printouts of Constant's phone logs, address book, texts, emails and his photo gallery,' she said. 'From the intimate pictures, he obviously had a very close relationship with a young woman. I imagine she's Lara Saatchi with whom he shares very explicit texts. I emailed them all to J-J as you asked.'

Bruno poured her a kir and had begun skimming through the printouts when Balzac barked again, signalling the arrival of the Baron's car with the Mayor in the passenger seat. The Mayor offered a bottle of Monbazillac from Château Bélingard and the Baron presented a chilled bottle of a white wine from Les Verdots whose label read simply *Vin*. Each man greeted him then Juliette with a kiss on either cheek.

'I'd better decant this wine first,' said the Baron, heading for the kitchen.

Bruno poured a splash of cassis into the waiting glasses and added white wine for his guests, murmured that he had to check something and went back to his study to review the text messages for that Sunday when Lara Saatchi's cell phone had placed her at Driant's farm. His eyes widened as he read.

He called J-J and said, 'This is now beyond just putting a fright into Sarrail and Constant. We've got them. Lara Saatchi texted Constant at eight twenty in the evening to say Driant had signed the insurance contract and backdated it. And she added that he shouldn't worry – she'd be sure to use a condom. Then at nine seventeen she texted, "He's collapsed. I'm leaving." Then Constant texted her back, "Leave no traces."'

'Where is Constant now?' J-J asked.

'I left him at Château Marmont about three hours ago and I have his phone and ID card. Do we arrest him? Or do we have to call the Brigadier first?'

'Let me call him. And I'd better talk to Prunier. I'll let you know. Which is the nearest gendarmerie if we do have to pick him up?'

'St Cyprien,' Bruno replied. 'I think the law is clear. You have to arrest him. This looks like conspiracy to defraud and to conceal a homicide. And now that Yves has found the cocaine I'm tempted to call it murder.'

'I'll call you back.' J-J ended the call, leaving Bruno staring at his phone in frustration.

'If I understand what I just heard, she screwed the poor devil to death and left him,' said the Baron, standing in the doorway. 'Sorry, but I was in the kitchen. I couldn't help but hear. Do you want me to keep quiet about it?'

Bruno shrugged and led the way back to the table where Juliette and the Mayor were chatting over their drinks. 'I think this may be a moment when four heads are better than one.'

He read the key texts from the printout, and explained why the role of the *fisc* and of the Brigadier meant that he could not be sure Constant would be arrested.

'That can't be right,' said Juliette, shaking her head.

223

'We don't know what the larger issues are, and whatever they may be they are the responsibility of General Lannes and the Minister of the Interior,' said the Mayor. 'But look on the bright side, Bruno. This makes it certain that Driant's heirs will win their civil case and probably with punitive damages.'

Bruno toasted slices of bread, put on the kettle to boil water for the rice, and led the way into the dining room for the foie gras with glasses of the Mayor's Monbazillac. For the benefit of Juliette and the Baron, Bruno explained the case from the beginning, the lunch with J-J and Goirau from the *fisc*, the Russian oligarch behind the insurance company, French government concerns about the sale of passports and insurance scams, and his own renewed secondment to the Brigadier's staff.

'I can't help but feel that if the Brigadier is this involved, there has to be more to it,' Bruno concluded. 'His real concerns are national security and intelligence.'

'This oligarch Stichkin, Russia and Putin – that could be the real issue here,' said the Baron as Bruno stacked the plates and went into the kitchen to cook the main course.

He splashed olive oil into a saucepan, added the rice and stirred until all the grains were lightly coated. He added boiling water and put the lid on the pan. Then he took out the casserole, removed the chicken thighs to a warm plate and covered them with tinfoil to retain their heat. The rice water was boiling so he turned the heat down to a low simmer. Then he strained the sauce from the casserole dish through a sieve, poured the sauce into a sauté pan, added a wine glass full of crème fraîche and some lemon zest and put it on the heat for about five minutes to reduce. He fluffed the rice with a fork, put it into one bowl and the chicken with tarragon sauce into another and took them to the table, where the Baron was pouring the Verdot into fresh wine glasses.

'Delicious,' declared the Mayor, just as J-J rang back to say that Commissaire Prunier had decided that Bruno's confiscation of Constant's phone meant that the evidence had been improperly obtained and thus would not be admissible in court.

'You screwed it up, Bruno,' said J-J bluntly. 'Worse than that, you tipped him off. You took his mobile but that won't stop him warning Lara and Sarrail and everybody else what you're up to. You were told to frighten the little bastard, not send him into a complete panic.'

22

Bruno passed a miserable night. He was unable at first to sleep and then dozed fitfully, waking to the acceptance that he had destroyed the chance of a conviction by seizing improper evidence. But then he began to question this. It was not improper. He had not formally seized the phone, simply used routine police methods to obtain the damning evidence it contained. And the real problem, he told himself with a surge of self-pity, was that he'd been given ridiculously vague orders by the Brigadier. He'd been the terrier sent down the burrow to frighten the rabbits out to the waiting hunters. Then he dozed again to wake knowing that he'd behaved in a way he wasn't proud of and couldn't defend. There was little relief even in reminding himself what nasty tricks Constant and Lara had played to get Driant's signature on that contract.

He sat up in bed, recalling that he had ways of dealing with these occasional moments of self-questioning. When in doubt, he told himself, do something. The sky was still dark but dawn came early in late May and even before his cockerel had crowed Bruno was up, in his tracksuit and whistling for Balzac to join him on their morning run. He set himself a punishing pace through the fringe of the woods and then along the full five-kilometre length of the ridge where he could watch the sun rise over the Massif Central far to the east. When he reached the rocky outcrop that looked down over the valley he sank down and did ten fast press-ups, jumped to his feet and jogged back, meeting Balzac on the way.

As always, the sight of his dog running with his tongue lolling out and his long ears flapping made Bruno smile. He profoundly admired Balzac's determination to keep up with his human companion, despite his short legs. Bruno stretched out on the grass and waited for his dog to jump on him and slather his face before tucking his head beneath Bruno's neck. He hugged his basset hound, enjoying the familiar smell, and hearing that sonorous, affectionate growl of contentment deep in the dog's chest. In the face of such absolute love, Bruno thought, it was impossible not to feel better about the world. He rose and they trotted back, side by side, Bruno keeping to Balzac's pace.

He showered, shaved, dressed, then turned on the radio for the news as he made coffee, boiled an egg and toasted the remains of last night's bread, sharing it with Balzac. All the chicken from last night had gone, so at least that had been a success, and Bruno tipped the last couple of spoonfuls of rice into Balzac's bowl. Twenty minutes later he was at the stables, greeting Hector with his morning carrot and watching his horse and his dog exchange their usual courtesies of greeting, sniffing one another while Balzac wagged his tail and Hector flicked his own.

Then Pamela's dogs, Beau and Bella, came into the stables, waiting politely until at some signal of welcome from Balzac they came to the door of Hector's stall. Bruno smiled at this canine etiquette as he began saddling horses for himself and Pamela, not sure if anyone else would be joining them. This was the weekend when the season of summer rentals began for her *gîtes* and there might be strangers wanting to take part in the morning exercise.

'You're early,' Pamela said, suppressing a yawn and stamping her feet to settle them into the tight riding boots. 'Jamie and his girlfriend aren't here yet and we'll take it easy because Miko will be joining us and she's still a beginner.'

'Is Miko learning to ride?'

'Yes, she's been taking lessons, beginning with Miranda on the ponies. She's such a slim little person but very keen. I like her, she's always cheerful, and the horses like her, too. I'll put her on the Andalusian and we won't do much more than a trot. If you want a gallop go off ahead. How's that Driant business you're working on?'

'More complicated than I thought,' he replied, saddling the Andalusian and then checking the girths before leading them out into the yard as Ivan's battered Renault Clio came along the lane, followed by Jamie's minivan.

'*Bonjour*, Pamela, *bonjour*, Bruno,' said Miko. Bruno had to bend down quite far to reach her cheek and even though the Andalusian was a small horse, he had to boost Miko to get her into the saddle. Her purple hair flared out from under her new riding cap like the tendrils of some exotic tropical anemone as she waved at Jamie and Galina.

Hector set off at a gentle pace led by Pamela until they left the outer paddock. Then he took off at a fast trot that within a couple of strides had become a canter and then a gallop. Even Galina was left far behind. The rush of air in Bruno's face was just what he wanted and he whooped with joy as they raced off and up to the entrance to the bridle path where Hector finally slowed, turned and, head high, neighed at the plodding horses behind him as if to show them what a real horse could do.

Half an hour later, Bruno was in his office, going line by line through the printouts from Constant's phone and making notes of the relevant texts and emails. They made a powerful and damning case that Constant, Sarrail and Lara knew exactly what they were doing to Driant. He also wrote a brief report to J-J on his questioning of Constant and how he had obtained his phone, using the standard phraseology that every young cop learned in training. 'I asked to examine his phone, saying that if he refused I would consider him to be obstructing justice and would seek a magistrate's warrant to obtain it. He then withdrew his objection and I gave him a signed receipt for his phone. It was returned to his residence this morning and a signed and dated receipt for it was obtained.'

When she had called to thank Bruno for dinner, Juliette had confirmed that she'd delivered Constant's phone to the retirement home before starting work, and demanded and received a receipt. Bruno then drafted a short summary of what he learned, with some timed quotes from the texts, and emailed it to the Brigadier's office, noting that it contained clear evidence of conspiracy to defraud. He then attacked a pile of paperwork while waiting for J-J's inevitable call.

'Your Mayor is a piece of work,' said J-J when he called just after ten. 'He's told Prunier he wants to use Constant's texts in a letter he's sending to the Finance Minister on the need for closer supervision of insurance firms. He also reminded Prunier that as a former Senator he had the privilege of direct access to any minister. Then he said he just happened to have seen the texts as part of a routine time-and-motion study in his capacity as your legal employer. As if that wasn't enough, General Lannes has reminded Prunier that you've been seconded to his staff and are thus covered by the emergency regulations. I imagine Goirau will also be giving him a call so I think you're in the clear. I'd say you have the luck of the devil except I suspect you'd already planned this.'

'A good man, my Mayor,' Bruno replied, and replaced the phone. He heard a chuckle behind him and turned to see the man himself. He wasn't sure whether the Mayor had been amused by Bruno's remark to J-J or by the enthusiastic welcome given him by Balzac, who had slipped out from where he'd been dozing under Bruno's desk.

'Thanks for your message to Prunier,' Bruno said.

'We take justice seriously in St Denis,' said the Mayor with a wink, rising from Balzac's greeting. 'I did enjoy that chicken dish last night. Where did you learn that?'

'From Florence. She says it's her kids' favourite.'

'I'm glad you're finally starting to realize how fine a young woman she is,' said the Mayor, and left before Bruno could retort that it was he who'd found Florence her teaching job and brought her to St Denis. Nor could Bruno add that this was supposed to be his day off.

The buzz he'd enjoyed after his morning run and the ride with Hector was fading and Bruno felt tired. He finished the essential paperwork and, with Balzac trotting along behind, he headed downstairs as the Mairie clock struck ten. Bruno's bad night worried him. He'd always thought one of the most useful things he'd learned in the army was the ability to sleep wherever and whenever he wanted.

He stopped at Fauquet's to buy a restorative slice of apple tart. Back at home, he put a slice of Cantal cheese on top of the tart, squeezed the juice from a couple of lemons into a glass and filled it up with water. He strolled slowly around his garden, looking in on the chickens and geese, eating his tart washed down with lemon juice and enjoying the day. Then he stripped off in his bedroom, closed the curtains and settled down to get some sleep. His thoughts drifted to the next day, when he'd be taking Balzac to lose his virginity and seeing Isabelle. Knowing he was smiling, he drifted away.

He woke just after two in the afternoon, feeling splendidly refreshed. He showered, dressed in civilian clothes and checked his phone, which he'd left on silent. He had three calls. The first he returned was to J-J, who said that Commissaire Prunier had referred the issue to the Procureur, the top legal official in the *département*. The Procureur said that after consultation with his magistrates, he'd be prepared to argue in court that the evidence was admissible, if backed up by France Télécom records. The second was to Annette, his magistrate friend in Sarlat, who said everyone on the Procureur's staff was discussing it and she'd found precedents that made such use of phone records admissible in conspiracy cases, and forwarded them to her boss. The third call was to Rod Macrae.

'Bruno, thanks for calling back. Chateau Rock has a buyer.

And it's a private sale so we don't have to pay commission to the estate agent. And here's the good part. It's staying in the family, sort of. Jamie and Galina are getting married and Galina is the buyer. How about that? I knew she was loaded but I didn't know she was that rich. She's buying in *en viager* so I can stay here till I die, but she owns it. Then it's hers, or rather hers and Jamie's. That means tonight's dinner after the rehearsal will be a kind of celebration, so don't miss it.'

Bruno was so startled that he sat down. *En viager*; it was often used by elderly people so they could stay on in their homes with a large percentage of the cash they would get from a sale. He wasn't sure what he thought about the deal but knew he'd have to say something. 'Well, congratulations, both to you and to them, and to Meghan as well. It seems everyone gets what they want.'

'Yeah, it means Meghan will have enough cash to buy a decent house in Britain and it looks as if I'll be moving into the cottage, which will suit me because I'll still have the recording studio. Jamie and Galina are planning to set up a residential music school, once she graduates from the Conservatoire, to host students from London and Paris for the summer concert season. My old booking agent in London called to say it looks as though my comeback album is going to happen. One more thing, Kirsty has told me about her plans to go into the wine trade. Since she'll still get a university degree I'm happy with that. Kirsty and Galina say we have to call the wine Chateau Rock, with a picture of me in my wild days on the label.'

'*Mon Dieu*, this is all happening very fast,' said Bruno.

'That's what Meghan said, until Jamie reminded her that she

was a lot younger than him when she married me. We'll see you tonight. The champagne is on me.'

'Have you told Nathalie? She won't be happy at losing her commission.'

'I haven't reached her yet but I'll make sure she gets something out of the deal. Gotta go, Bruno. We're off to Brosseil's office to sign the *compromis de vente*. See you at the rehearsal.'

Bruno called the Mayor to inform him and to ask whether Jamie and Galina ought to be warned of the possible complications of the *bail agricole*. Since Brosseil had drawn up the vineyard lease he knew all about it, the Mayor said, and would adjust the deal accordingly.

Three hours later, saddling up the horses with Pamela, Fabiola and Gilles, who was just back from Paris, Bruno passed on the news. The two women agreed that while they were glad the Macrae family would stay, Jamie and Galina were far too young to marry. Gilles, who had been trying to persuade Fabiola to marry him since their affair had begun, was all in favour of the plan. He appealed to Bruno for support, but Bruno ducked the question as he usually did in such matters, suggesting it all depended on the individuals.

'It's not as though they have much in common,' said Pamela.

'They have a shared passion for music,' Bruno replied.

'Yes, but she's Russian and Jamie is Scottish by ancestry and French by upbringing and education.'

'Not exactly,' said Fabiola. 'When we were going through Meghan's family medical history she told me her grandmother lived till the age of ninety-five and she was from Ukraine. Apparently during the war she worked as a kitchen maid for a

German family who were trying to settle in Poland. She went back to Germany with them, and after the war she married a Scottish soldier and moved to Glasgow. So Meghan is one quarter Ukrainian.'

'But Meghan goes to church here so she must be Catholic, not Orthodox,' said Pamela.

'The Uniate church in Ukraine considers its worshippers Catholics and the Pope agrees,' said Gilles. 'He even made their Patriarch into a cardinal. I had to do an article on it, years ago.'

'And although her parents are Ukrainian and Russian, Galina is a citizen of Cyprus, at least that's what her passport says,' said Bruno.

'What a jumble we are all becoming these days,' said Pamela, laughing.

'It's good for us, mixes up the gene pool,' said Fabiola.

Bruno found himself thinking of the number of Ukraine connections that suddenly seemed to have gathered around Chateau Rock. There was Meghan herself, Galina and her father and Bertie, plus Gilles's book. Bruno smiled, thinking of Pamela saying that whenever she came across a coincidence, it was just like London buses – none arrive for ages and then three or four come at once.

An hour later, they were seated on spindly wooden chairs in the small twelfth-century church in the hilltop village of Audrix, already a third filled by the St Denis choir and the musicians from Chateau Rock. Behind them, the rest of the nave filled with locals and relatives of the choristers. Father Sentout began with a few words on the church's history, used as a fortified strongpoint overlooking two valleys by both the

French and English during the Hundred Years War, and then signalled to the choir to begin with Mozart's 'Laudate Dominum'.

When the last notes died away, Jamie strummed the first four opening chords of the 'Concierto de Aranjuez' and Galina came in with the flute. Then the strings came in. The acoustics were perfect, the harsh echoes of the stone walls softened by the people filling the nave. Bruno closed his eyes and let his mind drift with the captivating music.

Then the choir sang Tchaikovsky's 'Cherubim', and tears gathered in Galina's eyes while the strings played the Schubert quartet with guitar that they had rehearsed. She kept her eyes on Jamie, and he kept his on hers, as they launched into Schubert's opus one hundred with the strings, keeping it as lively as a march or perhaps as a formal dance, the flute punctuating each step. It was a good way to end the concert, Bruno thought, a cheerful yet haunting tune that the crowd could hum as they left.

And then came the surprise. Jamie rose from his chair, propped his guitar against it and moved across to something Bruno had not noticed, an electronic keyboard on a stand, and pumped out what sounded like a trumpet playing the opening notes of the 'Marseillaise'. Then the choir came in chanting 'Love, love, love' and choir and strings all together launched into the Beatles' song, 'All You Need Is Love'.

First Father Sentout stood to roar out the words, followed by most of the rest of the audience. Bruno turned to see the people of Audrix behind him, including Nathalie, arm in arm with Philippe Delaron, joining in with the singing. Nathalie blew him a kiss and Bruno blew one back as Philippe hugged her close.

Then Rod came from the back of the choir with his electric guitar and played the riff that George Harrison had made famous. The stones of the old church resonated with the voices, the instruments and the choir together as if after nine hundred years the church itself was rocking with the music.

'*Mon Dieu*, that was magnificent,' said Bruno embracing Pamela, Fabiola and even Father Sentout. In a moment, everyone in the church seemed to be embracing everyone else, clapping and cheering as they began to leave. Suddenly, another riff came from Rod's electric guitar, instantly recognizable from his greatest hit. He repeated it a few times and the crowd fell silent.

'Thank you all for being part of this wonderful evening and it's not over yet,' Rod shouted in his primitive French. '*Non, c'est pas fini*. Tonight we celebrate not only music but also love because my son Jamie, the wonderful guitarist, and Galina, the beautiful young woman on the flute, have decided to get married. So you are all invited to help us celebrate at the auberge next door, where I have booked out the entire terrace for champagne and a buffet supper for us all. *Bon appetit, et vive la musique, vive l'amour*.'

23

Bruno was still smiling at the memory of the music and the celebration as he began his patrol of the market, Balzac at his side, shortly before eight the next morning. Everyone, including some of the merchants setting up their stalls, seemed to have been at the Audrix church, or at least they'd heard about it. The stall selling tickets for the summer concerts of the Conservatoire students was already surrounded by eager buyers.

'That was a great evening,' said Fauquet, serving Bruno his coffee and croissant and bending down to give Balzac a corner of doughnut. 'And today's the day for this little guy, I hear.'

'Where did you hear that?' Bruno asked and Fauquet pointed to a corner of the café where the Mayor was enjoying his own breakfast and reading *Sud Ouest*. He waved Bruno over, clearing away copies of *Le Monde*, *Nouvel Obs* and *Figaro* that awaited his attention.

'Philippe told me he'd be running a piece about last night's concert in the paper tomorrow,' the Mayor said. He looked down at Balzac who was gazing hopefully at Bruno's croissant. 'Do you think he has any idea about his fate? It is today that you take him to the breeding kennel?'

'Yes, I'll set off after the market closes. But no, I imagine it will all come as a big surprise for him. But he's old enough and he couldn't be in better shape. It's not as though it hasn't happened to millions of dogs before.'

'It's always different when it's the first time for your own dog. Tell me about this new citizen of the region we're getting: Galina. I know she's a talented musician and very lovely but how did she get a Cyprus passport?'

'Her very rich father bought citizenship for his family, presumably so she could live and work in Europe and perhaps as a precaution against things going sour in Russia. She also has Ukrainian citizenship through her mother but she was brought up in Moscow.'

'Where did his money originally come from?'

'Russia – mines and auto dealerships is what I heard, and an old friendship with Putin.'

'That worries me,' said the Mayor.

'Me too, and I told you about the *fisc* taking an interest. And our old friend the Brigadier, but the only instructions I've had from him were to keep up the pressure on Constant and Sarrail.'

'That sounds promising, and my best wishes for Balzac's big day and let's hope it's the first of many.'

'Big day?' asked Yveline, the local gendarme commander who had just come into the café.

'This afternoon Balzac will be initiated into one of the great mysteries of life,' said the Mayor. 'He's off to a breeding kennel for his first mating.'

'Oh, the dear little fellow,' Yveline said, smiling broadly.

'Put me down for one of his daughters and I don't care what she costs.'

'Join the queue,' said the Mayor.

Back at home after the market closed at noon, Bruno changed into jeans and a polo shirt and packed a cool box with a home-made pâté of foie gras and a bottle of Monbazillac from Clos l'Envège, of the vintage when he had been on the jury that awarded it the prize of Best of the Year. He added a Tomme d'Audrix cheese made by his friend Stéphane, a bag of cherries plucked in his garden and a dozen eggs from his chickens. In a separate cardboard box he placed a large paper bag full of his home-made dog biscuits, a bottle of Château de Tiregand from the Grand Millesime year of 2011, and a glass jar containing *confits de canard*, sealed in their own fat, that he'd made the previous winter.

He left food and water for his geese and chickens and checked that his shotguns were securely locked away. He put his own official handgun into the small safe he'd been required to install in the boot of his vehicle and removed from the roof the blue light that identified his car as that of a police officer on duty. He tossed his own overnight bag into the back, helped Balzac onto the passenger seat and set off. Installing the CD Rod Macrae had given him into the player he had added to the veteran Land Rover, Bruno began to enjoy the drive through a Périgord that was surging with the full thrust of spring, when roses seemed to flower from tight buds overnight and the green of new leaves was so bright it almost dazzled the eye. The air was fresh and clear and when he drove up onto the plateau, he felt he could see for ever, east to the dead volcanoes of the Massif Central and north to the great forests of the Limousin.

He had time to make a pleasant trip of it, going through Montignac and Terrasson. He took the old road to Brive, avoiding the autoroute and wondering how his brief reunion with Isabelle would go. He knew that however much passion and delight there might be, he would make this return drive feeling a deep sadness at what might have been, what should have been between them. But Isabelle was married to her career, and she claimed he was wed to St Denis. As long as neither one of them could resist the chance of catching these brief times together, Bruno knew he could never fully give his heart to another woman. He suspected it was the same for her. Could they someday summon the determination to make a final break, to give each of them the chance to find another love? Would the sound of her voice on the phone, or seeing one of her laconic postcards in his mail, ever cease to excite him?

It would be so much simpler if I were a basset, thought Bruno, glancing at Balzac, who was sitting up, alert to watch the passing world as they entered the suburbs of Brive, probably the largest city Balzac had ever seen. They had twenty minutes before Isabelle's train arrived. Bruno parked by the station and took Balzac for a stroll up the Avenue Jean Jaurès and across to the park opposite the post office where Balzac lifted his leg. Then they went to pay their respects at the Monument des Morts. The first city in France to liberate itself by its own efforts in 1944, it had been a key Resistance centre. Indeed, the Resistance had started here, on June 17, 1940, the day before De Gaulle's speech from London, when Edmond Michelet had delivered a call to resist to every mailbox in the city. Michelet was taken to Dachau but survived to become Minister of Justice in 1959. Now, groups of old men were playing *pétanque* around the monument.

The train was on time and Isabelle, looking wonderful in black slacks and a red turtleneck, an overnight bag on her shoulder, dropped to one knee on the station platform and opened her arms wide. Even before she called out his name Balzac was thundering towards her, with little yelps of delight. Bruno stood, smiling as he watched, until it was his turn for a welcome that was very nearly as fond and lasted almost as long. He doubted if anyone in the station but him knew that this glorious young woman was running the team that coordinated antiterrorist operations for the European Union. He took her bag and, arm in arm, they went back to the Land Rover, where Isabelle insisted on sharing the rear seat with the dog.

'We'll go by a place you'll remember,' he said when they got onto the road heading north-east out of town, after Isabelle had commented that she didn't know this part of the Périgord. They drove along, chatting easily for a while, until the talk turned to work and Bruno was reminded that, despite their intimacy, Isabelle was a cool, self-possessed career woman who was rising fast in French security.

Isabelle explained that the previous day she'd attended a meeting in Brussels with her own group and General Lannes, who gave a briefing on the latest Russian operations in Europe.

'You remember the Dutch caught a bunch of Russian military

intelligence guys trying to hack into their computers,' she said. 'This was after they used the Novichok nerve agent in England. Lannes introduced a Ukrainian counter-espionage official who gave us a lot of details on Russian sanctions-busting. The Ukrainians want Europe to get tougher and so do we. And the interesting name that came up was Stichkin.'

'But Stichkin's operations in Cyprus, Malta and Luxembourg give him some protection,' said Bruno. 'That's three EU votes in his favour, right there.'

'Exactly, so we'll need something else. Remember what J-J always said? Trace it back the other way, in this case from the Ukrainian end. The experts on Ukraine are the Poles, who have a love-hate relationship with most of their neighbours, including Ukraine. But they love France so they tell us things.'

'Why should they love France?'

'History,' she replied. 'Did you know the Polish national anthem is the only one in the world that mentions Napoleon? That's because he created the Duchy of Warsaw with the promise of independence after they had been carved up between Prussia, Austria and Russia. Polish legions fought for France, even at Waterloo. And like Britain, France went to war against Hitler to protect Poland.'

'And what do the Poles tell us?'

'To watch out for trouble from extremist Ukrainian nationalists, some of them with very discreet backing from the military and some of them Ukrainian expats who hate Russia. We have a few in France that we keep an eye on. You know at least two. One is that estate agent Nathalie de Villiers, born Nataliya Vershigora, whose elder brother was one of the scores shot dead in the Maidan in Kiev in February 2014. The other is Matviyiko Bondarchuk, known to his friends at London's Royal College of Music as a Canadian called Bertie. The Brits tipped us off about him when he came to an exchange semester at the Conservatoire. He had a cousin among the dead. Ukraine considers them martyrs, the "Heavenly Hundred".'

Bruno digested this, thinking back to Bertie's abortive fight with Sasha. 'Anything known about Meghan Macrae, wife of the old rock star?' he asked. 'She has a Ukrainian grandmother.'

'Not yet, but get me a family name, something I can give the Brits so they can check their records.'

'Galina, Stichkin's daughter. Is she Ukrainian, Russian, Cypriot or what?'

'Yes to all three. Stichkin is of Russian origin but born, like Galina, in Donetsk, in the eastern Ukraine. The city used to be called Stalino, after Stalin. Since the region declared itself independent of Ukraine and the war began, posters of Stalin are now back openly on the streets, along with Russian troops in plain clothes. But her father bought her a Cypriot passport which gives her European citizenship.'

Isabelle paused. 'Our sources on this are not just Polish. The most reliable sources are Dutch. They've taken a close interest in Ukraine since the pro-Russian separatists shot down that Malaysian Airlines flight from Amsterdam in July 2014, killing three hundred civilians, two-thirds of them Dutch.'

Bruno nodded, remembering the story. 'What do the Dutch say?'

'They tell us that Galina's mother, Bohdana, is a Catholic from Lviv, in western Ukraine. Bohdana has a nephew, Galina's cousin, who was also one of the Heavenly Hundred. The Poles tell us Bohdana divorced Galina's father because she supported Ukraine and he was loyal to Russia. He's the same age as Putin, grew up in Leningrad like Putin and he and Putin were in the same judo club. Putin joined the KGB and Stichkin joined the air force as a bomber pilot and saw action in Afghanistan. When the Soviet Union collapsed, the air force shrank fast and Stichkin went into business in Leningrad with his old friend Putin. They've been close ever since.'

'A guy from the *fisc* told me he thought Stichkin had left Russia in Putin's second term.'

'So he did, but he made sure to stay in Putin's good books and he goes back to Moscow often enough. We suspect he's still close, Putin's man in the West, able to keep an eye on those oligarchs who really went into exile. Putin got him involved in the restructuring of Aeroflot, and in nickel mines, but he made his big money in car dealerships before he branched out into life insurance.'

'When we played tennis, Galina told me she didn't want to grow up like her father,' said Bruno. 'She rebelled against his ambition for her to be a tennis star.'

'From all we know, Galina takes no side for or against Ukraine. She stays in touch with both her parents, calls them regularly, and since she's a person of interest, we listen in. That's why I know she's buying this chateau near you. She called to say she'd found the guy she wants to marry and she promised to bring him to Daddy's yacht after the concert season.'

'The real reason we're interested in her father is that he has a base in the West and we think he's helping look after the money Putin keeps outside Russia,' Isabelle went on. 'Stichkin seems to be accessible and reasonably friendly to us. Since Russia is the biggest geopolitical threat Europe has, we stay in touch. If anybody can give us an inside view of what comes after Putin, it will be him.'

Bruno slowed the car as it topped a rise and pointed to a chateau with pepperpot towers.

'Remember this? I thought we'd stop to give Balzac a walk around the ramparts.'

'You and I came here, that wonderful summer when we fell in love,' she said, and reached forward from the rear seat to put her hand on his cheek. 'Hautefort.'

A magnificent late-Renaissance chateau that looked as if it might be more at home on the banks of the river Loire, Hautefort was for Bruno a personal shrine. He could still recall that magical sense of being newly in love as he and Isabelle had strolled in the gardens and walked together through the magnificent old rooms. They could barely keep their hands off each other.

'Let's stop here, off the road,' she said. 'I brought a picnic.'

Bruno took a path to a copse and parked out of sight from the road. He grabbed a picnic blanket from the boot, while Isabelle took a baguette from her bag along with ham, cheese, apples and a bottle of Viognier. Bruno pulled out his picnic basket while Balzac sniffed his way all around the edges of the rug.

'This is very domestic of you,' he said, smiling.

'I wanted us to have some time to ourselves before we reached the kennels,' she said, almost shyly, her head down as she began slicing cheese.

Bruno reached across, put his hand under her chin and lifted it a little so he could look into her eyes.

'And you want to spend that time eating?' he asked, and edged close enough to kiss her.

'Of course not,' she said, kissing him back and tossing aside the bread and cheese.

24

As the imposing roofs of Hautefort dwindled in the rear-view mirror, Bruno pondered whether Balzac might feel any such moments of tenderness or cherish such memories after his own forthcoming tryst. He knew that Balzac responded to Bruno's moods and he felt a powerful sense of communion with his dog, that the two of them understood one another perfectly when they went hunting together. But other than sensing when Balzac was hungry or sleepy, happy and wanting to play or just gaze at the sky and the birds, Balzac's interior life was a mystery kept private behind those deep, dark eyes.

So were Isabelle's, he thought as he raised her hand from his thigh and pressed it to his lips. She was sitting beside him, Balzac alone now on the rear seat, watching Bruno as he drove. There were moments, he believed, when there was something between them as intense and intimate as those looks he had seen between Jamie and Galina as they played music together. Then Isabelle seemed to close some kind of mental door and the other, official, Isabelle would take over. Perhaps he was the same, he thought, the old soldier's distinction between being on or off parade.

They were approaching the small and sometimes wild river

known as the Auvézère, which the Baron claimed offered the best fly-fishing in the region. As they reached the river at Cubas, he turned east, following Claire's directions. After another junction and a few kilometres he saw the hand-painted sign for Chenils Mornier and turned up a dirt road that led to an old stone farmhouse, two storeys high. The windows had blue-painted shutters and the front door was open. The house was flanked by two large barns that formed a natural courtyard covered in gravel. It contained a wooden table and folding chairs. Half a dozen old wine barrels, sliced in half, held scarlet geraniums. A pigeon tower guarded the entrance to the courtyard and various outbuildings were scattered behind the barns. They might once have been stables and pigsties. Tucked into the shelter of a small rise where it would catch the sun for most of the day, the farmhouse looked down to the river. A battered Renault Kangoo van was parked outside one of the outbuildings and Bruno drew up alongside. Isabelle put Balzac on his leash and they climbed out.

They were greeted by a chorus of familiar basset howls – in which Balzac instantly joined – followed by much deeper barks, which Bruno assumed would be the Malinois, the Belgian shepherds. To his surprise, since Balzac was usually docile on a lead, his dog began to pull Isabelle urgently towards the small outbuilding that Bruno thought might originally have been a pigsty. She had to exert her strength to restrain him. Had Balzac been wearing a traditional dog collar, he'd have choked himself in his determination to advance. But he was wearing a harness, and the leash was attached to a ring above his shoulders so his throat was not constricted.

'That must be Balzac and he's pulling so hard because he can smell that his lady love is in heat,' came a cheerful voice.

Bruno turned to see a plump and smiling woman carrying a wicker basket filled with vegetables. She was wearing green rubber boots, grubby jeans and a checked flannel shirt, the sleeves rolled up above her elbows. Her thick brown hair was cut so short it was almost a crew-cut and while she wore no cosmetics that Bruno could see, she had a generous mouth and shrewd eyes, large and dark in her weatherbeaten face.

'Welcome, Bruno, and Isabelle, good to see you again. Balzac has really grown since you came to collect him at Suippes. What a handsome young hound he's become.' She bent down, put the basket to one side, and took Balzac's head in her hands, scratching that special place behind his ears. She looked into his mouth and ears and cast a knowledgeable eye over the rest of him before saying, 'He's turned out even better than I'd hoped.'

'Thank you. You must have quite an impressive *potager*,' he said, gesturing at the overflowing basket and holding out his hand.

'Since our dogs are going to be intimate, you might as well give me a *bise*,' she said, coming close and offering her cheek to be kissed, first one and then the other. She did the same to Isabelle.

'That's the bridal chamber, where your hound was heading. Diane de Poitiers is already inside, waiting for her new suitor. They both seem pretty eager but first come with me while I put the vegetables into the kitchen.'

Claire led the way into the main house, through a tiled hall which opened onto a large old-fashioned kitchen with a wood-burning stove that seemed to glow with warmth. Bruno thought that in winter it must be a comforting way to heat the room and much of the house. On this afternoon in late May, it was close to stifling even though the rear kitchen door and the windows were all open. The stove was flat-topped, with a large *fait-tout* pan steaming on the hot surface. Below it on one side was a baking oven and on the other a heavy iron door. She opened this door to reveal a glowing furnace into which she tossed another log.

'I need to keep this stove going all year round,' Claire said. 'It's how I get hot water and with dogs whelping every few days, I can't do without hot water.'

Bruno nodded acknowledgement and looked around. The big table that stood in the centre of the kitchen was covered with a waxed cloth, a pile of newspapers, a half-empty bottle of wine with a cork stuck in the top and a ceramic bowl full of apples. There was enough space for him to put down the box of food and wine he'd brought. A venerable dresser dominated one wall, handsome old plates displayed on its shelves. Most of the walls were covered in photographs of dogs, many of the mothers with litters of pups nursing at their teats. To one side of the sink was the oldest refrigerator Bruno had ever seen and to the other a working surface covered in zinc with cupboards below. Above the work surface a well-maintained Manufrance shotgun hung on two pegs in the wall, the wooden stock polished and the barrels gleaming with oil.

'I keep the ammunition securely locked away,' she said, watching her guests scan the room.

'Good for you,' Isabelle said.

'Shall I show you around? You might want to keep your dog on a leash otherwise he'll run back to pay court to Diane de Poitiers and howl outside her door.'

'I love the name,' said Isabelle. 'Do you name all your dams after royal mistresses?'

'No, that's just the pedigree line she's from,' Claire explained as she led the way from her rear terrace. 'Another one is called Margaret Thatcher because she's from an English line. Then there's Ingrid, for Ingrid Bergman, because she's bred from the Swede Sun line. Your Balzac will bring in some fresh stock to add to my Old Big Bone sires, that's why I'm so happy to have him here.'

They turned a corner behind one of the two barns to see a field of rough grass and shrubs surrounded by a wire fence. Bruno and Isabelle laughed in delight at the sight of an entire pack of bassets sleeping, lolling, gambolling and sniffing each other. There were white and reddish brown ones. Others were black, white and brown like Balzac and some were plain black and white. Although the pups were kept separate until they'd had all their vaccinations, the field contained young bassets, solemn elders and every age between. He stopped counting when he reached thirty. A dozen low doors had been cut into the wall of the barn, each one opening onto a narrow yard close to two metres wide and about five metres deep. Each yard was fenced off from its neighbour and had a latched gate that opened onto the field.

'These are all your bassets?' he asked.

'All except the ones with red collars. They are boarders, just here for a week or two while their owners are away.'

'Your food bills must be quite something,' he said. 'That's why I've brought you a sack of my home-made dog biscuits. I thought Balzac might offer some to Carla, I mean Diane de Poitiers, as a courtship gift.'

'Thank you, that's kind, and thanks for all that food you brought,' she said. 'The other barn is the same. That's where I keep the Malinois but their field is larger because they need more space. You can't see it all from here but there's more than a kilometre of wire fencing here. I dug all the postholes myself.'

'*Mon Dieu*,' said Bruno, deeply impressed. 'How long did that take you?'

'Two months. Fitting out the barn took even longer but I had some help from the apprentices at the construction school in Excideuil. One of the teachers is a cousin and he persuaded the director that it could count towards their coursework.'

'Did you buy the place?' Isabelle asked.

'No, I inherited it from my mother. I was an only child and I could never have afforded it otherwise. Now I make a modest living although I'd be in trouble without my military pension. This is what I always wanted to do.'

Claire showed them how a corner of each stall had been roofed into a large kennel, each about one metre by two. 'Dogs like the sense of being in a cave. It makes them feel secure and that's very important when the dams are nursing their pups.'

'You run all this on your own?' he asked.

'I get a day a week from two youngsters studying to be veterinary assistants. Next year I'm hoping to have four and that will make a big difference once I have them trained.'

'I take my hat off to you, Claire,' he said. 'You've done a fine job here. I just hope Balzac fulfils our hopes.'

'He looks pretty good to me,' she said, bending to stroke him. 'You saw how his penis came out of its sheath when he smelled Diane de Poitiers? I think Balzac is ready, willing and able. Shall we take him to her boudoir?'

'Perhaps we should call it the honeymoon suite,' Isabelle replied.

'I hope you're not expecting soft lights and romantic music,' Claire said, laughing.

'Why not?' said Bruno. 'Nothing but the best for Balzac. And you did promise music when we spoke on the phone – Carla Bruni, as I recall.'

The boudoir, as Claire called the small outbuilding which she confessed had indeed been a pigsty in her grandparents' day, was the place whose tantalizing scent had already attracted Balzac. He strained at the lead again as they headed towards it. She opened the door and Bruno was surprised to see that the light inside was indeed a soft and rather romantic red, from the infrared lamp which Claire had installed, she explained, for newborn puppies. *Bridal chamber and maternity ward in one*, thought Bruno.

'Oh, she's beautiful,' exclaimed Isabelle as she saw the female basset who had risen to greet them.

'Don't touch her, she might snap at you. It's a dog she wants now, not a human,' said Claire firmly.

Diane de Poitiers was magnificent, mainly reddish-brown and white, with long strips of black fur running from her ears to her haunches. Her ears were even longer than Balzac's and they shared the same noble head and long muzzle, which Bruno always thought gave bassets a distinctly aristocratic look. The smell of her oestrus was now powerful and as Balzac began to whine and paw the ground, she helpfully turned her back towards him and lifted her tail.

'Diane knows what to do,' said Claire. 'She's already had one litter. Balzac looks eager but Bruno, you may have to use your hand to ensure that he goes where he should. Isabelle, stay back by the door, please.'

Claire kneeled at Diane's head, speaking softly to her and stroking her head and shoulders as Bruno released Balzac from his leash. His dog, panting hard and visibly ready to do his duty, almost leaped onto Diane's haunches and at once made what Bruno perceived was the right move and began thrusting powerfully, his head at first raised as he did when he howled on the hunt. But then he lowered his head and began nuzzling at Diane's back in what seemed to Bruno like real affection.

'Oh, he's a natural,' said Claire, holding Diane close as the dam began making soft whining sounds. 'You won't need to help him at all. Just stand by.'

Balzac raised his head once more and delivered a full-scale howl that must have struck terror into the heart of every fox and boar and badger for miles around and then slumped onto Diane's back, his pounding haunches slowing to stillness.

'Now ease him slowly back and out,' Claire said softly. 'Sometimes they get stuck but I think it will be fine.'

Bruno did as he was told and the dogs separated, Balzac looking rather baffled as he backed away and then sniffed once more at Diane's rear where her tail had now lowered. Claire motioned Bruno to reattach the leash and take him outside.

Balzac was shaking his head and sniffing at his own genitals and then at Bruno and Isabelle as if wondering what on earth had just happened to him. Then he turned and looked at the door to the bridal suite and threw his head back and howled and then stared at Bruno who bent down to stroke his back and murmur comforting words.

'Do you think it's comfort he wants or would he prefer a rematch?' Isabelle asked, kneeling beside Bruno to scratch Balzac's head.

'Probably both,' Bruno replied, caressing her back with his other hand.

25

After their evening meal, and a second successful encounter for Balzac and Diane de Poitiers, Bruno was on his phone. He was scribbling something on a pad when Isabelle came out of the shower. She was wearing a dressing gown with a towel wrapped around her hair. Her face and eyes were shining and Bruno had a sudden image of Isabelle as a young girl at a fancy dress party. He muttered a quick word of thanks and closed the phone, enjoying the sight.

'I have something for you,' he said. 'Meghan's date of birth. I remembered her telling me she got a speeding ticket last year going to Bergerac airport to pick up her kids. I called J-J and he found it in the database with her French driving licence, which gave her place and date of birth in Glasgow, Scotland. With that, your British colleagues can get her family names and data and they should be able to get her grandmother's name.'

'*Merde*,' she said. 'It's Saturday night.'

She picked up her own phone, checked the contacts list and called. Bruno heard a male English voice. Isabelle apologized for the timing but said it was really urgent and gave him the details.

'That Ukrainian guy at the briefing you mentioned,' he

said. 'Do you think he'd help if you tried to trace Meghan's grandmother?'

'Trace what? That grandmother was a teenage kid working for German occupiers in a war when millions of Ukrainians were being killed, and not just the Jewish ones. Lord knows what archives remain.'

'I was thinking,' he said. 'The German family took her back with them. They must have liked her, protected her, and they were probably high-ranking. Who were they? Where did they go back to? Presumably they fled to Germany in '44 when the Red Army overran Poland. Where and when did she meet her Scottish soldier? In Berlin or somewhere else? We can get that from their marriage certificate and then British army records.'

'I'm not sure I see the point of tracing this Ukrainian grandmother.'

'A lot of Ukrainians who hated Stalin did more than just collaborate with the Germans. They helped run the death camps, did some of the killings, even had units that volunteered to fight for the Germans. There was even a kind of Ukrainian puppet government under the Nazis. A girl trusted enough to be hired by a German family and taken back with them to Germany would probably have been well connected, certainly seen as pro-German. And there was a Ukrainian anti-Soviet resistance for years after the war. I remember reading about one of their leaders, Bandera I think his name was, murdered by the KGB with a cyanide gun in the 1950s. It was state-of-the-art murder technology in those days.'

'That's not just a long shot, that's outer space,' she said, but looked thoughtful.

'It was Meghan who hired Nathalie, the estate agent whose brother was shot in the Maidan demonstrations in Kiev. Maybe just coincidence. But why would Meghan go to a new agent rather than someone local? And how did she just happen to come across an agent of Ukrainian origin with a martyr for a brother?'

'There's not much we can do about this until Scotland Yard calls me back.'

'Yes there is.' He took out his notebook, thumbed back through the pages and found the card with the number of Nathalie's drone permit. 'Civil Aviation HQ must have a duty officer, even at this hour. Get him to check the permit which will list Nathalie's *carte d'identité* with birthdate and so on. From that you can find her parents. Nathalie's dad was a Frenchman. Who was he? Where and how did he meet her mother? What was her background? Is she a French citizen, was she naturalized? How does she feel about her son being killed? What do we know about him? And when did he return to Ukraine?'

Isabelle sat down on the end of the bed, called the duty officer at the Interior Ministry, introduced herself and explained what she wanted.

She looked up at him. 'Shall I call Lannes or do you want to do it?'

'You have the rank,' he said. 'And I don't even know how far I'm supposed to be briefed on all this Ukraine business. The Brigadier likes to keep me in the dark, even though he told me he knew I was seeing you this weekend and why. He even sent Balzac his best wishes.'

'That's because he still thinks I can get you to marry me and bring you back to Paris to work for him,' she said, almost casually.

He stared at her. 'You would do that?'

She looked back at him defiantly. 'Yes, but not for him. I'd do it for me. For us.'

'We've been through this,' he said. 'In Paris, I wouldn't be the Bruno you know down here. No horse, no chickens, and I wouldn't keep Balzac in some tiny Parisian apartment. And what would children do to your career?'

'*Merde*, Bruno. We always end up having the same conversation. And if I came back to the Périgord and succeeded J-J – which wouldn't happen if I started having babies – I'd be miserable and start blaming you for losing my career.'

He looked at her and nodded and then threw up his arms and laughed. 'I love you but logically we're doomed.'

She laughed back at him and shook her head. 'And I love you but we have no future.'

'But we have the present,' he said, rising to loosen the belt of her dressing gown.

The next morning they were woken by a knocking on the door and Claire's voice calling them to breakfast. Bruno checked his watch: seven thirty. 'Coming,' he called back. They showered and dressed hurriedly, Isabelle running her fingers through her short hair and shrugging as Bruno let Balzac out into the courtyard, remembering just in time to keep him on the leash. In the kitchen, they found Claire with hot coffee, warm bread and croissants and ice-cold orange juice.

'You went to the village for these?' he asked. 'That was very kind.'

Claire shook her head. 'A neighbour and I have a deal: he picks them up one day, me the next. After breakfast, I have to attend to all the dogs, then take the visiting ones on a walk, which you're free to join with Balzac, and then we can put him to Diane again before you go. And thank you for that lovely wine at dinner last night. It sent me right off to sleep. I hope you both slept well.'

'Very well,' said Isabelle. 'Country air. Slept like a log.'

After the croissants there was home-made apricot jam with the baguettes, cheese and hard-boiled eggs. Bruno ate well and had a second cup of coffee while Isabelle packed. Then they joined Claire, each taking four leads for separate bassets, and set off on a route that took them down to the riverbank and then on a gentle rise back to the kennels. It should have been a simple stroll but the multitude of bassets had them tangled in leashes as the friendly dogs got to know Balzac, wandered away to follow intriguing scents and stopped to roll in the grass. At one point Isabelle sat down, laughing as she tried to untangle a Gordian knot while the bassets crawled over her, vying for caresses and attention.

When they got back to the kennels and left the other bassets in their fenced-off field, Claire made more coffee and then led them back to the bridal chamber, where Balzac once again needed neither guidance nor urging. Like a gentleman he began by nuzzling Diane where she lay on her side until she rose, presented her rump and lifted her tail as if this were the most natural procedure in the world. As indeed it was, thought

Bruno. This time, after Balzac had finished, Diane graciously nuzzled him as if returning a compliment and the two lay amiably together until Claire said she had to go and look after the Malinois.

'Thank you so much for your hospitality, I've had a marvellous time and wouldn't have missed it for anything,' said Isabelle. 'Any time I feel Paris getting too much for me I'd like to volunteer to come back here and help you walk the dogs. I can't think of a better place to restore my spirits. You ought to offer weekend breaks here. You could make a fortune.'

'You'd be welcome, both of you,' said Claire. 'If all works out with Diane's litter, as I'm sure it will, I'd like to breed Balzac again and welcome you all back, but I can't be sure I'll have rabbit on the menu next time.'

'I'd be happy to cook,' said Bruno, hugging Claire and saying goodbye. '*A bientôt.*'

They stripped the bed and left a twenty euro note discreetly on the pillow, with a message attached saying it was to buy a treat for Carla. They loaded the car and set off back to Hautefort to walk Balzac around the formal gardens and stroll through the small town that nestled beneath the chateau walls.

'The only thing I missed was waking up this morning in time for you make love to me,' she said, nestled into his arm as they walked. 'And soon I'll be back in Paris, trying to track a Ukrainian granny and work out just what her granddaughter and her friends have in mind.'

'I thought at one point it might be about holding Galina for ransom but I don't see Meghan doing that to her future daughter-in-law,' said Bruno. 'Then I wondered if there might be a plot to assassinate Stichkin, but I doubt whether he'd come here. He'd want the wedding on his own ground, Cyprus or Monaco, or perhaps on his yacht.'

'I don't see the point of killing him, even if they weren't so obviously prime suspects that they'd be caught,' Isabelle replied.

'What role did he play in the Ukraine troubles, anyway?'

She explained that Stichkin had been close to Yanukovych, the pro-Russian President who tried to block Ukraine from reaching an association agreement with the EU and then fled to Russia during protests that followed the Maidan violence. Stichkin and Yanukovich both came from Donetsk and Stichkin, with support from the Kremlin, then helped finance and coordinate the Donetsk declaration of independence from Ukraine and then the clandestine Russian support. When the ceasefire came, Stichkin had moved back to Cyprus along with his Ukraine assets in time to escape sanctions.

'So why would the Ukrainians target Stichkin now?' Bruno asked. 'He seems to be out of the game.'

'I don't know, Bruno. The Dutch say there are rumours that he was behind the secret police snipers brought in to shoot the Maidan protesters, but no more than that. And Kiev is always full of rumours. If Lannes succeeds in recruiting Stichkin, maybe we'll find out, for what good it does us.'

'You sound bitter.'

'Lannes is a good man but he's from the Cold War generation, like Putin, like Stichkin, playing the old Cold War games.' She looked up at him. 'Look at Europe now, with Romanians, Bulgarians, now the Balkan countries coming in. Can you honestly say that's been good us for us, the traditional Europeans? And now people talk of bringing Ukraine in as well. We have enough trouble with the Italians and the Greeks, not to mention the Brits. You ought to hear the Eurocrats in Brussels talk grandly of the United States of Europe, the new superpower. It scares me sometimes, the sheer unreality of it. I believe in Europe but it will take years, maybe generations.'

'So you weren't just being polite when you told Claire how much better you felt at the kennels.'

'No, I meant it, but after a few months I know I'd go crazy. It's the difference between the same, placid contentment every day for ever, and me aiming at something in the future while dealing with a new crisis every week.'

'Aiming at what? Lannes's job?'

'No, I don't think so. I'd rather play in the European stadium than on the little French pitch. Why not? Somebody has to do it. And I'm ticking off box after box – police, ministerial staff, EU justice coordination, counter-terrorism.'

'And you're good at it.'

'And I'm good at it so I'm going back. How long before my train?'

'Five hours, which gives us time for a sumptuous lunch.'

'After our country breakfast I'm not that hungry.' She reached up to kiss his cheek and whispered, 'I'd rather have another picnic at that place we went to yesterday.'

'I know you,' he said, hugging her. 'It's that little thrill of risk that you want, the possibility of being caught.'

'Of course,' she said, laughing, taking Balzac's lead and running back towards the car. 'But not only that,' she called from over her shoulder.

*

On the way back to the station at Brive she pulled out her phone and began replying to calls, pen and pad in hand. On the first one she spoke English. On the second and third she spoke French. On the fourth it was German.

'We have Meghan's grandmother,' she said. 'Elisaveta Tereschuk, married in Glasgow, 1946, to Company Sergeant Major James Angus McPherson of the Scots Guards, five children, and we're checking on all of them. He became a schoolteacher. She was secretary of the Glasgow branch of the Association of Ukrainians in Great Britain, founded in 1946 and she wrote for their newspaper, *Ukrayinska Dumka*.

'We also have Nathalie's mother, who returned to France from Canada after her son was killed in the Maidan. She was born in Kiev in 1958, somehow got a visa to study Polish literature in Cracow and left for the West in 1980 during the Solidarity upheavals. She was given a French student visa and married a French-Canadian student who had French nationality. In 1991, when Ukraine became independent, she returned to visit her family in Kiev where she gave birth to her daughter. One year later they moved to Canada.'

Bruno pondered all these individual epics, so many people leaving one country and moving to another to start new lives and new families while keeping their links to their roots. *That's what history is made of*, he thought, *all those little personal decisions driven by fear or ambition, war or hope for self-improvement, adding up to vast social changes*. The historians focus on the mass when in fact so much of the underlying reality is individual men and women trying to shape their own futures, like so many seeds carried off by the winds.

'We're getting nowhere on Lara Saatchi,' Isabelle went on. 'She hasn't been tracked coming into any European border post. Of course, once she's inside it's all the Schengen area so she doesn't need to show a passport.'

'Does that include Monaco?' Bruno asked. 'Even if she comes in by ship?'

'Certainly. So either she was born inside Europe and never left or she got her passport inside the EU and never left.'

'Widen the search to driving permits, education qualifications, health care,' he said.

'We already did. Nothing. That happens with refugees, particularly if they're worried about retribution against their families back in their home country. They can file their first registration under a false name, or pay a bribe to register a new name. She might even have two passports under different names. Meanwhile, we've asked for a search of the German military archives at Karlsruhe for Elisaveta's German employers,' Isabelle added. 'That will take a while, we're told. And now just one more call.' She turned away and dialled.

'Bonjour, J-J, it's Isabelle,' he heard her say. 'What's happening with this guy Constant? Is he talking?' Pause. 'He is? Good.' Pause. 'So he volunteered those documents and said so in his statement. Excellent.'

Bruno heard a final exchange of pleasantries before she closed the phone and said, 'Constant is singing like a bird, took J-J's guys into his office and voluntarily let them into the computer and into the files. He claims he simply carried out Sarrail's instructions. And he only met Stichkin once, in Monaco, at a cocktail party on the yacht.'

265

'Is he being charged?' Bruno asked, as he pulled into the parking area near the station.

'Yes, but J-J says he'll be listed as a cooperating witness.'

She leaped out of the Land Rover, dived into the back seat to hug Balzac and tell him what a fine dog he was, grabbed her bag and turned to embrace Bruno.

'Please don't come to the platform,' she said, holding him. 'I hate that kind of farewell. It makes me think of war movies and I start to cry. Thank you for sharing Balzac's big moment with me and for twenty-five wonderful hours and for everything. We'll stay in touch on this Ukraine business. *A la prochaine, mon coeur.*'

He drove home, feeling happy that he'd been with her and sad that she'd left as she always did, but delighted that Balzac's breeding had gone so well and that Claire had been such an admirable and hospitable woman. He'd also been interested to see Isabelle at work and impressed by the range of her contacts and her skill at amassing and processing the vast amounts of data available to the security services. But he wondered whether all this data should be taken at face value or if there should still be a place for the human factor, for personal judgement and the knowledge of people. Bruno knew that his work as a policeman depended almost entirely on the fact that he knew most of the people of St Denis and that the majority of them trusted him.

At the back of his mind he felt a small, nagging doubt about the Ukrainian connections that Isabelle had tracked down. Was it sinister, or all just coincidence? He knew Meghan to be a good woman. Bertie seemed a decent young man, even if he was hot-headed. He couldn't see any of them as the cold-hearted, fanatical killers of which terrorists were made. Nor could he see them all secretly engaged in some grand conspiracy.

Once back home, he checked on the chickens and geese, refilled their food and water bowls, fed Balzac and spent a pleasant hour weeding his vegetables and thinking. He went to his laptop, logged on and looked up the Ukrainian Association in Britain that Isabelle had mentioned. It had been started by a Canadian army officer as a support group for the thirty thousand or so Ukrainian prisoners of war, refugees and displaced persons who had ended the war in Britain for one reason or another.

He looked at a section called Patriot Defence, a fund-raising arm to buy first-aid kits and provide training courses for young Ukrainians in how to deal with combat wounds. In the circumstances, that didn't seem a bad idea. There was a section on the *Holodomor*, the great famine of the 1930s that Stalin had imposed when launching the collective farm system. Bruno had read enough history to know the website made no exaggeration.

He could understand why people started and maintained such an organization, how it could nurture and discover links and family connections in far-flung diaspora. Inevitably that would inspire young idealists heading back from France and Canada and Britain to take part in the Maidan demonstrations against a deeply corrupt government that wanted to keep Ukraine under Moscow's thumb and block any advance towards a closer link with Europe. Equally, Bruno could understand how such an organization could become a vehicle for violent, even extremist militants, and how it could become a target for the

Kremlin's own shadowy security arms. When he applied this to people he knew personally, he wasn't sure it added up. In their search for a Ukrainian connection, was Isabelle barking up the wrong tree?

Such thoughts did not prevent him falling at once into a deep and satisfying sleep. If he dreamed, he had no memory of it when his phone startled him awake some time before dawn. Speaking urgently over the sound of his truck's siren, Albert, chief of the *pompiers*, said there'd been a bad car crash with some deaths on the back road from St Cyprien. How soon could Bruno get to the scene?

26

It was not the worst road accident Bruno had ever seen. Pile-ups were the most gruesome, the most far-reaching in their consequences. But for a single car crash, he had never seen anything quite like it. At least, he thought, the car had not burned, despite the pungent smell of oil and petrol.

Huge logs of fresh-cut wood were scattered and clumsily piled across the bank, the road itself and into and around the ditch beyond. Bruno was reminded of a children's game, spillikins, in which wooden sticks are tossed down into a jumbled pile and each one has to be removed without disturbing the rest. The car seemed to have hit the logs soon after or even at the very moment they had spilled onto the road. There were no signs of braking on the tarmac, at least not in the harsh glare of the arc lights the *pompiers* had rigged.

The largest piece that remained of the car, the squashed and crumpled passenger compartment, was more than a hundred metres down the road. Other parts, a crumpled tailgate here and a wheel and door there, the engine block, were scattered at almost regular intervals behind it. These shreds of what had once been an automobile reached all the way back across a carpet of glass pellets from the car windows. They gleamed like tiny diamonds in the lights, all the way up to the tumbled heaps of logs which had presumably caused the crash.

Bruno tried to make sense of the sprawl of debris. Perhaps the car had hit the logs, leaped into the air to turn somersaults, before bouncing rather than crashing down. But it must still have been moving so fast that it took flight once more, bounced again and flew another few metres through the night air before it finally landed on the road and skidded to a stop half on the road and half in the ditch.

The *pompiers* were working with giant metal cutters on this last heap of tangled metal. Up ahead, at what Bruno assumed was the first point of impact, Fabiola had already spread a blanket over one very small bundle. He lifted the blanket to be sure and almost reeled back. It could have been something hanging in a butcher's shop. A young woman's body lay amid the pitiful contents of a burst suitcase; clothing, a toothbrush, a smashed hair dryer, a single shoe, male. Bruno had not known that Fabiola was the doctor on duty and instinctively he moved to join her as she bent over another crumpled form.

This one was a man, the remains of a shirt around his shoulders and the rest of the body bare except for a pair of jeans that were still attached to his one remaining leg. The torso was a mass of bloody wounds and the head bent at an impossible angle. That was two deaths. An expensive-looking briefcase was attached with a chain and padlock to this one's left arm. The case itself was locked. Bruno used his phone to take a picture of the case before Fabiola draped another blanket over the body. She paused, wiped away some of the blood from the caved-in chest, and pointed.

'Did you ever see tattoos like that?' she asked.

A large crucifix emerged as she wiped the dead man's chest. It was topped by a saint's head and flanked by a church with a tower topped with an onion-shaped dome. There were more tattoos on the arm that held the briefcase, a large star on the shoulder, and on the wrist a series of dots, four arranged in a square with another dot in the centre. Below the church were some letters that seemed to spelled CEBEP.

Baffled by this, Bruno took more photos.

'I'd better get to the car, what's left of it,' Fabiola said. 'The *pompiers* think the driver is still inside but they're sure he's dead.'

'That would make three in the car,' he said. 'No other bodies. The small one you put the blanket on. What was that?'

'Female and young but that's all I could tell,' she said.

Bruno shook his head but said nothing, thinking that if he took enough photos of the scene, he should be able to reopen the road before morning. His first job had been to close the road, put up temporary diversion signs and liaise with the traffic police. Then he'd called Lespinasse at home, waking him to say his breakdown truck would be needed before dawn to help clear the road. Now he called the owner of the funeral parlour to say they had at least three dead. Then he walked back with Fabiola to where the *pompiers* were working.

'The driver is in there, dead,' said Albert, the fire chief. 'When the car first bounced, the engine must have come up and damn near cut him in half.'

'I took one look,' said Fabiola. 'I think he was male, white, enough of one hand left to say he'd been professionally manicured.'

'So we confirm three dead,' said Bruno. 'Any sign of another passenger? Or any ID?'

'Not on the road. Maybe you can find something from those burst suitcases,' Albert said. 'There was a woman's handbag under the passenger seat with a fancy bamboo handle. We haven't opened it yet but you might find some identification in there. It's a Gucci, so I assume expensive. We'll take care of the photography. I'll let you do the search for ID. All I can tell you is that the registration number starts with M, but I don't know if that stands for Monaco or Malta. And the car was a Maserati, must have cost a couple of hundred thousand euros.'

Bruno was scribbling down the registration number when Albert spoke again. 'The speedometer was stopped at nearly a hundred and forty kilometres an hour. Even if he'd seen the logs, the damn fool wouldn't have had time to slow down, let alone stop.'

'And there were no skid marks on the road so no signs of braking,' Bruno said. 'Maybe the logs began falling just in time for him to hit them. That's a hell of a coincidence.'

He called the traffic police operations room again and gave them the registration number and then retraced his steps, much more slowly this time, looking for luggage. Within thirty minutes, he had found the body of a mature wild boar and two young *sangliers* pinned beneath logs. He had also collected two burst suitcases and one larger cargo bag of heavy-duty canvas, its zip open and filled mainly with women's high-heeled shoes, of different sizes. He had the handbag that had been found under the car seat. Could there have been another woman in the car?

He kept searching and found a second handbag in the ditch, along with a chicken head. What on earth was that doing there, around hungry wild boar? Maybe they hadn't finished eating when they were killed. The bag was black leather, with the name Michael Kors on the flap in small gold capital letters. That meant nothing to Bruno but a second handbag could mean a second woman so he continued searching, walking along the ditch from the logs to the wrecked cockpit that contained the driver.

He walked back up the other side of the road, shining his flashlight into the undergrowth along the bank and the shrubs and young trees above it, until he reached the log pile again. He clambered gingerly over the unstable baulks of timber, each at least three metres long and up to thirty centimetres thick, aware that with a slip or one false step he could break a leg. He saw nothing except shards of glass.

He scrambled up the bank to where the stack of logs had been, knowing that with daylight he'd have to try and establish just why the pile had tumbled and destroyed the Maserati. Various possibilities had already flashed through his mind: a rabbit warren that suddenly collapsed under the weight of logs; wild boar rooting nearby until the logs became unstable; somebody loosening the pile as they tried to steal some timber. But his immediate priority was to search for the possibly missing woman, although the kind of woman who was travelling in a Maserati could have owned two handbags.

Could she have landed up here? He looked down towards the

wrecked tailgate, close to where the man with the briefcase had been found. Suppose the car had hit the logs, catapulted into the air, losing the tailgate as it landed and spilled out the man with the briefcase in the rear seat. If a woman had been in the rear seat, she could have been hurled from the rear of the car and her momentum would have taken her forward. He pushed through the undergrowth on top of the bank, his flashlight scanning from side to side. Suddenly he was aware of broken branches brushing against his head. He shone his flashlight upwards. The branches were freshly broken. He turned right, following the trail and saw a flash of white. He pushed forward again, careless of the scratches to his face and hands.

'Fabiola,' he shouted. 'There's someone else here.'

He bent over the half-naked woman, legs askew as if broken, streaks of blood on her badly battered face and on her body. She was wearing only one high-heel shoe and a gaping white bra, the kind that opened in front. He put a hand to her neck and felt a faint pulse.

'She's alive,' he roared out and bent to start giving her the kiss of life until Fabiola appeared, half-helped and half-dragged by Albert. She told him to keep going and put a stethoscope to the girl's chest. Then she pushed Bruno out of the way to prise open the girl's eyelids and peer into her eyes.

'We need a stretcher here right away and get that ambulance as close as you can,' she ordered. 'Bruno, keep giving the kiss of life until we get an oxygen mask up here. Albert, call Dr Gelletreau and say I'll need him at the clinic and then call in Mireille, she's the best nurse. Then call the hospital in Périgueux and tell them the road may be closed so they'll need to send us a helicopter. Severe concussion, multiple broken limbs and ribs, probable chest damage. I'll do an X-ray at the clinic so they'll know what they're facing. Please stress that I want Decourcy, he's the best man on chests. With a lot of luck, we might even be able to save this one.'

Bruno kept blowing air into the stricken woman until a *pompier* took over. At Fabiola's instruction, Bruno and Albert then stamped down the undergrowth around the woman until the stretcher came and was placed beside her on the flattened ground. They moved her carefully onto it, the oxygen mask was placed on her face and the firemen moved off, Fabiola following to where they could scramble down the bank and into the waiting ambulance. Fabiola climbed in and the vehicle roared off, siren starting to howl.

'*Merde*, she was lucky you found her,' said Albert, mopping his brow. 'What the devil inspired you to look up here?'

'I found a second handbag, which suggested a second woman.'

'A good thing you did. We'd have been in big trouble if she was found in a day or two, dead from exposure or something.'

Bruno's phone vibrated in the pouch at his belt. It was the traffic control room. The Maserati was registered in Monaco to a Maltese citizen named Alexander Dimitrovich Fallin. The police in Monaco had been informed and would follow up.

Bruno informed them that a fourth passenger had been found, a young woman, badly injured but alive and now in an ambulance heading for the local clinic but with a helicopter expected to take her to Périgueux. He would forward any other names of passengers once he had examined the various bags and whatever papers he could find. Once daybreak came, he would take a careful look at the place where the log pile had stood and how it had been secured. The owner could be in serious trouble.

He put both handbags into his van and borrowed the heavy-duty metal-cutter from the *pompiers* to sever the chain that attached the briefcase to the dead man's arm. The case itself was sealed with a combination lock so there was no point assuming he'd find the key somewhere among the various possessions. He put the case in his van, thinking he might have to force it. He had tools at home. Then he went to each burst suitcase, gathering what belongings he could find, and put them in the van as well. The funeral parlour staff would strip the bodies. They knew they should keep clothing and contents, particularly any wallets, for Bruno to collect. When all that he could see remaining on the road were wooden logs and chunks of Maserati, he found Albert and asked when he could sign off on the site and call in Lespinasse to clear the road.

'Another half-hour should do it,' Albert said. 'I'll have the bodies taken to the funeral place first and then we'll do a last search. Will you take care of the ID papers and possessions?'

Bruno nodded. 'I'll let you have a copy of the inventory. The car was registered in Monaco but the owner was Maltese, with a Russian name.'

'One of those,' Albert grunted.

'How do you mean?'

'There was something on TV about it, some European inquiry into countries selling passports and citizenship to rich foreigners, a lot of them Russians. Malta was mentioned along with Cyprus.'

Bruno pursed his lips. 'And with one of those passports the owner could live and work anywhere in Europe.'

'That's it. Always the same, one law for the rich. I bet you won't see those people with the fancy passports working all night like us.'

'Probably not, but we're alive,' said Bruno, seeing the first streaks of dawn to the east. 'And here comes a new day.'

Bruno went home, first to take a run through the woods with Balzac, just as the sun rose and the birds exploded into song. He fed his ducks and chickens, plugged in the kettle to make coffee, had a quick shower and put on two eggs to boil. He grilled the remaining half of yesterday's baguette while listening to the national and international news before shifting to the local news. The accident and road closure was the second item, just after the latest complaint from various local mayors about the way central government was chipping away at their prerogatives.

Bruno dipped his grilled bread into the runny yolks, a bit for Balzac and a bit for him, and then filled one of the dog's bowls with fresh water and the other with dog biscuits. He squeezed two oranges for his own pleasure and added a spoonful of honey to his morning coffee. Breakfast over, he went out to his van to look at the lock on the briefcase.

The combination required two sets of four numerals. He put on some evidence gloves and tried all zeroes, all nines, and then one to eight. Then he tried the system a thief of his acquaintance had taught him. He rotated each of the numbers until they seemed to lock and tried to open the catches. That usually worked on cheap locks with just three digits but this time he had no success. He tried the second method, straightening out a paper clip and poking it into the catch to try to depress the tumbler. That failed, too. He tried the third method, inserting some strong fishing line into the catch and pulling it sideways while he tried again to get the rows of numbers locked. No luck.

The last method he knew needed a strong light on the locks. He used the paper clip to ease the first number to the right and saw the glint of metal to the left. That was the tumbler. He moved the code buttons one digit at a time until he saw the tiny indentation in the otherwise smooth tumbler. The digit was four. He moved to the next one, turning the second code until he saw the telltale indentation again. That was seven. The third digit gave him two and the next one three. The lock didn't open, But he knew he had the tumbler lined up so he advanced each of the four buttons by one digit. When he got to six-nine-four-five the lock opened. The same four digits worked on the second lock. He opened the case to what looked like files filled with documents.

On top of them was a clear plastic envelope containing a cashier's cheque from a bank in Monaco for three hundred thousand euros, made out to Notaire Brosseil, for a client escrow account. Below that was a file containing computer printouts of a letter from Brosseil, a draft contract to buy Chateau Rock *en viager*, and a copy of the relevant section of the commune *cadastre*, the map showing the location and lot numbers of the property to be sold.

There were other files relating to other properties, to the retirement home, to insurance contracts, property tax returns and the like. At the bottom of the briefcase lay temptation. Neat rows of green one-hundred euro and brown fifty-euro notes stared up at him. He'd never seen so much cash in his life. The notes had bands of paper around their centres, each one printed with the digits 100 x 100, 100 x 50, just as if they had come from a bank. That would mean ten thousand euros in each band of hundred-euro notes, five thousand in the bands of fifties. There were eight bands of notes, side by side, facing him, four in each denomination. That would be sixty thousand euros in the top band. He gingerly picked up a wad from the first band and found another identical band below. That would be a hundred and twenty thousand euros in cash.

Briefly, he thought what he might do with such wealth. A house, but he had a house. A car, but he had his police van and his elderly Land Rover. Travel? But why would he want to travel away from his beloved Périgord? Bruno remembered an evening with his friend and hunting partner Stéphane, with whom he played the national lottery each week. Talking of what they might do if they won, they had, to their mutual surprise, agreed that neither of them would change his life much. Bruno closed and relocked the briefcase and picked up his phone to call J-J.

'*Bonjour*, J-J,' he said brightly as a sleepy voice answered him. 'You may not have heard of the Maserati that crashed near St Denis last night. Three dead and one young woman badly hurt. One of the dead men, with a Russian name and a Maltese passport and the car registered in Monaco, had a briefcase chained to his arm. I just opened it. The case contains a lot of cash. Shall we head off to Monte Carlo? Or do you want to come here and help me go through the rest of the belongings?'

Bruno was answered by grunts and splutterings and a deep sigh. 'Give me a minute,' J-J said and Bruno heard bathroom sounds, running water, drinking. Then he said, his voice once more familiar, 'Repeat that.'

Bruno did so and could almost hear J-J's brain grinding as he processed all this. 'Have you been up all night?'

'Since I was called out to the crash at about two this morning.'

'How much in cash?' J-J whistled when Bruno told him and whistled again when he mentioned the cashier's check. 'I'd better come down to you with Yves and the forensic team. Have you finished the inventory? Do you have any other IDs for the dead?'

'No and no, and the three dead are at the funeral parlour. The injured woman has been taken to Périgueux hospital by helicopter.'

'You start the inventory and we'll be with you in about an hour. Where will you do it?'

'I'll need a big table so I was thinking of using the council chamber in the Mairie. And Fauquet's should be open by the time you arrive so you can get some breakfast. Meantime, I'll send some photos to your phone. There are some very distinctive tattoos on one of the dead.'

27

Bruno made five trips up to the council chamber with the various belongings he had collected. He took a roll of plastic sheeting from the storeroom and taped it over the table. He opened the windows to dilute some of the stink of petrol, donned a fresh set of evidence gloves and started work. By the time he heard J-J's voice down in the parking lot, he had a series of almost neat piles. There was the briefcase, then each of the two broken suitcases, the big canvas bag and the two handbags. Another pile was of obviously female garments and a second one of male clothing that seemed to have come from the suitcase. A badly ripped leather jacket, recovered from beneath the front passenger seat, was set apart. On top of it Bruno placed the Maltese passport he had found in the inside pocket, in the name of Alexander Dimitrovich Fallin, aged thirty-five according to the birthdate in the passport, and born in Odessa, Ukraine, when it had still been part of the Soviet Union.

Alongside it he put the bloodied pair of jeans, in whose pockets he had found a Mont Blanc wallet which contained four hundred euros and credit cards from Deutsche Bank and the Bank of Cyprus, both in the name of Alexander Fallin.

A battered Samsung smartphone had a smashed screen but technicians might be able to get something from it.

Beside the Gucci handbag where he'd found the smartphone, he placed a tattered document in Greek, French and English that identified the owner, Leilah Soliman, as being granted refugee status in Lesbos, Greece. It was dated eighteen months earlier. From the listed birthdate, she was eighteen years old and born in Aleppo, Syria. There were two stamps on the document and Bruno found a magnifying glass to study them. One seemed to be from the Greek police and the second was from Médecins Sans Frontières, presumably the refugee camp. He took a photo of the form with his phone.

There was also a residency permit for Cyprus, with the same name and details, dated seven months ago, and a Visa credit card in the same name from the Bank of Valletta in Malta. The bag also revealed an intact iPhone and what looked like a diamond bracelet. From an almost hidden pocket at the base of the bag he removed an envelope that contained 1,500 US dollars in one hundred dollar bills and 2,000 euros in notes of fifty euros. A pack of birth-control pills, half-used, cosmetics, mouthwash, a lace-trimmed handkerchief and an Hermès silk scarf made up the rest of the bag's contents.

The Michael Kors handbag held no identification documents of any kind, only tissues, cosmetics, a thong in red lace that had been wrapped in a small plastic bag and a pack of Dunhill cigarettes plus a Dunhill lighter that looked to be gold.

As Bruno was completing the inventory J-J pushed the door open with his shoulder and entered with a tray carrying half a dozen paper cups, steaming and smelling of coffee, and a heap of croissants and *pains au chocolat*. Yves, head of the forensics team, followed with another tray holding glasses and bottles of assorted fruit juices. An old friend of Bruno's, he nodded approvingly at the piles of belongings Bruno had sorted. Two more members of J-J's team followed them in, carrying plastic evidence bags and a couple of official police laptops.

'Get those gloves off, Bruno, and have some breakfast,' J-J said. 'But first, where's the money?'

Bruno pointed to the briefcase. 'The cashier's cheque is made out to a local *notaire*. Stichkin's daughter Galina is buying herself a chateau, or rather Daddy is buying it for her.'

'We should all have such thoughtful fathers,' said J-J, eying the money. 'And thanks for the photos of the tattoos. I forwarded them to the operations room at the Ministry of the Interior who put me on to the organized crime unit. They're Russian, unique to professional criminals called the *Vori v Zakone* or something like that. It means "thieves in law" and the tattoos are done in prison or in camps. Those letters you photographed are the Russian word *sever*, and that's only done in one of the Siberian prison camps, using soot mixed with urine for the ink. They have a very strict code, no cooperation with the authorities, won't even switch on a light bulb if ordered to do so. The organized crime team is sending someone down here to look it all over. Is this everything you found?'

Bruno washed down the last of his croissant with coffee and shook his head. 'The dead bodies, in what clothes they still had, were taken to the funeral parlour. Fabiola signed the death certificates but told them not to touch the bodies until the forensics team arrived. Maybe Yves should go there and look them over. Now you're here, I ought to head back to the scene of the crash and see if there's anything else to be found. I also want to determine why the pile of logs fell when it did. And I must type up the inventory notes. Have you opened a case file yet on the computer?'

'No, not enough time,' J-J said, speaking around a half-eaten croissant. 'I'll do that later and you can file your report directly to it. And none of this should get into the media yet. As far as the press is concerned, it was an accident, involving persons unknown. If you're asked, we're still trying to get registration details from Monaco and we suspect the car may have been stolen.'

'That won't stop a keen reporter,' Bruno objected. 'And the crash has already been reported on the radio. They know it was a Maserati, which is so expensive that it's news in itself. And a medical helicopter landing here around dawn won't go unnoticed. There's a message on my voicemail from Philippe Delaron of *Sud Ouest* and you know what he's like.'

'Refer Philippe to the press office and no off-the-record chats. This has to be kept under wraps. Anybody else know about the money?'

'No. Only you and me but Fabiola saw the tattoos and she's the kind of woman who will look them up out of curiosity. And you know Gilles, her partner, who still writes for *Paris Match*.'

'*Putain!*' J-J said tiredly and shrugged. 'I'm just passing on orders from the Commissioner and he'd had a call from Paris so all this is now way over our heads.'

'More because of General Lannes than Goirau, I would think,' said Bruno. 'But the *fisc* will have to be involved – Monaco car, Russian criminals, all that cash – don't tell me this isn't connected. And there's another thing. One of the women is a Syrian refugee. I don't know if it's the dead one or the one in intensive care but Lara Saatchi had a slight Arab accent.'

J-J shook his head. 'That's not our business. We just do the standard police work. So I'll get people working on the phones and credit cards and see if there's anything left on the car's GPS. Maybe we can find out where they came from. The speed they were going, they probably had to fill their tank on the way. We're dealing with four people but I only see two phones. Keep an eye out for any phones when you go back to the scene.'

'You'd better check with Lespinasse at the garage,' said Bruno. 'He may have picked up a phone with all the other stuff when he cleared the crash from the road. I'm hoping he or the funeral parlour can come up with some ID for the driver. From what I saw, most of him was crushed by the engine.'

J-J shrugged again. 'Poor bastard.' He looked around. 'How long can we use this council chamber as a work room?'

'I'll ask the Mayor but there's no council meeting until Thursday.'

'It's Monday so we should be done by then. Report back here after you've checked the crash site. Will you need more manpower?'

'We'll need a fingertip search of the area. Perhaps you could ask Yveline if she can spare a couple of gendarmes.'

'What was done with those dead boar you found?' J-J asked. 'I presume they could have destabilized the log pile.'

'I'll let you know when I've inspected the site.' Bruno turned to go but he stopped at the door. 'The idea that a boar just happened to accidentally knock over that pile at the very moment the car was passing strikes me as more than unlikely.'

'You're the country boy, Bruno. Is there no possible way that could have happened?'

'As I said: I'll let you know when I get back.'

The road had been cleared and was open to traffic, the logs all pushed to the ditch. A man Bruno didn't know was standing beside them, scribbling notes on a pad. He was dressed like a hunter, khaki pants and shirt, rubber boots and a sleeveless bright red gilet. Bruno half-recognized him, perhaps from a hunting dinner. He introduced himself, learned the man's name was Henri Contamine. They shook hands and Bruno asked if these were his logs.

'Yes, and so is this land, all the way from the road to the ridge up there. I have a permit for the log pile, plus a certificate from the forestry inspector for its stability.'

'So how do you think it collapsed?'

'That's what I've been trying to work out. The bottom row is secured by iron stakes at each corner, front and rear. The rear ones are still there but I can't see the front ones though there are gouges in the earth where they used to be. They might be under these logs here.'

'Or the stakes might have been swept up with the metal from the car when they cleared the road,' said Bruno. 'Could boar have done this? There was a big dead one and a couple of young *sangliers* among the logs last night.'

'You were here then?' Contamine asked. 'Must have been a hell of a mess. Three dead, I heard. Yes, I suppose boar could have done it but it would have needed two of them, digging out the front stakes and then some more rooting at the back to push the pile. Even then they'd have needed to work at it.'

'Can you show me?'

They clambered up with the help of two upright logs that had fallen oddly and rested against the slope. Contamine showed Bruno the two deep holes in the earth where the stakes had been. Bruno bent down to sniff but there was no smell of explosives and no sign of fire or charring. There were some old rabbit holes in the bank but no fresh droppings.

'We put terriers in to clear the rabbits when we put the logs here,' said Contamine. 'The ground is stable enough.'

'Part of it gave way,' said Bruno. 'And the rest is torn up. Could that have been boars, a whole herd trying to scramble up the bank to get away from an oncoming car, maybe dislodging and uprooting the stakes in the process?'

Contamine took off his flat cap to scratch his head. 'Maybe, I suppose it's possible, but you'd still have needed somebody at the back of the pile to push it over and I don't see boars doing that.'

They turned at the sound of a police siren, and a van driven by Sergeant Jules with four gendarmes halted near Bruno, who showed them the area where he wanted the fingertip search and then turned back to Contamine who was struggling to move a heavy log.

Give me a hand to move this log standing on its end, just help me push it over – Jesus!'

As the log toppled it revealed a hole behind it full of loose earth where the stake had been. Bruno scoped out some of the earth and looked at the sides of the hole. They were suspiciously smooth and flat.

'Would you say that had been made by a spade? Dug deliberately?' Contamine nodded and Bruno asked him to check the other perpendicular log while he photographed the sides of the hole.

'It's the same here,' called Contamine. 'Somebody dug away the stakes from here as well. *Putain*, this was deliberate.'

'Suppose you were planning this,' Bruno asked. 'How would you have got the boars here?'

'Food in the ditch and on the road – mushrooms, acorns, chickens, eggs and they love mashed potatoes. Boars are always hungry, they need two or three times more calories every day than we do. Pull out some of that loose earth, see if there are any chicken bones.'

They found chicken feet, heads and bones plus some broken eggshells. They went to investigate the back of the pile and found two deep grooves on top of the highest remaining log.

'That means men did this and they used levers,' said Contamine. 'Bloody vandals. Do you suppose they waited until a car came along and then levered the logs off? That makes it murder.'

'It certainly does,' said Bruno. 'But I'm not sure about the levers.' He pointed to a number of small square indentations, that looked as if they had been made by some mechanism on the ground below the grooves. He took a photo of them with his phone, and asked Contamine, 'Have you ever seen a hydraulic jack, one of those ones that truck drivers use to raise a heavy vehicle to change a tyre? It's a bit like a miniature fork-lift truck.'

'Something like a fork-lift truck would do it, and it would account for those grooves,' said Contamine. 'But were they trying to kill people in any car that happened along or were they waiting for a particular car? If so, they would have needed someone ahead, a spotter, to tell them it was coming.'

'You're right,' said Bruno, but he was thinking there were now phone apps that could track the movement of a car. He took out his phone, recorded a statement from Contamine about the boars, the stakes and his interpretation of events and made an appointment for Contamine to come to his office and sign it once it had been transcribed.

Then Bruno called J-J to brief him and was told that the fingerprints of the manicured hand of the man who had been crushed by the car engine had been taken, and matched those taken from the desk drawers and phones in the office of the Périgueux *notaire*, Sarrail. A DNA check of hairs from the back of the dead man's hand and those from a comb in Sarrail's desk was being done but J-J said he was in little doubt of the corpse's identity.

'So we have one Russian hood in the car with Sarrail and two women with very expensive handbags and diamonds,' said J-J. 'One of them is a refugee, the other is clinging to life and we don't know which is which until the live one is out of intensive care – if she makes it.'

'Check the eyebrows,' said Bruno. 'Get a policewoman to do it, or a nurse, one who knows about threading eyebrows. Lara had carefully threaded and sculpted eyebrows. When her face is cleaned up, take photographs, close-ups, and show them to the woman in the beauty parlour by Sarrail's office. Even if the face is too battered for recognition, she'll recognize her own work on the eyebrows.'

'Good idea. I'll get Yves onto it. He can take a photo of the dead woman at the funeral home and her eyebrows and we can show it to the woman at the beauty parlour. The question remains, who wanted to kill Sarrail and what was he doing with all that cash?' asked J-J.

'I'll get back to you,' Bruno replied. He checked the address book on his phone and called Brosseil, the *notaire* of St Denis, and asked him to stay in his office until he arrived.

He contacted Juliette in Les Eyzies, and asked her to check local equipment leasing companies for any recent hires of hydraulic jacks. Then he called the security number for France Télécom and requested a fix on his own cell phone, by triangulating the signals from the various cell towers in contact. Ever since the terrorist attacks in France that had triggered an official state of emergency, such almost-instant phone location systems had become an important tool in police work. He then asked them for the number and registered owner of any cell phone that had been in the same location for more than a brief period throughout the night. He waited less than a minute before the duty officer came back with a number. The phone's SIM card itself was prepaid and had been bought in Cyprus where French law was not enforced so the owner was not registered.

'Could you trace where that SIM card might be now?'

'If it's switched on,' came the reply. 'We'll call you back.'

He left Sergeant Jules and the gendarmes to their work and drove like the wind back to town, Bruno parked half on the pavement outside the *notaire*'s office and rushed in. 'Did you have an appointment this morning about the sale of Chateau Rock?' he asked a startled Brosseil.

'Yes, at nine. Monsieur Macrae, his wife and son and the son's future bride were here waiting for half an hour past the appointed time. They are very upset. The deposit cheque was to have been presented as the initial part of the transaction.'

'Did it have to be a cheque?'

'No, but it always is, a bank cashier's cheque.'

'Would cash be acceptable?'

'In principle, yes, but with these new controls on amounts over ten thousand euros, it would have been held pending the usual verification and enquiries.'

'How much was the deposit to be?'

'Three hundred thousand, ten per cent of the agreed sale price.'

'Suppose you had been handed part of the deposit money in cash?'

'I would have accepted it pending the official authorization, banked it in my client escrow account and let the bank take care of the necessary procedures against money laundering.'

'How long have your clients been gone?'

'Twenty, thirty minutes, but they're staying in the town in case the other side turn up and I call them back. You'll probably find them in the café. Why do you ask? What do you know about this, Bruno?'

'You heard about the crash on the St Cyprien road? I think it might have been the people bringing the deposit money. They had a lot of cash with them and a cashier's cheque made out to your client account. Officially you don't know that. The cash and cheque are currently in the possession of the chief detective of the Police Nationale.'

Brosseil's face was impassive. 'I see. What should I tell my clients?'

'That there is an unfortunate delay. But since Mademoiselle Galina is the buyer, I imagine her financial resources will eventually prove sufficient.'

Standing on the street outside, Bruno phoned the Paris headquarters of Médecins Sans Frontières and asked for Mathilde Condorçel, a press officer with whom he'd worked on a previous case. She greeted him warmly and he explained about the crash, the two women and the ID paper from the Lesbos refugee camp. Could she help? Mathilde said she would transfer him to a colleague who had worked there and would let her know that Bruno was a friend.

'Monsieur Bruno, *bonjour*. I'm Sandrine Ducannet. How may I help?' came a new voice. Bruno gave her Leilah Soliman's name and the date of the registration.

'The Moria camp on Lesbos is pretty awful. Even now there are more than eight thousand in a camp designed for a third of that number. But it's in better shape compared to 2016, when over half a million people, mainly Syrians, flooded into Greece from Turkey. God only knows how many died.'

'I remember the photo of the little boy, dead on a beach,' said Bruno. 'I don't know how the Greeks coped. Their economy was in bad trouble at the time.'

'It still is and now the EU is investigating administrative fraud. Greece received one and a half billion euros from the

EU for refugee assistance and not much of it came to Lesbos. There were several suicides while I was there and a lot of young people just disappeared, some of the girls onto visiting yachts. We asked the Greek police to investigate what we thought was sexual trafficking but they were overwhelmed just trying to keep order. Hang on, I'm checking the computer for that name and date she was registered. Was she born in Aleppo?'

'Yes,' said Bruno and gave Sandrine the date of birth on the form.

'That's her. We have her listed in the computer, but she disappeared soon after, along with seven others on the same day. I remember it because it was such an obvious case. There was a big Russian yacht in the harbour and we found witnesses who'd seen the girls taken on board by crew members after they'd been bought a meal at one of the tourist beach bars.'

'Do you have the name of the yacht and the date this happened?'

'Yes, it was June the seventh, just a week after Leilah was registered, and the yacht was called *Galina*.'

Bruno closed his eyes when he heard the name. That could hardly be a coincidence.

'It was registered in Cyprus and we made some enquiries,' Sandrine went on. 'It was owned by a rich Russian but the Cypriot police did nothing. We suspected they might have been paid off. You have to realize this was happening all the time, attractive young girls and boys, given a way out of those dreadful camps, wined and dined and given new clothes and a promise of a new life in Europe. In their shoes, I'd have taken that chance, even if I had to screw some fat old lecher.'

Bruno took down the names of the other girls who went on board the *Galina*. But Lara Saatchi's name was not among them, nor could Sandrine find it on her computer.

'Saatchi is quite a common name, Ottoman origin, it means watchmaker,' she said.

'Thanks for your help. May I come back to you if I have more questions?'

'Please do, and I'm sorry about the dead woman and if it's Leilah I'm sorry that she's just a name to me. She didn't stand out among all those heartbreaking faces, fleeing from war and finding themselves in something almost as bad. It made me feel ashamed to be European, how little we did, how little our politicians cared.'

'Except for Angela Merkel,' said Bruno.

'I suppose so, except for her.'

Then France Télécom called back. The SIM card of the phone he had asked about was currently at Bergerac airport.

28

Bruno found the Macraes and Galina at Chez Monique, the wine bar on the Rue de Paris. The place had just opened and Macrae, Jamie and Kirsty were being served glasses of Les Verdots by Monique herself. Meghan and Galina were having coffee.

'Congratulations on your engagement, Galina!' he said, pulling up a chair to join them. 'I'm looking for Sasha. Do you know where he is?'

'*Moi malenkyi zhelonyi chelovechek*,' she said mockingly, and shrugged. '*Ya ne znayu.* I don't know. I thought he might have been there this morning.'

'My little green man?' asked Meghan. 'Is that what you called him? Was that what Sasha was? One of Putin's secret soldiers in Ukraine?' She looked alarmed.

'Sasha worked for my father in Donetsk and before that he was in Crimea when Putin took it,' Galina said and shrugged again. 'Little green men is what they were called – green uniforms, no rank, no identification, just green, with Russian weapons and special flak vests that were only issued to Spetsnaz, special forces.'

'I thought you said he was a distant cousin,' said Jamie.

'My father told me so and maybe he is. But he's really my watchdog, my security man,' Galina said casually, as though this were not unusual. 'My father worries about me. He sent the plane for Sasha on Friday and said he would be back today. I thought it was to arrange the deposit money for the sale but my father told me some other people in his company had to bring a car back so he'd send it with them.'

'What plane is that?' Bruno asked.

'My father has a business jet, usually based in Cyprus, but my mother thought he'd probably send it from Nice to Bergerac. Then he told her the money would come by car.'

'It must get confusing, keeping track,' said Rod, drily.

'Have you heard from Sasha today or yesterday?'

Galina shook her head and then looked at Jamie. 'I am so sorry. I am sure it will all be settled. I tried to call Sasha from the *notaire* but there's no reply. Maybe his phone is on mute. I will try again, or call my father.'

'I'm sure he'll turn up,' said Bruno. 'Maybe he sent it with the other man who works for him, Alexander Fallin. Do you know him?'

'Yes, the other Sasha. Sasha is short for Alexander. Fallin is some business friend of my father, usually in Malta so I think of him as Malta Sasha. The one who came with us is Cyprus Sasha. How do you know him?'

'And Leilah, Leilah Soliman,' Bruno went on. 'Do you know her?'

Galina looked uninterested, as though this had nothing to do with her. 'Yes, I think so, from the yacht. She was Malta Sasha's girlfriend.'

'What's this about, Bruno? All these names of people, who are they?' asked Jamie.

'There was a car crash near here last night, a bad one, and two of the dead were Alexander Fallin and a woman we think was Leilah Soliman. They had a briefcase that contained a cashier's cheque for your deposit.'

Galina clapped her hands like a child, then reached out and squeezed Jamie's hand. 'You see, Jamie, I told you it would work out.'

'Two people are dead, Galina,' Jamie replied coldly, and at that moment Bruno began to wonder whether this marriage would take place. And if it did, would it last?

'I should call my father,' Galina said, abashed. 'Yes, I'm sorry. I did not think. This is very sad.' She reached for her phone.

'Not just yet,' said Bruno. 'I'm afraid you'll have to come with me to the Mairie where there's a senior detective who needs to talk to you and see if you can identify the bodies. I'm sorry, but it's the law to identify the dead as soon as possible.'

'I am sorry, I could not,' she said, shaking her head. 'I could not stand it, dead people. And they must have horrible injuries.'

'Don't worry, I'll come with you,' said Jamie, taking her hand. 'Bruno's right. You have to identify them.'

Bruno led the way to the Mairie and left them in his office before going to the council chamber to brief J-J on the boars, on Contamine's conclusion that the crash was no accident and on the link with Stichkin.

'We have no grounds to arrest Galina, J-J, but I said you'd need her to identify Fallin and maybe the girl. She knows them both. I'm pretty sure the dead woman is Leilah Soliman, a Syrian refugee from some grim camp on Lesbos who was spirited away on Daddy's yacht. Galina is in my office with her boyfriend.'

'She can't see the bodies now,' said J-J, rising to his feet. 'Yves is at the funeral parlour doing the forensics with Fabiola. Still, I'd better see her, get some details on Fallin and the girl. What about you? How do we get some kind of confirmation that this car crash was no accident?'

'I asked Juliette to start looking for places that lease or sell hydraulic jacks. I thought I'd better check on a private plane that might have brought Sasha here. He's the ex-Spetsnaz bodyguard. If anybody in all this is a killer, he's the likely candidate.'

'You and your hunches.' J-J sighed. 'Where will you be?'

'I'll stay here. You may want to bring Galina in, see if she recognizes any clothes, get a statement from her about the cashier's cheque and her own movements. But as soon as you can we need her to identify the bodies.'

Once J-J had taken Galina and Jamie from Bruno's office, he checked his computer for the special security number of air traffic control. He used his desk phone to call the number, identified himself and gave his identification code. He was told to wait while this was checked and then a brisk voice asked for his birthdate and army number. Bruno gave them and was then asked what he needed. He asked whether a Cyprus-registered private jet had flown from Malta or Cyprus to Nice and Bergerac in the last three or four days.

'Cyprus? That's a VQ-C registration. Let me check.'

Bruno heard the clicking of computer keys but within a minute, the voice was back.

'We had one incoming, one of the new Embraer Phenom business jets, into Nice on Friday afternoon, refuelled, then to Bergerac at nineteen hundred hours and back to Nice forty minutes later. It came back to Bergerac again late yesterday and it's still there.'

'Is there any way you can ensure it stays there? This is a murder inquiry and I think our suspect may be trying to take that plane.'

'Delay it? Is this a formal police request?'

'Yes, on my authority as a member of the special task force of the Interior Ministry. You can call the Minister's office and ask for General Lannes.'

'We can block any flight plan and ask the airport manager to have that aircraft held but he'll probably want to see a warrant unless you want to invoke the emergency regulations.'

'I'll do exactly that, thank you.'

Bruno then phoned a friend, Jean-Max, a businessman who owned and ran half a dozen prehistoric caves as commercial tourist sites. Jean-Max used his own helicopter to get from one site to another.

'Jean-Max, I'm in St Denis and need to get to Bergerac airport as soon as possible. It's a murder inquiry and there's a suspect about to board a private jet.'

'OK, Bruno,' he replied. 'I'm at the Roque St Christophe and can be with you at that landing place behind the medical centre in fifteen minutes, then another fifteen to Bergerac. Will that do?'

'Perfect, I'll be waiting. Thanks.'

Bruno called Yveline at the gendarmerie, explained briefly and asked if she'd come along, armed, and to get Sergeant Jules to inform the security chief at Bergerac airport of their arrival to investigate the private jet from Cyprus. What's more, they might need support from the detachment of armed troops now on call for security duties at all commercial airports. Bruno picked up his personal weapon and two spare magazines, called J-J out from the council chamber and briefed him quickly.

'*Putain*, Bruno. This is thin. It had better be on your own head.'

'Do me a favour, J-J, and call the Brigadier to let him know what's happening. Commandant Yveline of the gendarmes will be with me, both of us armed. This is a special forces veteran we're dealing with.'

'*Merde*, Bruno, take care. I hope you're sure about this.'

'So do I,' Bruno called as he ran down the stairs and across the bridge to the medical centre and the landing pad behind it. People were already looking up at Jean-Max's descending helicopter whose sound was almost drowning out the siren of the gendarme van. Bruno and Yveline reached the pad at the same moment, each holding onto their caps against the prop wash.

'It's not meant for three,' called Jean-Max as he landed, keeping the engine running. Then he saw Yveline's assault rifle and waved them in. She was wearing a flak vest and carried a second in her free hand which she tossed to Bruno. He donned it, clambered in and inserted himself to crouch behind the two seats while Yveline took the passenger seat. Bruno reached up and grabbed the spare headphones to speak to Jean-Max.

'Many thanks for this, Jean-Max. If you could put us down really close to the Embraer business jet, as near as possible to block it from moving.'

'*Putain*, Bruno,' came the thin, crackling voice through the headphones. 'Are we going to get shot at?'

'I hope not,' Bruno replied. Jean-Max let out a low whistle and then increased the throttle, adjusted the collective for full lift and as the helicopter left the ground he gently brought in the cyclic to put the nose down so that they could get forward motion as they rose. Within less than a minute they were cruising at a hundred and twenty knots over Limeuil and then headed almost due west, above the lazy bends of the Dordogne river, the vineyards of the Pécharmant unfolding to their right.

Yveline gestured to Jean-Max that she needed the headphones and once they were on she asked Bruno, 'Do we have rules of engagement?'

'I'm seconded to General Lannes's staff again, so we're under emergency rules. We're looking for a Russian, Spetsnaz-trained, and I think he set up that car crash this morning that killed three people. I need him held under *garde à vue* and get a forensics check while we interrogate him. I would guess he's trained not to talk but the forensics will get him.'

Yveline nodded and was about to return the headphones to Jean-Max when Bruno shook his finger and said, 'He might not be alone. I've asked Jean-Max to take the chopper down to block the take-off of a private jet that's supposed to take them away. I've arranged with air traffic control to delay the flight.'

'Is he – are they – armed?' she asked.

'Probably.'

The helicopter passed over the Poudrérie, the huge old ammunition plant that was built in 1916 to feed the hungry guns of the Western Front and was now a placid business estate. They were almost there. Jean-Max gestured for the headphones and Yveline handed them back. Bruno heard Jean-Max saying he was a civilian flight carrying two armed police officers on security duty for an emergency.

'Permission to land granted. We are aware of the emergency situation. Repeat we are aware,' said the control tower. 'Security forces standing by.'

Merde, thought Bruno, hoping that message had been sent on a closed channel. The last thing he wanted was for Sasha to know that the net was closing in. As Jean-Max came in to land, heading for the small aircraft parking area by the flying school hangar, Bruno saw the steps of an executive jet start to fold back into the fuselage.

'Get down fast, they're going to try to take off,' he said to Jean-Max, pointing urgently. Jean-Max nodded but continued dropping slowly and under complete control and heading for the space in front of the jet. Its door still not fully closed, the jet began to move, its nose wheel at an angle to turn it away from the incoming chopper. Three French soldiers, armed and in uniform, were shifting their eyes from the chopper to the jet but making no effort to intervene. *They must be waiting for orders*, Bruno thought.

'Jump out and roll, as soon as you can,' he shouted into Yveline's ear. 'You move right and I'll go left.'

She nodded, checked the safety catch on her gun and when they were still a good metre from the ground she jumped out and rolled to her right. Bruno squeezed himself out from behind the seats and followed, rolling left, in the direction the Embraer was taking. He stopped, lying flat on the ground and drawing his SIG-Sauer automatic as the jet's engines howled and it crept towards him. He took aim, and fired double taps, two shots at a time, into the nose wheel.

It took three bursts, but then the nose of the jet dropped as the tyre shredded and the metal struts of the nose wheel began grinding into the tarmac. The aircraft stopped. The engine noise faded as the pilot throttled back and cut the engines.

Only then did Bruno see the red cross on the nose of the aircraft and on each side of the fuselage beneath the cockpit, along with the logo *MedicAir Trans-Med Service*. Could he have made a terrible mistake?

29

What now? Bruno asked himself. He had to push the doubt from his mind and assume there would be aircrew aboard as well as Sasha so he might be facing a hostage situation. There was a drill for that. The airport would be closed, the public evacuated and a specialist team of *gendarmes mobiles* brought in along with negotiators and ambulances. Bruno realized that he was a sitting duck for anyone in the cockpit with a gun. He crawled forward until he was by the broken nose wheel, in the cover of the jet's fuselage, and gestured to Yveline to get under cover.

Then he heard the sound of jet engines and turned to see another executive jet on its final approach to the runway. He recognized it at once from the two engines at the rear and the third on top of the fuselage: a Dassault Falcon 900 with its distinctive high tail. It was the standard transport for military top brass and high government officials. *Mon Dieu*, he thought, that was all he needed, some French politician flying into this mess.

The door of the Embraer jet above him began to open and the steps were unfolding automatically. An angry-looking man in a pilot's uniform leaned out from the doorway and in strongly accented French demanded to know what the hell Bruno thought he was doing.

'Preventing you from taking off,' Bruno said, introducing himself. 'Air traffic control had ordered your aircraft to be held here and I want everybody out now and on the tarmac, starting with you. Are you the pilot?'

'I'm the co-pilot and the owner of this aircraft and I'm staying aboard.'

'Are you Monsieur Stichkin?' Bruno asked.

'I am.' He was a burly man of about sixty, tanned and healthy with iron-grey hair cut short, pale blue eyes and improbably white teeth. 'What's this about?'

'We are searching for a suspect named Sasha Kozak who works for you. Is he still aboard?'

'No, he left two hours ago on a commercial flight to Paris.'

'In that case, you won't mind if I check,' said Bruno climbing the stairs and pushing his way past Stichkin. The interior of the aircraft was evidently designed for dual-use, part executive jet, part emergency medical station. He noted four luxurious lounge chairs at the rear while the compartment he had entered was fitted with two bunk beds, one above the other. On the walls were the kinds of monitors he usually saw only in hospitals.

Other than Stichkin and a young woman dressed as a nurse these two compartments were empty. A pilot in the left-hand seat of the cockpit had turned and was watching Bruno nervously.

'We were not taking off, just obeying the control tower's orders to move away from the terminal and park beyond the flying school,' the pilot said. French was clearly his mother tongue.

'Can I enter the baggage compartment from inside this aircraft?' Bruno asked.

'No, the rear is a cold space for medical supplies with freezers for carrying organs for transplant. We've been waiting for a delivery from Sarlat hospital that I'm taking back to Nice where there's a patient waiting.'

'Can you open the baggage hatch from the cockpit for me?' Bruno said. 'I need to search it.'

The pilot fiddled with a catch and Bruno went to the door to see Yveline standing there, her weapon at the ready. The army corporal and two troopers seemed to have placed themselves under her orders. One was standing at the tail, the other two at the nose.

'Both holds should be open now, nose and rear,' said the pilot.

After a few moments Yveline reported that the rear hold contained only suitcases and the front hold contained small cardboard boxes labelled for swabs, syringes and other medical supplies.

There came a roar from the runway and Bruno looked out to watch as the Falcon landed with a burst of smoke from the tyres followed by a screech as the engines were switched to reverse thrust. Bruno turned to see Stichkin sitting in one of the lounge chairs, his hands clasped over an ample stomach. He was looking very pleased with himself as he stared at Bruno with a half-smile on his face. The woman who was dressed as a nurse sat opposite him, her back to Bruno.

'Kozak should be at Orly by now and then who knows where he's gone?' he said. 'But I know you. We were not introduced but I've seen you before at a chateau near here. It belonged to a friend of mine and the event was his ninetieth birthday party – Marco Desaix, a great pilot and a war hero on the Russian front. You were pushing a famous old woman in a wheelchair, the Red Countess.'

Bruno nodded. Stichkin had also been a pilot and there had been Russians at that party. It made sense that he would have known Desaix. 'Marco was a great hero of France, a legendary man. I went to his funeral,' he said.

'I gather you also know my daughter,' Stichkin went on. 'She speaks well of you.'

Bruno's nerves were still jangling as the adrenalin rush died down and he felt out of his depth at the sudden transition from gunfire to the kind of polite conversation he might expect in a drawing room.

'You must be proud of her,' Bruno replied. 'Galina is a very gifted musician as well as the best tennis player I know. But right now my priority is a multiple murder that was made to look like a car crash. Three dead, each of them connected to you.'

'How very sad,' said Stichkin.

'The evidence suggests that Kozak was responsible,' Bruno went on.

'Had I known, I would have tried to delay his departure. He asked for emergency leave to visit his sick mother back in Russia. But I shall stay. I want to see my daughter, this chateau she's buying and this boy she wants to marry. I gather you know him, too.'

'He's a fine young man. But I thought you were about to fly some organs to Nice.'

'They don't need me for that. Another co-pilot is coming to replace me, should be here by now. I have a meeting arranged here with some senior French officials. I imagine they will be on that jet that just landed.'

Stichkin shifted in his seat as if uncomfortable, put a hand behind his back and pulled out a mobile phone. He looked at the nurse. 'Is this yours?' She shook her head.

'It's not mine. It's an android. I use iPhones. Kozak must have forgotten it.' Stichkin offered the phone to Bruno. 'Maybe it will help your enquiries.'

Bruno took out a handkerchief, accepted the phone, wrapped it and put it in his chest pocket. He had the unsettling feeling that he was taking part in a play in which Stichkin alone knew the script.

'Bruno,' called Yveline urgently from the aircraft steps. 'You'd better come.'

The other aircraft had halted some thirty metres away. It carried the colours of the French Republic and descending the steps were the familiar figures of General Lannes and Isabelle, both in civilian clothes. His heart sinking, Bruno went down the steps, saluted and waited to be called to an extremely difficult encounter.

'Over here, Bruno. And you, Commandante Yveline,' Lannes called. The moment they reached him, Lannes gave Bruno a glacial stare. 'Is Stichkin inside?'

'Yes, sir. But Kozak has gone. He's the murder suspect in the car crash J-J will have briefed you about.'

'That's your problem, not mine. Is there any evidence that gives you reason to detain Stichkin?'

'His aircraft brought Kozak to Bergerac yesterday. He came back here this morning and left his phone on the plane, probably assuming we would use it to find him. The three dead seem to have been people who were putting Stichkin's insurance company at risk, which is to say that Stichkin had a motive to silence them. There is also a question of his yacht being used for trafficking Syrian refugees.'

'How strong a case do you have against him?'

'Enough to put him under *garde à vue* and then it would be up to a magistrate.'

'I agree with Bruno, sir,' said Yveline. 'There's enough for a conspiracy charge.'

'Good, so we can put some serious personal pressure on him. What about that nose wheel? I presume you did that, Bruno?'

'Yes, sir,' said Bruno. 'The aircraft had been held by air traffic control even before J-J informed them we were in pursuit of a suspected murderer. I shot out the front wheel to prevent what seemed to be an attempt to take off. This is entirely my responsibility, sir. Commandante Yveline simply agreed to support my request to come here in hot pursuit.'

'I see.' Lannes turned to Isabelle. 'Do you have any questions for Bruno, Commissaire?'

'Not immediately, sir. But we'll need to debrief him fully later. We'll also need to issue a European arrest warrant for Kozak. If Bruno has any photos of him, that could be helpful. We can run them through the archive of the fighting in Ukraine using the new facial recognition software. After they lost so many people when the airliner was shot down, the Dutch are eager to bring war crimes charges before their court in the Hague.'

'Understood. Very well, Bruno, I'd like an unmarked police car as soon as possible ready to take me and Stichkin and the commissaire to somewhere private, civilized and nearby. We'll also want a discreet exit from the airport. I imagine by now the press will be on their way. Could you take care of that while we go and have an initial chat with him?'

'Yes, sir. His pilot says they are waiting for a delivery of human organs for transplant to be flown to Nice. I doubt whether there'll be a replacement nose wheel available here. You might need another medical plane.'

Lannes nodded and followed by Isabelle he climbed the steps into Stichkin's aircraft. A few moments later, the pilot and the nurse came down the steps and said they had been asked to wait in the terminal.

Bruno turned to Yveline and said, 'Sorry to have dragged you into this. It's all my fault.'

'Don't be silly, I'm responsible for my own actions and you did the right thing, whatever the Realpolitik games being played inside that aircraft. But what's the antiterrorist coordinator doing with General Lannes?'

'I imagine it's several different things, starting with that Malaysian passenger jet that she mentioned, shot down by a Russian missile over Ukraine in 2014,' Bruno said. 'The Dutch government is holding Russia legally responsible for the three hundred dead. They say it's state terrorism and a lot of European governments agree. More recently there was the use of nerve agents in an English country town against a Russian

defector. So what we're involved in here is French security officials setting up a back-channel negotiation with the Kremlin,
or maybe with just one of the factions in the Kremlin.'

'*Merde*,' Yveline said. 'Meanwhile we have our orders. I'll
arrange for the car.'

'Any idea where we can take them?' Bruno asked. 'I was
thinking of one of the nearby vineyards, maybe Château
Tiregand. I know the count who owns the place. There's a
closed courtyard where we can put the cars.'

'Sounds good. I'll arrange a car from Bergerac.'

Bruno contacted the count, explained the need for a discreet
meeting place for an impromptu high-level security meeting
and was told they could use the chateau dining room. Yveline
reported that an unmarked car was on its way. She called the
airport control room and asked about alternative entrances.
At that moment a 4x4 vehicle that Bruno knew only too well
pulled up outside the airport fence. Philippe Delaron climbed
out, camera in hand. Another familiar car slowed as it passed
Philippe and J-J waved from the passenger seat before his car
rolled on to the airport entrance.

'So much for discretion,' said Bruno, steering Yveline out of
Delaron's line of sight. 'We'll have to screen the aircraft steps
when they come out. One of the fire engines could do it. Try
the airport manager.'

Bruno's phone vibrated. The screen told him it was Juliette.
As he took the call, a fire engine began moving forward to block
any sight of the two executive jets from the airfield perimeter.

'One heavy-duty hydraulic jack with broad blade, suitable
for lifting containers with a single operator, was rented from

Bergerac Leasing, just down the road from the airport,' she said. 'Six hundred euros paid in cash, lease secured on a Bank of Malta credit card issued to Euro-Trans-Med Logistics in the name of Sandro Cosacchi, whose identity was verified by a Maltese passport in that name. The jack was booked by phone on Saturday, picked up yesterday by special arrangement when the payment was made and the jack returned to the yard before they opened this morning.'

'Sandro Cosacchi,' Bruno murmured. 'Alexander Kozak. Sorry, Juliette, I'm thinking aloud. Thank you. I owe you one.'

He put the phone away as J-J approached to shake his hand and greet Yveline.

'Kozak flew out to Paris-Orly first thing this morning, having returned the hydraulic jack he rented to push over the log pile,' Bruno said. 'He paid in cash but had to show a credit card issued by a company owned by the Russian who's inside that aircraft with General Lannes and Isabelle.'

'And from Orly he could catch a plane anywhere,' said J-J, shaking his head in frustration.

'He's got passports in his own name and an Italianized version of it, and probably others,' said Bruno. 'I'll give all this to Isabelle. She may be able to use it to put pressure on the Russian.' He paused. 'Any word on the girl who survived the car crash?'

'Not yet, she was still being operated on but they don't sound hopeful.'

'Have you heard anything from Prunier?' Bruno asked, referring to J-J's boss, the police commissioner for the *département*.

'Not since he was on the phone with Lannes. Just a text

message to say I should accompany Lannes and arrange security as required, so I suppose I should take you along, Bruno. At least you're armed. How long do you expect them to stay inside that plane?'

'Until the unmarked car arrives from the Bergerac gendarmes to take them to Château Tiregand for more discreet talks,' Yveline said. 'They'll use a special exit at the far end of the runway. And since they're using a gendarme car, I'll go along.'

'Bring your car onto the tarmac and then we can follow them out,' Bruno said to J-J. 'The Russian is planning on staying here for a bit. You'll need to check whether Lannes wants to lay on continued security for him.'

J-J nodded just as his phone began to ring. He listened, grunted, and grunted again before muttering, 'Understood.'

'*Putain*,' he said as he closed the phone and stared hard at Bruno. 'Your reporter friend, Delaron. He's on the local radio news saying the police suspect that car crash was no accident. He's spoken to the owner of the log pile who said you and he agreed that somebody pushed those logs into the road deliberately.'

'It's true, and don't say I didn't warn you,' Bruno replied. 'But I haven't spoken to Philippe and if I had I'd have said no comment and our enquiries continue, just as you would.'

'As if I don't have enough on my plate, Delaron is here, trying to get photos of the people on those planes,' said J-J, and raced off to bring his own car onto the tarmac. Isabelle called Bruno to ask if the cars and new location were ready, just as the unmarked gendarme car appeared, J-J's Citroën behind it, and the two cars drew up close to the aircraft steps. Lannes and Stichkin came down the steps and squeezed into the back, Yveline taking the front passenger seat. Isabelle and Bruno climbed into the next car, behind J-J and Josette, his usual aide. They drove out to the far end of the airfield where one of the mechanics stood waiting for them beside an open gate.

As they took the back road towards the *route nationale*, Bruno told Isabelle about Kozak's hiring of the hydraulic jack with a credit card on one of Stichkin's companies. 'That puts Stichkin in the frame for a charge of conspiracy to murder.'

'Interesting, but of course Stichkin can deny knowledge of this, put it down to a private feud on the part of Kozak,' she said as they crossed the River Dordogne and caught sight of Château Tiregand, perched overlooking the valley on the long Pécharmant ridge.

'You mean he's just going to walk away from all this?' Bruno asked.

'This is bigger than your murder by car crash, Bruno, or of your old man Driant. The Dutch are pressing hard for us to widen the sanctions that currently target Putin's associates to include Russians who bought themselves European citizenship, mainly in Cyprus and Malta. If France throws her weight behind the Dutch, Stichkin stands to lose everything. That's why he's talking to us now. He needs our protection.'

'And what will he have to give us to get that?'

'Putin's money and where it's hidden. We're pretty sure that Stichkin is the bagman who knows where the billions are buried. That's what this is all about.'

'So Stichkin and his stooges get away with murder?' Bruno demanded as the turn-off to the chateau came into view.

Isabelle shrugged. 'Sarrail is your top stooge and he's dead.'

'And so is that girl that was in intensive care, ' chimed in J-J, turning round from the front seat. 'I just got a text message. They couldn't save her.'

Once inside the chateau grounds, the gendarme driver ahead pulled in to let J-J take the lead and Bruno steered him past the main chateau entrance to a side gate that led to an enclosed courtyard. The Count de St Exupéry was waiting to greet them

'*Bonjour*, François-Xavier,' said Bruno, climbing out to shake hands and thank the courteous aristocrat who made one of the finest wines of the region. 'This is very kind of you and I'm sorry I can't explain more.'

'No need,' said the Count, shaking hands with the others. He led the way indoors and then through a long corridor into a stately dining room, its walls painted red, furnished with Chinese antiquities brought back by some ancestor who had been an ambassador in imperial Peking. There were two open bottles of wine, fruit juice, coffee and mineral water on the table along with cups and glasses.

'If you need anything else . . .' the Count said.

'Thank you, no,' said Lannes, steering Isabelle and Stichkin to chairs on opposite sides of the table. 'We'd better get to work.'

The Count withdrew, Yveline stayed outside the door and Bruno and J-J went out to the courtyard where the gendarme driver waited by the cars, checking his handgun.

'What do you think they're discussing?' Bruno asked as he and J-J went to the courtyard entrance to keep watch.

'What new sanctions Europe is going to put on the Russians,' said J-J. 'There was something about it in the papers, more

Russian businessmen banned from travel and now there's talk of limiting the access of Russian banks to the international clearing system. But with half of Europe dependent on Russian gas, that probably won't get very far, whatever Putin's thugs do. But I take seriously what Isabelle said about Stichkin being Putin's private banker.'

'I imagine Isabelle will at least bring up the Kozak business,' Bruno said. 'She suggested putting out a Euro-wide arrest warrant for him on murder charges.'

'I'm sure she will,' said J-J. 'She's still a cop at heart. And don't forget I trained her.'

Then the press office called J-J again to say that local radio news was reporting a top-secret security conference between French and Russian security officials at Bergerac airport.

'Your damn Philippe Delaron again,' said J-J. 'Can't you bring him under control?'

'Not at all, he's far too useful doing what he does,' Bruno replied. 'Don't you believe in the freedom of the press?'

30

The conference at Château Tiregand was into its third hour and Bruno had ignored three calls from Philippe Delaron when his phone vibrated again. The screen said it was Rod Macrae.

'We have a situation here, Bruno,' Rod began, his voice high-pitched and nervous. 'Bertie's got Galina and he's got a gun.'

'What? Who?' Bruno was confused but the intensity of Rod's voice got his adrenalin pumping.

'It's me, Bruno,' said a woman's voice. Meghan had taken over the phone and was speaking calmly. 'We were listening to the radio when they reported that security meeting at Bergerac airport. Galina said she thought it must be her father since he'd called to say he'd see her this evening. Then I said something about Galina mentioning the little green men and Bertie hit the roof. He grabbed the shotgun Rod uses for rabbits.'

She paused to catch her breath. Bruno could only admire her self-control.

'You're doing fine, Meghan,' he said. 'Take your time.'

'Bertie dragged Galina to the terrace and said she'd better get her dad here or else. He's been shouting about the war crimes court at The Hague. Jamie and I have tried talking to him but he's threatened to shoot us. So we thought we'd better call you.'

'What's Galina doing?'

'He's got her sitting on the floor of the terrace and he's on a chair, his back to the wall, the shotgun on his lap. She's got her phone and she's tried calling her dad but his phone is switched off.'

'Keep calm and don't do anything. I'm on my way,' said Bruno. 'Just hold on a second, though.'

He turned to explain to J-J, who simply gaped at him before saying, 'Stichkin's daughter? Held hostage by a Ukrainian nationalist with a shotgun? Are you serious?'

'This guy, Bertie, he's a friend of the Macraes' son Jamie, the one who's going to marry Galina. He's called Bertie because he's from Alberta in Canada but his real name is Bondarchuk and Isabelle knows about him.'

'What do you mean, she knows about him?'

'She mentioned him by name when we were talking recently. One of her jobs is to keep tabs on Ukrainian nationalists and the Brits tipped her off about him. Apparently some cousin of his was killed in the fighting in Ukraine. '

'When you say you were talking recently . . .'

'Don't ask. But we have to get a message to her inside that room.' Bruno pulled out his notebook and began to write. 'Knock and call Isabelle out and give her this, say it's urgent. And give me your keys so I can take your car.'

'You're going there yourself?'

'Do you have a better idea? I know them all – Galina, Bertie, the whole family. At least they'll talk to me. And we need time to set something up. This guy Bertie, he's on the rear terrace of Chateau Rock with a shotgun. We need time to get a sniper in place, just in case, and I can win us that time. Come on, J-J, you know it makes sense.'

'Hadn't you better wait till Isabelle comes out?'

'She'll want to know that we have a solution in hand.' Bruno ripped off the page on which he'd written his message. 'You give her that note and then arrange for a police sniper and a hostage rescue team to get to Chateau Rock. She'll have to decide whether to tell Stichkin.'

Shaking his head, J-J handed over his keys and headed back inside the chateau. Returning to Meghan, Bruno told her he was on his way. He raced to the car and took off up the drive, past the riding school and onto the back road to Sainte-Alvère. At this stage he could use the siren but first he called the fire station at St Denis and asked Ahmed to bring an ambulance as quietly as he could to the entrance of Chateau Rock and Bruno would meet him there. As soon as he ended that call he saw he had an incoming call from Isabelle.

'What do you plan to do?' she asked.

'Keep things calm until you have a sniper in place and the usual hostage rescue team. I can keep him talking, even promise him I'll arrange to get Stichkin brought there. Whatever it takes. Are you going to tell Stichkin?'

'Not yet, he'd drop everything and take off for the chateau. I'd rather present him with a solution than a problem. Be careful, Bruno.'

He made a return call to Rod Macrae's number to say that a specialist hostage rescue team was being alerted. Macrae began demanding details so Meghan took the phone again and said they'd hold on.

It was a fast road as far as Sainte-Alvère but then it slowed with traffic and he was getting too close to use the siren. Trying to remember the long-ago police academy lesson on hostage situations, he could recall only the rule about securing the scene until the experts could arrive. He knew the ground and the people involved. With Jamie doubtless thinking of heroics to rescue his beloved, his mother and all the other young people who would be there, he knew there might be so many liabilities.

Bruno thought he could probably count on Meghan, Rod and Kirsty. But for all he knew, the French musicians might be filming it on their mobile phones and livestreaming it to the world.

His phone rang. It was Isabelle again.

'Our oligarch is taking a toilet break,' she said. 'Thanks for your message. I told Lannes. He says to leave it with you for the moment but we're not telling Stichkin. J-J has the hostage rescue team from Bordeaux coming in by chopper but they'll land away from the chateau. They'll be there in about an hour. I'll text you rather than phone.'

Ahmed was waiting at the entrance to the drive with a small ambulance and another medic. Bruno briefed them and then led the way up to the entrance where he'd first met Bertie and Sasha and the whole drama had begun to unfold little more than a week ago. One of the double entrance doors was open and he told the two medics to stand by.

The hallway was empty but he could hear the sound of female sobbing from the sitting room to the right, and looked in to see Kirsty comforting her mother. Meghan's face was red and awash with tears. That startled him. He'd thought of Meghan as the rock he could count on. Bruno put his finger to his lips for silence.

'Are Bertie and Galina still on the terrace?' he asked Kirsty in a whisper. She nodded and shushed her mother, who took a great gulp of air as she saw Bruno and tried to rise but then choked and began to hiccup. Bruno patted her shoulder and told her in a whisper that she'd done well. Then he asked Kirsty where he'd find her father and brother.

'Kitchen,' she mouthed. 'They've been trying to talk to him.'

'Where are the others?' he asked.

'Ippo went out on a bicycle ride before all this began and I don't know when he'll be back,' Kirsty whispered. 'Pia tried talking sense into Bertie but he sent her away. I think she's in the kitchen, maybe planning to try again. They aren't getting on well. After that stupid fight Bertie had with Sasha, Pia demanded a separate room.'

He squeezed Kirsty's shoulder and thanked her before going into the kitchen, his finger still held against his lips as Jamie and Rod rose from the kitchen table when they saw him. Pia was hovering over Jamie with a bottle of antiseptic ointment and some cotton wool. He had a swollen cheek and jaw.

'What happened?'

'I thought at first it was some stupid joke,' Jamie said. 'Then I tried to take the shotgun and Bertie gave me a punch that knocked me down and damn near knocked me out. He's as strong as a horse.'

Rod shook his head and led Bruno into the hall. 'We tried offering him a drink that we'd loaded with sleeping pills but he threw it away after the first sip. He was trying to make some calls but his phone battery is dead. I think he made one but he was speaking Ukrainian so I've no idea what he said except that he said something that sounded like "press conference".'

'How's Galina?' Bruno asked, thinking that if Bertie had planned this he'd have had a fully charged phone. It sounded as though Bertie had taken a spur-of-the-moment decision rather than planned this operation. Either way, trying to call a press conference would make sense from Bertie's point of view.

'She cried a bit and asked for Jamie but Bertie won't let anyone else onto the terrace. Bertie demanded her phone but she refused to give him the code to open it. He kept trying and I think it got locked. Anyway, he gave up and he's furious that we won't give him our own phones or chargers.'

'Are you sure the shotgun is loaded?'

Rod nodded grimly. 'Both barrels. I loaded it before this began because Bertie said he wanted to pot some rabbits in the vineyard. He grew up on a farm so he knows how to use it.'

'Do you have the number of his phone?' Bruno asked, and Jamie read it aloud from his contact list. Bruno called the France Télécom security number and asked for traces on all calls from Bertie's phone that day. He took off his uniform jacket and his belt with the phone pouch and holster, checking his gun to be sure that the safety catch was on and entrusting it to Jamie. He braced himself and walked out of the kitchen door in his shirtsleeves, his hands in the air.

'Bertie, as you can see I'm unarmed and hoping we can work this out. Hello again, Galina.'

The young woman tried to rise, her face suddenly shining

with hope but Bertie slammed a large foot into her chest to force her back to the floor. Bruno winced to see it. He'd expected Bertie to be under stress but he was showing real aggression.

'*Mon Dieu*, Bertie, she's a friend,' Bruno said. 'You know she's not your enemy.'

'You can let me have your phone, otherwise just go away.' Bertie was now pointing the shotgun at Bruno.

He was sitting on a wooden chair, very solid and rustic, in the far corner of the terrace with the chateau wall behind him. The place was well chosen, with no windows to overlook him and a thick trellis of ancient vines protecting one flank. He was at least five metres from Bruno, with more of the chairs and the long terrace table between them. Bruno glanced out to the garden, sloping down to the pool, and the tree-covered ridge rising beyond. Snipers would have no trouble getting clear shots from within two hundred metres. There was a window about ten metres above where Bertie was sitting. Maybe he could use that.

'I must have left my phone in the car,' Bruno said. 'But that's not the point. I think all this was a spontaneous decision you took. You haven't planned this at all, have you?'

'That's where you're wrong, Bruno. I want Stichkin himself,' Bertie said, his voice flat and his expression determined. 'When he comes here, Galina can go free. And then I want a press conference right here so he can explain what he did in Ukraine and then he has to face justice at the war crimes court. Ukraine's parliament voted for that trial. Then I'll turn myself in and face justice. This isn't a kidnapping, Bruno. It's a citizen's arrest of a war criminal.'

Bruno was trying to work out what was really in Bertie's mind. He must have known he was in trouble. With no phone and no allies, he'd know that he would eventually be outgunned. Whatever his original goal might have been he must realize his only threat was to kill Galina. But everything else, from his own survival to his own original goal, depended on keeping her alive.

'Legally speaking, you're a foreign national so you don't have the right to make a citizen's arrest here,' Bruno said. 'So what we have is a stand-off. All you have is the threat to shoot Galina and I truly don't believe you'll do that. You may shoot me or anyone else who tries to take that shotgun away from you. But your only real weapon is her and your belief that we're decent people who'll do what we can to save an innocent young woman.'

'It's simple. Bring her father here. Him for her. If you don't know what that bastard did, Bruno, you should. He was Putin's man in Ukraine, the man pulling the strings in Kiev, pushing those secret policemen to open fire on the protesters in the Maidan. He should face trial.'

'I know about the Maidan, Bertie, the snipers gunning them down, the churches throwing open their doors so the protesters had somewhere to flee. And it's Europe, Bertie, just as it was Europe in Sarajevo when I was a UN peacekeeper, and I still got shot. As far as the politics are concerned I'm on your side. But not while you have Galina under a gun.'

'This isn't about Galina,' Bertie snapped back. 'It's about that murderous father of hers.'

'You've made it about Galina,' Bruno replied, his arms

starting to ache with the effort of keeping them raised. 'There's a difference between what you think should happen and what will happen. Within the next hour there will be a hostage rescue team in place here. At that point you are out of options. You'll either be shot dead or badly wounded and arrested. When you're in prison, you will almost certainly be killed. You and I both know Russian intelligence can arrange that.'

'You can live with that, Russians organizing killings in French prisons?' Bertie shouted back. 'Russians spreading nerve agents in England? Shooting down airliners? Gunning down innocent young people at Maidan who only wanted freedom? You want to defend those bastards?'

The tighter Bertie was wound, Bruno knew, the more unpredictable he would become. But he was still making sense, still speaking coherently. Bruno told himself to stay calm.

'In the few minutes before the rescue squad gets here, Bertie, you can put down that gun, go outside, take my car and disappear. I suggest you try for Italy or Spain and then make your way to Ukraine from there. Your name and passport number are already on watch lists so you can't fly anywhere. That is your only choice.' He turned to Galina.

'Galina, is there anything you need? Water? A blanket?'

'I need to go to the bathroom,' she said quietly, looking at Bruno.

'Piss in your pants if you have to,' said Bertie. 'Nobody leaves here until your father arrives and we get the press conference. I'll want that friend of yours, Gilles, the one writing the book.'

'Bruno, there is something,' said Galina. 'Maybe I could

have some cigarettes.' She was looking at him so fixedly Bruno thought she was trying to send him a message

'You don't smoke,' snapped Bertie.

'This seems a reasonable moment to start,' she replied.

'Let me see if I can find some,' said Bruno and went back to the kitchen. Wordlessly, Rod handed him a pack of Marlboros and a book of matches. Bruno put his mouth close to Rod's ear and whispered, 'That window above his head. If all else fails, or if he shoots me, could you drop something heavy onto him?'

Rod's eyes widened. Then he nodded and Bruno took his gun from the holster where he'd left it and tucked it into his belt at the back. He heard the sound of furniture being shifted on the terrace, raised his hands in the air again and went back out. Bertie had overturned the heavy terrace table and positioned it to give him and Galina some protection against bullets. He was squatting behind it, the shotgun barrels pointing at Bruno.

'Toss the cigarettes over the table, Bruno,' Bertie said. 'Then separately toss the lighter.'

'No lighter, just matches,' Bruno said, tossing the cigarette packet over and then deliberately threw the matches short so they fell at the foot of the table on his side.

'Sorry,' he said, and bent down as if to retrieve them but then dived into the cover of the table and reached up to grab the shotgun barrel. He twisted it to one side and then hauled it down with all his strength and heard the deafening blast as it fired, both barrels. He rose, still holding the suddenly hot barrel and slammed the wooden stock into Bertie's chest and then onto the bridge of his nose. He opened the breech and tossed the gun aside, vaulted over the table, turned Bertie onto his stomach and brought his full weight down onto Bertie's back to pump the air out of him. He pulled Bertie's arms up and crossed his wrists at the back of his neck as he shouted for Rod to bring him his jacket.

Jamie was the first there, scooping the sobbing Galina into his arms. Then Rod arrived with Bruno's jacket, saying, 'You got him? How did you do it?'

'Plastic cuffs in the side pocket,' said Bruno, panting with effort as Bertie squirmed powerfully beneath him. Rod gave him the cuffs, Bruno put them on Bertie's wrists and it was over.

'How's Galina?' he asked.

'I'm fine,' she said, her voice muffled as she huddled into Jamie's chest. 'But I really need to pee.'

'Get the medics, they're waiting outside,' Bruno said. He stood up and stared at the gouged terrace floor where the shotgun pellets had blasted a tight circle. 'They'll need to look at the guy, I hit him hard in the chest. Please pass me my phone.'

He called J-J to say Galina was safe and the crisis was over. The hostage rescue team could be stood down but he needed St Denis gendarmes with their van to take the suspect into custody.

'One last thing,' he said, as Meghan and Kirsty rushed onto the terrace to embrace Galina and lead her off. 'Has Stichkin been told of the situation yet?'

'I don't know,' said J-J. 'Isabelle hasn't come out of that meeting since you left.'

Bruno texted Isabelle's number: 'Crisis over. Girl safe. Suspect in cuffs and alive. Will take him to St Denis gendarmerie.'

He pocketed his phone, helped Rod put the table back in

place and asked him for a big garbage bag into which he placed the shotgun. Then he helped Ahmed turn the semi-conscious Bertie over. The Canadian's face was a mask of blood where the shotgun stock had broken his nose.

'You might want to look at the girl as well,' he said to Ahmed. 'She must be in shock. She's in the bathroom.'

His phone dinged, the signal of an incoming text. From Isabelle, it said simply: 'On our way with papa. General says well done but whatever you do, don't arrest anyone yet. And media blackout. That's an order.'

Epilogue

Four weeks later

The secret had been well kept until that morning, when Philippe Delaron had the story in *Sud Ouest* and on *France Bleu* local radio. That allowed some heavyweight music critics from Paris and London to reach St Denis in time for the surprise comeback concert of the legendary rocker Rod Macrae. So instead of the usual concert on the quayside bandstand of St Denis for three or four hundred people, Bruno and Rod had time to arrange a makeshift stage on the back of the town's largest truck and the biggest and best sound system in the *département*. It had been erected on the bank of the river opposite the aquarium, where the parkland offered room for four or five thousand. It was packed by mid-afternoon and Rod was not due on stage until twilight.

It was Tuesday, market day in the morning and the town's usual summer night market in the evening, with the pizza kiosks, salad stalls, beer tents and barbecues that were already doing a roaring trade. Hubert's wine cave was staying open until midnight and the town vineyard had organized a shuttle service to ferry extra cases from the *chai* where the wine was made and stored. Bruno had arranged for forty portable toilets, extra bins for garbage, a first-aid tent and another for lost children. The town's rugby teams – the first and second men's teams, the juniors and the women's team – were acting as stewards and had all been issued with armbands that read *Bénévole*, volunteer. The gendarmes of St Denis, along with extra colleagues from Sarlat and St Cyprien, were managing the traffic and the extra parking that was filling the fields around the town.

To keep the crowds amused until the main event, at seven p.m. the town band started to play its entire repertoire. This was followed by the town choir. Then the town's own rock group, Panama, were going to play the golden oldies that most of the crowd knew by heart. With the town's choirmaster on keyboards, Jean-Louis from the garage on drums and Robert the retired architect singing and playing guitar, their mix of Brassens and Jacques Brel, The Beatles and and Francis Cabrel was well-known to all the locals – and none the worse for that.

It was, Bruno thought, the first moment that he could relax after the two weeks he had spent organizing it all. He had been pleased to have been invited to Galina's wedding, but simply unable to take the time off at the height of the tourist season and with Rod's concert as his priority. He comforted himself with the thought that Monaco and a luxury yacht were not what Pamela would call his *tasse de thé*. Nor did Bruno wish to renew his acquaintance with Igor Stichkin, particularly since General Lannes would also be there, cementing the new back-channel relationship with the Kremlin that had been his objective all along.

Rod, Meghan and Kirsty had returned from the wedding on

Sunday. Determined not to miss Rod's concert, Jamie and Galina had flown in a few hours ago, with that soft and dreamy look that suggested they had hardly stopped making love since the wedding. Jamie had told Bruno proudly that Galina had insisted that they postpone their honeymoon cruise around Italy on the yacht that had been named after her.

The sale of Chateau Rock to Galina had been completed before the wedding with a bank draft from Cyprus. The extra cash in the briefcase that Bruno had found in the crashed Maserati had been given to Galina to fulfil what Stichkin insisted had been its original purpose: to pay for the restoration of the cottage on the chateau grounds where Rod planned to live and whatever new decor and furniture Galina wanted for the chateau. Bruno and J-J privately thought that the cash had really been put into the car to lull any suspicions Sarrail might have of Stichkin's plans for him.

Only one arrest had been made, of Constant, the insurance agent, at the behest of Goirau and the *fisc*. Along with the papers that had been in the suitcase, their phones had provided abundant evidence that Constant and Sarrail had planned Lara's seduction of Driant, along with sufficient Viagra and cocaine to almost guarantee a heart attack. Constant admitted they were counting on the money from the sale of Driant's farm to cover the losses on the retirement home. He confessed that he and Sarrail had been terrified of Stichkin's anger if the project failed. Bruno suspected that Constant's cooperation in unravelling the tangled skeins of Stichkin's European investments might yet keep him out of prison.

Galina had been instructed by her father not to bring charges against Bertie, who had been diagnosed by a carefully chosen and suitably expensive psychologist as mentally unstable and under intense stress. General Lannes had arranged for him to be sent quietly back to Canada.

Kozak, if that had ever been his real name, had disappeared. But Isabelle's facial recognition programmer had identified him giving orders at political demonstrations and skirmishes in Kiev, Crimea and across Ukraine in previous years. Bruno and J-J were convinced he had killed Sarrail on Stichkin's orders, to save Stichkin from the embarrassment and public scrutiny that Bruno's investigations had already threatened to bring, with the prospect of worse to come. Stichkin's usefulness to Putin depended on his discretion, his ability to remain in the background. Sarrail's embarrassment over Driant and the retirement home were putting that at risk.

Bruno could not understand why the other Sasha and his girlfriend had also been considered expendable, until J-J suggested they had been sent along, like the money in the briefcase, as a kind of reassurance, in case Sarrail suspected that he'd outlived his usefulness. Isabelle had reminded Bruno of the murder of Maltese journalist Daphne Caruana Galizia. She had been killed by a bomb placed beneath her car in October 2016, after exposing the scandal of the widespread sale of Maltese passports to Russians and the bribes and corruption involved. Maltese Sasha had long been a suspect so perhaps Stichkin feared the police were getting uncomfortably close.

Once General Lannes had become involved, the police had attributed the crash of the Maserati to the unfortunate action of wild boars. Bruno was not surprised. A curtain of official discretion fell over what was now deemed a tragic accident. At least the Préfecture had announced sensible new controls on the placing of log piles too close to roadsides.

The Driant heirs were delighted with the generous financial settlement offered to them by the insurance company, so Bruno felt at least a small fraction of justice had been done. The thought of those two dead young women, struggling as best they could to make their way in a Europe that was growing tired of its own compassion, still troubled him. He had mentioned this to Gaston and Claudette when they invited him to a splendid dinner at La Tupina in Bordeaux, to thank him for his efforts in securing their inheritance. A few days later, Claudette had emailed him a copy of the receipt from Médecins Sans Frontières for her and her brother's joint donation of ten thousand euros.

In the performers' tent behind the stage truck, Rod was tuning his guitar when Bruno arrived, once Panama had finished their set. To their delight, Rod had asked the three of them to be his backing group and they had been rehearsing all week using Rod's own tapes.

'Ça va, Bruno?' asked Amélie, rising from the chair at the dressing table where she'd been checking on her hair and make-up. She looked terrific, in the spangled white dress she had worn at her Josephine Baker concert and her hair fluffed out into a giant afro. She gave him an air kiss on each cheek. 'I can't tell you how excited I am to be doing this.'

'Rod loved that vocal you did over his tape,' Bruno said. 'All your own work, nothing to do with me.'

'This whole concert is everything to do with you, Bruno,'

said Rod. He put his guitar across his knees and began rolling a cigarette.

'It's really just a rehearsal,' said Bruno. The official premiere of Rod's new album was to take place in London the following week. 'Your comeback tour of rock festivals is going to be great, but we're honoured to have the grand rehearsal. Which reminds me, the Mayor wants to say a brief word of welcome as you go on stage.'

Rod shrugged. 'Okay, I guess. But it's time to get on with the music.' He bumped fists with Robert and Jean-Louis as they headed up the steps onto the stage and told them to break a leg. '*Merde*,' they replied in the customary way. The Mayor put his head around the tent flap, and asked, 'Are we all ready?'

'You bet,' said Rod. 'Break a leg yourself.'

The Mayor headed up the steps, holding a roll of parchment from which dangled a red ribbon and seal, tapped the microphone, welcomed everyone to St Denis, and told them he had a brief announcement.

'By the authority vested in me by the people and council of St Denis, I hereby proclaim that Rod Macrae is now an honorary citizen of this commune where he and his family have lived for more than twenty years and where he has continued to write and make and perform the music that has made him an international star.'

The crowd erupted in cheers and applause as Rod emerged on stage through the curtain, accepted the roll of parchment and the Mayor's kiss on each cheek, thanked him, and said into the microphone, 'Well, I guess this is where I belong, these days.'

The cheers and applause doubled in volume.

'Thank you all for coming,' Rod went on when he could be heard again. 'We're going to play some of my old numbers and a few of my new ones, and it's great to be working with these guys from Panama and this brilliant young vocalist, Amélie.'

As Rod picked out the familiar chords of the global hit he had made nearly thirty years earlier, Bruno left the tent and climbed up the steps beside the medical centre to get a view of the crowd. The parkland was full, and so was the bridge and the quay on the far side of the river. There were dozens of boats and canoes on the water, which was so slow at the height of summer that they stayed in place with an occasional paddle stroke. He had no idea how many people had gathered, certainly more than five thousand, perhaps the biggest assembly St Denis had ever known.

A short buzz came from the phone at his belt, an incoming text message. He pulled it and saw that it came from Claire at the kennels.

'Good news, Bruno! On the stethoscope today I heard the heartbeats of Carla's nine new puppies. Estimated birthdate a month from today. Congratulations to you and to Papa Balzac.'

Acknowledgements

There were three triggers for the ideas that came together for the plot of this book. The first was the assassination by car bomb of the brave Maltese journalist Daphne Caruana Galizia, in October 2016. She had for some time been working on the various scandals surrounding the sale of Maltese passports, and thus in effect of European citizenship, to Russians and others. Since such a passport required proof of a Maltese residence, some cheap public housing tenements were being rented out at hugely inflated sums to the profit of local figures. Rumour has it that the Russian mafia were involved in her murder. The second trigger was the outrageous use of a nerve agent in a quiet British town by two Russian intelligence agents seeking to kill a Russian defector, Sergei Skripal.

The third trigger was much more pleasant. It was hearing of a number of rock stars heading for Miles Copeland's Château de Marouette. It reminded me of some very happy years in the 1970s when I became friendly with Miles's father, a CIA man who had become legendary for his close relationship with Egypt's President Nasser. Our gossipy lunches on the rooftop restaurant of the London Hilton were always interesting. At around the same time the then-editor of the *Guardian* indulged my wish to write about rock music, on the condition that I did so in my own time. I was fortunate to attend the premiere of Pink Floyd's *Dark Side of the Moon* at the London Planetarium; David Bowie's first incarnation as Ziggy Stardust; the launch of *Quadrophenia* by The Who; to go on an American tour with Procol Harum and Steeleye Span; and to attend the ball at Blenheim Palace for Mick and Bianca Jagger. Those fleeting brushes with rock stardom came flooding back as I began to plan this tale of Chateau Rock.

The book also owes a great deal to the many classical music concerts in the Périgord which these days are rather more my speed. It may owe even more to the riverside concerts that enliven our summers and to the local bands and musicians like my friends in the group Panama. Robert the singing architect, Jean-Louis the *garagiste* on drums and Stéphane on keyboards, have given me great pleasure over the years so I'm delighted to commemorate them here.

Rod Macrae, his family and Chateau Rock are inventions, and so is Balzac's breeding kennel, the Château Marmont retirement home and the Stichkin family. But there are such Russian oligarchs and many of them have acquired rights of residence and influential roles in Europe along with some protection for their wealth. One understands their motives; Vladimir Putin is an uncomfortable leader and a dangerous neighbour. His forces have invaded two neighbours, Ukraine and Georgia, occupied Crimea, launched a dramatic cyber-attack on Estonia, deployed nerve agents in Britain, shot down a civilian airliner and sent troops, ships and warplanes to sustain its odious Syrian ally. It is not entirely Putin's fault that international tensions have increased so sharply but one understands why Western intelligence agencies have been scrambling to rebuild their Kremlin-watching capabilities. Just to be sure my imagination wasn't running away with me, I ran the outlines of this plot past some old contacts in the field who had better remain nameless.

As always, some of the key characters were originally, many novels ago, inspired by some real people in the Périgord before being filtered through my imagination. But these fictional people quickly took on for me lives of their own as they confronted new plots in new books. And time passes. Some of the original figures have died, others have retired or changed their jobs. Businesses have closed or been sold. New winemakers and restaurants have emerged. Children are growing up. St Denis is sufficiently real in my head that I understand the place and that its people have to evolve.

I am hugely grateful to my friends and neighbours and the welcoming people of the Périgord for providing such a perfect place and inspiration to write. Thanks in particular to Raymond and Francette for looking after the garden and the basset hound when I'm travelling. I owe an incalculable debt to my wife, Julia Watson, a professional food writer who keeps a close watch on Bruno's cooking and who is co-author of the Bruno cookbooks. When not covering Grand Prix races, our daughter Kate maintains the brunochiefofpolice.com website. When not working on her poetry and plays, our other daughter Fanny keeps track of all the characters, meals, skills and relationships, a task which becomes more complex with each new book and short story.

Bruno would not have become an international success without my agent and friend, Caroline Wood, nor without Jane, Jonathan and Anna, my wonderful editors at Quercus in London, Knopf in New York, and Diogenes in Zurich. Alongside them stand small but devoted armies of copy-editors, proofreaders, designers, publicists, marketeers, printers and sales teams. And we'd all be in trouble without the booksellers, book reviewers, librarians, bloggers and book clubs who bring them to the most crucial people of all – readers like you.